75

Books by Paul Darcy Boles

THE STREAK

THE BEGGARS IN THE SUN

GLENPORT, ILLINOIS

DEADLINE

PARTON'S ISLAND

A MILLION GUITARS

I THOUGHT YOU WERE A UNICORN

THE LIMNER

THE MISSISSIPPI RUN

GLORY DAY

GLORY DAY

PAUL DARCY BOLES

GLORY DAY

Random House New York

Grateful acknowledgment is made to the following
for permission to reprint previously published
material:

Edwin H. Morris & Company: Excerpt from
"Sweethearts on Parade" by Charles Newman and Carmen Lombardo.
Copyright © 1928 Mayfair Music
Corp. Copyright Renewed, assigned to Edwin H. Morris &
Company, A Division of MPL Communications, Inc.
International Copyright Secured. All rights reserved.
Used by permission.

Library of Congress Cataloging in Publication Data
Boles, Paul Darcy, 1916-
Glory day.
I. Title.
PZ4.B688Gn [PS3552.0584] 813'.5'4 78-57126
ISBN 0-394-50198-5

Manufactured in the United States of America
2 4 6 8 9 7 5 3
First Edition

BOOK DESIGN BY LILLY LANGOTSKY

TO DOROTHY

AND THE MEMORY OF MY GRANDFATHER,

C. R. B.

GLORY DAY

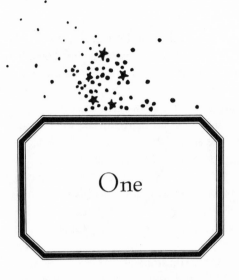

One

No town sleeps. Someone is always awake; as someone was in Arden, Ohio, on this morning of the Fourth of July, 1929.

From where he stood outside a limestone cave in the valley under the woods, Cy Bellaman heard the train whistle. He nodded to himself with his head lifted. He had fair, light-yellow hair, almost a jonquil's in color, and his face was a good hunter's—shut up, sealed, nearly without expression. His eyes were slate-gray with blue glints, and his hair was neatly clipped and tight to the scalp. He wore nondescript trousers, dark snub-toed boots, a jacket flapping open over a white shirt. His right hand and arm cradled a rifle, beautifully made, its stock polished by the heels of the hands so the grain of the wood appeared to flow like a living animal's flesh. He carried it as though it were weightless, a continuation of his body. He breathed the freshness of the morning, the light rank scent of the river, the smell of the still-wet night leaves. After a moment as the whistle sounded again he moved back into the cave. Now he could not be seen, and could well not have been there to start with.

On the plank-boarded station platform in Arden, Marty Broom, who had been asleep with his head on a mail sack, came awake when he heard the whistle. He was sixty-three and given to catnaps rather than drowned, full sleep. He hawked and spat, holding one wing of his grizzled mustache aside. Around him the station and its platform assumed shape; its old red bricks held the sun on their cheeks and turned peach-colored. Marty heaved himself to his feet, stamped on the echoing boards to get out the pins and needles, gave a huge stretch which he felt all the way down to his least corns, and hauled up the mail sack to hang it in its place on the hook. Surveying the eastern sky he said to himself, "Not a rain sign. Be a dinger of a Fourth."

A dog came up the steps; it was beggar-wise, large, fat; with a curly coat, burred and snarled. It ambled forward. Marty hunkered on his heels to pat it. "Stay out of the line of fire, Sam. Get a can tied to your tail otherwise." He and the dog stood waiting, Marty's eyes narrow. "On time," he said over the train whistle's noise. "Don't have to look at a watch to tell. Way the sun hits the rails shows it."

The train was rushing close now. Its noise filled the morning. Then it was there alongside, the locomotive sudden as a tornado, black, huge, screaming, the whistle sounding again in two heavy blasts, the cinders and smoke sweeping back along the locomotive, and the car roofs like the backbone of a dragon. The cars stuttered and leaped past, their window blinds shuttered. In the wake of the observation car, a warm rush of air settled over the track, full of cinder-and-coal leavings, the only remnants of time and distance. The mail-sack hook hung stripped of its burden. Marty said, "Get on the downwind side of me, Sambo. You been into sheep. No mail runnin' after this, no trains through till it's over. I'm goin' down to Flute's and get some breakfast. Come on."

He and the dog clumped down the platform steps. Along the street, sunlight was roving now, glancing into those shops which would remain open for the holiday—Flute's Café, Soames's Pharmacy, and because it opened on call and there had been business for it this morning, Melton's Funeral Parlor.

In the Arden hospital, halfway down the lane behind Front Street, Phyllis Bellaman lay in an iron-railed white bed on the second floor. She had been asleep for a time, dreamless, opening her eyes at the whistle's call. Her left shoulder was hurting a little now. She sat up in bed, arranging a pillow to support her, and turned down the shoulder strap of her blue silk slip; she had come there in the clothing she'd been wearing the night before. She touched the bandage. It was tidy, as neat as the wound itself. The wound was only a nick, drilled through the flesh above the left clavicle where it would for a time disturb muscle and tissue, but after healing, Dr. Bowen had said, would leave only a small, firm scar. She liked the craftsmanship of the bandage. Dr. Bowen's thick fingers could be deft. So could his tact. He had said very little as he drove her there. She'd said nothing—there was nothing to say—as she watched the limousine hearse from Melton's Funeral Parlor pull away ahead of them, toward Front Street, in the clear moonlit night. Dr. Bowen had said he'd come by or call later in the morning to tell her whether she could go home or not. She intended to leave in any case, but because she had known Dr. Bowen all her life, she was grateful for his silences, for everything he had never said.

She lay back again, arms at her sides, looking at the fresh patterns of the sun on the whitewashed ceiling. Some of the sunlight entered the lower windowpanes, to touch her heavy-textured blue-black hair, to bring out, like slowly revealed sculpture, her cheekbones, which were classical in shape, and illuminate her generous mouth. Under the stark whiteness of the sheets her body was benevolent, neither small nor large, its fluid lines made to be joyful, to articulate in sweet freedom. After the last fierce whistle of the locomotive, she remained quiet for a while, the sound of her own breath resuming more strongly, making her more deeply aware of herself—of Mrs. Cyrus Bellaman. She kept still as death for these seconds. Presently she did stretch, raising her arms, watching the sun slide over her hands, slip through her fingers and warm her shoulders. Her motion disturbed a magazine on the bedside table; it fell into bed with her. She picked it up—a fairly old copy of the *Saturday Evening Post* with a Leyendecker cover, a handsome man with a smooth white collar and a golden head. It was very like Cy himself, she thought, though it lacked his strength and the implicit character in his eyes.

A few blocks from the hospital, which was firmly administered by his Aunt Alice, Nick Cloud also heard the final whistle of the Monon Special. His naked flesh—he had thrown back the sheets during the night—was brick-dark with sun stain. He regarded his sex with complacency. Virginal—but that was not unusual, for his age, in this town. He could see the sun on all three window sills. Winters, with all the windows shut tight and sealed, the train's whistle would have come here like a far-off, muffled bugle. This morning it could have sounded upward from the basement, where jars of Harky's jelly stood on rough board shelves in long rows, and where the coalbin opened its mouth next to the enormous storage bins. It could have sounded from the attics on the fourth floor of the old house, where dust-covered horsehair trunks had been abandoned years before. Or it might have emanated from the first floor, where his grandfather lay in the tall old room, with the nurse asleep on her cot in one corner.

Nick crossed his fingers behind his head, allowing the sense of the day to fill him. The Fourth; it was here. The room was gathering light like an opening flower. The milkman would have come while it was still full dark, come and gone without special notice. The water wagon would have been snailing along, its pipes hissing, filling the street with a flood and laying the dust from curb to curb. It started out on Front Street, and its second street was always the Cloud Block. Nick sat up sharply. He could no longer stand being in bed. His heels hit the warm dappled flooring. This is the *Fourth*, he told himself —trying to recapture something partly gone now, something that even last year, when he was fifteen, and certainly the year before, would have surged behind his ribs.

As he stood with his knuckles taut, cupping light, arms extended, belly curved out, in a monumental stretch, the first of the fireworks went off. At least a six-inch salute, the brawling roar seemed to break the morning in pieces.

"Damn now!" Nick said admiringly. But he said it with regret as well, that it no longer stirred his blood.

In his bathroom he turned on the shower in the cavernous tub. Water lit up his muscles, bringing out their long whipcord ridges, the tough bulges of the thighs and calves, the stomach's flat silk, the otter-black hair and inquisitive eyebrows. He opened his arms to let the water drum on his chest, feeling in love with the day, wanting to sing about it; he looked down, approvingly, at the water streaming around his testicles, then straight up, shutting his eyes, taking the shower's force against his high-bridged nose, like a ship's bow in a storm.

A minute later he stood before his dresser mirror—Federal, with eagles around its frame—and ran a comb through his hair, splashing drops on his faded shirt, worn flannels and gym shoes. Sunlight, higher now, spread over the wallpaper, which showed in measured, repetitive sequence the journey of a great many pioneers through interesting countryside. The paper had been hung there at his mother's bidding, years ago. Marna Cloud was an actress, her dramatic sense reflected in this design, which, on one of her few visits, she had decided had just the right heartiness for a growing boy.

He had grown tired of the pattern over the years, and had added to it, in several shades of Prang crayon, a fleet of Cloud automobiles—the celebrated Clouds, the ones his grandfather had manufactured before the Cloud Shops had been sold. The massive cars stood out like gleaming chariots against their company of Conestoga wagons. Not far from them he had, this spring, drawn a nude portrait of Melissa Gardner. He had never seen Melissa without her clothes, but there she was on his wall, dominating cactus-strewn plain and struggling pioneers, her legs by comparison to their horses and oxen twenty feet high, a naiad rising from the western horizon. She had, in the portrait, basketball breasts, a marvelously tiny waist, a navel that might easily hold a pint of wine, a large amount of pubic hair, and a faintly ecstatic, if not quite foolish, smile.

Once when Harky Lucas came in to clean Nick's room she had complained about the portrait. "S'pose she came over, visitin', some afternoon. How'd you like it if she saw this?"

Nick said that he doubted if Melissa was coming to visit in a hurry, that her father wouldn't let her even if they were chaperoned by a couple of ministers.

"All the same," Harky said, "that picture's a disgrace."

But she let it alone; Harky would express herself, forcibly, about what she didn't like; then she would allow the object of her displeasure to go on living.

Another fusillade of salutes went off outside and Nick wrinkled his nose, sniffing gunpowder, faint on the already heating, pollen-laden air. Not long from now it would hang over the town, a faintly noxious but somehow invigorating pall that would stick inside clothing for days to come.

As he left his room—on the third floor, remote, oversized like all the other rooms up here—he looked back at the wallpaper where he had drawn Melissa. She towered in sexual fantasy; the sunlight glared at her charms. But she wasn't merely Melissa; he had known that while he was working on her. She was a Jungle Queen, a dark desire, Helen of Troy; and to be a little more specific, and honest about it, Phyllis Bellaman. It was hard to let oneself know about this yearning for a good friend's wife; but it didn't even have to be thought about, not any of it. It was there—that he was sixteen, Cy's friend, that she was thirty-one, Cy's wife. Cold baths and Galahad examples didn't do a thing to take it away.

In the hall from a twelve-foot-high armoire scrolled with

wooden birds and carved with Victorian flora, he picked up the two large paper bags with their fireworks. The third, filled with rockets, pinwheels, sparklers, fire balloons, jewel fountains, he left where it was, for the dark. All of the fireworks had been carefully, even pickily, selected from the Tribe of K—the Kaplan brothers' wondrous and lofty and counter-jammed hardware store on Front Street.

He skimmed down the long oak staircase, stepping off the last tread where the staircase took a grand curve. He paused again in the living room, cool with night and spacious as an armory, the fireplace at the far side holding lightly gilded cattails and bullrushes arching from large jars; the painting of his father over the hearth, done from a photograph after Rex Cloud had been shipped back from France and buried. The painter had been famous for his time—a follower, it was plain, of John Singer Sargent. A stripe of sun lit up one eye, a portion of the lower jaw, touched the smile. If the sniper outside Amiens hadn't been so well trained, his father would have been marching today in the World War contingent of the parade. Behind the Civil War veterans—they, as usual, would come first.

Nick supposed he would be pressed into service as a driver for those who couldn't, or didn't want to, walk. Among them were always a few from across the river, the Kentucky side, the *other* side, who were friends of his grandfather's, and who would join their ancient enemies on parade—scoffing, chewing, detesting time which had taken its will of them. But Noel Cloud, himself once one of the youngest generals in the Union Army, wouldn't be joining that group. He would remain in his room, with Nurse Angela Riffon keeping guard over him as if her starched cuffs depended on it. She might allow Noel Cloud to have a few, a very few hand-picked veteran friends in the room to see him, considering what day it was, but that would be all.

He turned from gazing across at his father's cleverly painted features and headed along another hall which, eventually, led

9

to the dining room and the kitchen. The rooms branching from this hall were numerous. Among them was a glass-roofed retreat which, back in the days immediately after Noel Cloud had built the house, had been known as a conservatory. While Noel Cloud could still speak, before the third stroke had clutched him, he had sometimes mentioned the soirees that were held in this house, first when the Clouds built buggies, then in days following the Civil War, when they manufactured the great Cloud cars. The conservatory had several fountains in it—one still worked, if you could find the crank that opened its pipe.

Padding along, Nick paused at the door of his grandfather's room. For all its amplitude, it wasn't as large as the baronial bedroom on the second floor, where Noel Cloud had slept with Grandma Marie. Noel Cloud had only been moved down here with the third and nearly fatal stroke—the one that had left him unable to speak. But it was a large-shadowed place, crosshatched with suggestions of outdoor light moving in under the drawn curtains.

Nurse Angela Riffon had caught sight of Nick and called in her sickroom tone, "Nick! He's awake. He'd like to see you."

Oh, hell, Nick told himself. How does she know? He can't say what he wants or doesn't want.

He set down the fireworks and went in.

Angela Riffon had made her cot bed, and also the massive fourposter under the window. In spite of the size of the man in it—he had not seemed to diminish with sickness, but rather to have grown, his beard still with a touch of jet black, the hair sleek as the wing of a young white bird—he appeared small in its length. The light comforter was drawn up over his nightshirted chest, but his hands lay outside. They were large yet agile-seeming hands, each bone exposed by their thinness. Dark-brown spots on their backs stood out against parched flesh. The sun stealing under the curtains lit the room with an undersea secrecy. Noel Cloud's eyes drew Nick as though they beckoned him. They were brown-black, like his, with Indian steadiness. Eye color had skipped a generation; from Noel, by-passing Rex, to Nick.

Smelling the odor of medicines flattened by sprays meant to alleviate it, Nick watched his grandfather, the eighty-nine-year-old man. From the intricately carved footboard of the bed he said, "Good morning, sir."

Noel Cloud didn't attempt to answer. After the last stroke he had tried for a time to be understood, then given up in dignified disgust at the animal noises that came out of his mouth. Sometimes a crease showed up in the full width of his forehead, a line drawn there as if cut by a sharp knife. Nick had decided that when this happened, the urge to communicate was so severe it could hardly be tolerated. But now only the eyes tried speech; under the heavy, upflaring eyebrows they bored into Nick, but there was nothing blaming, impatient about them.

Nick felt himself rising, a trifle, on the balls of his feet, as if with physical effort he could project himself into the eyes and through to the brain of the old man.

These were the eyes that had watched in the Wilderness while the cartridge belts of men wounded and unable to stir caught fire and exploded on their bodies. This was the sensibility that had plotted and achieved escape from Andersonville. These the initiative and skill that had started up the Buggy Works—the Shops. And built the Cloud automobiles, with their ash frames and their strong engines and their dependability. This was what time did to you, even if you defied it.

Nurse Angela Riffon's voice sounded like a pigeon's, with that somehow mindless amiability. "He says Happy Fourth of July, Grandboy!" She had gone around close to the shoulder of Noel Cloud, bending a little, her crisp uniform protesting lightly with starch. Once Nick had heard her telling Noel Cloud, "Now we have to go potty, don't we?" He found it difficult to forgive her then, or now—as she said to the man in the bed, "Isn't that just what you say, old honey?"

Noel Cloud's eyes didn't move to her. They remained fixed on Nick.

Nurse Riffon said to Nick as if in confidence—as if Noel Cloud were deaf, as one spells out confidences around a small child, "Our temperature's way down this morning. So maybe we can just have some of our old friends in to see us today."

Nick said, even though he hadn't meant to, "Please don't call him 'honey.' Or 'old honey.' He's General Cloud."

He felt himself flush, felt the high red spots on his cheekbones. It was ridiculous to blame Angela Riffon for trying. All the same, his own lower jaw had thrust out. For a few beats of time he gazed on Nurse Riffon's slightly shocked, hurt and suddenly angered eyes, her air of guardianship assaulted.

To his grandfather he said, "I hope it's a good day for you, sir. All around."

The heel of his right gym shoe squeaked as he swung to leave. But he was too late to avoid Nurse Angela Riffon's response. She followed him swiftly to the door. "Now, if you don't like how I do my duty, you can keep a civil tongue in your head!" She was murmuring it, but it was all the stronger for that. "I do what I'm trained for, and do it right. Which doesn't include havin' to take orders from a teen-age smart alec! Even if he is the last of the men Clouds, and thinks he's better'n anybody else!"

It was patently untrue; it hadn't been the reason for Nick's request. But he could feel his own anger burning. He swallowed, moving away. She called after him in the same hard, affronted whisper, "And just tell Harky we both need our breakfasts, me and General Cloud! She's ten minutes past time already!" She added one more shot: "*I* don't get no holiday today, I can tell you that, Mister Man!"

He felt a shaft of dislike for himself—it would have been right to hold his tongue in there. Harky had grown up with Angela Riffon; she said Angela was the only one of the Riffons who'd amounted to a hill of beans, pulling herself up by solid will power. He should have remembered that, before he spoke.

He heard the door shut now with a malicious-sounding snap of its lock.

Light danced through the dining room, gilding the long table, which also held reflections of the oaks and elms leaning near these windows. On another fireplace at the far side of the table an ormolu clock, with figurines of a pair of winged horses ramping at its flanks, stood manteled and timeless, no longer with reason to be wound and mark the hours.

Swinging open the kitchen door, he breathed in the smell of hot cakes sizzling. Harky stood over the wood-burning range, her face rosy with range-warmth, her eyes a dark, smoky blue. There was another, gas-burning range alongside; she refused to utilize it. The wood burner was coal-black, its nickelwork shining in hot stabs of brilliance.

"Kind of late, ain't you? Figured you'd be up and about with the birds." She fiddled a pancake turner under one of her creations, examined its underedge with careful, quick assessment, let it fall back for more heat. "You were last year."

She had caught a glimpse of the fireworks sacks as he set them down and drew up a chair.

"Well, you got deviltry there, anyhow. Hot cakes ready in about two minutes. I suppose that woman's hollering about her breakfast, and the General's."

"She's fractious," Nick said. He reached for a hot biscuit from the basket already on the table. Something about Harky seemed held in this morning, simmering with more repression than even the day's excitement warranted.

He could catch a whiff of her gingham work dress through the rich food smells. She washed all her work things in Fels Naphtha. A clean, carbolic scent.

"Won't hurt her to wait, and God knows the General must get little enough joy out o' that mush they make him eat." She half turned to Nick, the spatula angled up from her hip, held like a short sword. "You was over at the Gardners' too late last night to be told anything. So I'm goin' to tell you now."

She rounded all the way to him, folding her arms tightly

under her bosom, and took a deep preparatory breath. Nick sat very still. Her face was as grave, as bothered by circumstance as it had been when she had told him about Noel Cloud's third stroke.

She said, "Cy Bellaman shot Henry Watherall dead last night. He winged his wife, too. Caught her and Henry together at the Bellamans'."

The substance of her words burst much more loudly around Nick than the first salute of the daylight had sounded. It went on echoing for a moment inside him as if it had exploded in his veins. He wished, for a second, that he could start the morning over—go back a few minutes in time. But things couldn't work out like that; they were what they were, and this feeling of being suddenly frozen, this dryness inside his mouth came from facts, not little-kid fancies.

Everything about the day had changed. The same sun was filling the kitchen, and in a short time Wid Lucas, Harky's husband, would be coming in for his own breakfast; but all this was now a glittering holiday surface. Beneath it, Nick felt as if he had been knocked down and lay dazed. He could feel blood slowly coming back into his face. He stared at Harky, as yet unable to comment, letting his eyes do it for him.

"It's true enough, Nick. Phyl Bellaman called Sheriff Potter right after it happened—right after Cy lit out. And Jerome Potter got the Vigilante Committee together. They all want to keep it quiet till they've found Cy—don't want no big dust-up, 'specially on the Fourth of July." Brooding, she wheeled and flipped over three cakes with three turns of a powerful wrist. "Wid'll fill you in a little more. He was out with the Vigilantes last night, and he's goin' to join 'em again this mornin'. And Phyl ain't hurt bad. She's in the hospital . . . but ain't it a cussed rotten thing to happen right now, on the Fourth? The *glorious* Fourth, like they say?"

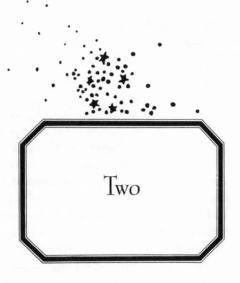

Two

Noel Cloud's hearing had always been acute. In the heat of action he had been able to distinguish the voices of his own men from those of other troops, even through shot and shell and the overriding cacophony of war. In the Shops he had been able to tell a good day of production from a bad just by a tempo in the air; his foremen had been aware of this, and sometimes asked him if what he heard was all right. He had answered truthfully when it was or was not, and this both awed them and amused them.

But since he had been robbed of speech he had learned to read overtones, as an orchestra conductor does as he isolates the brasses, the strings and the woodwinds in their varied interpretation. He had heard, beneath the altercation between Nick and Angela Riffon, her sharp anger and his grandson's outraged sense of decency. Now he managed to shut out the drone of the locusts in the night-moist trees and concentrate on Nick.

Nick was indelibly like Rex in face and body, and he suspected the boy had Rex's temper, too: a certain affability of good manners covering a passionate conviction of right and wrong. But there had been more than that in the final rift between father and son, in the frenetic quality of Rex's life before the world broke apart in the Great War. Perhaps it had been that he was the offspring of an acknowledged war hero, that he knew the county expected high deeds of him. In any event, Rex had certainly been swift to enlist, but there had been a fatalism about him during his last days at home which had bothered Noel even then, because it did not sit well with his own ideas of what a man should and should not be. It was a diamond-hard energy that was also an awareness of being cheated—a laughter that had brittle edges, as if it expected death. Noel had lived through enough death around him and in a thousand forms—death for which he was responsible and for which he only felt responsible—to know that the laughter was essentially false, that it masked a sense of being horribly uncertain.

He recalled the night before Rex left for New York and embarkation for Europe; he had been home on leave for a week, brightly male in his tailored first lieutenant's uniform. He and Marna attended a Damn-the-Kaiser dance somewhere in town; they arrived home late, climbed the stairs whispering, and with soft, excited laughter looked in on Nick, a sleeping young child. Noel heard them from the living room, where he sat, unnoticed, beside a low fire; he told himself he would say a decent goodbye to Rex in the morning and lingered by the fire, in a mood of memory and regret. Telling himself he had never had genuine time to be with Rex, that he had never even taken the time to formulate carefully, and pass on to Rex, how he truly felt about battle—that all a man could do was attempt to travel through it with as much care and skill as he could summon, and that whatever the speechmakers said about it afterward, this was the single truth.

Presently he was aware that Rex had come down the stairs alone and slammed out of the house, his footfalls knocking clearly against the porch, and that from abovestairs Marna Cloud was calling after him, her voice brilliant, as if even in anger she was aware of a possible audience, "Go on, go to her!"

Noel had been unable to sleep until Rex returned, which was late indeed; then he snapped on a lamp and in its light inspected Rex. Neither man was at his best; Rex's face was drawn, his bright-blue eyes haunted; his uniform jacket hung open over his dress shirt. Noel heard himself saying, stupidly, as though commenting to a subordinate whose reactions he mistrusted, "I guess I'll say goodbye tonight. I know you must leave early; and I'll have to be at the Shops." The Shops were full of war work, hastily converted to the production of tanks.

Rex sat down, throwing one handsomely booted leg over the arm of a divan. "My God, Father, you never leave them, do you? You come home, sir, you're the patriarch, the head of this family. But all the time you're back in the Shops, you've never left them." He'd leaned forward. "Tell me, sir, when you were at Manassas—the night before, was there some good girl you thought about? Someone on whose—well, call it bosom—you wanted to lie down for a while? Just to say to hell with it and act like a common man, to take a vacation from virtues for once in your life?" Rex wasn't smiling; his face was like gray paper in the soft light.

Noel remembered his answer; it started out of an anger that he carefully suppressed. Now he was not so sure he shouldn't have given way to it even if it had meant losing his sense of fairness and consideration. He had said, "I wish you well, son. I don't think we ought to part on this note. As to your question —yes, I've been burned by self-doubts, before a battle and after it, what man hasn't? I didn't happen to console myself that way. But perhaps I considered it."

There was a silence; then Rex leaned close to him, his breath ripe with alcohol. "Sir, I'm sorry. I'm a godawful rotten son. And a pretty sad father myself, come to think of it. I believe I'll make the hell of a soldier—I think I know how to die."

"Oh," Noel said, sitting higher, wishing to reach for his son but unable to. "That's the simplest thing anybody does. I had an aide, Custis, who said that dying was always overrated. It's living that's much more difficult." The moment the words were out, he regretted them; he had always detested the sanctimony of dress parades, of speeches. But he only added quietly, "Custis died before Appomattox. Quite unpleasantly, of dysentery."

Rex kept on watching him; then he got up, and as he stood there, Noel stood too. He hadn't expected Rex to lean forward and kiss him, as the boy would do when he was small, scrubbed red from a bath, ushered into the room to say a quick good night, and peck his father on the cheek. But now Rex did just that; then lifted a hand and was gone to the staircase; but before he rounded the curve and was drawn from sight, his boot heels stopped making that abrupt noise and he faced downward. "Good night, General," he said, and then turned again, and was gone. His voice had been half sardonic, a touch drunken. Noel went on looking up toward the stairwell for some time afterward. When he himself climbed to bed, dawn was arriving.

He had always wondered who it was that Rex went to that night before leaving Arden—as it turned out, forever. He hadn't been able to see him off in the morning; there was a shop emergency, and he had scarcely shut his eyes before he was out of bed again. And now he would very much like to tell Nick all this, even though it had no heroics in it. Now that he knew he was dying.

Harky was calling outside the door, "Come on, Angie! Give a woman a hand! I got the General's breakfast here, and yours, and the tray's a handful!"

Nurse Riffon whipped her novel, a confection by Grace Livingston Hill, neatly under her chair and out of sight. She got up, all starch and speckless whiteness, like a white hen, Noel thought ungallantly, and started for the door, while Noel Cloud with great effort, not perceptible from an inch away, contracted the muscles of his right eye—and felt the eyelid draw down with the aching minuscular progress of a turtle's— so that, with luck, he could appear to be winking at Harky when she was let in and, with luck, she could see it.

• • •

Wid Lucas came into the kitchen by way of the back door. Once inside, he looked only at Nick. He sat down, a man smaller than Harky in size and weight, his nose a billhook, his eyes steady and gypsy-black, his face the color of sun-warmed amber stone with nets of red veins over the cheekbones. He adjusted the straps of his cornflower-blue overalls with his thumbs and said gruffly, "All right, I can see you heard. Guess Harky told you."

Answering "Yes," Nick was surprised that such a small word could cover quite as much.

Reaching for a biscuit and a knife and butter, Wid kept his gaze on Nick. "Goddamn it, Cap, I knew how it'd hit you. Right in the gut. Me too, only I guess I ain't ever been as close to Cy and Phyl as you have."

He glanced away, glaring at the coffee pot. "I *like* Cy though. I like Phyl. I liked the hell out of Henry Watherall. He's at Melton's Funeral Parlor. Jerome Potter's got the right idea—find Cy, and keep this quiet till we figure out all the ins and outs of it. After Potter rounded us up last night we poked around the bushes quite a while. Couldn't find a hair of Cy. Rest of the Vigilantes've gone out again now, still lookin' for him. I'll join 'em again in the next hour."

His eyes moved back to Nick, level and urgent. "Sure, some folks think the Vigilante Committee's a joke. Think we set around and guzzle home brew and swap lies. But when somethin' like this comes up, I'm glad we're on deck—not hollerin' and rousin' the whole town, just findin' him."

Nick nodded, knowing Wid wasn't so much defending the Vigilantes as he was trying to take the edge off the shock. He appreciated this, as Wid went on through a bite of biscuit, "Findin' him for his own sake as much as anything. Ain't a jury in the county'll convict him for this. He killed Henry in a real cause—no two ways about it."

This time Nick found his voice, hearing it as though it were very far away. "Wid, Cy's my best friend, outside Buck Bolyard. And Phyllis . . ." He was quiet for a few seconds, before he could go on. "And Henry—he was a *good* man, he never hurt anybody."

He wasn't aware that Wid had gripped his wrist until Wid's fingers locked around it. "Christ alive, Cap, you think only bad people get hurt? Get killed, like in the movies? Think some of the people a man likes best don't get wound up in their own kinds of hell?" Shaking his head, he released Nick's wrist, and Nick could tell that in his own way, Wid was as disturbed as he himself was. "Oh, hell, I'm sorry, Cap. I know you're old enough to know that. I'm talkin' like some fool Dutch Uncle. Well, look—best thing for you to do right now is eat some o' them hot cakes . . . you may not want 'em now, but it's a long time till the picnic and we all got to have somethin' solid in our bellies." There was a pause, and in it, Wid addressed himself to hot cakes, now watching Nick out of the corner of his eye; Nick took a bite and found, again to his surprise, that it was possible to eat.

Wid looked out the window. "Great weather—way it ought to be every Fourth . . . Expect you and Buck got somethin' special planned?"

Nick brushed a fireworks bag with one foot. "Sure we have, but now—it seems kind of silly . . ."

"Why? There ain't a thing you can do to help with Cy, except keep your mouths shut about this, and hope for the best from here on in."

There was still a constriction in his throat muscles, but Nick's voice was steady again. "Wid, was Mrs. Bellaman—Phyllis—did she have a lot of men? Some people say it's so, but I never even liked to think about it . . ."

"Well, hell, Cap, I don't know. I hear rumors, just like you. Kind of general batshit some people talk. Even if she did, I guess it was her right, and between her and Cy—not any of my business, just their own."

Nick said, "Not long back, Eugene Fisher was talking around, saying he and Phyllis—"

Wid brought a fist down on the edge of the table, making it jump a little. "Consider the source, Cap. That piece of smarm, he'd say anything. Hope you gave him his comeuppance."

"Sure I did, I smacked him. So did Buck—we did it one at a time, fair odds. He'd been telling it around that he was going to . . . you know . . . with Melissa, too."

Wid said casually, "You know, it's too damn bad it wasn't Eugene got drilled last night. His daddy—Eugene's—was one of the nicest birds I ever knew. In the Rainbow Division, with your daddy. But I wouldn't worry about young Fisher—no stayin' power in his pecker, I'd judge, just between you and me and the gatepost." His forehead creased. "Cap, I just want you to know I know how close you feel to Phyl, and Cy, and how sorry I am this happened. But try not to let it faze you."

Nick said slowly, "I'll try. It's just—Cy's always been fine with me . . . and Phyllis—" He said suddenly, "She's like a Paul Scarlet rose . . ."

Wid's eyes opened very wide and then he said, "That's real nicely meant and real nicely put, Cap," and he was still staring at Nick as Harky came back in. He glanced up at Harky, back to Nick, and added, "Yessir, I can see how you'd feel that way about her—'course, I don't pretend to know a thing about women myself, includin' present company."

Harky said with force, "I don't know what you're talkin' about, but you'd better set out them sprinklers before you go back with the Vigilantes, Widdicomb Lucas. This day's hot! Gonna burn off all the portulaca if it ain't wetted down." She leaned over the table. "He greeted me," she announced proudly. "The General, just now. Winked as clear as a jaybird, and twice as sassy."

"He never," said Wid.

"Life in him, shootin' out of him. Had I his doctor rights, I'd bake up a rhubarb pie and see he et it to the crumbs." She stooped hugely and spread open a sack-mouth. "Would you look at all them bombin' materials! What you got cooked up for this year? No more explosions in the courthouse tower, I d'voutly trust?"

Nick said, "No, this is different. It was mainly Buck's idea."

"That boy'll be governor or hanged, it's the Lord's tossup," Harky said. She inspected Wid. "What you sitting there moon-eyed for?"

Wid shrugged; then his eyes met hers directly and he said, "You really want to know, I'm thinkin' about Phyl Bellaman. Somethin' Nick said—her bein' like a rose. I was sayin' to myself, a woman like her, a man doesn't even have to know her. Sees her once, and feels somethin' in his fingertips. Somethin' in his head, like an old tune."

Harky shook her head vigorously. "It's a tune that always ends up one place, and most of the time somethin' like this here tragedy happens. I ain't blamin' Phyl Bellaman," she said heavily. "I'm blamin' others."

For a second Wid's and Harky's eyes met again. But nothing was said and Harky looked away, readjusting her apron. "Well, Angie says, in her great gen'rosity, she'll let some of the General's friends in to see him awhile. They're already gatherin' out to the side. Relatives bringin' 'em, like shepherds showin' off the flock. I'll make lemonade and some cookies."

She stalked to a cabinet and bustled there. "When you two get through, put your plates in the sink. Wid, you bear in mind you got to help set off the park cannon come noon—no matter if it takes time from vigilantyin', it's important. Mayor'd blow himself up without you. Nick, you be back here in time to dress up for the parade, and drive them veterans in it." She glanced around as she swept a dozen lemons into a bowl. "And take care, the both of you. I dread this day. Children maimed and mortified. Poor little Ricton boy, couple years back, took out the whole side of his jaw. Had his jujube candy in one hand, torpedoes in the other. Was watchin' Tom Mix, and got 'em confused. Ain't been able to say the multiplication table since."

Wid plucked a toothpick from the cut-glass holder and murmured around it, "Way you're sittin' there in the sun you look more like Rex Cloud 'n anybody'd say was possible, Cap. Come on, let's get out in it—we're bein' shagged."

Nick got up, went to the sink and set his plate in it. The sink had water taps, which connected with the town water supply; but the red pump installed when the house was built was still used for all Harky's rinsing and naturally for drinking. He picked up a tumbler, held it beneath the pump spout and agitated the handle. Drinking, he seemed to see Phyllis Bellaman's eyes reflected in the water, and to taste the hint of sulphur.

He put the tumbler down, leaning back against the sinkboard. Wid was placing his own plate in the sink. Nick said softly, "How about Cy's dog; how about Merlin?"

Wid said, "Locked up, but raisin' Cain when we left there last night." He made a mouth of disgust. "My God, we sure thrashed around them woods under Carmian. Couldn't find a booger in a bear trap in that mess. Mebbe we'll have better luck this morn." He lowered his head under the spout, gestured to Nick to pump and growled as the water sluiced over his head and ears.

Fireworks in hand, Nick went over to Harky where she was slicing lemons on a board, kissed her on the warm moist hairs at the back of her neck, and joined Wid in the doorway. As they went out together he thought of Cy, who couldn't show himself to people in all this sunlight on this golden day, and a shiver passed through him.

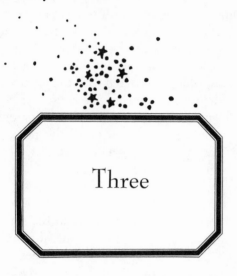

Three

Few people knew exactly how many limestone caves there were along the valley under Carmian's Hill; cool in the hottest noons, their walls shining with the glitter of yellow salt and drops of moisture, they lay secret and biding. They had a sharp, woodsmoke smell like flint arrowheads.

Cy had been in the cave since two o'clock in the morning, making for it instinctively, remembering it as if it had always been there for use in emergency. As light gathered and plunged through to the floor of the woods, as the train whistle called, he had stepped outside to mark the quality of the day; it would be steadily hot.

He sat on a log well inside the mouth of the cave; the rifle, barrel up, stood against the wall.

Stripping off his jacket, finding among loose cartridges in its pockets a couple of chocolate bars, he had eaten one, saving the other for later. He felt no fear of being discovered and taken by Sheriff Jerome Potter and his committee, though they were good woodsmen, and old friends. The one man who could have found him—who, with intuition that had no need for ordinary hunters' logic, would very possibly have come directly to this cave—was Henry Watherall. And Henry would never step into the woods again; he would never sit, amiably silent like a shadow, for hours on end in a duck blind, or quiet beside a deer run, or move like fog through a dark morning as the trees came out of their dimness.

Cy had known Henry since they were both nine years old. Henry's schooling had been sparse, like that of most Ridge people; but he and Henry had gravitated together as if in some past life they had known each other well, and this new relationship was merely taking up where the other had left off. At Henry's home on the Ridge, Cy had eaten fatback and possum, squirrel stew and dove, venison and river perch; at his parents' home, in town, Henry used to show up for supper like a shy ghost, watching Cy and Mr. and Mrs. Bellaman with alert care so he wouldn't make terrible mistakes of etiquette, speaking carefully when spoken to, and only becoming himself again when they escaped the constricting atmosphere of the house and were together once more on familiar trails.

It was Henry who saved his life—though Henry wouldn't have put it like that—on the morning after New Year's Day when he fell through river ice and went under like a rock, his new strap skates weighing him down. Henry always in the background, silent, supporting, through the death by cancer of Cy's father, and later the death of his mother, and when he had gone off to college. During the war Henry returned badly wounded, with an important medal he kept, thereafter, in a tin box under a floor plank in the house where he and his mother lived on the Ridge, along with a pile of frayed hunting magazines Cy had passed along to him.

Invited to Cy's wedding, Henry came in his private's uniform, the cloth leggings insecurely wrapped, the uniform already beginning to fade, but clean. During the reception he sat in a corner, sipping claret cup. The enormous Wolfson house, constructed by Pierre, Phyllis' great-great-grandfather, seemed to dwarf him, the jazz band imported from Dayton for the festivities to assault his ears. It was a frantic time, stormy with bad news—the month before, Rex Cloud had been killed in France. His older sister, Alice, had been engaged to Cy for a year before the war, but she attended the wedding anyhow. A tall girl in green silk, she took charge of Henry, taught him, with his dragging foot, a few rudimentary dance steps. Marna Cloud, flushed and funny, did her famous imitations of town characters, surrounded by an applauding group of well-wishers, all flown with Wolfson champagne.

And through it all Phyllis, now Mrs. Bellaman, had moved like a dark torch, her eyes burning and her hands possessive upon Cy.

He couldn't believe the way she had loved him that night. It wasn't against nature, but it went into a core of fierceness, annihilation and rebirth that made him, in the morning, look at her, sleeping, as though he contemplated a miracle—that this much passion, shameless, demanding, giving and asking more, could be compacted in one bright body. Her nightdress was ripped where she had torn at its lace to get it off, throw it away; her hair spread as if lifted by a vast wind, her lips were moist, her breathing steady and deep, her eyes when they at last opened, staring up into his, amethyst and still hungry. She had smiled as if the smile were wrenched from her, and arched herself up to him, her fingertips caressing his nape and spine, then their nails tightening, her nipples warm, and she'd said, in her voice that was forever a promise even when it perhaps didn't mean to be, "Oh, fuck me, love. Fuck me, give us a baby."

It was not coarse, not shocking; but it was a plea and a need nearly terrifying in its strength. And it was little enough to what she began saying later on: words, language, mocking questions dealing with his prowess in bed; the jargon of whores, which he recalled from secretive trips to the bad houses of his college days. But the difference was wide; the whores did it to stimulate their weary customers; Phyllis meant it. Presiding at a supper for her ailing father, Tom Wolfson, she was the soul

26

of attractive, matronly rectitude; in white lace, she poured tea from the Revere service, laughed with the men about her; that night she was a lovely bedroom demon.

She stimulated him to greater, even heroic feats; ashamed of not being in the Army—though he had been confined to his engineer's job by the government—of living safely in Arden while the men for whom he made tanks in old Noel Cloud's shops died in them abroad, he had also this saving joy in her. And she, apparently, in him.

By the time, the following spring, that Tom Wolfson died, leaving the Bellamans alone in the house on Wolfson Block, she had changed again. There was still intimacy, still the things they laughed at together, knew together; yet at the Shops, sometimes, he would look up past his drawing board, pencil gripped tight in his fingers, and murmur to himself what the shop workers would have said, "She's kicked me out of bed."

But that mood of hers didn't last, either; they turned to each other, blind as strangers on shipboard, in the lilac-drenched nights, as if shooting stars ran fire in their blood. She spoke no more about the child that never appeared. She blew hot as a sirocco, then cool as Iceland moss. She had been eighteen when they married; on her nineteenth birthday, during a long, loud party to which all their town friends came—the news was good from Europe, the tide had turned, that bastard Kaiser Bill was heading for a great fall—she disappeared and it was not till a few days later that Cy, nudged by well-meaning male acquaintances, found that Link Savage, a tough-bitten young shop foreman he'd always liked, had been missing too.

He took Link out behind the Shops—a usual place for settling differences, well out of sight and earshot of old Noel— got the defiant truth from him and beat him senseless.

At home that night he brought it out as brutally as he had to Link. She gazed at him quietly, as though he had asked the correct time. She said, "I think we need some time apart. I'm signing up for some courses in Cincinnati, I don't want to be half ignorant all my life. I'll be leaving in the morning. I've asked Tessy Morton to come in and keep the house clean and make supper for you while I'm gone. If you want to make love before I go, I'd like to. If you beat me, I'll never come back."

How, he never knew, but he found himself in bed with her then; it should have been demeaning, but it was not. That week, after she left, he took up again with Henry. He walked into the clearing on the Ridge, and leaning in the sagging doorway, nodded to Tilda Watherall, who was stringing dried gourds, and to Henry, cleaning a rifle beside the hearth. He said only, "Let's get some doves."

Henry hobbled over to him and said, "Thought you'd dropped into the quarry or somewhat," and they spent the rest of the evening discussing their dove approaches.

Now, on the log, observing the span of sunlight as it began to penetrate the mouth of the cave, a hot, inching semicircle, Cy said aloud, "Oh, my Jesus, Henry. Oh, my God . . ."

Making his way to the Flute Café's rest room, Marty Broom passed a couple of truckers in one of the booths and overheard them, as they argued about the best routes to Columbus, mention that the town they were in had once produced notable cars. "Sure," one of them said. "Clouds. Some bus."

Marty shut the rest-room door on them indignantly. To him, calling a Cloud a bus was blasphemy. He unbuttoned his pants and belched a breath of Grady Flute's bacon and eggs. If those dumb out-of-towners had ever worked for the Shops in the great days, they'd have had some respect for an automobile that could have stood up to the Duesenberg, the Stutz, the Rolls.

An amazing automobile, a shining beast of a car, fairly expensive, not too many made by the week, but a mile above the black Tin Lizzies Henry Ford rolled off his chattering Detroit assembly lines. Marty'd never been even an assistant foreman, but he had swung his lunch bucket with the best, felt a confrere of old Noel himself when the old man marched through with a sheaf of shop prints under one arm and a word for everybody.

The day the craneman made a mistake and Marty's left leg was crushed between half a ton of bedplate and the wall, Noel Cloud stood over him, talking with quiet encouragement, until the doctor arrived. He'd paid all the bills, too, and made Marty a night watchman afterward, with no cut in salary. But when Noel had that first stroke and the Shops were sold—to out-of-towners who produced niggling cars made to last a few years and head for the boneyard—Marty quit the Shops for good.

Better being a good, able town handyman, hauling mail for the post office, working for Miss Alice Cloud at her hospital, assisting the Kaplan brothers in their hardware store, than have any part in producing crap.

He was buttoning his pants when, looking out the window above the trap, he saw five men climbing a path leading to Carmian's Hill. He leaned and scrubbed with the heel of his hand at the murky pane, not doing much good. But he recognized the men, all right, though they were already diminishing in the early sunlight. One was Sheriff Jerome Potter, another was Carl Bolyard, wide as a barn door, still another Tommy Beavis, the sheriff's only full-time help, but out of uniform, and the last two were Muff Raintree and Phil "Slim" Thomas, taciturn men from the Ridge, good with guns, knowledgeable about the woods. All of them carried weapons.

By gow, that's no hunting party, Marty told himself sternly. That's the people call themselves Vigilantes, and think they're so big-chested secret. There ain't a law on earth says I can't follow them.

At the counter he settled up his modest check swiftly, impatient when Grady wanted to chat. "Ain't got time to chew the rag," he flung over his shoulder as he stepped into Front Street's sunlight. Sambo, the dog, got up from where he'd been sprawled under the awning and followed a few paces in back as Marty headed alongside the café to the rise of land behind it.

Oak shadows pooled in a cadence like music over the side lawns of the Cloud house. The old veterans seated on the bench murmured among themselves, so many sun-praising bees. When they laughed the noise was sudden, cackling, elfin; there was no reservation in it, even though some of them were from across the river in Kentucky. But against the warm thick dark blue of their fellows, the Confederate gray they wore had a slaty, muted cast, like granite beside basalt. Under a clump of oaks at a distance from their charges, the ladies who had accompanied the veterans to the Cloud place were gathered, in dotted swiss and eyelet organdy and voile, some of them Daughters of the Grand Army of the Republic, some Kentucky-bred Daughters of the Confederacy, some also wearing the ribbands that marked them as Daughters of the American Revolution. They were the caretakers, relatives and friends come to show off their prized and long-lived possessions. They talked in steady undertones, keeping alert for aberrant or dangerous behavior from the honored and senile. Over all, the locusts shrilled—the trees flared points of voluminous green.

Nick stood with Wid, watching the flag on the deep front porch, where it gave a ripple on its horizontal lanyards and then hung still again. Then he looked at the veterans, their campaign hats proudly creased, buffed and dusted; the boots shinier than they must have been on any field of war; the uniforms threadbare but elegant. He thought of his Grandmother Marie's Waterford glass, brought out now only to praise, never to use. Some of the veterans were turning their heads toward him and Wid, hands loose on their knees, quids safe in their cheeks, relaxed but conscious of their day of celebrity.

Wid stretched, his rooty hands going up to cup and clasp the sun, his heels set as if he was linked forever to the flowers, vegetables and grasses he lived with and tended.

"Poor old devils . . . well, Cap, got to set out them sprays. Harky's right, this day'll burn the monkey where it hurts. I know where you're goin', but 'fore you leg out for Buck's, how about a little dram? I got a nice new jug in the storehouse."

He jerked a thumb toward the carriage-house garage and

sheds. There grape arbors cast latticed seines of shade, the roofs decanted shadow to the driveway as if to distill the sweltering heat. Ancient lilac bushes, long past their season's blossom, covered the carriage-house walls. Snowball and night stock sparked from the pleasant gloom. Foxfire and salvia, portulaca and gladiolus waited in stipples of sun for the day to end, for their leaves to feel the cool dew. Beyond the arbors, the strawberry and rhubarb and sweet-corn patches baked in an oven of air.

Wid said impatiently, "Well? Ain't aiming to get you dead drunk and besotted. Just thought it might lift you out o' the dumps a little. Ain't no day for the dumps." He bent over and uprooted a dandelion before he went on. "By the way, Cap, if you're plannin' to drop into the hospital and see Phyl Bellaman —go real careful and tactful. Your Aunt Alice don't lose no love for Phyl. Doubt if they've exchanged half a dozen words in so many years. And this thing about Cy ain't goin' to improve matters."

Nick said, "Aunt Alice was engaged to Cy once, wasn't she?"

"Sure was. Back when the war was hottin' up good. She don't talk about it much, and I bet a silver dollar *he*'s never mentioned it to you. Phyl took him away easy as pie from a doorstep. Them things cut deep—she has it in her mind, you can bet. Prideful lady, your aunt, and she thinks a hell of a lot of *you*. Bear it in mind if you're goin' to go oozin' sympathy around Phyl."

Nick said, "I wasn't going to take her any calf's-foot jelly or anything. I might drop in to see her; might not."

"Don't get your back up with *me*." Wid put a hand on Nick's shoulder briefly, then took it off. "Want that little innocent drink or not? Won't strike you blind. It's one o' Renfrew's good batches."

"I think I'll give it the go-by till later," Nick said.

"Sure Mike. It's in the old rabbit hutch. Where Harky can't roust it out. Just reach down till you feel the energy."

He turned and walked toward the carriage house and sheds. Even overalled, he had what people termed a military bearing, but a point of sure pride with him was that he owed the government nothing and that it owed him a good deal. Nick supposed he would be carrying his government-issue Springfield rifle, with its own sling, when he rejoined the Vigilante Committee later in the morning; when he spoke of the weapon he was always careful to remark that he had paid for it, hadn't lifted it as any souvenir.

Nick went on toward the bench to perform his duty; something the Civil War veterans would expect from him, as General Cloud's one living male relative in direct line of descent. As he moved toward the veterans he was aware of the onerousness of duty and its grave demands, but at the same time he was thinking about the rabbit hutch. Wid's mention of it had brought back remembrances that for a few seconds swarmed through his mind.

Buck and I were eleven then, he thought. Winter, and snow had patched the earth around the carriage house. The sky was steel-gray, twilight hanging over the ground like an iron hood. Buck said on impulse, "Let's let the rabbits out." They were Belgian hares, familiar only with the limited freedom of the chicken-wire run nailed to the hutch, fat with lettuce, doped with raw oatmeal and carrots from Harky's winter stock.

Nick said "Sure" without a pause. The hasp of the door built into the chicken wire was cold-burning on his fingertips. The first hare hesitated in the open door, ears laid back, soft warm nose wrinkling; then it gave a lumpy leap and landed on the floorboards of the carriage house. The second hare followed, looking around at a tire of the magnificent green Cloud buggy, a bumper of the Cloud limousine beyond, wearing a cosy-Grandma look straight from Beatrix Potter. Then both of them went in slow hops toward the sill board, out into the sharp dark air. At which Buck's half-mastiff, Albert, made one ripping sound in the back of his heavy-furred throat and shot out after the first hare. At first what was shocking wasn't Albert himself

—it was that the plump domestic pet could move so fast. For four great but ever-narrowing circles it stayed ahead of inexorable Albert, dodging and turning like a zigzag piece of lightning; then, much worse, just as the dog caught it up and broke its neck, it screamed. Nick and Buck could not move; they were frozen. When Albert caught and killed the second hare there was, again, that quick awful unavailing cry.

After a while Nick found a couple of Wid's garden spades, and Buck helped him break the tough rinds of earth; they buried the hares, the sacrifices, and after that they didn't mention anything about it to any adult, and not till much later, even to each other. When he found them missing, Wid said he guessed somebody'd forgotten to latch their door. Noel Cloud heard about them being gone, and asked Nick if he'd like another pair. Nick declined.

Nick went over to the veterans, nodding to them now, and stopping beside the bench. Deep within himself he asked, Why do I think of Cy and Phyllis when I remember the rabbits? And of Henry Watherall—easygoing, shy-eyed, coming around from the Ridge sometimes in a slat-wheeled vegetable wagon, dickering with Harky at the back door; a man with dignity and good close-mouthed sense—who would go limping with Cy into the woods.

I'll see Phyllis this morning, he thought. I have to see her. He hoped his Aunt Alice wouldn't be angry about it, or disappointed in him.

The old man nearest him leaned from the bench, nostrils flaring around white nose hairs, faded eyes inspecting him closely under the shadow of the gilt-tasseled hat. He remembered this gray-clad veteran's name, Rance Todman. From the pump another veteran, in sweltering dark blue, came walking back to the bench, wiping his mouth with the back of a sere and leathery hand. Lieutenant John Strite, who had served with Noel Cloud, wavered for a moment on uncertain legs, then made a dart to the bench and unceremoniously rumpbutted Todman to make room for himself.

33

Rance Todman gave the Yankee a chilly, glinting glance and held out a hand to Nick. "Hey, boy."

Nick pressed the dry, lizard-cool, frail-boned hand. "Captain Todman," Nick said.

"Yeah," said Todman. "And I'm goin' in to see your grandpa. They can't keep me out. Tried to bar the way last year, 'cause I talk too much. Huh! He can't answer nohow, now. What difference'll it make? They said I tired him out last year. He c'd answer me back, then." He leaned out over the bags of fireworks. "Just smell all that goddamn powder! Stinks like Cold Harbor."

Beside him, Strite wriggled humped shoulders. "Shee-ut." He put out his own hand to be shaken. "Listen at him, reg'lar Reb talk, thinkin' every scrap he got in was special. Ought to know damn well they all smelled the same. Couldn't tell one from another—just roll the meat wagon around after, and count the bodies. Gettysburg same as Shiloh."

Nick shook Strite's nearly weightless hand as Strite said, "*I'm* goin' in to see Noel too. Let a Reb in, they can roll out the carpet for me . . . I fit with him, alongside him—they got to remember it!"

"That's a fact, Lieutenant Strite," Nick said.

He passed along the line, shaking hands. As he reached the end Rance Todman said loudly, for the whole benchful to hear, "Noel's the only bluebelly I ever respected—ain't cause he was a goddamn brevet general, just 'cause he's a good man to live cross-river from. Wouldn't be here today if he wasn't! Hell, some folks don't even celebrate this here Fourth, my side the river. It's the day Vicksburg fell!"

Laughter rippled down the bench.

Nick had paid his respects; he shifted the fireworks to the crook of his left arm and started to leave. But behind him John Strite bellowed in a deaf-man's voice, "How's your mama, son? How's Marna? Still runnin' around the big cities actin' in plays?"

Nick felt the watchful ladies nearby listening closely. They

34

didn't exactly lean out from the shadows to hear better, but they were waiting for his answer. Marna Cloud's name often appeared in the gossip columns of newspapers; there'd been a recent interview with her in the *Delineator*, whose readers liked to know how actresses lived, or how they said they did. Nick remembered that the week before, when he was having supper with the Bellamans, Phyllis leaned across the table, patting his hand, saying in her throaty voice, "Never mind. You'll live it down, darling."

He spoke loudly for Strite and the rest. "My mother's in Chicago—we had a letter last week. She can't come home for a while because she's in this play—*Candida*. She said to say hello from her."

Strite was grinning with yellow teeth like old corn nubs. "Knowed her when she didn't hardly reach my bootlatch. Always dressin' up, puttin' on a show. Sure some elocutionist! Beat the hell out of Chautauqua! 'Curfew Shall Not Ring Tonight!' Done it up brown as johnnycake!" Then he roared out: "Shame she don't get married again—woman with her fire —Rex gone all these years!"

There wasn't anything to say to that. And the good ladies were still listening.

Nick searched for a decent comment, then didn't have to— because Harky came out the back door, with a huge tray of lemonade and cookies. His audience diverted, Nick walked off. Ice clinked through the chatter behind him. He brushed by the bridal-wreath bushes under the front-porch railing, noting that their tiny blossoms looked like the rosettes Melissa Gardner's mother used to trim her many dresses.

The spirited sound of fireworks got louder as he stepped off the curb at the end of the driveway. The paving stones of the street were murky but clean, still touched with traces of water left by the wagon. Nick walked to the middle of the street, set down the sacks and shook out a twelve-inch salute. It had a satisfactory weight in his hand. He spread the fuse, the gimlet eye of gunpowder black inside its fluffy string. By mutual agree-

ment with Buck, whoever did the actual selection of the fireworks got to shoot off the first one; this year he'd done the
buying.

He fixed the base of the salute firmly between paving stones.
It looked like the excited penis of a noble redman. He found
a little, tidy box of Swedish matches, taking some delight in its
perfect shape, its miniature tray, struck a match, lit the fuse
and moved away, scooping up the sacks as the fuse started a
healthy fizz.

The noise was superb. It rang in his head for a few seconds;
paper scraps settled, a lively stench moved under his nostrils.
Up through the lower leaves of the overhanging oaks the smoke
lifted and joined the sunlight. But when he had turned away,
making for Buck's, he didn't look back. The year before he
would have, walking backward, still marveling, until the blackened smudge where the salute had been was out of sight.

Over the back fences of the lane leading to the Bolyards,
hollyhocks and sunflowers leaned with leaves thick as jungle
growth, in a kind of ripe passion. Outside the Bolyards' gate
a new garbage can dazzled the eye.

Carl Bolyard was large-boned and firmly knitted, his flesh so
full of dark blood it sometimes appeared to take on the coloring
and texture of one of his own prime sirloins. Besides Bolyard's
Meat Market, where Buck helped out summers, Carl ran the
Bolyard Slaughterhouse—west of town, discreetly set apart
from other enterprises, since its smell was, in the warm
months, unbearable. All three Bolyards—Buck, Carl and
Maidy—shared the gift of enjoying one another, laughing at
each other, no matter how slight the cause. Their enjoyment
in themselves seemed to reach above any tribulation, minimiz-
ing and scaling down even success. It was whole, sufficient, and
Nick liked being part of it.

He went up the walk, past the garage window where Carl's
green Dort automobile shone, hosed down and polished and
decorated with streamers for the parade. Carl had once told

Nick he'd have liked owning a Cloud, but it would have cost him too much; he preferred putting the money he saved into short, eventful vacations—to Turkey Run in Indiana, Starved Rock in Illinois.

Close by the walk, behind their wire, Cochin-Chinas and Rhode Island Reds picked over kernels of corn. They stared at Nick, squawked as he passed, and went back to their foraging. Buck sat on the back steps, a ginger-furred kitten occupying one overalled knee. He was smoking a cigar butt of respectable length, Carl no doubt having left it so on purpose. He puffed a mouthful toward the kitten, which retreated and batted a paw at him and arched its spine. Buck fanned smoke away and gathered the kitten closer to his bare chest. He said mildly, "What held you up?"

Nick sat down alongside him. "The old vets—you know."

Buck nodded, carefully shifted the kitten and took the sacks from Nick. With his left hand he offered the cigar to Nick. Nick shook his head, and Buck replaced the cigar, his lips long, with thoughtful, deep lines at the corners, his eyes fire-blue, his hair short, Indian-flat, soot-black.

From a sack he pulled up a cluster of cherry bombs, dangling them above the kitten's nose. "Good. Just fine. Like we said, these'll go in under the edges of them fool old urns. I got the rest of it all figured, where to put the big stuff. Okay." He gave Nick a glance, and went on peering into the sacks. "How much?"

Nick said, "With the night stuff, eight dollars."

Buck made a sling of his right hand under the kitten's belly and set it down on the walk. The kitten minced away, hardly casting shadow, tail rigid as if it stalked all mankind. Buck dug into a pocket, brought up a handful of dollar bills and counted out four. Folding them into his own pocket, Nick said, "I'll pick up the night stuff before the parade and bring it along."

Buck's eyes creased into slits. "A real nice thought came to me when I got up this mornin'. Daddy was home and takin' a rest 'fore the Vigilantes started out again—ain't it awful?—

so it about got driven out o' my head till right now. But what say we do it"—he flickered a glance down at the bags, upward again—"just when they fire that ol' cannon off, over in the park? Just on the stroke of noon?"

Nick took a pleasurable breath. He was often surprised by Buck's endlessly fertile vision. Blowing up the cemetery urns was an idea they had both thought of; this refinement on it had Buck's special dab of polish. The urns, ugly and useless enough to deserve extinction, would die as the cannon bellowed in its traditional rite—making a sound fit to roil the dead and astound the living.

Buck said, "You can hear the courthouse clock from the cemetery. Hear it from the park, too—that's when they light the cannon fuse. So?"

"So sure," Nick said. After a second he added, "It's just about ideal."

"Didn't think it was any bad thought." Then Buck's face changed. "Figured Wid'd tell you about the other thing," he said softly. "I feel right bad about Cy." He shook ash from the cigar. "About Phyl, too—Mama, she was sayin' this morning, Phyl Bellaman ain't no bad woman. No Hoor of Babylon, anyhow. A woman don't have to sing in a choir and go to box-lunch raffles for the starvin' Armenians, to be a wonderful lady. *I* don't care what she done."

He traced a bare, fawn-dark toe over the step. "Daddy said he agreed. Said a woman like her was worth ten of the kind always lookin' corner-eyed to see if a thumb's on the scale. Jesus, but I feel sick for Hank Watherall. Bet you, though, wherever he is, he figures it was worth it . . . I just can't see a man like him goin' to Hell. Hope he's around someplace—tryin' to tell Cy he's sorry, anyhow, and a long way from Melton's Funeral Parlor. That's where they took him."

He sat back, shoulders looser, his face blunt and humorous again. "I'm takin' Candy Pruitt to the parade, and the dancin'," he said. "You takin' Melissa?"

Nick had been thinking of Phyllis Bellaman. It was as if, for

38

a few seconds, a hand had been laid over his loins, which felt a strange ache. Phyllis, Cy, Henry . . . He said abruptly, "Oh —no. Melissa's father wouldn't let me. Anyhow, Eugene Fisher asked her first." He amended this: "I mean, Mr. Gardner *said* Eugene asked her first. That's what he told me last night—only it was morning, pretty late this morning—when he kicked me off their porch."

"I'd like to *do* somethin' about Gene Fisher," Buck said musingly. "About Mr. Gardner, too, except he's too old to swat." His eyes slid to Nick, and he said almost offhandedly, "Expect you'll want to stop by your aunt's hospital and see Phyllis a minute."

"It won't take much time," Nick said.

When he pulled his prized Ingersoll watch from his overalls, Buck disturbed several other articles which clinked and shuffled there. Until reaching a point when it turned futile, he and Nick had been indifferent boy scouts in a troop scoutmastered by Roy Gardner, but Buck's notions of preparedness went far past those of the official manual. He went equipped for desert island or distant planet.

"We got enough time. Even stop off at Melissa's a spell, 'f you want to."

Buck looked up at Nick. "I been thinkin' somethin' else," he said. His face was warm, solid bronze. "Didn't mention it to Daddy. He'll likely think of it himself, or Sher'f Potter will." His mouth curved up. "Daddy's got that *shot*gun. The one we us'ly keep behind the cold-cut ice chest. Ain't shot it since the time them out-of-staters tried to hold him up. Hit a side of beef, we picked shot out of it for a week. Wouldn't take his good gun, said it wouldn't be fair to Cy. Anyhow, what I was thinking . . ." His voice went down. In the Bolyard's house, past the screening of this door, Maidy Bolyard was singing "Brighten the Corner Where You Are." Her full, yolky contralto sailed up and down and around the notes, but did it blithely. The Bolyards liked music and comedic patter and played their fumed-oak Sonora phonograph most nights after supper, favoring Moran and Mack, the *Two Black Crows,* as well as Paul Whiteman's *San, Hindustan,* and *Rhapsody in Blue,* and Enrico Caruso and John McCormack, with selected "Family and Operatic Favorites." And they had a player piano whose rolls were apparently without end.

Cutting an eye at the screen, Buck kept his voice down even farther. "I just bet Cy's down in the woods off the hill, under the cemetery."

Nick said as quietly, "I don't think he'd be any place else. They were *his* woods." He felt his throat tightening again. "And Henry's," he added.

Buck took up a sack, stood up and put his face close to the screening. "Mama—Mama, we're goin' now!"

Maidy Bolyard broke off. "Well, you just have a fine time —you too, Nick! Tell Wid and Harky if there ain't room in your car with them vet'rans ridin' with you come the parade, we'd be glad to haul some of 'em with us!"

Nick could see her shadow through the screen door. He called, "I'll tell them. See you in the park, anyhow!"

"My Lord, the park picnic—I'll wager Harky's got all her bakin' done for it already, and I ain't even started!" She laughed. "Look at you, Buck Bolyard, like a ragbag, and Nick neat's if he'd just come out of a bandbox! I'm goin' to press your new suit after I work on your daddy's. If you can't stay out o' mischief, stay out o' jail!"

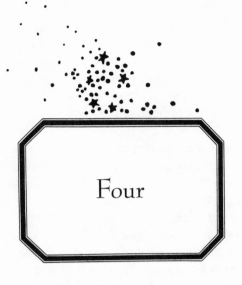

Four

From where Marty Broom had paused for breath—he was wheezing slightly and had a stitch in his side—he could see backward and down from the path's hill slope over a great deal of Arden. Over the trees rose the steeples of churches, from Front Street the tower of the courthouse, and northward a few roofs of the Shops, across the street and down an incline from the school. He could make out the general shape of Front Street and the Cloud Block and the Wolfson Block; the leaves glittered like sharp mirror glass. The dog, Sambo, sat down beside him, idly searching out fleas.

Marty had kept the five members of the Vigilante party in sight for a while, with difficulty; now the party was out of sight in one of the dips of the land. Thinking of this Vigilante group, in its self-importance and secrecy, he became more indignant by the minute. Who in merry hell do they think they are, he said to himself, obviously trailing some wrongdoer—else why the guns?—and not telling the rest of the town a thing about it? Just because they all fought in the war, think they can run the town and stay quiet about it, ride roughshod over the rights of the rest of us. No better than so many Prussians, themselves.

But then, the town itself was going to hell in a handbasket; in Marty's estimation, outside the Clouds and maybe the Kaplans and certainly the Bellamans, the place was sliding into decay. Nobody was as good as they used to be.

He pulled a stem of timothy grass and sucked the sweet end. He still couldn't see any of the committee coming out of the valley and up onto the last approach to Carmian's Hill. He turned his attention back to the east, to the town; not one explosion could be heard from down there at this distance. He thought about the people he liked to work for the most—Miss Alice Cloud, at the hospital, because she treated him as if he were as smart as she was. The P.O. because it was important government work even if the pay was pretty poor; the Kaplans because they believed in quality merchandise in their store and were mighty funny people; and—he bit the timothy stalk in two and spat it out in strong self-agreement—and the Bellamans.

Fondly he thought about Cy and Phyllis. Of course, he'd had a lot more to do with the missus than with him, but Cy was a quality man. He kept to himself, and since the selling of the Cloud Shops, apart from the rest of the town, outside chumming around the woods with that Henry Watherall; didn't have to worry about money, there'd been plenty of that from the Wolfsons, with Phyllis the only heir, and besides, he'd made plenty as the top engineer in the Shops, in those solid days, and had probably saved a good bit.

Marty frowned heavily at the remembrance of the way some people talked about Phyllis Bellaman. He himself refused to listen to such talk, considering it mostly came from slack lips and yokel minds, from what passed for workers in the Shops these days. Maybe Phyllis Bellaman didn't always toe the Methodist and Baptist line the way people were expected to, but there was no need for her to. She was a law unto herself, and Marty approved of the law.

He'd worked around the Bellaman place—that fine old

house in its fifteen-acre grounds—for around a dozen years now, give or take a few months; he recalled the afternoon a couple of years back when he showed up late on a June-blessed day, and going to the shed for the hoe and rake, heard a splashing over in that natural rockpool in the middle of the grounds and walked over there to consult with Phyllis about weeding out the phlox borders. She didn't always want him to weed; she liked the grounds half rough, and said the things people called tares should be given a chance, that they were just as beautiful, very often, as the trim and accepted flowers. The gentle splashing stopped as he got closer to the pool. It was shadowed like a grotto by birches and wild hickory, and a place not many knew about now that the Bellamans didn't entertain anymore or throw those big parties.

When he caught sight of a body through the warm gilded leaves he didn't at first think it was Phyllis at all—thought it was some kid who'd sneaked in there and gone bare-ass for the fun of it, leaving his clothes on the bank. Then he took another step forward and she turned around where she sat, her legs dangling down toward the water, a twin of her sparkling from the polished, still darkness of the water, her hands back on the rocks, her head back and her wet hair flowing over her clean brown shoulders and down along her spine. He couldn't help seeing all she had, and though it should have embarrassed him, somehow it didn't.

Maybe it was because she didn't make the hint of a fuss about it, just sat there looking over at him. After a breath she said, "Hello, Marty. I forgot you were coming today." She got up, not fast, and reached for her slip, and he thought he'd never seen anything more perfect. Not a spare ounce on her, the breasts not so cow-big that they got in the way, but not so meaching that they got lost in the rest of her, either; the legs turned so fine that any man who respected craftsmanship would have felt a warm shock in his balls. Marty had never married, and he wasn't religious, either; but he had standards he liked kept up. She hadn't let them down an inch.

When she'd put on a little dress and was buttoning it, she walked around to where he was and said suddenly, "Thanks for being nice," and kissed him on the lips, in a friendly, quick way. Marty wouldn't ever forget the tingle of that feeling right through his mustache, and her not seeming to mind his sweaty work clothes.

Then as they walked back toward the house and the sun-rioting gardens, they discussed the case of the phlox borders. She didn't want too much edging, just enough to give the plants room, and he agreed, though as a rule he might have argued a little just for the fun of it. A woman like that you couldn't fault. For a while she helped him weed, squatting beside him as though they were both about ten years old and grubbing industriously and happily in the deep-black loam; and yes, sure, he felt little flickerings of fire along his spine—sixty-odd wasn't an age when you lost that need, whatever you were supposed to lose—and when he got up to go get the wheelbarrow, he felt hard and urgent. But there was a friend-ship, too, all around him, stronger than he'd ever thought it could be, even for this fine woman. It was something he valued like a gift he'd been given right out of the sky. And he wasn't going to have anything take it away or put a stain on it. So let them talk. Maybe she'd had a lot of affairs—there was enough sweet smoke about them for there to be hot fire under it—but he'd bet his life that most men who'd known her didn't talk about it. And he wouldn't listen to anything about it from those who *didn't* know. He'd just shut his ears or tell them to take their talk and stuff it.

Maybe her spirit was something like what that ancestor of hers, Pierre Wolfson, must have had when he was first settling this territory, before the town was even called Arden.

Now he turned his head around again to the west. Well, well, well. There they came, small in the distance, heaving themselves up the last of the path onto the hillside out there, Sheriff Potter in the lead, Tommy Beavis toiling behind him, Muff Raintree and Slim Thomas snaking behind them, big

44

Carl Bolyard in the rear. Where was Wid Lucas? He was part of this bunch; working for a man as good as old Noel Cloud, he ought to know better, but he had a dumb side. Maybe he hadn't caught up with his buddies yet this morning.

They all looked as if they were headed for the trestles. From the Ridge to the south above the river—where the colored folks lived on this side and the white hill dwellers, like Henry Watherall, on the other—the three trestles headed across Carmian's Hill northward, carrying the tracks down, finally, through Arden. If a man wanted to walk the trestle bridges, he could save some time going north; Marty figured that's what they aimed to do. All right, boys, he said to himself; all right, you bunch of heroes, we'll just see what we can see.

He took off his cap, whacked it on his knee and fitted it on again, purposefully. When he started climbing again, Sambo was at his side. Thinking about Phyllis Bellaman had warmed him as though he'd had a shot of good neat whiskey.

Nick and Buck came out on upper Front Street. Some of the wooden slat-boarded sidewalks behind them held heat like slabs of oven-warm bread, but the heat rising from the paving stones was stronger. For three blocks along Front Street, to the south, sunlight went beating toward the town square; past the fountain in the middle of the square the courthouse tower offered shadow for half a block around it, its four clock faces looming above into the full light, its limestone blocks long discolored by patches of bronze. The fountain was a wide dark-green iron saucer, over which iron cherubs and birds resembling failed phoenixes held smaller saucers.

The awnings of Flute's Café, Soames's Pharmacy and Melton's Funeral Parlor were down, oases of shade under them, as was the awning over the fire-station door. A bumper and a touch of scarlet paint from the La France fire truck, known as the Baby Doll, gleamed in the shadows. The broad façade of the Tribe of K, its awnings raised, flashed plate-glass reflections so fiercely that it could only be inspected under lowered eyelids.

As they crossed the street and turned north into the lane toward the hospital, Buck said, "Hey, they got a wing-walker over in Barlton." Barlton, Kentucky, the nearest town across the river, was distinguished only by its smoldering rivalry and resentment toward Arden. It was self-contained and had its own idea of festivities. Nick thought there might be honest and reputable people living there, and Buck concurred, but neither had ever met any, with the exception of the Confederate Civil War veterans and their female handlers. The wing-walking innovation was, Nick thought, one up for Barlton.

He said, "I'd like to see it. My father wanted to get in the Lafayette Escadrille. He didn't, and I guess the Rainbow Division was just as good . . ." But when his aunt told him about it, he hadn't really felt it had been as good. Alice Cloud was the only family member who relayed bits and pieces of the past to him, the only one who had been nearly as young as his father during that time, who had known it all at intense first hand. And she didn't like to talk about it much—only when she took him to Cincinnati on trips. She said she wanted to let him grow through his eyes and ears, and they would go to the opera, to *Aïda* and *The Barber of Seville* and *Rigoletto*. After he had learned what was going on onstage, he began enjoying it. She once mentioned the time of the Great War, cagily. As they sat in their hotel dining room one night she said, "It wasn't romantic, you know. Not any of it. Rex thought it was, he had the notion he was fated, touched by the plume of death—all very gallant, very *au désespoir* . . . but it wasn't like that, and it's a mistake to think it might be. Rex was like that all his life, but I don't think you are. Are you?"

Cautiously, watching smoke rise from Aunt Alice's Murad, Nick said, "I don't know. I'd like to know what war *feels* like."

"Yes, you would. You're the grandchild of a warrior. But that's not what I meant. It's an attitude of mind, a certain craziness—Father has none of that, he never did have. I hope you won't." Then she smiled briefly. "When you're in college, maybe some summer we'll go to France and you can see the approximate place where Rex was killed. I think you'll understand better then. It's so serene. In the absence of your mother —and you must always know what she does is necessary to her, more necessary than being with you—and because I'm closer to your age than your grandmother and grandfather, I've taken you on, Nick. I'm a highly interfering woman."

But she didn't actually interfere. What she said that one time had brought them closer than they'd ever been, even though they'd always had a closeness that didn't need a lot of surface-kissing to prove it was there. Just deep respect . . .

Buck was saying, "Oh, hell. I'd rather a million times scrap on the ground than go piroguin' around up there in the sky. I like the feel of somethin' under me."

Buck looked jauntily up into the crowns of the oaks. Down the lane children squatted beside a flat rock watching the ashy worms called snakes curl up from tiny gray sharp-smelling cones. On other blocks, explosives boomed and snapped, and somewhere a dog cried out in pain or fear.

Nick took a small breath and said, "Here we are," and they went up the walk to the hospital.

Julian, Leon and Aaron Kaplan gave a simultaneous jerk, heads bobbing forward and then back, as Julian, at the wheel of the Cloud roadster, braked at the curb in front of the Tribe of K.

In the parade, by custom and a certain easy protocol, the Kaplans would fill the roadster and drive it directly behind the Cloud touring limousine and its load of Civil War veterans. Back when the hardware store started to show real profit they'd bought the car, a superlatively handsome machine. They used it now mainly for ceremonious and joyous occasions, which, among the Kaplans, came more often than they did to most Arden families. They felt that by possessing it, and showing it off, they were paying a little homage to Noel Cloud, the town's most illustrious citizen. But they were also proud of it in its own right, as they were proud of themselves, of their lives, their children, their town and their place in it, and what they did for a living.

Julian and Leon stayed in the car. Aaron, the eldest, resplendent in a white linen suit, flung back the door, and swinging a set of keys, hurried into the Tribe of K. Behind its sun-glared windows an amazing variety was on display: plowshares and mower blades, windmill vanes and sickles, milk pails and jute bags of cattle feed. From the doorway a breath of the hardware fanned into the street: clean oils, the sweet musk of tempered steel, rich grain.

Julian leaned from the open roadster and called, "Bring plenty of them! Ten, anyhow!" He wore a fawn-checked jacket, a bright cravat in patriotic colors, trim spotless flannels and a Harold Lloyd straw skimmer; Leon was dressed to match.

Aaron was striding along an aisle flanked by counters heaped high with fireworks. As usual, because they loved fireworks, they had overbought.

In the car Julian said to Leon, "First thing tomorrow we got to shift that stock down cellar. Don't matter if we get a rush on, it's got to be done."

"I have it in mind," Leon said comfortably. "Don't worry about it. Lookit," he added, turning around to gaze along the block. "Melton's is open. Somebody has died."

Julian turned around too. "Well, a great shame to die on a holiday."

They looked at each other. "It wouldn't be General Cloud?" Leon asked.

Julian shook his head. "No, I called Miss Alice at the hospital this morning to tell her we would handle the main fireworks in the park. I asked about the General. She said he's no better, but as far as she knew, no worse. Holding his own." He spread his hands over his well-creased trouser knees. "She's furnishing the music for the dancing. The colored boys from the Settlement, from Reverend Bates's church, like last year. Very gifted young boys," he added approvingly, humming a bar of "A Kiss in the Dark" in a round baritone.

Leon leaned out and shouted, "Hey, Aaron! It takes so long to make up your mind? Ten of them, the big ones, it's all we need!"

Julian broke off his humming. "Better make it a dozen. In case we spoil one or two putting them together."

"Right," Leon said and bawled, "A dozen!"

From inside the store Aaron called back, "Hold your water out there! I already got about fifteen!"

Julian smiled. He said, "A very good idea, Leon. One of your best."

"Thanks," Leon said. "It just kind of came to me; I was shaving and thinking about over in Barlton, where they got this fellow who walks on the wing of an airship. Then it came over me, whiz; I could see it in front of my eyes. A rocket made of ten rockets, all lashed up like one. Five in front, five behind. With a main fuse stuck in so they all go off smooth and shoot up and out together." His hands planed up into the light, described a wide curve. His eyes, shining like blackberry currants, inspected Front Street with enormous pleasure. "It's bound to be seen in Barlton, and they'll know where it came from."

Julian laughed. "Oh, will they ever! They'll think, them Kaplans, they outfoxed us again! A fine signal from us to them, sailing over the ground of Kentucky!"

"They'll think about this whole town putting one over on them," Leon said. "It ain't just *us*. So, we haven't got a wing-walking gentleman, but this nice effect we have got. I should have thought of it sooner . . ." He shrugged. "But it's like the man invented the clothespin—he didn't plan for it ever since he was a small child. It flashed into his head." He motioned his head toward the hardware store. "My God, is he taking inventory? Give him a toot."

Julian gave the horn a tap. Its sound was noble and peremptory. It coincided with a barrage of salutes from about three blocks away and with Aaron's emergence from the store. Aaron held a large cardboard box overbrimming with fat long skyrockets, which he placed carefully in the back seat of the car before he got in. "I bought more than any dozen," he said, "closer to a gross. So there's room to experiment." He waved to Julian. "Home, James. Get a wiggle on, Mister Barney Oldfield."

Julian replaced the lilac-shade silk handkerchief with which he had been patting his high-domed forehead, arranging it correctly in his breast pocket, and put the roadster in gear; the engine gave an eight-cylinder roar as he made a U turn, and they rolled back up Front Street. Over the sound of their royal progress Julian was humming again, and after a little while Aaron and Leon joined in, in fair harmony.

Sheriff Jerome Potter had pale witty eyes under heavy lids, with deep folds beneath them. He was as hard-grained as hickory, and not out of middle age, but he resembled, in some lights, a bloodhound. Now, sweating profusely and heeling out on the first of the trestle bridges, the southernmost, and its gangling weathered spider legs reaching down to the creek below, he stopped, and turning around, stared back at Carl Bolyard, and Tommy Beavis a few ells behind him, and Slim Thomas and Muff Raintree strung out behind them. Good enough men, he told himself. But damn the fact that we're here, and damn Cy Bellaman, and damn you, Phyllis.

He said, "Want to ketch your breath a mite, Carl? 'Fore we head on across?"

Carl Bolyard, wet-faced, shook his head. He had the steady eyes of his son Buck, but his muscles were buried under tough fat like sides of bacon. The double-barreled shotgun, a Lakeside, seemed diminished by his heaviness. "Hell, no, Jerome. Let's make right along. If he's around the water tower, now's the time to find out."

Over Carl's shoulder Tommy Beavis said, " 'At's right, Jerome. If he's there, he ain't goin' to wait on us. Makes sense he might be there. Layin' up, waitin' for the midnight train out, it bein' a passenger train, like the ol' special, and the only one through today since that."

Potter reflected, looking at Tommy, his official subordinate, that he looked better out of uniform than in, though he'd have to swaddle himself in heavy dark-blue wool and that police cap later, for the parade.

Behind Tommy, Phil Thomas said in his husky, Ridge-man's voice, "Stands to reason, since he didn't take the car from home, he's got to leave some other way. Ain't no buses 'less he'd leg it to Barlton, 'cross the Kentuck' bridge, and that'd be takin' too much chance."

Muff Raintree leaned the butt of his squirrel rifle on his shoe cap. "Was I him, I'd take that train out. He couldn't o' been on the early one; it don't stop for water. He'll have some cash on him to pay the fare."

"Never knew him when he didn't have cash," Phil Thomas said. "He never throwed it around, but when a body was hard up for a few bucks, he put out."

Potter said irritably, "Jesus Jenny, Phil, he ain't dead. You're talkin' about him like he was on ice. Henry's the one who's dead." He swung around, sun in his eyes, and Carl said, straining behind him, "Watch out, Jerome, fella can put a boot 'tween these ties without thinkin'. Done it myself when I was a young sprat—come up here to put Injunhead pennies on the rails, wheels used to flatten 'em so every Injun had the mumps. Scared me to hell, but wasn't no train comin', and I got myself free in a minute or so."

The sheriff was walking with care, but at a good pace. Far under him in the creek he made out his shadow, rippling as it was obscured by ties and then revealed again, the Winchester single-shot angled over his shoulder, tiny as a toothpick in green-black water. The next bridge would be easier; it was bedded with ballast. The last bridge would be the hardest; it was the highest, and the creek it spanned, Foe Killer, had a mean chime on even the stillest day. It abutted the old quarry, where just a few of the Colored Settlement people now worked, gouging out a living.

He said without turning his head, "Your foot's too sizable to fit in between ties these days, Carl."

51

Carl laughed. "Yours ain't, Jerome."

Phil Thomas said, "Wid allowed how he'd bring a jug with him when he rejoined us. Ain't seen a hair of him yet."

The sheriff said, "I ain't supposed to listen to that kind of bootleg gospel without doin' somethin' about it. One day soon I'll have to shut down Renfrew's still, just to keep him thinkin' honest."

Carl's boot soles, hitting the ties solidly, made his two hundred and twenty pounds sound like a ton. The bridge was shaking gently, but then, it always did.

Tommy Beavis said, "Inchworm on your shirt back, Carl. Measurin' you for a new suit."

"Got a suit I ain't wore yet 'cept for the tryin' on," Carl grunted. "Buck got one exactly like. Sears, Sawbuck. Light-blue stripe, and they got white vests to 'em."

"Buck'll knock the eyes straight out o' little Candy Pruitt," Tommy said. "She'll go *ee-ee-ee* and turn up her heels."

"Don't take store-bought to make her do that," Carl said. "She's a right fine piece, or I'd 'a thought so at Buck's age. When he takes a mind to make it legal and quit school and settle down, I'll give him half the butcher shop."

"S'pose he don't want it?" Tommy asked.

"Hell, he's a Bolyard. He'll run it good. Same as Nick could have with the Cloud Shops. Dumb shame the Gen'ral couldn't've hung on a few years, long enough to hand the Shops to Nick."

Tommy said, "Can't tell so clear about kids today, Carl. Rex never wanted a thing to do with the Shops in his time. Told Gen'ral Cloud so. Can't tell about kids *any* time, seems to me."

Ahead, striding off the last bridge tie, the sheriff wheeled around. His eyelids made sharp, dark creases; his eyes were cool.

"I dunno," he said as Carl and Tommy halted. "Sometimes I think this committee's feather-headed. You can see what you all seen when I called you to Bellamans' last night, and still talk like you're so many old women gabbin'. Goddamn it, men, let's can the chatter. Cy's a lot of things, most of 'em good up to now, but he ain't no fool, or deaf, either."

Carl said, "Don't have to be so tetchy, Jerome. We can hold it down. Somethin' we said about kids and how they fuck around stick in your craw?"

A light like a gemstone showed in Potter's eyes. "No sir. Kids'll always fuck around, and sad to say, they don't always stop it when they get our age. Or Henry's, or Phyl Bellaman's. Let's have a little silence around us the rest of the distance, okay?"

Carl nodded good-naturedly. Patches of sweat the size of saddles shone under the arms of his chambray shirt. Softly, as the sheriff turned again to face the next stretch of grounded track, the second trestle bridge showing ahead through oak and chestnut boughs, Carl said, "Hurts all right, Jerome. I know. Sorry I'm a loudmouth."

The sheriff didn't answer; as he went ahead, his shoulders straightened, tightening the straps of his galluses.

On the ballasted bridge he quickened the pace for himself and the rest of the men. No one talked; there was only the creak and slurring of boot soles on the dried-out ties. Then they were in full shadow again, out of the searing light. In front of them Foe Killer sounded as if ice were continually crushed under its rocks. At the far end of the next bridge the water tower was hidden by a tall stand of chestnut trees. Behind Carl's muted puffing, Tommy said, "Yonder's Wid."

"See 'im," Potter said.

He lifted a hand, upward and out to Wid, who, in his turn, lifted a mason jar. Potter motioned to Wid to stay where he was and to keep silent. Again the sheriff went ahead, again his shadow was cast downward, on fast water this time, and from a much greater height. As they reached the approximate center of the bridge, Tommy muttered " 'Oddamn," stumbled, then caught balance. Potter half turned, without slowing down, then wheeled back and went on. When they were all off the bridge, Wid came forward along the ties and whispered,

"Figured you'd reach here about now. I come up by the trail the other way. Drink?"

Phil Thomas gazed wistfully from a crag-jawed face, but the sheriff said, "Not right now." He couldn't be heard two feet away. "Fan out," he told Carl and Tommy. "You two around b'hind the tower; Phil, you and Muff down east and west; you and me, Wid, from here. And for Christ's sake don't shoot him. If he's there and *he* shoots, I'll handle it. Just close in."

Hoarsely, embarrassed, Tommy said, "Bootlace, back there, like to flung me. 'Pologize, Jerome. I'd take 'em off if it wasn't for snakes."

The sheriff faced southward, taking a last glance at Foe Killer bridge before proceeding. But as he stood there, his pouched, diamond-shaped eyes altered, an expression of pain and anger filling them. He was staring back to the trestle.

"Well, my God," he said.

The other men gazed with him. Marty Broom was ten yards out on the trestle, advancing from the other side. He moved slowly, seeming scarcely conscious of the six men watching him. His cap was drawn down tightly, its bill stiff over his invisible eyes. Reflecting his terror, each motion of his body was rigid, strained, as though performed under water or in a vat of glue. Behind him Sambo padded, tongue out, paws spraddling the ties.

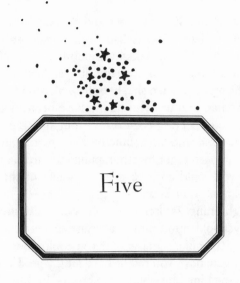

Five

Two women watched Buck and Nick come up the hospital walk and go out of sight momentarily as they stepped onto its porch; one was Phyllis Bellaman, the other Alice Cloud. Phyllis saw them from the window on the second floor. She had found the clothing she'd come in, a blue cotton dress, English walking shoes, dressed swiftly and taken a chair in the sun under the window, looking impatiently for the battered maroon Auburn of Dr. Bowen to show up in the lane below. She had decided to give him another ten minutes and then she'd just go downstairs and walk out, hoping Alice Cloud didn't see her from her corner first-floor office, but not caring much if she did. Alice had been home in bed when Phyllis and Dr. Bowen checked in at about one the morning before; Goldy Fisher, the night nurse on duty, hadn't been told anything but the fact that Dr. Bowen wanted Mrs. Bellaman to rest in peace and quiet.

But Phyllis was perfectly aware that Alice Cloud would have been informed; there was damn little Alice Cloud didn't know. She didn't dislike Alice, she never had; in truth, she admired her: her capability, her efficiency and the way she'd carved her life back into shape after it had been broken—after Cy had thrown her over. Phyllis thought sometimes, when she thought of Alice at all, that it was a shame it was Alice who'd had to drop by the wayside when she, herself, went after Cy; they were the two women in town who should have been friends, intelligent friends, respecting each other; they had the same sense of style, natural and unassumed; they might have laughed together and been eager together, pulled toward each other like sisters. If you could go back to those weeks of the war when you ached in all your bones, and grief sat on you like a muddy vulture tightening its dark claws on your chest, and your raw eighteen-year-old mind aimed at marriage—the anodyne for everything, the quick surcease—if you could do that, knowing what you knew now, you might have let Cy go. He'd deserved Alice, and she him. She would have buoyed his life, lifted it and opened it out; they'd have made the kind of couple people point to as quietly joyous.

Phyllis knew that Alice would have grown from her green years into even more than she was now. Maybe she wouldn't have taken over this house, and with her own money, converted it into a hospital. Nor might she have developed so fiercely General Cloud's own formidable talent for organization, nor the sort of mind that could overcome obstacles, and slice through local apathy with razor logic.

But she'd have given Cy as much in bed as I ever have, Phyllis thought, and a whole and trusting faithfulness, and would have got from him all the things he had to give which I never wanted.

Oh, God, he was beautiful then, and I didn't even see it.

He was the second most beautiful man I'd ever known. The one I had to reach out for and take, the way you'd see somebody else's apple, and wrest it away, and not give a damn that it was the only thing somebody'd ever wanted . . . and the seeds never grew in my barren ground.

She leaned forward suddenly—she was aware of others

around her, of their reverberations from her, and hers from them, as she hadn't been for a long time. She could hear Goldy Fisher walking by in the hall on quiet rubber soles and she thought, I ought to tell you never to let your rotten nephew come around anymore, Goldy. Never let your foul little Eugene come near my house; his only talent is for sustained intercourse, and his mind is yellow inside, like suppurating pus. The last time he quoted Epworth League Scripture to me, I nearly called his mother Milly to tell her to come and get her long-cocked darling and wrap him up and send him far away, to the Dry Tortugas; I'd have paid for it.

From the hall she heard Goldy talking softly with Birdy Mathews, who must have just come on duty; at their muted, commonplace tones—she couldn't hear what they said—she sat back, thinking, Henry, oh, Henry . . . I wish it was Eugene that Cy had killed, I wish it wasn't you.

She turned her eyes into the lane again and saw Buck striding to the porch, a paper bag of fireworks in the crook of his arm, and beside him, also with a sack, Nick.

Dear Christ, she thought. He's coming to see me. Wid's told him about it.

Her eyes were on Nick's foreshortened face, his black clipped hair, the quick motion of his shoulders, the angle of his jawline. She was leaning forward again, listening to the front door open, and then she sat back, feeling a kind of intense sunlight, which had nothing to do with the heat on the window sill, flood her, as if she was helpless in its force.

Alice Cloud wore a white shirtwaist, to which was pinned a small gold watch, its shut case engraved with her initials. Her summer suit, tailored and pale-green, caught a flash of pane light as the front door opened; it also touched her red-gold hair, her broad cheekbones and her wide, assessing brown eyes. She turned a little from the rolltop desk, long firm legs pushing back and causing the chair to roll a few inches. The office was small, and but for the mildly scarred big oak rolltop and a bright Audubon print of tanagers on the wall, would have been sterile. She'd just had time to see Buck and Nick approach, and to prepare for it. Without notice she might, when they appeared at her open office door, have said something she would have been sorry for. As it was, she had the opportunity to reach for the day's schedule and to poise a gold pencil above it, so when they looked in, she could look up at them, as though surprised. Mildly surprised, not angered. She had long since learned to arrange her features into the expression she wished her face to wear, a politic defense and practical, a vast distance from the naked, charming, slightly plain face of the girl she had been. She had once overheard her mother, Marie, remark to Harky, "Alice is so vulnerable, Harky, it's all there in plain sight. I wish she'd learn to lie a little, like other people."

Harky had said, "Fine thing, Miz Cloud, wantin' your own daughter to fib. But I know what you mean. She wears it all out in plain sight. Sun's either in or out, nothin' in between."

But now her eyes were nearly complacent, only a trifle aloof, as she inspected Nick, nodded to Buck. The rage she felt at Nick's being there was well-banked; it wouldn't, she hoped, show to him. Still, he often read more of her than she bargained for. He had his mother's intensity of recognition without words, a trait Marna used very well as an actress. Rex had usually been so full of himself he didn't bother to guess what others might be feeling. All the same, she thought, I'm shaking inside; I wish I'd told Wid *not* to tell him. I could have called Harky and Wid this morning, and cautioned them, right after Dr. Bowen called me. For a second she looked into Nick's eyes —Rex's exactly, aside from the color—then back to a sun-swimming point between Buck and Nick. Then she said, "Good morning, gentlemen."

And Nick, looking at her steadily, said, "I'd have known, anyway. Buck would've told me."

She made up her mind at once: he had read her own mind, with full accuracy, and he was quite right. The spring of tension inside her was released. She said mildly, "Of course he would. If I were you, I'd have expected him to tell me."

Buck blinked as though remotely aware of being caught in a crosscurrent, and faintly uncomfortable about it. He said, "We ain't goin' to bother nobody, Miss Alice. Leave the fireworks right down here with you while we go up and see her."

She let the pencil click on the desk and said dryly, regretting the flat sound of it, "I hadn't expected you to set them off upstairs. Old Mrs. Tensicott's in bad shape; she's in the room on the end. Mrs. Bellaman's in the first room next to the stairs. If you walk on the inside of the risers, next to the wall, the stairs don't creak so badly. I'm going to have Marty Broom rip them out before winter and put in something that won't deafen everybody."

Nick stood listening to her with an overt patience that bothered her as much as anything else; as if he had to suffer through this, wait for her protective wall to let down a little, before he could do what he had to. She flicked a glance to him, and away. Over them all lived something sentient, waiting upstairs; luckily, Nick wasn't looking at her now—her anger, touched with fear, blazed in her eyes as they all gazed out and up at the stairway. But it was only Goldy Fisher coming down, her footfalls on the wall-side treads thoughtfully muted but making ancient boards complain anyhow. A slim, heavy-eyed woman in her night-wrinkled uniform, coat over her arm, she said in the doorway, "I'll be goin' along now, Alice. Birdy's got things under control up there. Feel like I could sleep forty days and forty nights." She waved at the boys. "H'lo, Nick—Buck. Guess I'll see you in the parade, or at the park, both or one. Eugene's takin' M'lissa to the picnic and the dance. Maybe all you kids is goin' together?"

Nick's nostrils had widened as if merely to take in the hospital odors more deeply. "No, I guess not, Goldy," he said. "We'll be there, though."

"Sure nice of you"—Goldy leaned against the doorjamb, prepared for a good chat, letting down after duty—"to arrange for them colored players, Alice. Some people don't have no

59

feeling for jazz. Milly for one. Turns up her nose at it, won't let her pi-anna students play it and gets mad if she hears they've backslid. She's got to pound it out herself, for them comedy movies at the Argus, and I guess it gets to her—so she welcomes a nice sad picture, like *Tess of the Storm Country.* But what I say is, it's the kind of thing, jazz, gets you out o' yourself. Eugene's an awful good dancer; he's startin' to teach me, when he's got the time. Wouldn't even think he wants to study for the ministry, way he dances . . . but he says it ain't against God."

Buck slid an eloquent look at Nick.

Alice Cloud said, "Better get as much sleep as you can, Goldy. We'll have the usual burns and contusions, perhaps worse, before tonight."

Goldy shifted away. "Alice, did Dr. Bowen call back in yet? He's out at the McBrides' . . . that baby started movin' in Rose McBride 'fore she thought it would—must've dropped by now."

"I've read the schedule," Alice said, with no evident impatience, "and he hasn't called yet. I think I'll call out there in a few minutes and see if I can raise him. Have a lovely Fourth, Goldy."

"Going to try. Land, that's a darb of a suit, Alice. You bring that back from Paris last year?"

"From Florence. It wouldn't quite fit, so I had to slim into it."

"You, you don't need slimmin'. Some people's large-boned by nature. Like your daddy. Well, give me a ring in case of emergency."

Again she started away. Then she looked back. "Told Birdy just what Dr. Bowen told me last night: not to look in on Mrs. Bellaman but let her sleep till he gets back. He didn't say if it was a case of bad nerves, or what. Give her a sleep shot and that was it. Looked like she was real dazed, sort of walkin' in her sleep when she come in." Her eyebrows were arched; she wasn't asking, but she was waiting. "Like she was drunk or run over," she added.

60

No one in the office spoke or moved. Goldy firmed her lips, nodded once more to everyone, and Alice and Nick and Buck waited until the front door had opened and shut before they stirred. Then Buck and Nick put their fireworks down on a low table under the window. Buck said, looking out after Goldy, "A secret is awful hard to keep in this town."

"Yes," Alice Cloud agreed, "but it has been done." From the desk she picked up a package of Murads, found a match, lit one and blew smoke, noting that her hands were remarkably steady; rage didn't have to be evident, after all. Through the smoke she said, "All right, go on up—don't stay long. I don't want this hospital to be the center of a scandal."

"We don't either," Nick said. His eyes were clear on hers. "I think Cy'll be all right," he said. "All they want to do is get him back as soon as they can."

Alice found herself unable to answer. She stayed quiet as he came over to her and kissed her on the cheek, then she returned the kiss, a very light brush, and it was as though both were embarrassed by it, as though they had subtly violated some pledge to each other that ran deeper than demonstration and did not have to ask for it. Nick and Buck went out without looking back, Buck's naked feet a whisper quieter than Nick's as they disappeared up the stairway, keeping near the wall.

Alice swung around to the desk and picked up the telephone. As she waited for Velma Temple, day operator at the phone company, to come on the line, Cy moved in her mind, as, no matter what, he had moved there for many years. Her face relaxed and her body softened to a feeling against which she had no reliable armor, which lay, for years, below most consciousness, beneath even how she felt about Nick.

At the stairhead Buck took a paper cup from beside the cooler and poured himself a drink. Over the cup's rim he said, "I'll stay out here if you want to go in, see her by yourself." He spoke softly, as if in the company of the very ill.

At the far end of this upstairs hall Birdy Mathews waved to

them and disappeared into the room where old Mrs. Tensicott lay, presumably dying.

Nick said, "No, you come in. She'd like to see you, too." He whispered it positively, more surely than he felt it.

Buck said "Okay" and made an over-the-shoulder basket with the empty cup into the waste container.

Nick went a few inches ahead of Buck to the first door. He thought about rapping, decided it would waken the patient if she was sleeping, and opened the door a slit. All he could see was the bed—no one in it. He swung the door open all the way.

Across a wave of sunlight Phyllis smiled at him. She sat on the chair with her hands in her lap, like a child at her own birthday party. Her face was so filled with light and greeting that it was as if she touched him and absorbed him.

He knew nothing about perfume; it was something some women, some girls—Melissa—wore to advantage; on others it was just vaguely present. He didn't know the name of Phyllis' perfume, or if it was more than the perfume of her body itself that quickened the air around her. He had once, at the Bellamans', gone into her bathroom by mistake; knowing, immediately, that it was hers, even though there were no monograms on the towels, no special womanly scented soap cakes. There had been a light, fresh, enveloping scent, a presence that said Beauty.

He stood before her and said without looking anywhere but at her eyes, "I'm sorry. I wanted to say so."

Her voice reached to take him in as her eyes had already done. It had such grief in it; and such gladness, running together. "I saw you coming up the walk. Oh, Nick, I'm glad to see you."

Buck said quietly, " 'Morning, Mrs. Bellaman. I'm real sorry too."

She took him into her warm, aching circle. "Thank you. Thank you for coming with Nick. Right now it means more than I could possibly say."

Nick thought, You didn't get caught with Henry Watherall

last night. You didn't do what people say you did—even when they're nice about it, like Wid—with anybody else, either. You didn't do any of it, it's a big mistake. And in his loins, in his bloodstream, in the heat of the window, he knew the thought was false; but this real knowledge did nothing to stop his pity and his reaching out for her. She didn't look stained, nor even lightly smirched.

Yet he felt a harsh sorrow and longing which shut off whatever he might try to say now, and a kind of tide-rip of loss as she looked away from him, at Buck. "Buck, I wonder if you could bring me a cup of water."

"Yes'm," Buck said at once. "Be right back."

Buck's feet were hushed on the floor; the door opened and shut with near-silence.

The little cords in Phyllis' throat stood out suddenly. The throat was like a creamy column; her mouth was unsmiling. She lifted a hand to Nick, and he took it; it was delicate but sturdy, strong-fingered. His hand fitted lightly around it.

"Nick. Will you come over and see me tonight, at home?" Her voice, its sense, hardly reached him, but it was like thunder.

He nodded. "When?"

"After the dance. I suppose you'll be going."

Again he nodded.

"About eleven, then. By yourself, if you don't mind. I need you there. I don't want to be alone. I do need you, Nick."

In his mind Nick said, Yes, you need me, I know. Maybe it's the way you needed all those others, maybe it's true even about Eugene, but I don't care. Because it's me you need now, and even if all the others felt just as I do now, that doesn't matter either. Not even Cy matters.

"I'll be there."

With her free hand, her left, she touched his jaw, under the ear, then ran her fingertip up his cheekbone. The tip of the finger on his flesh seemed to have touched him before, not as if he had dreamed it or thought about it happening, but as if it had happened before and was, only now, remembered. Yet it was the first time they had touched, except casually and as if by accident.

She pulled her hand out of his gently; she could see Buck, behind him, coming through the door.

She took the paper cup and drank, sipping, then set it down on the window sill. In its watery circle, sun burned and the green of the leaves was reflected in miniature.

Buck said with low-keyed anxiousness, "Anything else we can get for you, Mrs. Bellaman?"

She shook her head, her dark hair racing with hot gold. Nick watched the same play of brilliance along the down of her arms, over the clean muscles in the evenly tanned flesh.

"No, you'll want to be on your way. It's an important day, after all, isn't it? And," she said casually, without malice, "your aunt won't want you to stay here too long." Her eyes were upon Nick's again. "I'll be leaving myself in a minute. I'll get some breakfast and then wander around a little. I may take a walk."

"Peach of a day for it." Buck sounded too earnest, too sociably compliant.

There was a line of small white stitches at the edge of her high-collared blue dress and Nick wondered if that brown-bronze, silk-gleaming flesh was the same all the way down. Earlier in the summer he and she and Cy had gone swimming in the grotto on the Bellaman grounds. The night was full of moonlight and blue deep shadows under the birches and in the water. They wore suits, of course, and afterward they sat on a rear terrace in garden chairs and played mah-jongg, in the cooling secret hours.

As he and Buck were leaving the hospital room Nick looked back. She hadn't moved and her eyes were the last thing he saw as he shut the door.

Alice was on the phone when they stopped to pick up their fireworks, but when she caught sight of Nick in the doorway she cupped the mouthpiece, saying, "Just a second, Len," so he knew she was talking to Dr. Bowen. "Nick, if you should see Marty Broom around, tell him I've got a little job for him today. The stairs and the hallways need washing down. Have a good time, and tell Harky and Wid I won't see them at the parade, but we'll all get together before the dance."

It was as if there had been nothing between them—no unseen battle, no Phyllis Bellaman upstairs. He felt fine relief, as though he had been excused some bitter assignment, but he wondered if after he went to the Bellamans' tonight, the guilt, the feeling that he had betrayed her, would come down again in force. He raised a hand to his aunt in a salute of understanding and went out onto the porch as Buck shut the front door behind them.

"Y' know," Buck said conversationally as they went down the walk, "I purely hate hospitals. If I ever get real bad off, I want it to be to home, where Mama can dose me and I can die quiet." After a few steps he went on, " 'Course, Miss Alice's is good as they can be. It wasn't around when I had my adenoids messed up, or I'd o' gone there. 'Member all them books you read me when I was laid up?" He didn't wait for Nick's answer. "If you'd look up, you'd see Phyllis still in the window, watchin' us. Watchin' you. She always looks at you like you was some kind of prince." It was a matter-of-fact statement, with no nuance in it, though Nick went on looking ahead, feeling as if his neck muscles were locked against staring around and up. It would have been good to have another sight of her before tonight, but it wasn't necessary.

"God, Lord, she's beautiful," Buck said fervently. "I don't blame no man for her, or her for no man. It's just Cy I feel sorry for, Cy and poor Henry." He snapped his fingers. "Yea-uh. That's wrong. I *do* blame one man for her—Gene Fisher."

In an effort to be fair, Nick said, "Well, sure, if it's true . . . but then, Gene's hardly a man."

"I reckon it's true, like it or not. And even if he's a dressed-up banana peel, he got to her and then he *talked* about it. Anybody talks about it oughtta have his thing cut off and hung on a windmill . . . Here." He handed Nick a bag. His eyes went half shut as he gazed ahead at the masterly groomed front lawn of the Gardners'. "Ol' Gene ain't smousin' around here right this minute, anyhow. There's Mrs. Gardner and Melissa around on the back steps, shellin' peas. You got a clear coast. Old man's out in front fixin' to raise his flag. Leave me keep him occupied, I kind of enjoy it."

"Appreciate that," said Nick.

In her office, Alice Cloud said to Dr. Bowen, "Just give me a call when you're through out there, then; and I'm sorry it's taking so long. There's nothing important yet at this end, but I'll know where to reach you if shrapnel hits us. I hope Dr. Miller's enjoying his fishing trip; *you* ought to take the next Fourth of July off. Try to nap between her pains; you can't have had any real sleep last night. I'll tell Mrs. Bellaman she can go, and have Birdy give her the pills—'bye, Len."

After she hung up, she went into the hall and climbed the stairs, even her shadow decisive. In the upstairs hallway she got the attention of Birdy Mathews, who was folding clean towels on a rack, and asked her to get the sedative pills Dr. Bowen had prescribed for Phyllis. Alice felt Birdy's shrewd green young eyes following her while she went along to Phyllis' door. It was as though Birdy knew her state of mind and might be considering her an old maid harboring an ancient grudge— which was ridiculous, since Birdy was the best nurse in the place, didn't listen to gossip and didn't, herself, indulge in it. Outside Phyllis' door Alice hesitated for only long enough to debate knocking or going in; then, as Nick had done, she opened the door.

At first, in the brightness, she could see nothing, but after a while she made out Phyllis Bellaman at the window. Against the sunfall, the thin cotton dress was a simple scrim, the deep-gold, supple body as obviously naked beneath it and the slip as if there were no cloth at all; Phyllis Bellaman, Phyllis Wolfson of that decade and more ago, stood without moving, apparently not hearing Alice as she approached. Then she turned around slowly.

In a beat of time before their eyes met, Alice knew she had been unprepared for this. It wasn't like passing on the street, casually nodding, often not even bothering to acknowledge each other's presence. In our enemies is our salvation, she thought: the realization that we have it in our power to unmake them as enemies and thus to become more of ourselves. Yet it was not a matter of forgiveness alone; before forgiveness, there had to be understanding . . .

I know why she had to have Cy, she told herself in this instant of meeting; I know it very well. I've always known it, and I've thrown it away as a rubbishy reason, a wild, girl's whim. But it was no more specious than my own terrible anger at betrayal, my own anger holding me up even when I went to the wedding, rubbing salt in the wound publicly and learning that salt has a lonely, prideful taste.

However Phyllis had answered her own old loss by replacing it with Cy, and then replacing him, in turn, with others, it had been no more self-damaging than Alice's answer.

She said very quickly, as if by saying it now, and only with haste, she could ever say it at all, "Phyllis, I'm so damnably sorry for you. I'm sorry. It's not something I'm just *saying*. For you, and Cy. All these stupid years."

She heard herself get it out, not a waver in it, which also astonished her. She had meant to come in here cool, polite, not an inch overpolite, either—to handle this as any routine matter of administration should be treated. The words were clear enough, but what they exposed must be appalling.

Phyllis' eyes, deeply intelligent, narrowed and then went wide. She took a step away, her shoes the only sound in the room, though outside, fireworks rattled and bellowed. She said, "I hope I can go now. I was going to leave, anyway. I don't need Dr. Bowen's go-ahead." She had thrust her hands into the pockets of the neat dress, a dress Alice noticed had no blood on it; her head was high, her expression fixed. "I stayed when

I saw Nick coming along. I enjoyed seeing him. Now I'll go."

Birdy Mathews looked in as Alice said, "You're certainly free to go wherever you want to, Phyllis. I asked Dr. Bowen about it. He wants you to take these; they'll help you sleep." Alice took the bottle of pills from Birdy and held them out. "One or two at a time for insomnia," she said. "Goodbye, Phyllis." Again, a hint of what she felt before she had first spoken surged up, but it was washed away now—compassion, understanding, forgiveness gone as if they had never rushed into her. But she knew they had been there.

Pocketing the pill bottle, Phyllis walked to the modest dresser and picked up a flat long scarlet leather purse. She hung it over her arm, gazed for a moment into the spackled mirror, smoothed her back hair with her fingertips, put her hands back in her pockets and looked squarely at Alice Cloud. "Just send the bill," she said, and then she was in the doorway. A few seconds later her heels sounded on the steps; she was going down them neither speedily nor slowly, just taking herself away. A hint of what could have been her perfume, cologne, powder, stayed in the bright air.

"She looks all right," Birdy said with caution.

Alice's voice had the deadness of all real anger. "Yes . . . doesn't she."

When Birdy went out, Alice could feel Phyllis' strength and bitterness in the room as if the other woman were still there. Alice thought, How gallant and implacable she is. How terrible as an army with banners. What a fool I made of myself. How lonely she is.

But she watched from the window until she saw Phyllis reach the end of the walk and turn southward, in the opposite direction to that taken by Nick and Buck. She waited until she could no longer see the dark shining head, the free-moving confident stride through the leaves of the elms. Then, from the window sill she picked up the half-emptied paper cup, and holding it as if it contained the germs of bubonic plague, she too left the room.

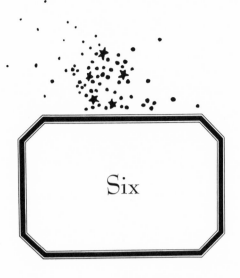

Six

Squatting at the north end of the trestle bridge over Foe Killer creek, Sheriff Potter cupped his hands tightly over his knees and kept his eyes on Marty Broom. The sheriff's face and body were aimed at Marty as though he could, by will and wish alone, suck him safely toward him.

Standing just behind him, not moving anymore than the rest of the Vigilante Committee, Wid Lucas had shut his own eyes a few moments before. He forced himself to open them. He'd always regretted his queasiness in the presence and even at the thought of heights; visiting Paris on the heels of the Armistice, on a day gray as a foggy cat, he'd made a prime ass of himself coming down by having to cling, frozen, to the ironwork of the Eiffel Tower railings, and it hadn't been just the *vin ordinaire* hangover, either.

There was Marty, with the dog behind him. He was about in the middle of the bridge and seemed to be in the grip of vertigo. Now and then, at long intervals, he would get up enough nerve to lift the toe of one shoe, letting it dabble over the air between the ties, then at last find footing and lurch that much closer. Every time this happened it seemed another miracle, which couldn't be repeated.

Now there had been no advance for many minutes. The men called to him with advice and encouragement, no longer keeping the silence Sheriff Potter had imposed. If Cy had been at the water tower before, he'd be long gone now.

Sheriff Potter spoke in a soothing croon, only a fraction frayed and tight. "Soooooo, Marty. You can come on ahead now. Lift up your eyes. Look at me. Don't look down." The sheriff might have been making love to somebody who held his life in fee.

Wid caught a little motion from the sheriff's right hand, a summoning in the air behind the sheriff's hip pocket. Puzzled, swallowing dry, Wid took a step closer. Without turning his head, his eyes or attention from Marty, the sheriff croaked, "God's sake, gimme the liquor."

Bending with extreme care, Wid placed the mason jar upright in the sheriff's calloused palm. The sheriff brought the jar around to the front as if he were presenting the grail. He lifted it, and its glass flashed in a sunburst. For a second the reflection danced like a butterfly on fire over Marty's sweat-drenched shirt. Then the sheriff got the right angle on it, arranging it so it wouldn't blind Marty, and called, "Come on, now, Marty. Got a nice drink for you at this end!"

Wid was reminded of a mule-mean captain who, crawling at his side, had talked him back to the trenches in the Argonne offensive and who had kicked him so hard as soon as they were home free that sometimes he still felt it.

Around behind Wid, Muff Raintree said in a whisper a half tone louder than the creek's white babble, "Both his shoe soles are loose, goddamn it."

Marty was trying again; his right foot was raised, and the sole flapped, revealing a glimpse of red woollen sock. Wid's jaws clenched. A dragonfly shimmered near Marty's lifted, searching toes. He brought the foot down. But it was the other foot that did him in as he dragged it onward, the left foot—the one he got bunged up in the Shops that time, Wid thought. It skidded on the tie and then slipped down between it and the last one, the loose sole crumpling sideward and upward like a foundered boat, Marty then half kneeling, with both hands flung out and gripping rail iron. Wid could see his knuckles, blue-white, like polished bone, around the hot rails.

The dog whined.

Wid took another step, nudged the sheriff with his leg, said "Pardon me, Jerome" as the sheriff looked up and then shifted to one side; unslinging his Springfield, Wid handed it to the sheriff and went out on the ties. His stomach, or whatever the mechanism was inside a man that made him wish he were eight feet under honest ground, didn't like any of this; but it could be controlled for a while; it could be mastered, provided a body just kept on going, paying no attention to the wilderness of sky and air.

When he got near Marty, it struck him how you could smell fear on a man as if it came out of a hell-brewed bottle. And this was a good thing to concentrate on, to know you'd soon be away from, because it also kept you from thinking. He said quietly, "Come on, Marty, get set. Gonna heave on you now; you can help me pull your leg out. You can do that much. Then, when you're up, I'm goin' to worm around a 'hind you, and me and the dog'll be right there, steerin' you home."

He managed to get his wiry right arm under Marty's left, his left under Marty's right, said "Let go the rails" and pulled up with all his strength. Marty's head went back, his eyes in the shade of the cap's bill like oysters long off ice, and when Wid saw the left foot slide free, a red creasemark over the draggling top of the sock, he made a ballet step around and took hold of Marty from the rear, under the elbows. From then on, it was just a backward waltz home. The dog got some slobber on his clean overalls, but nothing worse.

As soon as they were on holy ground, where their shadows didn't drop fifty feet to a kettle-boil of water, Wid said to the sheriff, "Go ahead and give him the drink, Jerome. Then I'll take one myself."

Sheriff Potter gave Marty a tap on the shoulder, and Marty raised his head. He took the jar from the sheriff and tried to get the tin rubber-ringed cap off, but suction and shaking defeated him until Slim Thomas helped him. He drank then, and coughed a little, and surrendered the jar to the sheriff, who said, "When you can talk some, I'd like to hear it. Guess you had some notion of helpin' us out."

Marty's voice was graveled, only workable, but outraged. "Big secret. Citizen myself. Got the right . . ."

The sheriff gazed away from him. "Like to know, would you." He was purring, humming. "If it'd do a whit of good, I'd tell you. It wouldn't. Half wish I'd left you out there." The sheriff brought his eyes around, and upward, to Wid. "Last thing I knew about you, you couldn't climb a stepladder without goin' blue in the gills."

Carl Bolyard said, suddenly roaring, his face a steaming platter-roast next to Marty's, "Ain't you goin' to thank Widdicomb Lucas for savin' you, and 'pologize to us for ruinin' everything?"

Marty's mustache, dank as it was, still bristled. "Nosir. Not'll you all tell me . . ."

The sheriff got on his feet. He was still inspecting Wid. "You all right?" he asked. He held out the mason jar. "Here, and you *do* deserve it."

For the past seconds Wid had been staring into molten air, high above the trestle where he had walked. Now it was as if he came down to earth, studying first the trestle ties, then recognizing the mason jar in the sheriff's hand, then the sheriff himself and the men around him. He shook his head; he seemed smaller now than when he had started out after Marty, appearing in all aspects himself again. A corner of his mouth lifted faintly. "Forgot my little weakness about bein' . . . up high," he murmured. "Almighty damn, what a man'll do." He pushed the jar aside. "Save some for me," he said. " 'Scuse me."

He walked away, decently upright, along the tracks toward the concealed water tower. Out of sight in the oak and chestnut shade, it soon was apparent that he was being very sick, but it was also plain that he didn't want to make a lot of noise about it. The sheriff had been looking after him; he wheeled, handed the jar and the Springfield to Carl, and said, "You people may as well stay here." He hitched his own rifle under his arm. "No need all of us to go carousin' around the tower now. Nobody'll be there, but I'll just take a sashay around, anyhow."

The sheriff swung away, passing Wid still in a clump of sugarbushes. He had no hope of finding Cy at the tower; it might have been a false guess anyway, thinking he would be there. It made sense to believe he was hiding up somewhere waiting for the midnight train out, since it was the only one that would make this water halt today; like the early-morning special, it didn't stop at the station in town. But the sheriff respected Cy, and while he'd hoped for some luck himself, he didn't believe he would so easily outguess him. If Cyrus Bellaman intended to take the night train, he might well be fox enough to wait for nightfall to approach the tower; it was what the sheriff himself would have done.

He did know how Cy's mind worked, and his own; the lamentable thing was that his mind had nearly always been a step or two behind the other's. As he paused, the tower's rust-red dome appearing on its iron stilts out of deep foliage, he recalled playing a good deal of chess with Cy, in the old days when they were pretty close. It had been possible to believe you were conquering Cy, that the very Capablanca or Morphy gambit Cy had taught you himself was going to best him. Then he'd come at you with a smiling and innocent pawn, and you'd be in the soup.

He hadn't played chess with Cy since about 1920. Jerome Potter wasn't married then, didn't have obligations. If he'd been married, maybe there wouldn't have been the Phyllis complication.

Or maybe there would. No man expected it to happen; it was only that with her, it did happen.

He fingered the trigger guard of his Winchester, worn to brightness under its darker steel, then walked on, going off into lean poison green grass beside the rails, keeping down, keeping quiet. When he was inside the shadow cast by the tower, it was like stepping into black water from a furnace. He could hear his own breath in the quiet, so long a way was he from the distraction of town celebration. Twenty feet from the tower he stooped in the rough-edged grasses and peered under it. There was room for a man to stand up there, or lie at ease and wait in some comfort for whatever might be coming from any direction.

After a moment he straightened. Nothing.

The baking grasses around him, the breath of cool limestone from the quarry, whose basin couldn't quite be seen from here, the sun's heat on the back of his neck, all had a spermy, caressing smell and touch. It made a man remember Phyllis as she'd been, in the timeless, love-drenched afternoons at the Bellaman place. A town landmark, he thought, and oh, eternal foolishness, it was a landmark for me. Then there was nothing in the world but Phyllis, naked and wet from making love, wanting more as soon as they swam back up to normal, straddling him, with her hair falling around his face, stroking up and stroking down, calling from him the last drop of giving, and afterward, saying, "Was it enough? You're sure it was enough?" As though she taunted him, as though she was laughing inside herself and might die of the laughter.

She had been with him, it seemed, since last night, when he and the rest had left the Bellaman place on the first of this hunt. He'd felt her with him along the river bottom and in the lash of the boughs overhanging the trails along Carmian. As if he'd been sap-young himself again, head over tokus in all her delight and power; even though she'd just been cool, and distant, and unfrightened, and a mile above him, while she stood there in the Bellaman living room and showed him and

Tommy where Cy was standing when he shot Henry Watherall, and they waited for Doc Bowen to get there and treat
her, and confirm what couldn't have been plainer—that Henry'd been gone the second he was hit.

But he'd felt her, as she'd been when they were still secret
and mutually ravaging lovers. He felt her even as he used the
phone to call up the Vigilantes and to call Melton's ambulance-
hearse.

The last he saw of her was when she got into Doc Bowen's
car. She looked a little stunned then, as if for the first time she
felt her life homing in and realized what had happened.

All the same, she was still in his bones; the whole goddamn
thing had come alive again, was creeping through him like light
searching out his skeleton. His blood felt that crazy, giddy
rioting again. He'd gone back, reverted to the time when he
had not even given a whistle for the friend he was cuckoo-
nesting, and both Arden banks could have been robbed and all
the churches sacked and the choir ladies raped and pillaged, for
all he cared—the time before she dropped him like a hot
buckeye chestnut.

Try to tell your wife about that sometime, Jerome, he said
warmly to himself. Try to tell Emma how it was—and is. She'd
listen two minutes and come for you with a frying-spider. She
wouldn't know, either, how it is out here looking for a man you
like and always did, pitying him in your guts, and knowing you
were part of what finally brought him to what he did last night.

He skimmed sweat from under his ropy, lean jaw with his
forefinger. "Cy?" he called out loud. Then he turned his back
on the water tower and walked away, not bothering to stay out
of anybody's earshot. When he reached the tracks he walked
straight back along them, kicking ballast, taking satisfaction in
the harsh abrasive sound.

Buck went a few steps ahead of Nick toward where Roy Gardner had started to attach a flag to his flagpole; Mr. Gardner had
the flag partially unfolded and was staring up at the galvanized

ball on top of the pole. A wren sat there flirting its wings and Roy Gardner was squinting at it as if, because it hadn't asked his permission to be where it was, he'd like to wish it away. He was shorter than either Buck or Nick, with three areas of firm obesity around his rear, his belly and jowls. His pale-gray trousers were held up by a white web belt with the insignia of the Boy Scouts of America on its buckle; his shirt was light pongee, set off by a Hoover collar and a carefully knotted black necktie. He was a strong supporter of the President.

Buck murmured over his shoulder to Nick, "Hope Melissa's got good sense today." He meant it in a good way; he considered Melissa fey and undependable. His own girls—with Candy Pruitt the brightest example—weren't flighty. They knew what he wanted, and gave it, without flaunting the fact or obviously undermining deep-rooted Calvinist conventions. They weren't known as bad girls, or drummed from the community. They enjoyed Buck and liked him, as he took sure pleasure in them.

Nick caught a teasing glimpse of Melissa and her mother on the back-porch steps: Melissa's legs and bare feet, in her lap the blue bowl into which she was shelling peas; Clare Gardner's less interesting legs. The toes of Melissa's right foot were turned up, somehow deliciously. Where Phyllis Bellaman made him think of a magnificent mare, finished, perfect, Melissa was a fresh and fragrant colt, skittish, unsure . . .

Over the freshly mown lawn, raked and shining, not a stub of dead grassblade left in its carpet, not a leaf or weed in sight upon it, its surface softly wet with the morning watering, the boys went up to Mr. Gardner at his flagpole.

Nick thought about the previous night's session with Melissa on the front-porch swing—which had been interrupted by Mr. Gardner every ten minutes or so. He would emerge abruptly from behind the front-porch screen door, always as if he'd been hiding there, in red leatherette slippers, bathrobe and pajamas, and heavily announce what time it was. Nick hoped the shock of his own reappearance this morning would be easily absorbed.

Perhaps Mr. Gardner had wakened smiling, benevolent, tolerant. He doubted it.

Buck cleared his throat. Mr. Gardner brought his head down and around, to take in Buck and Nick.

Buck said, "Mornin', sir. Great day for the parade!"

This man, who had been their scoutmaster—and who had seen them leave his troop with no regret—took a small backward step, his spotless white oxfords planted firmly, as if he had discovered in his flawless lawn the tunnel of a mole.

After a moment he pointed to the bag in the crook of Buck's arm. "Fireworks," he said. It was the tone he might have used, as president of the First Mercantile Bank, on a farmer whose crop-loan payment was late. Nick had sometimes wondered if he could persuade his Aunt Alice, who since Noel's first stroke had handled the Cloud moneys, to transfer their considerable bulk from the old Bank of Arden to the First Mercantile. He felt it would change Mr. Gardner's feeling about the Clouds. But this was as far from any possibility as Nick's becoming an Eagle Scout had been. Alice Cloud liked Melissa, considered her a child with potential, if at a chancy and trying age; she did not consider Mr. Gardner worth even disliking.

Across the lane, outside these precincts, a string of Chinese two-inchers was rapidly and gloriously detonated. Their racket, holding the drone of the cicadas at bay for the time it lasted, seemed to put extra force into Mr. Gardner's declaration. "Fireworks," he said, "should be outlawed. If we had a decent police department, they would be. If we had a good mayor and an efficient county sheriff. Both of you are too old to play with them. By using them, you encourage little chaps to follow your lead, and to get hurt."

It had become Buck's turn to step backward, which he did in a much more dramatic manner than Mr. Gardner had moved, reeling slightly and clapping a hand to his forehead. "Gol!" he said with what could by no one be construed as less than honest admiration. "You put your finger right on it, Mr. Gardner. Yessir, you *hit* it! Never saw it like that before. Tell you what—" He turned to Nick, his eyes innocent as dark-blue marbles, lashes like sprayed soot. "Nick and me, we'll dump 'em in the river b'fore another hour's out. Swear it," he said. "Scout's honor," he said. "Sir."

Mr. Gardner did not, quite, appear mollified or at ease. Perhaps he was remembering a fourteen-mile hike, conducted in Carmian's Woods during most of a broiling day and half the night, when Buck had led him in pursuit of a black bear which nobody actually had seen but Buck. The troop, with the exception of Nick, who knew where he was, had become thoroughly lost. Buck had also managed, as if inadvertently, to lock Eugene Fisher in an abandoned but noisome privy by jamming its door, and ended up a sort of hero for the day by leading them all out of the wilderness. At the outset of such trips into fantasy, Mr. Gardner possessed obvious reservations, but Nick could tell, by a certain slackening of the sparse lines in the pink Gardner forehead, a little letting out of the modest Gardner paunch, that Buck hadn't lost his touch. Nick would have used such flattery himself if he had had the key, but Mr. Gardner would have seen through his lesser artistry at once.

Buck said, "Gimme your ol' foolish toys, Cloud," and scooped in the bag Nick handed over. Buck swung both sacks in a circle. "Yesssir, we'll just drown these buggers. I been wantin' to have a nice chat with you 'bout a few things, Mr. Gardner—at my age, some things kind of prey on a person's mind. You know, about women and"—he lowered his voice— "diseases and such. Lemme just ask you a few things, couldn't even ask my own daddy. Cloud, you go on and go get your knife —it's his old scout knife, Mr. Gardner, he left it on your front porch last night, worried sick about losin' it—while me and Mr. Gardner talk private."

Mr. Gardner's eyebrows, wan blond caterpillars with little fur, arched suspiciously, but Buck had him nailed and was moving in, his voice low and intensely confidential as Nick walked off. Nick hoped Buck would get in a few licks concerning Eugene Fisher, whom the Gardners somehow allowed

Melissa to be alone with. The problem was that Eugene's bearing easily impressed certain company—mostly old ladies and his Epworth League colleagues—as did his often reasserted dedication to live his life in the eye of the Lord, his brilliant standing with the First Methodist minister, Reverend Keller, and with the principal of the Arden High School, Randolph Sutton; and his being the son of Milly Fisher and nephew of Goldy Fisher, both of whom everybody liked. His decorum as a First Class Scout, Troop 17, Beaver Patrol, would also stand him well with Mr. Gardner. Yet the reasons for caution were more widespread and undercover; to trust Eugene with any part of your life, and certainly with your daughter, was tantamount to chucking a king cobra under the chin.

Crossing the lawn now, Nick had the uneasy notion that Mr. Gardner was actually stubborn enough to consider himself a better judge of character than such wise heads as Wid Lucas, to name just one. Mr. Gardner's path had frequently crossed that of Alice Cloud on the school board, and Mr. Gardner had invariably been bumped aside by good sense; Mr. Gardner felt, too, that Marna Cloud's profession as an actress was, though remunerative and looked upon with admiration by many, suspect as an art whose practitioners were no better than they should be; Mr. Gardner also disliked Noel Cloud, who'd never paid him much attention. Therefore, though Nick himself was a Cloud, and had never felt welcome on this clipped turf, he knew a smoldering, baffled wonder at anyone who could sanction Eugene as a Fourth-of-July-parade and evening escort for Melissa. It had to be bullheadedness, the smugness of Being Right.

He'd found it didn't do much good to say what one really thought about Eugene; Melissa took it for sour grapes, wriggled uncomfortably and looked away. She might, he sometimes thought disturbedly, even be excited by the whispers that trailed like river bubbles in Eugene's wake, among other girls her own age. When he'd beaten up Eugene, a fair joust as long as it lasted—one couldn't pick up a man who wouldn't go on fighting, and prop him up and start over—he didn't mention it to her. It hadn't been done for Melissa's sake, not entirely, anyway; Eugene's crowing about himself and Phyllis Bellaman had been a strong part of it.

He stopped cold, sighting Melissa now, her mother beside her. In the fractional instant, he felt something that was less guilt than a shaft of knowledge. Hell, he thought. I'll be at the Bellamans' tonight. Alone with Phyllis; asked there by her. And now I'm here.

He walked the rest of the distance to the back-porch steps. Melissa's brief-skirted gauzy dress was sprigged with the pink rosettes her mother ran up on the Singer. Her hair was bobbed in a honey-colored bell, a style that had come stealthily to Arden, after Marna Cloud had had hers done in Al Bomasy's barbershop. Melissa's eyes were like sunlight through tortoise shell, tipped up at the corners, lashes heavy and dark, and they were wildly innocent. Since the time that Nick had become aware of her as a completely desirable girl, these eyes had, disconcertingly, been given to soft tears when she heard news which, to almost everyone else, would have seemed unexceptional. When the news was stirring, such as the time Charles Lindbergh landed at Le Bourget and the Atwater Kents and Crosleys crackled with it, Nick could understand this. But when she stepped by accident on a caterpillar, the tears flummoxed him. Between such abandoned reactions, she was a cheerful girl, radiant even. Coming out of the Argus one Saturday afternoon after a matinée of *Broken Blossoms,* they had met Alice Cloud. Alice looked once at Melissa, with clinical fondness, and sang in a whisper to Nick before going on, "Don't know what to call her, but she's mighty lach-ry-mose . . ."

After much persuasive exploration, Melissa would allow herself to be touched on portions of her breath-taking anatomy, as though she were unconscious of Nick and basking alone in some far Araby. When he attempted further intimacy she moved away, escaping any ultimate sexual touch with the dexterity of a young seal. Yet last night, during those sweat-soaked hours on the Gardners' swing, Melissa had at least twice murmured that she loved him. Nick did not know if by this she meant that a dim roseate future lay ahead of them, entered by way of the altar and a bridal bouquet, or if it meant that she would simply, in process of time, whim, circumstance, capitulate gloriously. He didn't think she herself knew which—and in this lay the wonder of the intrigue, the excitement of suspense for both of them.

What made it more complex was his discovery that he suffered with her in her resistance to him; it was very difficult to press his own cause when, simultaneously in the back of his own mind, he was pleading hers.

Mrs. Gardner, whatever she might think of him, was making a decent attempt at casual conversation. ". . . I'm so glad it didn't turn out thundery. We deserve a good Fourth. Remember how it rained last year?" Mrs. Gardner's hair, unbobbed, fine-spun gray, was held in check by a barrette. Beside Melissa, who seemed about to spring up and dash away across the back lawn without actually touching the earth, Mrs. Gardner was practically rooted where she sat; she forever gave the impression that she would have enjoyed liking Nick if only she'd had Mr. Gardner's permission.

Nick said he recalled last year's downpour and rejoiced in this dry air. Mrs. Gardner went on shelling peas. Nick kept her in his vision but actually reveled in Melissa—her splendid legs, polished to a bronze patina, her knees, only just revealed by the drooping hem of the dress, her slender feet, her amber hair—hair that would feel, in the downy fur at the back of the neck, like a newborn lamb.

Her eyes flew away from his like birds. Then they soared back, lighting on him for a breath. Then she shot up, almost overturning her own bowl of half unpodded peas, giving it to her mother, saying, with a throat catch, "The phonograph's running down!"

Nick became aware, then, of the sound of the phonograph

from the living room. The tenor had been singing "Sweethearts on Parade," his voice at best thin, strangely effete, as though, a castrated member of a caliph's court, he amused languid houris, but now it held a desperate quality as the record turned more and more slowly and the tenor was transformed, inexorably, into an ever-lowering basso profundo. Melissa was darting up the back steps, bare pink heels petal-like, flashing. She beckoned Nick to follow, follow. Nick said "Beg pardon" to Mrs. Gardner and caught the back door before it could flap shut again.

He entered the kitchen, where, on the porcelain-topped table, a chocolate layer cake bound with wax paper waited to be eaten in Arden Park after the parade. A canary of the breed known as Harz Mountain roller looked at him around a slightly nibbled cuttlebone through its cage bars. Following Melissa, he swept on through the immaculate dining room, past Mr. Gardner's Daddy Chair, Mrs. Gardner's Mama Chair, Melissa's Baby Chair—the same height and width as the others, yet ineffably hers. Nick couldn't recall ever having been invited for supper at the Gardners', or for that matter, to share a biscuit and jelly.

In the living room Melissa was furiously cranking the Victrola. Unlike the Bolyards' Sonora, which, though they took ceaseless pleasure in its use, was casually maintained, the Gardners' Victrola was polished to a metallic, black-a-vised gloss; the overgrown fox terrier staring into the morning-glory mouth of the speaker, in the gilt-and-blue trademark shining inside the raised lid, was as saucy as he'd been when the machine was delivered.

Nick advanced upon Melissa, standing behind her as she labored. She was putting a lot of muscle into it. Heels wide apart for leverage, body rising and dipping; the rosette-stippled dress hem sliding up and up, her thighs cream and gold, a wonderful triangle sheathed by a pale-yellow satin undergarment growing wider by the second at the apex of those underthighs. Perhaps the spring would slip a cog, and she'd have to start over. If so, he was willing to wait. She was more haunting and her body was speaking to him more wisely than any number of massive wallpaper nudes. But then the tenor regained his old insipidity, his nasal lamentation recognizable as words again: "Two by two—they go marching through—those sweethearts—on parade . . ."

She straightened and faced him in one motion.

At the same instant he understood she had meant him to see. She had become a Melissa reckless and headlong, a Melissa whose newness, like white willow with the bark suddenly stripped by lightning, might not last long in this air, but breathing joy and accepting it. She smelled of her mother's rosewater and her own bright flesh. He put his hands behind her head, brought her up and closer, her eyes starting to shut now, and as her lips fitted on his, as she crushed inward and up and heat spread through his belly and made his back arch inward like a bow beginning its stretch, he felt his right elbow brush against something alien. Then he heard whatever it was fall with a tinkling crash to the Axminster carpet, and he felt her slide away. It was as though he grasped after a smoke of promise, there so swiftly, offered and glorious, and gone.

He blinked down at what she was inspecting. The room was tightly furnished. All around were dark cabinets packed with pin trays, representational figurines, religious and secular— Joseph of Arimathaea and his staff saying hello to a brown-faced china pug dog—and many photographs. There were photographs of Melissa on a tricycle, crouching and muffled against weather, of Melissa in variant moods and seasons and rates of growth; of Melissa with Gardner aunts and uncles and her own parents. Of Billy Sunday with his jaw like a steam shovel of flesh, and his eyes truculently Christian. Of upright friends of Mr. Gardner's, those he knew in person and those he'd written to because he admired their principles.

The photograph Nick had knocked down—he bent closer to see it more plainly on the floor—was of Herbert Clark Hoover in his high, neck-clinching collar. He picked it up by a corner of the gilt-dipped frame. There was a large crack in the glass which traversed the President's pursed lips and slanted over an eye, giving him an oddly more human cast of countenance, as if he'd started to tip a wink to someone and to ask if anybody would care for a few hands of blackjack.

At the bottom of the picture was the prized autograph—*For Roy Washington Gardner, loyal American,* then the signature but no presidential seal. It had the dominant place in this room, standing out even over the many pictures of Melissa.

Nick said, "Look, M'liss, I can take it along right now. They can cut a new glass at the Tribe of K tomorrow . . ."

Melissa nodded fiercely, her hair bouncing up and down as Mr. Gardner's voice came from the dining room. Nick held the photograph in plain sight, like a salver, on the palm of his right hand. With the glass upright.

Mr. Gardner was saying, "Melissa, your mother and I think you better start getting ready for the parade now. We all want baths; there's the car to decorate; Eugene will be along before you know it . . ."

Mr. Gardner came into the room. His eyes, at first merely testy, then shocked, looked nowhere but at the photograph. He came on toward Nick, stooped above the photograph for another moment as if to check that what his eyes had first registered could really be true, took the picture from Nick and hugged it close against the chest of his creaseless shirt, standing between it and further assault.

The tenor, with the spring all wound up under him, was once more into a refrain, "An' I sigh—as they pass me by—those sweethearts on par-ade . . ."

Mr. Gardner said very softly, "You did this?"

"Yessir," Nick said. He realized he still held out his hand, fingers spread; he put his hand in his pocket. "Accident, Mr. Gardner. I was telling Melissa, I'll take it down to the Tribe of K, first thing tomorrow. They can cut a new glass in a couple of minutes."

Mr. Gardner's grip on the injured photograph became

tighter. "No thank you. I can afford to repair it. I'll see to it myself. Well, then." His nostrils were pinched, faintly white around the flanges; behind him, Mrs. Gardner looked in, then disappeared. At her father's shoulder, hovering in back of him, Melissa had started to cry—she wasn't making any noise about it as yet, but there was a lustre around her eyes. No longer the passionate and possessed and noble girl of those bare minutes ago, she was still enormously attractive, and Nick wanted to put his arm around her. He thought of Eugene Fisher—a darkling jar of Vaseline, full of scriptural arts and the wiles which only the truly gifted cynic could command—about to come to Melissa.

Nick made a short bow, which he had learned in dancing school, in a class run by Mamie Jernigan and for which the pianist had been Milly Fisher, Eugene's mother. It was a long time since Nick had made the bow. He said, "I regret any trouble I've caused you, and I wish you a very good day."

In the yard Buck was leaning against the flagpole. The wren had flown away. Buck slapped the sacks, handed him his and said, "Kept him as long as I could, but he started smellin' a rat when he heard the screen door open. Guess I'm losin' my touch. How'd it go?"

"About average," Nick said as they started away.

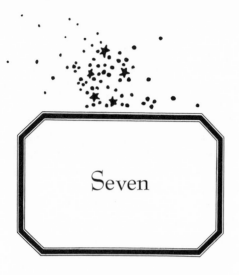

Seven

The circle of sunlight had moved farther into the cave, almost to Cy Bellaman's feet. He had the gift of full concentration, of applying himself completely to whatever engineering or hunting project was at hand. Now he was building his own past and Phyllis', as he might have laid out the preliminary drawings for a new clutch assembly; yet the deeper he got into it, the more he found himself sweating, even though the cave stayed cool.

Even from inside the cave he had heard a burst of the shouting far above him and to the west, from Foe Killer Bridge. Recognizing the voice of Jerome Potter, he had been surprised that Jerome had so little sense; then he realized it must have been an emergency. Maybe someone had dropped into a deadfall or tumbled off one of the trestle bridges. Cy sincerely hoped not. He expected to be trailed with some finesse; he had always respected a worthy opponent. He had thought that after the first blind hunt for him in the night hours, Jerome, and the rest—Wid, particularly, who had native shrewdness—would have settled on the water tower. They knew the railroad schedules, hands down—knew that there was just the early train on this holiday, and the late one, which stopped for water.

Jerome had probably figured out, as well, why he, Cy, hadn't taken the car. For one thing, it was eminently recognizable: a Cloud roadster, a good deal older than the proud specimen owned by the Kaplan brothers. For another, it would have flagged to those who hunted him that he was already out of town; he would then be beyond their domain, and it would be Jerome's duty to put out a general alarm. He knew the workings of the Vigilante Committee's collective mind. He was fully aware that they'd try to protect him by finding him themselves, inside the sheriff's territory. And on his own ground, and theirs, he intended to stay a jump ahead; at night he might be able to swing onto the train at the tower without being nabbed, and if he couldn't, he wasn't worth shooting. It was a mere game; he regretted having to play it, but he would play it with everything he had. If the morning train had stopped for water or at the town depot, he'd have been on that, and this damn farce wouldn't have to be gone through.

After he was on the train, let them put out all the alarms they had to. Let them rouse the town, tell the dirty truth, and whistle for him. He would drop off the train before the conductor could get the telegram. That would be at about Hamilton. After that he'd be on his own, anonymous, drifting awhile, maybe beating his way to the full north, disappearing into New York, dropping into it like an egg unidentifiable from all the other eggs in any big basket. Get rid of this rifle before he took the train. Pay his fare as soon as he got on board, give the conductor a little song and dance about somebody who was sick and whom he had to see in a hurry farther north; from that point on he would improvise.

The objective was to get away. Never to see Phyllis again.

If he let Jerome drag him back for an explanation and then the inevitable trial, he'd have to see her. She'd be in the courthouse, through interminable days, cool and above it all, and he would go sick inside, having to look at her even though he didn't want to, his body doing it for him.

He licked his lips, which tasted of salt. Walking to the mouth of the cave, he looked out into the raw sunlight. Tiny cabbage butterflies, about the size of snowflakes in a good wet Ohio storm, were dancing over the trail outside the cave. They swayed into sight and out again, lighter than feathers over the dark-green grasses and against the trunks of the oaks and chestnuts. He followed them as they vanished westward, remembering exactly where the nearest creek was.

His white shirt was no more obtrusive against the background of warm sun shafts and foliage than the hide of a white deer. He reached the creek, making very little noise as he went, in another minute and a half. It was one of those arrows of water that came out of the ground for a few yards and then ducked under again, cold, secret, old water the Indians might have known. He lay full length, holding himself on the palms of his hands, and drank with the neatness of an animal lapping. Then, dipping his hands in the water, he washed his face and splashed his hair and the back of his neck and stayed where he was a little longer, liking the cool near-silence and the way his skin felt as the moisture on it started to evaporate.

His mind clicked into gear again: he and Henry had often used this creek when they were nearby. The last time, that hunt last fall, when they had shot two bucks, he'd helped Henry take them home to the Ridge and helped him gut and clean and salt them down. There had been a fine satisfaction in doing that job well, alongside Henry. Henry's was the one place where everything else fell away and what remained, stark, was living itself; there was none of the nonsense of day-to-day emotion, of night-to-night agony. Henry never spoke of Phyllis or of Cy's life with her. Henry came to supper with the Bellamans. But the only time he could have seen Phyllis alone these latter days must have been when he drove the old horse and the vegetable wagon up the lane behind the Bellaman place to sell his stuff. That must have been when it started to happen.

It had hurt with every man in different ways. Starting with

that son of a bitch Savage, who quit his job at the Shops the day after Cy had pounded him half dead. Going on to Jerome. Maybe Jerome didn't realize it, but Cy had known almost from the start, had felt it with his testicles as much as with his intuition, and had not wanted to talk to Jerome about it, because he still liked him too much. They couldn't sit down at the same table together after that, even when it was good and over; they wouldn't play any more chess in their lifetimes. Whatever fool had said "Time heals all wounds" hadn't been a cuckold, or if he had, hadn't loved his wife.

Yes, loved her. Because every time when the man had been dismissed—and she lopped them off like branches from a dead tree—she changed again, came back to what she'd been right after the wedding, ardent for him, not even having to say it, only moving to him, not even having to touch him because it was all there, less an asking for forgiveness than a terrible silent cry to be sustained and valued. And he found himself telling himself, That was the last, from now on we'll start over; this is what it was meant to be in the beginning. Pride didn't have a thing to do with it. Pride was what you'd felt, younger; pride was a silly luxury. But when it was that Eugene Fisher kid— not a child, such people were born old—he'd packed up and gone away for three weeks. Telling old Noel, who hadn't had his first stroke then, that he needed a rest.

In Noel's office at the Shops, Noel had said, "Why, yes, take a holiday. You and Mrs. Bellaman ought to go to Europe; you could drop in at the Mercedes plant in Stuttgart, Cy—I have a few friends there, been in correspondence with them at any rate. Look around, take some notes. We'll write it off as business and it will be on me." Noel leaned back in his worn-castered chair. "They're an indomitable team, those Germans. They'll never go back to wartime again; the country's too poor; they were trounced too thoroughly. But they're making beautiful cars. Quality, precision. I'd like to take young Nick over some year soon. His mother's been after me to give him some polish; she calls every week from wherever she's playing—and

Alice has said she'd take him abroad. Truth is, I don't have much time for him. Not enough." Noel spread his hands. He spent most of his waking hours at the Shops, which, somehow, ran better when the men on shift knew he was there. He was a center of stability, expecting excellence; but Cy knew the old man was lost, hated to go home.

A dusty picture of Rex Cloud in overseas uniform hung on the wall in back of Noel's head.

Cy said quickly, "Oh, no, I just want to hole up somewhere close by. Just for thinking things over."

"I did that right after my war," Noel said. "I thought for a couple of days, then I met Marie Patterson at a river-boating party and married her the next week; and the week after that I was in Washington trying to scrape together enough to get the buggy works off the ground. Wartime friends—money was tight. They all advised me to step down from my brevet commission, take a colonelcy, and stay where it was safe. Safety. It's what most politicians, and a good many political generals, seem to have wanted more than anything else. Still seem to want. A never-ending boom. It wasn't like that with President Lincoln, you know. I saw him once . . ."

Cy waited, watching the deep-brown, nearly black eyes, the still-vigorous black beard. "Oh, it wasn't anything," Noel said. "It was when Little Mac had those gun emplacements around Washington, most of them logs—false guns—they wouldn't have kept out a troop of horse. I was waiting down the hall, I'd just mustered the regiment from around here, and I didn't have my wartime commission yet, didn't expect any—I'd mailed along some ideas I had about the South. I'd said I didn't think they would be easily buffaloed. I'd known too many. I'd said they had to be respected, and that puffing about patriotism wouldn't pull it off. A nation could have a lot of loud brass bands and fuss and feathers, but what it needed was just a few men of the caliber of Light Horse Harry Lee's son, and less shouting about hanging Jeff Davis. He came out then, walking rather slowly, hands behind his back—saw me, nodded to me, came over to me and asked me who I was, and when I told him I wasn't anyone, a farm boy from Ohio, and gave him my name, he grinned and said, 'I got your letters, Mr. Cloud. By some mischance, they were delivered to me instead of being waylaid. If you'll see my Secretary of War sometime today, when he can work you in through the grist, you'll find out how much I agree with you, and why you're here.' He teetered on his heels then, and walked off, and a second later, when I caught another look at him in the doorway light, he looked old and sick and heavy-shouldered. I never saw him again. It's nothing for memoirs."

Noel looked up again at Cy. "Have a good time, and take the time you need."

Now Cy remembered how it had been when he came home, to find Phyllis pledged to him again, as though some essence in her had never been away from him, never hated all men alive and him with them. That good time hadn't lasted, though he'd been crazy enough to expect it to. Before he understood that she'd gone back to that Eugene creature once more while they were still in the days and nights between, he tried, as he had never tried before, to get her to talk about it. "What happened?" he would ask. "Something, before you married me— before we made that choice. Somebody else—"

She would shake her head, folding into herself, not turning away but adamant. He himself had a good idea who her first lover had been. And he thought sometimes that Doc Bowen might know something about it, but he'd never been able to bring himself to ask him. Doc might know a great deal about the past lives of his patients, but he didn't open his mouth except to give out a prescription. He took the Hippocratic oath seriously, but he had so much respect for the privacy of others that he'd have kept quiet anyhow. Tom Wolfson had been a good friend of Bowen's, and Phyllis had gone to Bowen all the time she was growing up.

But would acting like some kind of detective, a Sherlock, have helped her? Would it have saved Henry?

If last night I could have stood outside it, he thought, if I could have seen it clear and cool, a problem, with me outside its middle . . . Goddamn it to hell, if I'd been just a little better engineer.

He wiped water off his hands on his trouser legs, got up and stood listening for a moment. All that blather from Foe Killer Bridge had faded away long since. He thought, I forgot to feed Merlin, too. Meant to do it before I went in the house, after I locked him in the run last night. But I decided I'd go in first and eat something myself, and feed him after I'd seen Phyl—sometimes she likes to watch him eat, along with me. A big dainty dog, a hell of a well-trained dog, the best setter I ever had. Ah, well, maybe somebody'll remember to feed him.

On the town side of Carmian's Hill, in the Colored Settlement, the Reverend Collis Bates opened the front doors of the church. Though the other Arden churches wouldn't be having services today, this one would have its celebration.

Nor was that the only way it differed from most churches. Within the memory of those old enough to recall first appearances, the church had been a very bright pink, like the highly colored cheek of a bisque doll; years of heat and winter had weathered it to this fragile rosy shading.

Its nave was high and wide, running through the arch straight to the altar, which was of rough boards sanded down and then, through time, worn smooth by elbows and hand-touch. The floorboards were pegged and as broad as the planking of the outside timbers; and no board had ever sprung of developed creaks. Along both sides were windows almost to the ceiling, and there was a rear window over the altar, all holding panes of clean plain glass.

But more than its flesh coloring, it was the angels that gave the church its special quality, its distinction. Under outside corbels springing from the peaked roof, at the four corners, the wooden angels leaned outward and forward, each with its trumpet against embouchure-strong lips, each blowing silent blasts to heaven.

The angels had wings that swept up in swan curves, tapering through primary feathers to wingtips, each angel with long, wide eyes looking at spring sky, shimmering summer heat, weeping autumn rains, the cryptlike silences of winter. Their carved curls appeared to support the roof and its boxlike tower, whose bell had come off a river boat, and which still had the commanding clang of a packet. The bell could be heard from Arden when the wind was right.

The angels on the east were continually facing Arden, those on the west sighting toward Kentucky, into the leagues of trees on the opposite river bank. In all lights they looked alive.

To the Reverend Collis Bates, a thick-shouldered man in his sixties, those angels nearest him, and above him as he swung open the doors, seemed to flare out in the heat and offer a certain greeting. They were, he thought, messengers by trade, directly in congress with the Lord. When he had the doors back, a draft moved over him, its air sweeping inward from the porch. He walked along past the benches. There was only one aisle, the bench ends on the outside abutting the walls. Like the pulpit, the benches were of worn pine, and backless. He went along to the bell room, closet-narrow but tall, and open into upper darkness where doves stirred and talked. Head back, taking a turn of the rope around his fist, he pulled. At first the bell gave out a mere *ting*, but at the warning the doves gathered themselves in the tower and aimed outward through the slats. On the next pull the bell clapper struck home. Reverend Bates got the rhythm then, and the bell called out steadily for a minute, reaching through the whole black settlement, over the Ridge into the white side, and down to the east into the woods.

His congregation had started coming in by the time he unwound the rope from his hand; Reverend Bates went out and climbed to the pulpit. On its lectern waited a Bible as heavy as a hearthstone, in which were recorded births, deaths, marriages and other high-water marks of his people. It also contained commentary about the flock as it had been in his father's and grandfather's time. Turning the yellowing, must-smelling but durable pages to the front, anyone could have found out that Pierre Wolfson, settling in the last of the 1700s, had released from bondage eleven slaves, six males, five females, and offered them their own township; Reverend Bates's grandmother had been with them. In crabbed, slow penmanship, it was also written that a score of Settlement men had accompanied General Cloud to war, as part of his regiment from Arden. In 1865 some had come back; others had died in towns scattered from Pennsylvania to Tennessee.

This morning, instead of opening the book, Reverend Bates placed his right hand on it, palm flat, and waited while he watched the people still gathering; nodding to one here and another there, and gathering his forces around what he wanted to say. It wouldn't be Scripture on this day, but music would be right. He watched as the last man, Grandpa Gordon, came in under the angels, navigated to the first bench by his grand-daughter guiding him by a frail elbow.

There was a shifting on the benches, a sound of muslin and overall-cloth, and a smell of hair oil and morning soap . . . a mild waving of palm-leaf fans.

He looked at the Settlement musicians on a bench to his left: cornetist, saxophonist, bass viol, trombone. Henny Dervis, the youngest musician and Reverend Bates's nephew, held his cornet bell on his knee, its mouthpiece pointed straight up. The oldest musician was Gladstone Phillips, bass viol; he was fourteen. He had assumed a crouching position, ready to stand and draw his bow across the strings, on signal.

Reverend Bates said to everybody present, "I'm going to speak about this Day of Independence. Just like last year and the year before and before that, it won't be any sermon. Just a few remarks I thought ought to get made. But before I make them, we'll warm things up with a hymn. I've got a hymn in my mind. It's 'My Lord, What a Morning.' "

There wasn't a hymnal in sight. As Reverend Bates lifted his right hand from the cover of the Bible and swung it down through the air, Gladstone Phillips came to his feet and pulled the bow of the viol across the strings, producing a C, a key everybody could accommodate to. Reverend Bates swung his hand up, and the four musicians hit the first bar like good horses out of a starting gate. The sound struck the ceiling and came down again, ecstatic, free, round as bird song and true. The first deep phrase came lining out of the horns and the bass, then there was a sucking in of air and a letting forth of the answer from the congregation. Everybody sang. Nobody sat back, mumbled, glanced askance at anybody else, did anything but join in and meld the words into passion that soared out of the open doors and made the sky, up around where the corner angels stood, reverberate with orison and gathered plenty. My —*Lord*—what a—*morn*ing!

Reverend Bates, singing himself, straw bass, could see out where the Settlement started, at the lip of the path leading up into the hillside, and twining down into the town of Arden. He made out a couple of figures climbing, still small in the distance, and thought for a flash that maybe one of them was Mrs. Cy Bellaman. She'd begun coming to the church quite a while ago, just showing up, sometimes taking a bench in the back, and usually leaving before everything was over. Once or twice she'd stayed until he was finished talking and shaking hands on the porch, and she'd given him some money for the church pot, which could forever use it, and asked him how things were progressing—very quiet, low-voiced, mercy and dignity stamped all over her. He didn't know if she was a member of the M.E. or the Baptist, but it didn't make a jot of difference. He understood that she didn't come because she thought, Real Quaint, or How They Enjoy Themselves. She didn't fool herself and didn't try to fool you. Like Alice Cloud, in that respect.

Reverend Bates had worked in the Shops a lot of his life. He had a natural bent for knowing just what made an internal-combustion engine tick and had an abiding respect for Noel

Cloud and for Cy Bellaman. He'd been a troubleshooter himself, appointed so, pretty young, by old Noel, and paid more than some of the whites there thought he was getting, not only because Noel liked him but because he was worth it. When the Shops were sold and began turning out gimcrackery, it wasn't what it had been under Noel. But he'd stayed on because he needed the job to help run the church—his father had been a quarryman, and his grandfather had been a shrewd trapper, and they had both served the church as ministers.

He sang from the hard stomach muscles, up and through the chest, and squinted a bit against the sun to make out the climbing figures on the road. Wasn't Miss Alice, not tall enough for that; anyhow, she'd be tied up with her hospital today, till time for the park dance this evening. He thought he'd say a few words about General Cloud in his remarks after the hymn; and if there was time later, during the parade or after it, he might go down and see the General for a minute. It didn't make a whole lot of difference that the General couldn't answer him; just sitting with him was the idea.

Reverend Bates could see now who the figures were; they had reached the ridge slope and were cutting across this edge, through the Settlement, on to the hill, evidently aiming for the white cemetery above the river. Nick Cloud and Buck Bolyard. He remembered how when Nick was born the General, fairly up in years for it, looking like it was a miracle, passed out cigars, saying, "I am at last a grandfather." The General's son, Rex, had dropped in at the Shops that day too, celebrating, one of the few times he'd ever come by except to borrow a new, fast model and run its guts out on the country roads.

Judge not, Reverend Bates admonished himself, that ye be not . . .

Nick and Buck had paused for a second or so, apparently listening to the singers. Then they went on into the trees, out of view.

The hymn ended, the last of it globed high and faraway in the throat of Minnie Apperson, who sang alto in a way to make the soul remember it when times were hard. Then there was a loose silence, everybody's eyes fixing on Reverend Bates, a shoe sole scraping, a cough got out of the way.

His voice took up before the warm air had settled. "Freedom," he said. "Freedom! Let's roll that around in our minds a little. It's a day for it. Let's praise the men we got it from, the men and women who always had it in their hearts, and I'm not talking only about pilgrims and pioneers . . ." He bent forward. His hands took hold of the lectern as a man takes hold of a plow. "I'm talking about Moses, Aaron, the burning bush, the lights in the darkness. I'm talking about the first light that shone out over the face of the deep . . ."

There was a rough stone wall below the schoolyard and above Shop Street. Phyllis Bellaman stopped here, sitting with her hands on the wall coping, leaning back, looking along toward Front Street. She had started for the Wolfson Block, but three quarters of the distance there she'd turned and come back the other way, thinking of the lonesome grounds today, thinking of the house itself, where she had been born; she didn't believe she could stand going back just yet. She could see automobile glass glinting as cars trundled down Front Street, most of them turning westward and aiming up the road toward the park, bound for the ceremony of shooting off the park cannon. As a little girl she had enjoyed that; the suspense was the best, the rather flat and abrupt explosion itself anticlimactic, but to see the men count the time on their railroad watches—the Walthams, the Elgins—and to feel a crawling delight as the watch hands moved toward straight up, noon, and then to hear the showering chimes of the town clock as the fuse hissed along into the black powder packed into the cannon—there was certain happiness.

On Front Street now, she saw Eugene Fisher appear and walk past the Argus, where posters, beside its arcade, advertised Richard Barthelmess in *The Patent Leather Kid*. Mr. Barthelmess was busy holding back a German tank with his bare hands. It glowered above him in titanic darkness against a scarlet star-shelled sky. Eugene, in that distance, walked proudly, wearing a fully buttoned blazer, white flannels, his own hair as black as Barthelmess' in the poster, his shadow printing along the windows of Soames's Pharmacy as he went under its awning.

She had vaguely intended going into Soames's herself in a few minutes; it was the one place open today where one might get a sandwich without regretting it. Flute's Café, a little way along, was something she didn't think she could face. Thank you, Eugene, she murmured to herself. Thank you for shutting off that avenue to me, too. For a second or so she thought about going in anyhow and cutting him dead, but it took too much out of the spirit. There was a wrenching expense involved in it—as there had been just now when she'd faced down Alice Cloud—and she shouldn't have been hungry, anyway. She thought, I think I ate something yesterday, just at twilight, just before Henry came. It might have been light-years ago, longer than a human mind could encompass.

The body was very tricky; here it was, a little hungry, as if it had no decency at all. Past Soames's and Flute's and Bomasy's barbershop, the awning above the windows of Melton's Funeral Parlor was a washed-out lilac. She had been in there, in the front room, the viewing room, when she was fourteen and her mother lay tricked out in rouge and lace, and she had been there again, with Cy, when Tom Wolfson lay there, made into a dubious clown. She would not go to this latest funeral, but she would have to see to it that, somehow, Tilda Watherall got money—she might send it along through Tommy Beavis, Jerome's man, if she could get hold of him soon; she hadn't thought of it last night.

She had thought of nothing much last night before Dr. Bowen washed her arm with cotton dipped in alcohol and then gave her the shot; and after it she had drifted, like after making love . . . until this morning and the sound of the train and the remembrance of what had happened. It was chasing her, the realization itself was coming at her, and around her, badly now, and if she'd ever taken much pleasure in drinking—there was very good brandy in the cellar at home—she would have started homeward again. But that wouldn't work; what she wanted was a dead man to be alive. Two dead men, now, she thought; Henry has been added. He is on my little list. Oh, Henry, I liked you very much.

The sun was hot here; the wall absorbed it as if the cement coping were blotting paper. On the street past the schoolyard, in the opposite direction from the Shops, a cherry bomb ripped the air, and its pale-fire explosion, against the sun, sent mirroring images of itself in the dark school windows. It went higher than the circular, silo-shaped, iron-enclosed fire escape, and scraps of it floated down into the foot-beaten grassless yard. For a second it also brightened the front hallway of the school past the worn doors. She remembered going in there in awe of the older girls and boys, clutching her blue lunch pail, smelling the strong odor of sweeping compound and moist wool and lunches and children's excitement. Someone her own age had whispered to her, "There's Alice Cloud; there's her brother Rex. She graduates this year; he's got a year to go. Aren't they—" But she already knew *who* they were. They were the reason why she had transferred to that school.

She was ten. Up to then she'd gone to school at Miss Ames's Academy, in Indiana; her mother balked when she said she wanted to transfer to the Arden school, mix with that bunch of nit-headed shop-workers' children, but her father said if she wanted to, she could; it was good enough for General Cloud's son and daughter, wasn't it?

They were the Clouds, that's all they were.

Everything.

If Alice Cloud knew how close I came to walking straight into her arms a few minutes ago, in her rotten half-charity hospital; if she knew how I nearly began talking, telling her I hated those years much more than she could ever be sorry for them, and that at the wedding I wanted her to stand where I was standing, to wear that ring when Cy put it on my finger —but then, Alice knew that. She'd known it a dozen years. She'd known why I took Cy—made him want me. She didn't know how much I tried with Cy, though. She'll never know that.

For the last few seconds a small boy had been looking at her. He'd been walking along toward Front, kicking a lard can in front of him, but the clatter had been beyond her thought. His eyes were hazel and his face was smeared with remnants of gunpowder, dust and a few cracker crumbs. A corduroy knicker leg hung loose. He said conversationally, "H'lo, Mrs. Bellaman."

"Good morning, Jimmy," Phyllis said.

He lived in the lane behind the Wolfson Block and was a selective admirer of dogs, liking some, discounting others as not worth his time. He had no dog because his mother, Mrs. Hargis, had four other children, and dogs made her sneeze.

He said, "Ain't goin' to the cannon. Goin' to the park later. Goin' home now. I'm clean out of firecrackers. Mama said git home by noon, git washed up, don't git killed." He added, "On the way, can I go in and see Merlin?"

Oh, God, she thought. Merlin; when the holocaust begins it takes in dogs, too. They get starved out. She leaned down to Jimmy and said gravely, "You can feed him. You know where the food is; you've watched Mr. Bellaman."

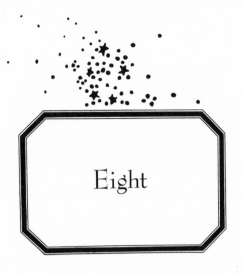

Eight

The front door of the Glid McBride farmhouse hung open to the heat, though the screen door kept out what flies it could. Dr. Leonard Bowen leaned an elbow against the faded cabbage roses in the blistered wallpaper and talked a few inches from the mouthpiece of the wall phone, which stuck out like the neck of an ebony duck from its box. It was a party line, and after activating the crank he'd had to wait two minutes before both he and Velma Temple, the operator back in Arden, had made the listeners-in hang up. He could tell when this was accomplished by the fact that the line force increased, getting clearer and letting a conversation go louder at both ends. He had Alice Cloud clearly now.

He said, "Breech delivery, I should've known it. I'm heading back now. Glid's drunk as a wet coot, out in the barn. Rose is all right—she'll be on her feet in a day. She's got food and drink handy, and a supply of stuff for the baby—weighs eight pounds. They're both asleep. Rest of Glid's kids have gone off to the park, but the oldest told me she'd be back before sundown." He listened a moment, then said, "Have Birdy wrap the burn in tannic acid bandage, and expect me in about twenty minutes. Got any other new cases 'sides that?"

At the other end Alice, sounding normal and level, said, "There's this fellow—one of the Linden brothers—who may have a broken neck. He says it is. I think it's badly sprained. I believe you die with a broken neck. He seems to have been with a girl in his father's loft, and they both fell out. The girl sustained only bruises."

"Lord," Dr. Bowen said, "what gets into people in this weather, on this crazy day? I hope they both enjoyed it while it lasted. No, you don't necessarily croak with a broken neck; depends where you break it. Tell Birdy to keep him quiet. Phyl Bellaman leave?"

There was a very brief pause. "She has gone on her way," Alice said.

"Best thing she could do," Bowen said. He'd felt the pause. "Alice, I hope you were easy on her."

"I tried to be. I was polite."

"Isn't what I meant. Now that she's—well, 'bereft' I guess is the word—it's no time to come upper-handed with her."

Another pause. And Alice said, "Am I so obviously unfeeling?"

"Only with her. And with stupid people—yes, you're high-handed as they come with ignorance. I got to go now, I'm sick of this pigsty. But it's a good baby; it'll flourish."

Alice said goodbye, and when she had hung up at her end, Dr. Bowen kept the line open until Velma spoke. "Anybody else you want, Doctor?" she asked.

"Velma, you went on at about seven this morning, didn't you?"

"Yessir."

"Took over when Liz Cooper went off, didn't you?"

"Yessir. And I'll be here right through the whole day because Arly Kinser isn't comin' in at all. She's goin' to the park dance, which puts me on till right about midnight when Liz comes in again. I done it for her 'cause she'd do it for me if I needed time off."

"All right," Bowen said. "What I'm getting at—listen a second, we're still on this line by ourselves, aren't we?"

Velma said, "Yessir. I'd hear the dip in the line, otherwise."

"All right, then," Bowen murmured. "Here's what I want to know. Don't fudge around or fib to me—I know you too well. Liz told you about the call last night from Phyl Bellaman, didn't she? The call for Jerome Potter. And she let you know about Jerome callin' the committee together. Just tell me plain."

Velma's voice sounded smaller. "Yes," she said. "And she told me about you gettin' called in."

"Sure Billy Bobtail, I figured she would have. It was news, and I don't blame you girls exchangin' news. I don't blame you listening in, either. I'd do it myself if it was the only entertainment I had on duty. All I want to ask you is to shut up. Don't let it out to anybody but the parties involved. I'm pretty sure Liz won't—she wouldn't, except to you—but I just want your word you won't, either."

Velma's voice was wounded. "Why, Doc—what we tell one another, up here, that's kind of sacred."

"Good girl," he said. "And if anybody gets snoopy, clam up. Got that clear?"

He hung up, and for a moment he leaned both shoulders against the wall beside the telephone. Then he heaved himself away, picked up his bag and went out. On the sagging porch he stood for a moment, the heat shimmering around his eyes and his white thatch of hair. Then he stumped along to his dust-covered Auburn, dropped the bag down beside him, knuckled his eyes and got the car going. It wasn't as good as a Cloud would have been, but he thought too much of the Cloud cars to use them for truck horses. He'd had this Auburn ever since his Cloud buggy had finally bitten the dust, and God knew, the buggy had lasted well for thirty years.

Driving along, he thought about Phyl Bellaman, and Cy, as

he'd been doing ever since last night, even during the Rose McBride *accouchement*. Phyl had been a lot narrower across the hips than Rose—but then, most people were. It was the only time he could remember when he'd gone ahead, on his own, and knuckled under to any request, no matter how desperate, to commit a criminal action. Right after Rex Cloud's death in France had been noised around, he was in his office at home, on upper Front Street. When he went to answer the rap on the door that evening, he was surprised to see Phyl there by herself, eighteen and wearing a mink tippet and muff against the early cold of that year. She stood beside the Franklin stove, taking her time about taking off her furs, no doubt flustered about some common female complaint, he'd thought.

But when she said it, straight, even though it was common —she was a long way past being flustered. "I'd like to keep the baby if I can. But I want you to tell me if that's possible—I've been feeling very ill."

He told her to undress, which she did behind the screen— he had no office nurse then, or ever; he would bring in a nurse only for difficult operations. Then, bending over her on the old leather-topped table, he thought that hers was probably the most beautiful example of a female body he'd ever seen. His own wife had been dead five years, and he was too busy and his fool gall bladder kept acting up too much for him to fret about affairs of the warm flesh anymore—but he knew sexual rarity when he saw it.

She didn't seem worried about any moralizing from him, but clearly, she was very frightened. And although she didn't know it, she had good reason to be; she was about two months along, and he didn't think she'd make it all the distance of the nine. The uterus wasn't fitted for bearing a child. He told her, and told her as straight as she'd talked to him; that was when she asked him to help her get rid of this thing that wasn't yet a child.

He could feel her pleading as though she reached right into him. He hadn't even considered the point that if Tom Wolfson found out about it, or anybody else, he'd be done for in this town and county and state forever, and that he was even then too old to go somewhere else and try to start over.

She said, "I'll have other babies, Dr. Bowen. I know I will."

He said, "No, you won't, Phyl. When I've done this, the only kids you'll ever have might be those you adopted. You won't have any of your own."

It wasn't that she didn't believe him; it was only as though she couldn't accept that. She didn't cry once; just kept her chin out and stuck to whatever she believed in the teeth of natural fact. He did the best he could; it was as though they worked together like a dedicated team, she trusting him, he trusting her. Now and then he remarked to himself, not out loud, that something about her reminded him of old Pierre Wolfson, in those steel engravings you saw in the local history pamphlets —a man, a dark forcible entity, who was going to dominate life and yet try to be fair about it. It was some generations from her back to old Pierre, but she was more like him than she was like Tom Wolfson, or her mother.

She was weak afterward, naturally, and he gave her tonic and made her keep something on her stomach, and she told him she'd stay that evening because Tom and Betty Wolfson were out of town for the weekend, and the servants thought she was spending the night with a friend.

In the morning after she'd got some sleep and looked fit to walk, she said she'd pay him as soon as she got her next allowance, and Dr. Bowen said, "If you ever try it, I'll spank your bottom." He didn't offer any sage advice, did not tell her that she had a good useful life ahead of her, and that this couldn't wipe it out or change it. It would have been a lie, and he'd tried for some years not to deal in lies just because they were easier. He knew how much she was changed. He wasn't a parson, or a poet. His trade wasn't lying.

It would have been nice to be able to do something for her, a lot more than aborting her. And nice to know she was still a friend, in all the years between then and now, but that would have been lying to himself. Because she never came to him again. She didn't go to the First M.E. services, either, when Rex Cloud got shipped home. She just went to all the parties anybody else gave, and gave a lot of them herself. Wild girl, smart girl, sweet but oh, so wild, everybody said; she enjoyed the whisperers who talked about her behind their hands and over their matron's chiffons and silks—enjoyed making them jump. When she took Cy Bellaman away from Alice, Doc Bowen had a crazy impulse to go to her and talk turkey, but it would have been a fool's move. How was he to know it wouldn't turn out fine for Phyl and Cy, whatever it would do to Alice?

A red-hot mama and a jazz baby, a flapper, she could have done worse, of course, than Cy. (He didn't think Cy could have done worse than her.) But it didn't cut the way he felt about her, the respect he had for whatever she wanted from living, the dream she'd had in those steady, very dark-blue eyes.

He turned the sweat-stained wood of the steering wheel and pulled up at the curb in front of his house on Front Street. Down the line the Kaplans were having a powwow in their backyards, running from one to the other; their houses snuggled against one another, and they were a clan always in and out of one another's places. They were gathering around a table in Aaron's yard, the women serving lemonade to the brothers while the brothers worked over some kind of assemblage of rockets. He left the engine running while he went past the overgrown myrtle bushes to his front door, wanting to freshen up a bit before he went on to the hospital. At the door he found a note from young Dr. Miller, stuck in between the doorbell and the wall, telling him one of Dr. Miller's patients, Mrs. Tensicott at the hospital, would appreciate him looking in on her while Miller and his wife were on their fishing trip. Dr. Bowen grunted and cast the note into the bush leaves. He couldn't do much about Bright's disease, which was Mrs. Tensicott's trouble—no more than he could do anything about Noel Cloud's last stroke. But he'd look in.

Toward lower Front, he heard a racket of firecrackers here and there, and glanced around to see Sheriff Potter's Willys-Knight, a 1922 which hadn't been improved by any of the country driving the sheriff did, coasting in to the curb near Soames's Pharmacy. The sheriff got out, and six men got out after him—one of them, Dr. Bowen was surprised to see, Marty Broom, who was supported, as he lurched to the walk, by Carl Bolyard on one side and Tommy Beavis on the other. Marty made a side-flapping motion with his hands, like a seal, and they took their protective weight away from him. They all stopped in a clutch of argument under Soames's awning. So much for that, Dr. Bowen told himself—I didn't think, when they first started out to bring him back last night, getting hold of Cy was going to be a cinch.

He saw Eugene Fisher come out a little way under the awning and stand there, leaning against the cool glass, listening and watching the arguing men. He felt a rill of pure detestation for Eugene. Count yourself lucky, you simpering Christ-using idiot, he said to himself; I guess it's all true, you got to Phyl, or she let you get to her, for a while. You can number her among your finest conquests, anyhow; one day those little girls will tell, one of them will blow the gaff before many moons, but Phyl won't mention it to a soul.

He opened the door and went in. The house smelled musty, and back in his office one of the cats was yowling. As he scrubbed his hands he looked out the bathroom window. Down past Melton's Funeral Parlor, and the Argus, the Baby Doll fire engine had been brought out from the shade into the sunlight, in preparation for the parade. Chief Ovid Gorseman was walking around it, admiring its flashing old bulk. Should have been a fireman, or a farmer, Bowen thought, holding his wrists up and letting the water run off. Wouldn't have got so linked up with other people then, and by God, I'd have got more sleep.

Eugene Fisher's left dimple was deeper than the other, but both were impressive. He had often been told he looked like the Charles "Buddy" Rogers of *Wings*. The Argus hadn't yet got around to showing *Wings* because it demanded special equipment for the recorded sound effects of planes snarling and machine guns ratcheting; Franz Otis intended to show *The Jazz Singer*, too, when he got the right equipment in. But one could travel across to Barlton and see, and more important, hear these wonders. Eugene agreed with those admirers who pointed out his resemblance to Rogers, though he thought he had the edge.

He stood carefully watching and listening as Sheriff Potter spoke quietly to Marty Broom. Marty's anger was steaming, uncontrolled. He was also incoherent.

The sheriff said, "Marty, you just go along now and settle down. Advise you to drop in and ask Miss Alice if she'll have somebody bind up your leg too. I really ain't got time to fool with you no more today."

Marty said, "Time! Sneakin' around lookin' for some criminal, keepin' it hushed up! Leggo me, Carl Bolyard!"

Carl had placed a weighty arm over Marty's shoulders. He didn't take it away. He said in bass tones, "Marty, don't fuck up what you don't know nothin' about. You're real fortunate you got saved; you'd still be up there on that trestle when the midnight Nickel Plate comes through, hadn't been for us." He held a steady finger under Marty's nose. "Hadn't been for *Wid*," he added sternly.

Wid said, "Don't need no thanks. Listen, Jerome—" He turned to the sheriff. "I got to toddle along. Harky'll raise the roof 'f I don't change and git over to the park and help the mayor fire off that blasted cannon. I'm cuttin' it fine as it is. If you want to get together later, after the picnic, I'll be ready then." His eyes still on Potter's, he made a motion of his thumb, indicating the presence of Eugene in the pharmacy doorway, and the sheriff gave a very tiny nod of understanding.

Tommy Beavis said, "And I got to get on my p'lice uniform. For the parade."

"Yeah," the sheriff said. "Reckon I'll be at the cannon firin' too. In case she finally blows up. You be on hand there, Tommy —help out keepin' the crowd back. Go along now."

Tommy gave a raw-boned half salute and wheeled and started away, toward the courthouse and the jail.

Carl said, "Guess I'll head home myself. I'm drivin' in the p'rade, with Maidy and Buck and Candy Pruitt." He shook his head and planted his fists on his hips. "Jerome, what we goin' to do with this feisty little mutt?"

Marty lunged forward and took a swing at Carl, which Carl absorbed by lifting his elbow.

Sheriff Potter said, "Oh, hell's sake, cool off, Marty. Go on in and I'll buy you a chocolate phosphate."

"Wouldn't touch it," said Marty, "if I was dyin' of heat-stroke."

"You kind of touched Wid's liquid refreshments," the sheriff said. "Maybe that's what's wrong with you, part of it. Heat's already got to you quite a bit. Listen—" He spoke to the others. "You boys go along. See you at the cannon in a while. We'll have a little kind of conference there, see what we'd ought to do next."

The men nodded and left, and the sheriff turned back to Marty. "Give you a ride down to the hospital. That leg ain't goin' to hold you up much longer if you don't get it tended to. Come on now."

"Go piss in a boot," said Marty.

The sheriff shrugged and got back in his Willys-Knight. He slammed the door heavily, not with any special commentary, since it always needed heavy slamming. The machine shook and protested as he drove off, and at the corner he turned left and westward, aiming for Arden Park.

Eugene Fisher advanced to Marty, who stood trembling and muttering. "Come on in the drugstore, Marty," he said. "You look in bad shape."

Eugene was seventeen, a year older than Nick and Buck. His tone was suited to homilies, pronouncing them as if they were fresh inventions. It was a muted voice wrapped in damp velvet that didn't quite go with his good looks. He laid a well-manicured hand on Marty's slumping shoulder. "Remember the Good Samaritan," he said softly. "Remember about Doing unto Others. You remember it, even if they forget it. Try to turn the other cheek."

"Oh, shit," said Marty.

Mild pain creased Eugene's forehead. It vanished as he turned to watch a couple of fourteen-year-old girls going past on bicycles which had stripes of crêpe paper intertwined in their spokes, making a whirling display of blue and red and white as they rolled. The girls were dressed in brief light cotton dresses which lifted in the wind of their lazy, gentle progress. They were licking pieces of chip ice, their tongues curling around the ice. They glanced at Eugene in the shadow, and they smiled back at him, shyly and yet with invitation.

Eugene licked his own lips, gently, but he had kept his hand on Marty and now brought to him his full attention once more. "Come on now, old chap. Let me buy you something—"

"Buy it myself," Marty said, letting himself be steered into Soames's. "And I ain't anybody's old chap. Start preachin' at me, and you can sit by yourself. I gow! First that bunch, now you. Why'n't you git yourself a gospel tent and hit the road? Git a steady job and help out your mama. Stop screwin' everything from a knothole to a sheep and act like—" He doubled up and stopped, a hand sliding down his left shin and his face contorting. "Ow! Jesus H. Christ, I got to sit down. Be limpin' like Hank Watherall 'f I don't."

Eugene patiently headed Marty toward a booth. "Sit down right here, Marty, and put your leg up." He helped him ease down and sat opposite Marty, drawing his flannels up with his fingers, pinching the creases as he sat. The booth table was marble-topped, and the partitions between the booths were high.

He could see past Marty to the magazine racks in the rear, where copies of *Captain Billy's Whizbang,* Hugo Gernsback's *Amazing Stories, Doc Savage* and *Black Mask Detective* were being read intently by four small boys. The out-of-town news-papers lay under the magazines, Hearst publications with red-bannered headlines speaking of the Yellow Peril, flagpole sit-ters, and bloody hatchet murders. From the racks and the newspapers came a smell of ink and pulpwood inviting to the nostrils, mingling with the scents of sweet soda from the long marble soda fountain and pharmaceuticals from the prescrip-tion department. Serried displays of D'jer Kiss perfume, Shu-White, Tanlac and Lydia E. Pinkham's Vegetable Compound lined the walls, along with cases of Lithia Water—whose bot-tles, emptied and washed, made ideal containers for home brew. Above them, Nujol and transparent amber bars of Jap Rose soap were available.

One of the ceiling fans, turning slowly on quarter power, each blade distinct as it came around, sent a drift of warm air over Eugene and Marty.

Marvin Soames came to the doorway of the prescription department and called out, "Anything, Marty?"

Marty stirred and groaned. "Cherry dope," he called back to Marvin.

"Make it two," Eugene said. "Easy on my ice."

Marvin's head, a polar bear's for whiteness, gave a shake. "Not till you pay up somethin', Eugene. I'm right sorry."

Eugene made an impatient, twiddling motion with his right forefinger and middle finger.

Marty's eyes shone with a flicker of amusement. " 'F you hadn't swiped ever'thing in sight, cleaned him outa condoms, you'd still be workin' here and have all you wanted." He inched around and said to Marvin, "Give him one on me. Plenty ice in mine."

Marvin, heading for the fountain, said, "Buck Bolyard and Nick Cloud was in a while back. Marty, Nick said if you showed up, Miss Alice's got a job for you at the hospital today."

"I'll think it over." Marty turned back to Eugene. "Feels better now. Just takin' the load off, it helps," he muttered, caressing his leg, fingers splaying flesh down to the ankle. As he straightened, cap askew, Eugene bent over the table even more solicitously.

"What happened on the trestle, Marty? What trestle was Carl Bolyard talking about? What were you on it for?"

"On it fur? Cat's fur to make kittens' britches."

"No, I mean it, Marty. You shouldn't be out in this heat, and on a trestle, of all things." He inspected his fingernails. He was prowling, waiting for an opening.

Marty hit the marble with his fist. "Son of a blue bitch. I'm sick of it. A citizen don't have a chance to get a vote on how things is run in this burg. 'F we'd made Gen'ral Cloud mayor back 'fore the war, when there was a move to, it'd a worked out good by now. But with our mayor so old he don't know his behind from his sister's teacups, you got guys like Bolyard, and them dumb Ridge runners, and Wid Lucas'd ought to know better, and Jerome Potter—and that dumb-headed Beavis. Runnin' it all! Ain't even constitutional. And this here's the Fourth of July!" He subsided, but the cat was out of his hot bag. "Aw, hell, they're lookin' for somebody—round about the water tower was where they was headed. Got to be serious, got to be somebody important—else why'd they try to squash it? Somebody waitin' for the night train to try to skip town, 's what I figure. And it's all I know. Nemmine what happened to me on the trestle . . ." His hand squeezed his leg again.

Eugene's smile stretched from dimple to dimple. "Well, well," he murmured.

When Marvin Soames had served the drinks in high-bosomed glasses with frost around them, and collected two nickels from Marty, Eugene drank his in a hurry and slid from the booth. He straightened his blazer lapels, leaned his head on one side and said, "I'm taking Melissa Gardner to the parade, and the park and the dance. Ain't she sweet, walkin' down the street? Won't be as classy as some others we both know, but I'll keep her from the foggy dew. Bank on it. 'Bye, old man."

Marty was half up, hands spraddled on the marble, eyes

furious. "If you're talkin' about somebody we both know, blabbin' again, I'll—"

"What'll you ever do?" said Eugene. "Sit down, you old fool.
Wrath is unseemly in the aged. Go to grass."

He walked out.

Marty looked after him, then sat back, stiff-bodied, eyes
moving from pure anger to a ghost of worry, his mustache
feeling clammier than usual. When Marvin Soames remarked
from the fountain, "Didn't even thank you for his dope, did
he?" Marty grunted. He felt foolish, and ill.

Jimmy Hargis considered himself past the age for fairy tales;
all the same, the Wolfson estate, where the Bellamans lived,
made him feel as though he entered enchanted grounds. With
Phyllis Bellaman's permission to feed the dog still in his ears,
he took the latch off the back gate and ran along the path. The
old house, its upper windows throwing back gold and its chim-
neys lofty and vine-wrapped, gazed down on him from its
distance; the grounds were shrill with locusts, a noise compounded by heat, but it was cool under the silk of leaves, even
cooler beside the nearly hidden pool with its willows and
birches and hickory around it. He went past the pool, his
reflection skimming it, and came around behind the house,
where the dog run waited. He couldn't hear any fireworks from
there; it could have been any day at all.

Merlin was in the doghouse at the far side of the run. Jimmy
went to a shed, opened the door, and chewing his tongue in
concentration, measured into a bowl three scoops of the mealy
dog feed, as he'd seen Mr. Bellaman do many times. He liked
Mr. Bellaman, who didn't say much, but tolerated his presence
without a lot of silly questions as to how he was doing in school
or if he liked baseball, and so forth. It was as if they talked
together without adult-to-children stupidity. He opened the
tap beside the shed, letting the water trickle in and mingle with
the feed in a kind of wet sawdust, which smelled good. Presently he turned off the tap, and walking toward the run, mixed

the food with his finger, now and then tasting it.

At the door to the run he set the bowl down and managed to get the latch up; he picked up the bowl, stepped in and went toward the doghouse. He was halfway to it, across the lengthy yard, when Merlin came out. Merlin was a Laverack setter, stippled with jet-black spots like random beauty marks on a coat as clean and white as miniver. He was two years old and he had been trained by a man who knew what he was capable of, and to whom he gave all of his considerable affection, as his progenitors had given their hearts to hunting men for three hundred years. He stood in the full light, a forefoot lifted, his tail feathering, not quite in a point, simply ready; then he came toward Jimmy with a sound of soft greeting in his throat. Jimmy set the bowl down.

The door was still ajar. Merlin saw it. He was around Jimmy as if he hadn't bothered to prepare himself for running, as if there had been no contraction of muscle and no instant aiming of bone and blood. He didn't touch the flanks of the gate as he went through. Jimmy could hear him quartering the yard outside, aiming for a scent, then he could hear him no longer. It made Jimmy feel unhappy but also exalted, as if he had done a great favor for a creature which didn't have words to ask it, yet had a tremendous need.

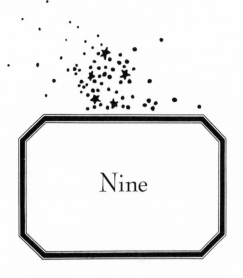

Nine

Buck chewed a last bite of the ice he had cadged from Marvin Soames when they'd dropped in at the pharmacy, shook the waxed cardboard container, heard a final tinkle of ice there and offered it to Nick. Nick drank the ice dregs and the cool water, and set the container on the ground. They had just come into the cemetery. The sound of Reverend Bates's congregation could not be heard; this place held a deep, cypress-tree hush, its gravestones and monuments taking the light in long slants of copper gold, its paths aiming among granite shadows to the retaining wall above the river.

The markers and monuments erected in the early days of the cemetery were simple enough, with only a few worn garlands and lambs for decoration. But the first simplicity had gone to perdition during the reign of Queen Victoria and its delayed but powerful effect on American design. Overdecorated vault and canting stele and crazy stone foliage rioted through the cemetery.

Everything culminated in the urns on the retaining wall. There they stood, four broad-lipped thundermugs waiting for four gargantuan bottoms. Nick recalled coming to the cemetery one Memorial Day with his mother—her swift trip home had happened to coincide with the day of tribute. His Aunt Alice was with them, and Harky and Wid, Harky bearing potted plants to put on Rex Cloud's grave. His grave was simple enough, as was Grandma Marie's; the Cloud plot was encircled by a low iron fence. Looking toward the urns, Marna said, "I don't think anybody *made* those. There's some sort of satanic underground society that grew them." Her becoming veil whipping a little in the soft wind, she held Nick's hand tightly. And Alice Cloud said, "Well, they could be taken care of with a little dynamite."

Nick thought it was a wonder that he and Buck hadn't got around to the natural act of doing away with the urns till today. And Buck's grand notion, the special fillip of synchronizing the explosion with the noontime park cannon ceremony, was truly brilliant. Buck was heading for the urns now, but Nick stopped for a second beside a remarkable monument, a tiered marble layer cake with a vine leitmotif. On its lower portion was chiseled *M O S S*. Eventually Arden's mayor would rest here. Mayor Moss would be down in the park now, to the south and well below the cemetery; he would be pottering around the cannon, with his sister at his shoulder, telling him not to burn his fingers.

Nick joined Buck at the wall. A granite bench ran along under it, and on this Buck had already spread out the contents of his sack. Nick upended his, and worked with Buck, separating the heavier explosives from the lighter. Buck had placed his Ingersoll watch on top of the wall; from time to time he cast a glance at it. His face was like a wet brown stone. His eyes were narrowed, wolflike, but with an amused glint. The smell of the river, gently miasmic but pleasing, wafted up over the wall and around the frowning urns. Buck reached under the bench and snipped some blackberries from the bushes whose roots crawled under the wall from the high riverbank. He tossed a few to Nick. Nick recalled an argument he'd once had with

Buck in this cemetery as to whether the blackberries and wild strawberries here got their good flavor from the fertilization given by corpses. Buck had thought so. It didn't spoil the taste; the blackberries in Nick's mouth now were overflowing with juice.

The fireworks laid out neatly, Buck drew from a pocket a pair of snub-nosed pliers and began crimping the fuseless ends of the larger salutes, moving along the wall and inserting these between the bases of the urns and the wall coping, and further decorating the urns by forcing more salutes in the interstices of their monstrous underbellies. He laid down the pliers and went back for smaller salutes and packaged firecrackers, slitting with a thumbnail the bright-red paper with its soft gold Chinese lettering, carefully shaking out the crackers and unwinding the interlinked fusework, and beginning to garland these in and among the big salutes. Nick picked up the pliers and finished crimping the twelve-inchers, carefully tamping them into and around and below the urns. After Buck had draped stringers of the Chinese crackers between the powerful salutes, threading the fuses one into another, drawing the mama fuse, which would ignite the rest, into a lean knot between thumb and forefinger, he stood back and regarded them with critical appreciation.

"Looks kind of like an old lady with a lot of corset strings hangin' down," he said. " 'Bout to go to a party."

"Four old ladies," Nick said, slapping an urn. "We can just drop the cherry bombs inside." He stood on the bench and groped inside the urn he had slapped. "Feels slippery, but there's no rain in the bottom. The cherry bombs'll go off with the rest, from the inside out, as soon as the salutes go."

"Bound to," said Buck. He and Nick selected clumps of cherry bombs, reaching far inside the urns, to the armpits, to place them. This done, Nick stayed on the bench, from this height inspecting the flow of the river fifty feet below, while Buck jumped down, looked at his watch once more, brought up another respectable cigar butt and lit it with one of the

Swedish matches. He took a deep draw. To Nick he said, "We got lashin's of time yet. C'n you see the park from there?"

Clinging to the inner side of the coping, right hand's fingers hooked to it, Nick swung himself out, his shadow small down past the bluff on the shining water. The shadows of the urns were down there as well. The river was a hundred feet wide at this point, black-green from the leaves on the Kentucky side, a green-bronze brightness in its center where the sunlight splayed. Looking southward, Nick could see a small tongue of the park, the diving raft bobbing on its oil barrels, the park scow drawn up and bottom-over alongside it, and a section of the marl beach curving outward and dark where the water deepened. The cannon was back toward the center of the park.

He swung upright again and shook his head. "Not much."

Buck arranged himself on the bench, leaning against the wall. He crossed his legs and gazed back through the cemetery as if he could see through its gates and down off Carmian's Hill. "When I kick off, be double damned if I want to lay up here," he said. "Better over in the Colored Settlement. Maybe up among the Ridge people, where Henry'll be goin'."

Nick sat on the coping, feet on the bench. "You'll have to settle for this," he said. "I will, too. This is just where we'll be put. If we stay around Arden, anyhow."

Buck's eyes were a trifle amazed. "Ain't you plannin' to? Sure, you got to go off to college, but—"

"Might have to make a living," Nick said.

"Go on! General and you and Miss Alice and your mama got enough to go till doomsday and live like Jay Gould. You know it. Daddy says Miss Alice got more invested in them gold-plate stocks, on Wall Street, than the law just about allows." He counted off on his fingers, cigar between his teeth. "Anaconda Copper," he said. "Railroads, Sam'l Insull utilities. This here country ain't ever gonna stop pushin'. Daddy—he takes a little flyer now and again—says it's a man's duty to aid prosperity."

"I don't know about those things," Nick said. "I mean, I never paid much attention. But I might want to go away, anyway, to Chicago or New York or overseas, maybe."

"Not for long," Buck said. He turned to watch Nick's shrug. "Take it all in all, there ain't no country like it, and ain't no *air* like Arden. Comin' back from Turkey Run, me and Mama and Daddy just fill our lungs with it, stop singin' 'Row, Row, Row Your Boat' when we hit the town limits, and start laughin' 'cause we can't help it, so glad to be back. And, hell, if you went outside the country, you'd run into Bolsheviks and God knows what all. No . . ."—he twiddled the cigar—"I'll lay here and like it, I reckon. Grousin' maybe, but kind of glad. I notice your Aunt Alice always comes back when she's been away a spell. 'Course she could go anyplace and stay her*self.*"

"She went overseas the first time because she wanted to see where my father was killed," Nick said. "She couldn't find the exact place, but the guide showed her about where. She said the best men in Europe, and a good many from this country, died there."

"Well, shitty ol' Kaiser Bill's done for," Buck said comfortably. "Ain't goin' to happen again. Rest easy." He tilted his head back, trying to read his watch upside down, then turned around and gave it a square look. "Couple minutes yet," he said. "Keep listenin' for the clock." He blew on the cigar end, then got up and folded his arms and stood waiting, eying the mama fuse. "Jesus, with the cannon and this here foofaraw, one on top o' the other, ol' Pierre Wolfson and John Carmian and Roberts and the rest of them pioneers might likely spin right 'round in their graves, your daddy and your grandma along with 'em. I don't think any of 'em 'd mind," he added sunnily. "Know I wouldn't, gettin' shut of an eyesore."

Nick could hear the watch ticking. He said, "What about Henry's mother? She'll have to get Henry's body."

Buck's eyes met his straight on, and his shoulders relaxed. "Yeah. Under all the rest, it keeps pickin' at your mind, don't it? Aw, Daddy said Sher'f Potter sent Tommy up there to the Ridge last night, to tell her. Tommy got back with the Vig'-lantes later, when they was scourin' around the woods, told 'em

Tilda didn't carry on none. She was quiet awhile, then said she'd always liked Cy Bellaman; he deserved a chance to be brought back decent and have a fair trial. She won't make no more fuss than Abe Melton, and he'll be trap-mouthed 'long as the sher'f wants him to. She's havin' a pine box made, and she'll carry it down to town tonight, late, and git him from Melton's to take back to the Ridge." Buck's eyebrows met. "Only boy she had left, haulin' him in the same wagon he sold garden truck from. Hell!" He glared at his watch.

Nick knew he wasn't blaming Cy, or Henry, or Phyllis. He was blaming what you couldn't get your hands around, couldn't control. The tornadoes that roared down the river valley, the stroke that had hit Noel Cloud. Circumstances that wrung your gut and for which there wasn't a name, even here in this place where cypresses looked down on tombs both simple and fancy.

The first chime of noon was sounding from the courthouse clock in Arden. Nick wheeled around alongside Buck, both of them squinting at Buck's watch. Its hands were nearly straight up. Its ticking persisted through the sweet, solid tones of the clock as they penetrated here, drifting around cypress boughs, monument and marker, along the paths. Three chimes had been accomplished; four came plain and round. Buck picked up the watch, returned it to his pocket. He brought the coal of the cigar, pale-orange in this heavy light, up under the mama fuse, holding it from touch as yet. Just as Mayor Moss, with the cautious guidance of Wid, must be doing with a match, at this living second, near the fuse of the powder-glutted cannon in the park.

The fourth chime rolled through the cemetery, went over the retaining wall and was swallowed above the river. A kingfisher that might have been disturbed by the sound soared up above the wall, then dipped from sight, a piece of jewelry with wings, gone as the fifth and sixth chimes trembled and passed by.

But the number seven chime hadn't quite finished speaking

before another noise joined it. It came from a corner of the sky to the north—out of heated blue space. Nick, staring there, brushed Buck's elbow, but Buck didn't move anything but his eyes. His hand stayed under the fuse.

Over the growing roar, Nick shouted, "Damn, it's the wing-walker! Right—over—the river—coming this way!"

Buck stiffened, but held his position at the fuse. He touched the cigar tip to it at the moment the plane came into full sight, which was also the second when, by counting inside his head, he had ascertained that the number twelve chime, now wholly drowned out by the plane, had finally sounded.

Then the fuse was fizzing, and Nick and Buck were running backward, still facing the river, neither able to tear his eyes from the retaining wall, the urns and the sky full of engine noise. The plane sounded as if it had run without oil for a couple of hours, and its dry bearings were screaming. It swarmed closer, nose slanting downward over the river, height now just a few feet above the wall and the urns, its course seemingly unplanned. It was a biplane of wire, wood and canvas, ragged Dutch-blue painted fabric seeming to moult as it staggered along, and a message lettered in red lead by an unskilled calligrapher on its port-side fuselage: *Barnes the Barnstormer.* Its belly rippled with waterlight. On the upper wing balanced a man, legs wide apart, helmet straps streaming like hound ears; the pilot crouched deep under that wing, half hidden by cowling; a mere white face-flash, mouth set in an *O.*

As the plane passed in fantastic profile in front of the wall, the urns blew up.

Their explosion had nothing to do with the plane, Nick thought; whatever trouble it was in couldn't have been added to now by any outside force. All the same, he felt an instant flash of wonder, as if he and Buck had, without meaning to, brought plane and urns together in a split second. He found that he was projecting himself inside the minds of the men in, and on, the plane, and realized that they might, in their obvious extremity, believe that they had been shot at from this bluff. In a kind of stopped time, an intense slow motion, he regretted this. And in the same slowed-up time, as the plane roared on downriver, he watched the end of the urns.

They rose with grace they had never before possessed, in bursting splinters and shards. Then the wall coping was there by itself, cleansed of them, and a thick curtain of smoke hung for a few seconds above the wall.

Nick and Buck advanced while the smoke lifted. Neither looked at the other. They gripped the top of the wall, kneeling on the bench where bits of burned paper and urn dust and other detritus crunched under their shins.

Nick realized, all at once, that he could hear again. It was as if he had had water in his ears, had struck both sides of his head repeatedly to get it out and had been rewarded by this warm flowing life that returned to them, this ability to make out words and the shapes of language.

Buck was saying, "I think I heard the cannon, too. Think it went off 'bout exactly the same second." Then Buck's eyes widened. And then he and Buck were, indeed, looking at each other.

The noise of the plane had stopped.

A good point about overalls, Nick was thinking, is that they're easy to drop. Buck took his off with a couple of impatient sideswipes at the straps. He emerged from them like a leopard moving, his ribs showing in faint lean blue steps in the ladder of his rib cage, muscles ridging in his brown thighs and arms as he strode to the coping, the flat blades of bones in his back standing out like incipient wings as he whirled his arms and lifted them. With enormous calm, considering everything, he said, "They're in the goddamn river. You stay here, and bring me my gear later. I swim best. I can get 'em out." He let out as much air as he could, then sucked in a breath that made his navel a tight ring and his stomach as flat as a walnut board. He was still taking in air as he dived.

•   •   •

Phyllis Bellaman had gone by wooden-slat sidewalks behind the short streets raying out from Front, along to the bridge at the end of town which led to Kentucky. She wasn't walking quickly, but as always, she took pleasure in the sheer fact of motion. It lulled thought and it might even do the body some good. She had stepped up onto the bridge a few minutes before, and was now moving westward.

The best thing, of course, was to turn off the mind, let it drift until nightfall. The clamor of explosives from the town was an indefinite echoing hullaballoo of no import or purpose, and over the grayed planking of the bridge boards, automobiles passed her without stopping. After one left the bridge just outside Arden, it was possible to by-pass the jog of cracked concrete leading into the town proper and go straight onto a highway going north. She wished Cy had taken the car and gone that way. But no—he'd probably sized the Vigilantes up very skillfully, and knew he could outwit them and then be gone anonymously, no easily identifiable car to trace him by, no more ties, no more Arden. For a second she envied him; she had often deeply admired him.

But she was allowing her mind to rove too dangerously. She again performed the trick of forgetting, of letting a little wall click down between herself and everything but the fact that, strangely, she was still alive. She had learned this trick carefully in the years of marriage to Cy—had learned, when she woke in the mornings, to push aside the terror and the feeling of sliding away and rushing toward some blackness . . . learned to treat each minute as a clever simulation of life-as-usual. The trick had come into being after she had let Link Savage make love to her—he thought he was very good, like all men in blood heat. They had gone in his car, with him smelling of liquor and the shop sweat he covered with talcum, to a hollow west of town and not far from Bolyard's slaughterhouse. She remembered, as they headed back, stepping over a cattle skull in the long grass. It had its own peculiar beauty, nacreous and frail between the ivoried horns, and much more appealing than the man at her side. The act itself had been quick and unsatisfactory. But after that she learned to remove herself from Cy as he raged at her, knowing even when he had knocked Link Savage senseless that it didn't matter much, that it was removed from her. So was the memory of the wartime past, of her lost child with no children to follow it, of her first and sincere and faithful love. Returning to Cy, she had tried to see him as he was, admirable and even gentle, a man totally in love with her, who rated far more than simply having been accepted as a substitute, an invalid's nurse.

It had worked for several months, until one day she understood that her life with Cy abetted her torture, that only one man could have stopped her rage. She'd been, as they said, *good*, with the mocking laughter going on behind her face, until Jerome Potter came to serve as her whipping boy and target, her toy, and another, temporary revenge on life.

Calmed and quiet in one of those rare spells between bouts of darkness, she also realized that Jerome was no Link Savage, that he had given her all there was of himself, a great deal more than the physical side. Very much the same thing had happened a little while back in the hospital, when she understood how much she had wronged Alice Cloud, and had been forced to assume coldness around her, to protect herself once again. Jerome had *loved* her; he was a man with many crotchets, but he was also someone other men trusted. He had a straight line of conduct they could appreciate and value, and this was what she had ripped apart in him when she brought about his betrayal of Cy. She doubted that any other woman would ever do it. That she had appalled her now. That incident, the slimy Eugene, the events of last night, Cy, Henry . . . but Henry was dead and Cy was gone and she could bear facing none of it.

There were benches on the bridge every twenty yards or so, where foot travelers could sit and rest. Here the girder shadows fell more steeply, and while the bridge railings were plastered for most of its distance with signs asking passers-by to try Cow Brand Soda, to use Doctor Hofstedder's Bitters, and to drink

Ne-Hi—this last adjuration accompanied by the silken-hosed kneecap of a flapper—the benches were solid and sustaining.

Perhaps I need Ne-Hi, she thought, sitting down wearily. For a time she held the scarlet purse in her lap, hands folded over it, face turned across the bridge, watching the current riffle around snags, rush around bone-white bleached stumps. Sometimes on holidays, in the right weather, excursion boats lively with Dixieland bands came under this bridge, their stacks just clearing beneath it, their noise romping and echoing from both banks, their banjos and clarinets growing wistful and tiny with distance as they left smoke and banana peels and a film of oil from a leaking engine sump stirring on the surface of the water.

After a while she turned to the north, looking down over the railing at the water directly under her, feeling its power and knowing that old sensation of illusory motion, as though the bridge carried her along while the current itself was suspended. On the railing beside her was mounted a telescope of sorts, with a shutter at the viewing end; she read its instructions: DROP DIME, SEE THE TWO-STATE HEARTLAND. She snapped her purse open, found the right coin and worked the dime into the bent slot. There was resistance, but amazingly, the shutter gave a flat snap and she found herself with an eyepiece clear for seeing. Behind her the Fords and Dodges and an occasional Reo and once an Apperson Jackrabbit flashed past, causing the bridge planks to rumble steadily. Once a man with a straw skimmer and a rufous face, leaned out and bawled, "Oh, you *pretty* thing!" She shook her hair back, placed her right eye close to the eyepiece cup, encountered a green-and-beige blur and found an adjustment lever with her right hand. The river to the north came into slow view, settling in upon her vision like one of those Easter-egg vistas, little pastoral vivid-green demesnes where rabbits, yellow chickens, and shepherds and shepherdesses in diminutive costume, played in a deathless crystalline light. She swiveled the telescope toward the Ohio bank. The steeple of the Reverend Bates's church, from this vantage point the only part of it visible, the angels under waves of trees, swam into her eye. She thought, I might go up there later.

She next made out the courthouse tower, with the hands on the clock face standing straight up, though she could not hear the slightly hoarse chimes of noon. The rest of Carmian's Hill lay in a thousand shades of green, all at their most splendid. She swung the telescope leftward, resenting the constant passage of the automobiles behind her, wishing she could study this map of her past in silence. She tapped the metallic circle of the eyepiece, bringing the Ohio shore more completely into balance. There was the park, almost back to the bandstand, the cannon in its center a glint of bronze, the park benches and tables a practical, blind public green. She could even see Jerome Potter, the manner in which he stood unmistakable, a tiny figure among figures, near the cannon, with the linen-clad form of Mayor Moss closer to the cannon, and Wid Lucas, bending beside the mayor. Jerome and Tommy Beavis were keeping the crowd back, obviously. Carl Bolyard was recognizable merely because of his size, a straw hat on the back of his head.

Phyllis thought, When I was five and six and seven, I'd go to the park by myself in the summer mornings, and after a while Alice and Rex Cloud might come along, sometimes with Marna Davenanter, and I could watch them, even if they didn't want me to play with them because I was too young. And when they and their friends, Jerome Potter and Cy Bellaman, would head up and back into Carmian's Woods to play Robin Hood, and Lorna Doone, and sometimes go back down into the limestone caves and play house—I guess it was house—I'd stay on the swings and look after them, and think that when I got to be their age I'd be their princess, everything would change. Marna was their princess then. She directed them, remembered the words when she was Titania and made Rex be Oberon, though he didn't like it. And once I saw her kissing Rex. They were beside one of those oaks right next to the cannon, and she leaned up to him—it was a butterfly kiss, but it made my stomach hurt a long time after. I didn't pay any attention to Cy. He was a lot more serious than the rest, with the solemnity boys get at a certain age when they're thinking seriously and don't even see the excitement around them. All he ever did that was interesting was pal around with Henry Watherall, who wasn't even a town boy. Henry smelled of tanning coon skins, had soft dark quick-looking eyes.

She scanned the park, and then slanted the telescope up toward the cemetery. She couldn't quite see it on its rise of land, but she could see the bluff and the four monstrous urns on the wall. At that instant something strange happened—she took it at first for a flaw in her own sight. The urns vanished in shadow, broke apart lazily, and were gone. At the same time a blue plane came in sight, dipping toward the water past the cemetery. And as she nudged the telescope again, a trifle this time to keep the plane in sight, the plane dipped and fell like a landing duck opposite the park landing. Then she saw a puff of cannon smoke go up past those little trees and drift out toward the plane as though the cannon had shot the plane down. Of course it hadn't; it was coincidence and illusion, but the effect was no less riveting—even though she knew the cannon was loaded only with powder.

My God, she thought, this is a magnificent telescope. What do they mean just charging a dime for its use?

The plane was floating like a celluloid dime store toy, the people who'd been around the cannon were racing down to the landing and out onto the raft. Someone upended the scow and put it in the water. She tried to see the plane better, but the shimmer of sun around it hurt deep into her eye, and she pushed back her hair, then tried again. This time she saw somebody swimming straight from the north toward the sinking plane. The man had a strong, steady stroke—a little flashing of whitewater around him as he came on. Dwarfed by the bluffs on either side, a mere intaglio of raised motion above the deeps, yet he was heading for the plane. The wings were facing downward, the tail thrust up like a mallard feeding.

In one of the good times, Cy had taken her on a fishing and hunting trip, just the two of them. He'd had his canoe and they'd gone far upriver, spending the night in a cabin he knew about up there; in the morning, which felt like cold glory around them that fall, paddling downriver to Arden, Cy started singing "There's a Long, Long Trail A-Winding." His baritone was good for a man who didn't sing much, beating back from both shores over the noise of the paddles. But she shattered the spell. "Please don't—I hate those old war songs. You weren't in it, after all—why do you have to sing about it?" He'd kept quiet then. Something was gone, had died again; everything re-died, everything around the real death, Rex's death, withered, continually.

The telescope's shutter fell. She groped in her purse for another dime but found none. She took off her left shoe; then, standing on one leg, reversed the shoe in her hand so its tough-sewn sole was a handle, and with the heavy leather walking heel, hit the telescope. She bent again to the eyepiece but the shutter had stayed in place. In the rippling of girder shadow and sunlight she walked steadily again, back toward Arden, head up and back, purse slung on her arm, hands in the pockets of the dress, living time away until the night came.

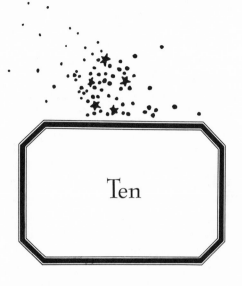

Ten

As he waited for Buck's head to show up in the river beyond the wall, Nick undid his shirt buttons, getting ready to strip and dive himself. Buck was right, he was the better swimmer of the two; fifty feet wasn't an impossible dive, but it wasn't anything to be thought of with sheer joy, either. Nick would have done it on a bet if the stakes had been high enough—say, the blessing of Roy Gardner and his own acceptance as fit company for Melissa. He would also have done it if Buck hadn't. He finished opening his shirt and had his belt buckle ajar, ready to do it anyway, when Buck's head, an otter's, bobbed up at a point a few yards outside the edge of the wall's shadow. Down there in the river Buck raised an arm and his voice was confident, quick and buoyant. "Don't folla me now! I need them damn' overalls! Got money and cigars in 'em!" The rest was drowned in splashing—in a powerful crawl, Buck was heading south. Nick watched him from the wall until the head and gleaming shoulders and buttocks and kicking feet were out of sight.

Nick jumped down from the wall and looked around a little

wildly. There was still a slight, annoying ringing in his middle ear, compounded by the plane bellowing and the aftermath of the explosion. It made him think of Franz Otis, who ran the Argus, and had been shell-shocked in the war. He'd gradually come out of it, but even today he would sometimes give a sudden start, glare like a steer about to be poleaxed and then apologize for his lapse.

There was still a heavy odor of gunpowder and a touch of engine smell in the air. Nick looked past the cypresses, along the rim of the bluff, and found the tree he'd been looking for. It was a grandfather oak, roots twining deep in the bluff, well beyond the wall, its lower trunk a natural footspace for climbing, its upper boughs leaning out over the water. Thirty seconds later, leaves rustling around him, he was well up into its crown, and crawling along a thick bough toward its extreme western tip. A squirrel chattered at him from higher up; bark drifted onto his chest and the back of his neck. He reached the last possible perch—beyond this one would have to be a bird or a squirrel or a tree snake to go. His legs dangled over the water, and with his hands he parted twigs. In another moment he made out Buck, whose progress toward the park had been very fast, and the scow, diminutive and clumsy, wallowing from the park beach toward the plane. He could just recognize Sheriff Potter and Carl Bolyard in its bow.

The blue biplane was still riding the current; if it had been a river packet, one would have said that its captain had better abandon ship. Its nose and the stilled prop were under water. Its lower wing was deeply awash, but on its upper, the wing-walker stood, tiny and fragile, a dot of life over a mighty river, under a huge serene sky. Buck seemed to be gaining on the plane only by inches as it swung like driftwood toward Kentucky. Then the pilot appeared, another speck; he crouched on the lower wing, and his boots must have been calf-deep in water. Then he jumped and went under. When he came up, beyond the leading edge of the rapidly submerging lower wing, he was fifteen yards from the scow—a length Nick could only guess at, but, he thought, roughly correct. The pilot's arms were a very small *v* as he flung them high. He went under again.

Buck changed course and was moving toward the pilot. The scow was crawling, thrashing, toward the plane. It bobbed in the lee of the upper wing, the men in its forward section evidently shouting to the wing-walker. When he jumped, it was so close to the scow that Nick couldn't tell whether or not he'd swamped it; then he could see the wing-man being lifted on board. And as he swung his attention to Buck, Buck reached the pilot, who had come up again, though he was obviously starting to drown. It was beyond understanding that anyone who could operate a plane couldn't swim. But it was manifestly so.

A pressure of heartbeat eased down in Nick's chest; he breathed more deeply. Buck had the pilot under the chin and was towing him, swimming half sidestroke toward the scow. There was a flash of wet oars lifted high, the scow, happily almost unsinkable, taking on more water as its crew crowded to urge on Buck, and then hands reaching for the pilot as Buck relinquished him. He was aboard. Slowly the scow turned around and headed for the park landing. In its wallowing wake Buck swam, more leisurely now; then, as he headed shoreward, speeding up in a last bravura display. At the moment he pulled alongside the scow, his buttocks showed brown-slick, in that distance, as he performed the naked-swimming action known as the Rising Moon.

All of them—scow, wing-walker, pilot, Buck—were being gathered in and welcomed by the crowd on the oil-barrel raft. Out toward the shadowed opposite shore the plane settled closer to the water's surface, its topmost wing under, its fuselage vertically canting. Then it seemed, even as far from Nick's eyes as it was, to be giving a final flirt of its tail assembly, as a widgeon or teal would do before diving, and then it was gone. The current closed over it. The river shone brightly and calmly as before.

Nick climbed down out of the tree, divorced from that shining distance, feeling allied with the squirrel, which was scolding once more, and answering it with a "Yah yah, yourself!" Back at the bench he scooped up Buck's overalls, making certain the pliers and the cigars and other paraphernalia were there and intact, and that the Ingersoll was safe. He folded the overalls in a pillow-sized package, tucked it under his arm and set off back through the cemetery. The presence of the graves around him, the sentinel shadows of the cypresses, the meaning of this place, were for the moment of no significance to him. He felt temporarily immortal. I'll go see Phyllis Bellaman tonight, he thought—because she wants me. *She* wants *me*. It was a holy tryst, so brilliant in its strength now that through it, he felt a cresting affection for Melissa, and even a brief second of head-patting distant tolerance for her father. He also felt a curling, reaching, satisfactory power in his loins, a dark joy—fierce, promissory.

He walked faster, then found himself running. He took the quickest way to the park, cutting across to one of the woods paths from the cemetery road, descending sharply, and slowing as he grabbed at slick-leafed sumac and hawberry. In another few steps he was under the surrounding foliage in a pepper scent of dusty leaves. After a few minutes the smell of a mint bed freshened by creek water filled the air. He knew where he was then. The park to the south and up, the caves to the east and downward. The creek was one he'd often visited with Buck, and he'd mentioned it to Cy one day when Cy happened to be talking about the deer runs here. Cy had said, "Well, Buck didn't find it first," and smiled a little. Cy never smiled largely, but his rare smile was somehow much more than other people's grins. He'd said, "Henry showed it to me when we were both younger than you and Buck. It's what Henry's people up on the Ridge call Lonesome Water. It comes from there, not river water, wells up in a spring just outside the Watheralls' clearing. Then it goes underground, and only rises for a few feet in the woods."

Nick stood still.

It might have been remembering Cy; might have been the weight of his own body, its warmth, the heat in it clustered around its center—as though by thinking even this much of Phyllis he had called up something in the air. And in the rush of gladness at Buck's still being alive, and himself somehow more alive as well, he'd forgotten to feel guilty and had trespassed beyond a certain invisible boundary.

But the heat remained. It was no longer anybody's business. None but his, and hers. People took it lightly; some talked about it to their friends, even their enemies. Eugene, for instance . . . how anyone could do that was a mystery he didn't want to investigate. It was as if some people were afraid of it and had to hide behind the sniggering. Like the younger kids thumbing through *Captain Billy's Whizbang* or the *Police Gazette* in Soames's . . . which he had done himself at that age, fascinated. But Buck knew what it was worth; he didn't speak of it except fondly and infrequently—as if he held it in too much regard, as did his girls. Candy Pruitt must be something . . .

Nick had no direct knowledge of the subject at hand, of the mystery, but he felt, in this green place, that somewhere in Phyllis was the answer, and that if he got the answer from her, he might then know too much. For a few seconds his brain went beating as wildly again as though peril were close-fitting around him, and as though he had known something for a long time that he didn't actually want to know.

Hell, he thought, there must have been somebody first—for Phyllis. Far back. And even if I think sometimes I know who it was, I won't go on in that direction. Not today, for God's sake, and not tonight. Maybe not ever . . .

He walked on, balancing on a fallen beech log and following it to its lightning-blasted roots, then leaped from the log onto the main course of the path again, impatient to see Buck, to hear the story of the rescue from the other end.

He could see the creek now. A magnetic shine of water

above dark leaves, vanishing into them again swiftly, teasing at thirst. He tried to shut his mind, close it to whispers of conscience. He knelt beside the creek, patches of mint green-glinting around his knees like scattered dollar bills, with gold pieces of the sunlight dancing among them. The Confederate bank notes, a sheaf of them in one of the attic trunks, were more beautifully engraved than money today, but they had always saddened him as he studied them, a quality about them doomed and gallant. Noel Cloud had said, "If a man had to choose his enemy for valor, he couldn't have done better than to select the South." He would try to remember to be especially decent to Rance Todman in the parade today, and to those other old men from across the river. Not all of Kentucky had fought with the Army of Northern Virginia; it was still a prickly job for them, living where they did.

He laid down Buck's overalls and cupped up some water. It was as good as he remembered from the last time. When he had drunk three handfuls, he flipped water off his fingers and was about to get up—his blood was cooled now, and his anxiousness—when he saw Merlin across the creek.

The dog blended almost perfectly with the background of shadow and light. His head was lifted, like Nick's. His coat in a slash of butter-gold light revealed a few beggar lice; he was panting but it couldn't be heard far off, a gentleman's panting; his loose home collar, which Cy wouldn't let him wear while he was working in case he got hung up on a fence or in briars, held a few weeds between his throat and the leather.

Nick said very quietly, "Merlin, it's me. Come on, Merlin."

After a moment the setter padded forward and started to drink with the quick serious lapping of a dog on a scent, using as little time out as possible. Nick reached over and took a firm hold on his collar with one hand, picked up Buck's overalls with the other and stepped over the water to join him.

At his time of life Jerome Potter did not want to be right. He only wanted to be as right as possible. The difference between these aims, sometimes called compromise, was, to him, wisdom. He had learned in the years of a demanding, poorly paid job, covering acreage which contained only one town, but which demanded a great deal of watchful enterprise, that to try to be absolutely right was to invite those sly, invisible, but always waiting obstacles. He avoided what the old Greeks had called hubris. But on occasion, the strain on a man's forbearance was terrific.

Mayor Harold Moss was standing beside the sheriff. His eyes were fuzzy, myopic; his well-groomed old flesh was scented with Bay Rum. For the sixth or seventh time he inclined his head, in its well-seasoned panama, toward the sheriff and asked in a confidential, pained voice, "Who is that boy?"

The sheriff said, "That's Buck Bolyard, Harold. You've seen him 'bout a thousand times since he got hatched. Maidy and Carl's boy. Helps Carl run the butcher shop, summers."

"But he's totally naked," Mayor Moss said. "He swam into the landing without a stitch on. I saw him. He didn't have any bathing dress at all."

"He ain't naked, this given second," Potter said. "See?"

He guided the mayor's attention over past the cannon, where the two of them conferred—the cannon was still warm from its firing, giving off waves of heat. Under a clump of oaks Buck stood chatting genially with his father, Wid Lucas, Muff Raintree and Slim Thomas; Muff and Slim wore their Great War uniform a little self-consciously, metal hats raked back, parade-ready jackets a few shades lighter than they had been when issued. Wid had changed to a fedora, purple striped shirt with coral sleeve garters, Sunday trousers and yellow snub-toed shoes shined to Harky's specifications. Carl Bolyard's white vest was tight on his Falstaff belly, but the coat to the suit was draped around his son, reaching most of the distance to Buck's knees, and considerably larger in the shoulders than Buck.

On shadow-cooled grass under the oaks lay the pilot of the late barnstorming plane, Peter Barnes. His scuffed, drenched flight jacket had been removed, but he dripped from most orifices; his leather cap, which he had prevented solicitous well-wishers from removing, appeared to be shrinking on his skull. His face was startling in its ferocity—it gave the impression that he had emerged from Hades a few seconds before, and would never be able to recount his adventures there. A blaming face, as well as haughty; there was silvery scar tissue around his eyebrows and down the bridge of the nose. He held a Lithia bottle half full of Carl Bolyard's home brew, the white porcelain pressure-cap open, its base balanced on his moist stomach, whose navel was exposed beneath his open shirt. As the people around him talked, now and then he threw them a bitter upward glance, then opened his mouth and let loose a startling sound; it was several seconds after each such noise that the hearers recognized it for a laugh. It was a bray, brass-edged, enormous, deeply atonic.

Beside him reclined the wing-walker, James Pringle, leather cap also still on, breeches sodden, boots wrinkled and muddy. He had snarled carrot-red hair and a battered face seared rather than touched with freckles. He held his own bottle of Carl's brew. Each time Barnes produced his remarkable laugh, Pringle managed a sketch of a salute—without putting the bottle aside—said "Check, sir," and took another sip. Barnes would nod then and say "Carry on, Sergeant."

Aaron, Julian and Leon Kaplan were gathered a short way from Pringle and Barnes, murmuring in low, concerned voices. Their roadster was drawn up at the park gates beside Carl Bolyard's Dort, both cars now decorated with twists of crêpe paper, flag clumps attached to the radiator caps. Carl had the Dort's trunk packed with home brew in anticipation of the picnic following the parade. Two Kaplan children, Rebecca, seven, and Mark, four, had been allowed to come along this year to witness the cannon ceremony. Rebecca, a pretty child in white dimity with a scarlet bow setting off her lustrous hair and eyes, was watching Barnes and Pringle with fascination. Mark was also in perfect white, his hair and eyes like matching velvet; frail, more vulnerable than his sister, he carried a celluloid duck, and from time to time circumspectly chewed a little of it. As Captain Barnes made the sound again, Mark touched his father's hand and moved closer to him. Aaron patted his shoulder reassuringly.

Twenty-five or so other citizens of Arden who had been faithful to the cannon firing and had, this time, been rewarded far past their greatest expectations, drifted around the park grounds and down where they looked out at the water as if the plane might somehow reappear and begin the entertainment all over again. A few people were now heading out of the park toward home to get ready for the parade and the picnic, dancing and fireworks that would follow.

All this Sheriff Potter observed out of the corner of his eye. He listened meantime to the mayor.

"Perfectly unclothed, in the buff," Mayor Moss said querulously. "You know we can't have that, Jerome. It just won't do. In my day when Brannigan was sheriff he'd have arrested anyone who appeared like that in public. He'd have clapped them straight in jail. That was in my younger days, to be sure, and we did things differently. There's a great deal of license and liberty around now, I know. Why—" He lowered his voice and gazed dimly toward his sister, Corabelle. She had plump, sun-polished knees and a pince-nez, and sat on the steps of the park pavilion in her Enna Jettick shoes, patiently waiting to escort him home so he could once more rehearse his Fourth of July speech. It had not changed throughout his mayoralty and it had never been heard in its entirety by a soul. But unlike the Gettysburg Address, it had never been published, so they never knew what they might be missing.

"Why," the mayor whispered, "Corabelle saw him, I know she did. Couldn't keep from it. A great many of our ladies must have seen him unclothed."

The sheriff started to lean on the cannon muzzle, drew his hand away just in time—the stinking old thing was always fit to fry fish on after its yearly gasp—and said, "Harold, that Buck Bolyard over there pulled the pilot out o' the water. Current would have took him real quick, otherwise. As it is"—he bent his attention to the recumbent fliers, just as Barnes loosed another false and terrible guffaw—"as it stands, those boys ain't in stellar condition. Shock, I'd say, largely. I sent Tommy for Doc Bowen. He'll look 'em over soon as he gets here, and if he says they ought to have a little rest, we'll take 'em to Miss Alice's hospital awhile. Asked Tommy to call the folks over in Barlton too."

The mayor's wafer-thin lips were fluttering. "Barlton? What on earth has Barlton to do with us, Jerome? We have our own celebration, and they have theirs. You know that. When Brannigan was sheriff, some of the toughs from Barlton tried to come over and mingle with our people, and you may believe Brannigan got their number in a hurry."

Sheriff Potter swallowed. His throat tasted dry; he shut his eyes a bit. "Godfrey Brannigan's been dead twenty years," he murmured just under the level of audibility. "He was sheriff when I was a little kid and it was a good day he could pound sand in a rathole. This is nineteen hundred and twenty-nine and I think I'm alive, but around you, goddamn it, I never do know."

The mayor said, "Eh?"

Potter raised his voice. "Said they came from Barlton. They got hired over there, the wing-walker and the pilot. So I asked Tommy to check with 'em over there—at least to let 'em know their employees came to grief with the plane but are in the land of the livin'. They ran out o' gas—oil too, way I get it. Maybe just out o' luck. Imagine people like that live on fortune, a good deal, just the way they did back in the war. That was a rag bag of a crate, Curtiss Jenny, but on its last legs and a step past."

Mayor Moss blinked. His eyes, the sheriff thought, are pretty much like blue robin's eggs. Nice if they had something behind them.

"I don't understand, Jerome. I don't pretend to. I leave it all to you. No more nakedness. Not even on this fine and special holiday. I have to go now—it's past my nap time, and

I need to study my address." He floated off a few steps, toward the pavilion and his sister. "It was a fine firing, wasn't it? That's a faithful old weapon, such a *hearty* sound."

The sheriff trusted himself to nod. Then, as Mayor Moss hooked arms with his sister and they began their placid progress to the gates, the sheriff started toward the group under the oaks. He was halfway there when Aaron Kaplan broke away from his brothers to stop the sheriff. "Jerome—ha, you're a little wet—"

"From the scow," the sheriff said. "We didn't have exactly a regatta crew goin' there, for a while. What's on your mind?"

"Julian and Leon and me, we've been wondering . . . these poor aviators, they lost their aircraft, maybe all they had—but it's embarrassing to just offer a little money to men like that, who fought for us and gave all they had. A man has his pride, he needs it worse than many other things. So—"

"Well, if you're thinking about getting up a Kaplan purse for 'em, it's a nice idea. See what you mean about the embarrassing side . . . but they may have to go to the hospital awhile. Why'n't you put the money in an envelope and leave it with Alice Cloud to give 'em when they check out?"

Aaron's hand pressure increased. "You are a good man, Jerome. You put up with a lot and this county should be indebted. I'm going to stir up things in this county, so are Leon and Julian, to get a real police force here so it ain't just you and Tommy having to watch over us. I said it before and I promise again. I wanted you to know."

"Thanks, Aaron." The sheriff waited.

"Now, there is a little thing. Tonight my brothers and me are as usual in charge of the big fireworks. So this time we decided—well, if Barlton has their wing-walking specialty, we should have something to compete. It seems they ain't got their specialty anymore, but what we did shouldn't go to waste because of that."

"All right, what did you put together?" the sheriff asked quietly.

"It's a rocket," Aaron said. Potter could see the largeness of the Kaplan brothers' combined vision in Aaron's eager eyes, even though his mouth was judicious.

Rebecca Kaplan had remained where she was, watching Captain Barnes and Sergeant Pringle. The smoke of the full-sized fresh cigar which Carl Bolyard had presented Buck after they'd landed drifted down across the intense faces of Barnes and Pringle. Mark Kaplan had come along to stand in his father's considerable shadow, bringing the duck with him.

Aaron was amplifying, "But not just a single one—ten, to tell the truth. All rolled into one. And when we shoot it off, it is bound to attract a lot of attention—"

"Yeah," Potter said, "with this place full o' people. So you want Tommy or me to kind of block 'em off from gettin' too close. One of us'll try to be on hand. If it backfires, we'll try to shovel the remains into some kind of respectable condition."

"Oh, no fear. I'm shooting it. It will be completely safe, safe as houses, as churches. It's only the little extra precaution, the just-in-case . . ."

"Got a trough for it?"

"Leon built it. The best lumber—heavy, and long."

"That's the ticket. Very patriotic. Big Bertha . . . Aaron—" A touch of impatience, at least its harbinger, moved at the corners of Potter's lips. "I got to break away. So do you. Parade time'll be here before you know it . . . and don't worry, we'll see that there's protection."

Aaron reached down for Mark and swung him high. He walked back to his brothers with Mark above his head, the boy's eyes ecstatic at this height, Rebecca circling toward them, shouting, "Me too, me too . . ."

Sheriff Potter went on toward the oak trees, brushed under their leaves and put his knuckles on his hips. He said to Buck, "Hey, hero, the mayor says I ought to lock you up. Indecent exposure. Tell you what, though, you didn't have to show your ass in that elegant way while you was comin' in. It's just like anybody else's—no gold platin' I could see. Next time save it for Candy Pruitt."

Buck smiled contentedly. "Nick ought to be showin' up soon with my overalls. Don't rightly know what's happened to him." He relished another pull at the cigar. "Kind of a good thing we happened to be nigh."

"Been mulling that over," Potter said. "I can't figure what you were doin' up in the cemetery and I don't intend to make a case of it. *Have* got a few other things on my mind." His eyes went around to the Vigilantes and when he spoke again his voice was muted. "I want a vote. Guess you got an idea about what, Buck. And I know damn well you and Nick'll stay quiet about it. Leave you here, Buck, to bask in your fame, reap praises from the multitude—you other men, step back here in the trees with me a minute."

Over the men had come another mood; the last tailings of the exhilaration of seeing Barnes and Pringle pulled alive from the river. Carl stretched vastly. Wid cracked his knuckles and murmured dryly, "Praises my patooty. Them fellas didn't even thank Buck. Didn't hear 'em renderin' no thanks to the Lord, neither."

Uncomfortable, Carl said, "Well, now, they got a lot on their minds. Guess they've cracked up before, but this must look like the end of the road for 'em. Don't nobody have to thank a Bolyard for a favor."

The sheriff walked ahead of the others, back into the trees. There were no benches here, but he put a foot on a stump and said, "I ain't smart or I wouldn't hold on to this job. Emma says if she believed in divorce, she'd divorce me—I'm not home enough to warm a skillet for. Anyhow, though, if you all feel the same about it, here's what I want to do." He looked at the ground as he continued, "I want to go on the rest of the way alone. Still think Cy's going to head for the tower when it's good and dark. But I've maybe worked out an idea to get him then. Want to do it myself—I've got a good many reasons, some of 'em not even halfway official, for wantin' to do that."

141

For a second his eyes lifted and went around to Carl. Potter thought, Yes, Carl remembers. He may be the only one of these men who really knew about me and Phyllis, even though the rest of them might have guessed something, back then. But Carl knows, because, back then, when she bounced me, he took care of me, though we never talked about what it was, breaking me apart then.

He said in a very low voice, "Part of it's just that Cy and I were awful good friends."

Slim Thomas spat a short sluice of amber tobacco juice into the grass. He had shaved close for the parade and his jaw muscles were a sleek blue in the shadow of his trench hat. There were a couple of dents in the pale mustard-painted metal; the sheriff remembered where he'd got at least one of those, working his way back through a bad sector.

Slim said, "It ain't any of us think you can't do it, Jerome. But we're here for you to use if you want us."

"Hell, he knows that," Wid said. "What he asked for's a vote. You boys gonna show hands? Up, for it. Stay down, against it."

Carl said slowly, "It'll kind of keep folks from talkin' more'n they done so far. They won't look around and count noses tonight and see we ain't on hand for the doin's. Make 'em sort of discount any blabbin' Marty Broom does on his own." He looked back at the sheriff. "Wasn't you even goin' to take Tommy?"

"Nope," Potter said. "And he's one man I don't have to ask yea or nay of. Marty's got no idea who we're lookin' for. He's a rare old coot, but he ain't a hard thinker—don't give yourself a lot of reasons, just say yes or no." He straightened up, shoulders back, a gallus badge gleaming. "Come on."

Carl's hand was raised. Wid's came up; then Muff's and Slim's, together.

"You yell if you change your mind," Wid said. "Send out a pigeon. And just hold on to all the guns for the time bein'."

The other men nodded in assent and Potter said, "Well,

thanks for present confidence." They were moving back to the park. The sheriff held a hand over his eyes and made out a battered Auburn pulling up outside the gates; behind it was his own reprehensible Willys-Knight. The Auburn was braked abruptly, and Dr. Bowen stepped down into the weeds. Tommy Beavis, now in thick official police kit, got out of the other car.

From his couch under the park oaks, Captain Barnes again made his raucous and hair-raising noise of donkey-sorrow in which no amusement stirred.

"Wish he'd stop doin' that," Wid said. "Sounds like the end of time and the earth. Maybe it is, for him. Damn, I wonder what on earth's holdin' up Nick."

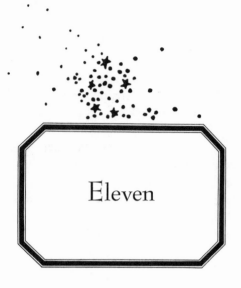

Eleven

Merlin stopped and pointed. It was a splendid point; his left forefoot curled back under his breast, his tail was a superb plume. Even his nostrils, expanded, were still.

Nick's own breath had come high in his throat and clotted there. So it was a cave, he thought. A long distance away there was a stir of movement in the day; birds shifting from bough to bough, changing positions in the dark webs of shadow through the trees. Here there was a circle of silence, irradiated by sunlight. When Cy had shot Henry last night, had there been such silence just before the rifle talked?

The mouth of the cave lay ahead, just below the rough trail. The smell of the limestone reached from it and blended with the syrupy odor of leaf and tree sap. A tongue of sunlight lapped into the floor of the cave. Hearing his own voice come out and wondering that it could be this quiet and softly urgent, Nick said, "Break!"

Merlin broke in a single bolt. As he entered the cave he made the only sound of any consequence he had made since the meeting at the creekside. It was a blind whimpering of great joy, followed by short, half-stifled barks. The sound trailed away, its cave echoes were swallowed. Nick drew in a deep breath and said to the cave and the air around it, "Cy— it's Nick Cloud."

There was a full moment of complete hush from the cave. In his head Nick could clearly see Cy's hand, palm out and down, hushing the dog.

Then Cy's voice came. It was quite gentle, only a touch of sardonic weariness in it. "You by yourself out there?"

"Yes . . ."

"Come ahead, Nick."

At first, as he stooped and went in, Nick could see only dark-green gloom, feel the coolness of the cave walls enclosing him. In the sunlight outlining him, patching the backs of his legs with brilliance, he stood and waited for his vision to clear. Then, swimming toward him was Cy's face. He didn't know what he'd expected to see. A demented, twisted face, a hunted one? Cy needed a shave, slightly; but his fair skin could take a day's beard without showing it much. There was a mere glint of golden furze around the chin and up the planes of the long cheeks under the cheekbones. His hair was a subdued yellow helmet. He was kneeling with Merlin's head in his hands.

He said reflectively, conversationally, "Sit down. There's a log." Nick found the log. "You know," Cy murmured, "I got a good one here. Sometimes they get so damn overbred. But he's turned out right." His hands rocked Merlin's head back and forth, slowly; his fingers reached under the collar and detached weeds, and went over Merlin's coat, taking out beggar lice and a few dock burrs. He said, "Your idea to let him out?"

"No, I found him," Nick said. "At the little creek."

"He might've jumped the fence," Cy said. "Don't think so —I built it about a foot higher than his capacities. But his kind can by-pass a lot of estimates. Lie down," he told Merlin. Cy came over to the log and for a moment stood there looking down at Nick. "Guess I've got to ask," he said then. "I don't know many answers today. You plan to try to turn me in?"

Nick was staring up steadily. "Not a chance."

"Don't get mad about it. I had to ask. You might've thought it was for my own good. The way the committee does. But you've never lied, as long as I've known you. Clouds don't very much. Your grandpa never did. Alice didn't, either." He sat down on the log; Nick kept his eyes away from the rifle, barrel up against the wall.

Cy thrust his feet out, boot heels cocked on the cool dark ground. "I gather there's no big alarm out yet."

"Far as I know, only the Vigilantes."

Cy had his hands braced on the log. "Heard a plane a while ago. Coming downriver."

"It wasn't looking for you," Nick said. "Barnstormers, from Barlton. It fell in the river but the men got out all right." He drew another far-down breath. It was astonishingly easy to be sitting here with Cy. On the other hand, it was very hard to know what one had to say—the things that needed to be spoken—and how to get them out. He was certain Cy felt the same. It was as if Phyllis were somewhere, listening. Merlin was curling around and licking down the roughed spots in his fur. Cy said, "If you'll take him back, it would help. Put him in the shed. I don't think he can make it out of there." He put his arms forward in a tight stretch. Then he asked, "How's Phyl?"

It was a short question, but not unconcerned, and not simple.

Nick said, "I stopped in at the hospital; I think she was getting ready to leave."

Cy nodded, now inspecting the ground. "I don't want to see her again, you know. I don't know what could happen. It's just better for everybody. I don't know how you feel about her, what talk you've heard. But I think it'd be a good idea if you stayed away from her. I've never given you any advice before, that I can remember. But I mean that advice—and I'm not saying it for my own good."

Nick thought, I feel like blushing, the way I felt when I

knocked Angela Riffon this morning. He didn't answer, though, and when Cy spoke again, the subject had changed.

"I'm not very easy around kids, since we didn't ever have any. But you're not a kid any longer. I wasn't, myself, at your age—and I guess I wasn't ever much for helling around even earlier. The woman I should have married was your aunt. I let her down. Shouldn't have." He shifted abruptly then. "Holing up here—it's a little like being in Plato's Cave. You studied that yet?"

"No, not yet."

"There's been time to think quite a bit. I feel as if I've got a lot to say, to somebody, but now is not the real time. I'll say it all to myself when I get out of this town. Jesus, I've loved this town, though I didn't know it until recently. And it wasn't just the Shops, when we were making something your grandpa could be proud of—that was part of it. Every time I'd get a good offer from somewhere else I'd study it about five minutes and then forget it. But it was—call it another quality."

"The air?"

Cy blinked. His lashes were white-gold, the eyes turning dark, a glittering blue, behind their slate.

"Buck," Nick said. "He was saying this morning, the air's better."

Cy shook his head. "Air's the same everywhere—sootier in Pittsburgh, and Gary, Indiana." He'd cupped a knee. "Good hunting's the same in a lot of other places too. No, it's people —somebody giving a damn about you. Even Jerome . . ." He was quiet. Then at the end of more quiet he said, "Henry . . ."

Nick thought, There can be so much to say, it can choke you. It's better not to try. He found he had stood up. "Cy, I'll take Merlin back. And I'll shut up."

"That's something I value," Cy said. He, too, was standing. He seemed to reflect for a couple of seconds, then put out his hand. "I'll be at the water tower about midnight, when the train comes through. If it hadn't been Independence Day and they'd been running regular schedule, it would have been a lot easier. I'd like to say goodbye to you then, the last time, if you can make it. If you can't, forget it. I'd just like to say so long to somebody then. There's nothing I want you to bring me—nothing I need. If you can't be there, it's all right—and we can say it now, in any case."

They shook quickly. Merlin was watching Cy, not Nick.

Nick felt the strength in Cy's hand, like Buck's, but older, wirier. There was still a callus on Cy's middle finger—he'd once called it an engineer's callus, from gripping so many sharp-edged pencils. Phyllis, touching it, had said softly, "It's a friendly callus," and Nick had felt envy and a sort of delight flooding through him as he sat after supper in the firelight with them. They had had those times of something so solid that it warmed a watcher; and the other times when neither had said much, or looked at each other much, but both had been solicitous and looking out for a guest's good time.

Then Cy said "Stand!" to Merlin, and Merlin was up; Cy walked over and took him by the slack of the collar. "My belt's a little too wide, but you'll need a leash," he said to Nick. "He'll go along when I tell him to, but good as he is, he might have second thoughts. I had a redbone once, took him with me duck hunting up around Xenia, and somebody stole him. Five days after I was home, he showed up again." His eyes studying Merlin were reflective, as if he remembered points about that vacation by himself.

Nick took off his belt, noting for the first time that the buckle was still open, that his shirt hung open, that he was still set to take off his clothes and join Buck in the river. He handed the belt to Cy, who slipped it under the collar, brought it around, made a flat knot and held up the end for Nick.

"Go on," Cy said very softly. "Both of you. See he's fed, Nick."

"Yes," Nick said. Now there wasn't going to be any goodbye outside that; he didn't as yet know if he would see Cy at the tower. He was sure Cy knew that he hadn't made up his mind about that. And all at once he was taking Merlin out of the mouth of the cave, the dog giving one reluctant backward pull, then moving with him, as Cy said "Go on!" to Merlin as well as to Nick. Then Nick and Merlin were in the dazzling swoop and strike of the sun above the trail, and when he did turn and stare back at the cave, there was no sign of anyone in it, its darkness was serene, no face and no hand lifting.

A tightness persisted in his chest when he went on. When he was a good deal younger he had sometimes cried out in the darkness, and at those times Grandma Marie would come in and lean over the night light—he slept in a room off his grandparents', and he had usually been thinking, or dreaming, of his mother, not yet used to her being gone so much. And Grandma Marie, a small, brisk-handed presence, would plump up the pillow and sing to him—"Froggy Would A-Courting Go"—soothing, surrounding him with sachet sweetness and robust power. But that soothing couldn't reach him now in this stringent loneliness. He wondered how difficult it was for Cy, how hard it had been, these years.

Grandma Marie's funeral had taken place on an edge-of-spring day with lilacs starting to show; his mother had refused to let him go into Melton's to see her laid in state, as they put it; all he really held of the memory was his Grandfather Noel sitting like a silent stone in the First M.E. Church, his hands on the back of the pew in front of him. That and the oily, rich, artificial scent of tuberoses.

The tightness stayed, but had diminished by the time he and Merlin were above the woods and going through a corner of Sutter's meadow. Goldenrod pollen was gathered on Merlin's flews. They came out on the road, dusty and silent ahead. On the telephone wires above it a long line of blackbirds watched with eyes like the polished black buttons on the ends of hat-pins. The wires, even on the most windless days, gave off a plangent humming.

He halted, Merlin patient with him, when truckboards slapping and an engine grinding erupted behind them. The truck came in sight. Travis Renfrew applied brakes with skill, getting the best out of thin linings, flinging open the passenger door. A smell of fish clung around the truckbed. The Model T's brassbound radiator vibrated, and Travis patted the rump-sprung seat. "Get in . . . fry y'self to a cinder out here!" He kept his whiskey stock under the floorboards, his current fish for sale in the comparative open under a tarpaulin. "Bring the dog up—Cy Bellaman's dogs behave good. Goin' straight to town . . . got a couple deliveries to make."

When Merlin and Nick were up, Travis made a few stabs with his feet at the planetary gears, and as they rolled on, Merlin put his chin on the window ledge and a stream of warm air lifted his ears lightly. Travis said, "Funny thing. Was takin' in my trotlines over on the Kentuck' side 'fore I started to town. Right across from the old graveyard. Looked up and seen them hellacious old urns is gone. Somebody's made off with 'em."

Nick blinked to show his interest.

"No respect for law," Travis went on, shaking his head sternly. "I'd 'a stopped and told Jerome Potter about it, but him and me don't pass the time of day much, bein' in different lines of work, as you might say. Anyhow, when I passed the park he looked to have his hands full."

Nick remembered that the cemetery bluff couldn't be seen from the park or the river opposite the park landing unless you climbed a tree on that other side—and even then, it would have to be a tree as high as the oak he'd climbed on this side. You'd have to have had hawk sight to make out both riverbanks clearly from the bridge. He felt that the missing urns would stay a secret from just about everybody but Travis until the holiday was over, which was at least something to be thankful for. He stroked Merlin's head and said, "What's the sheriff so busy about?"

"Buck Bolyard," Travis said proudly, "pulled a flyin' man right out o' the river, saved his bacon. Fella told me when I slowed up outside the park. Airplane went right down, swallowed up. Just about when the cannon went off."

"I wish I'd been there," Nick said.

"Likewise. Enjoyments like that put smack in a man's days. How's Gen'ral? Mama? Know how Wid is, seen him in the park."

Nick told Travis General Cloud was holding his own; it was a convenient embracing statement. He told Travis his mother was in Chicago.

"Al Capone runs it," Travis said. "May she steer clear o' him. Wouldn't touch them lead-salts they sell for Scotch, my life depended on it. Dirty friggin' place." Nick listened to him over the erratic chanting of the truck and watched dust purl from the balding tires. "How's your *aunt?*"

Nick said his aunt was in good health.

"Pr'pose to her myself if she'd have me," Travis said as he steered to the middle of the road to avoid an ambling cow. Farm children had embellished the cow's horns, patriotic ribbons dangling from them. "Strappin' figger of a woman, make y' stand up and start cloggin'." He smiled at himself in the cracked windshield. "Right over yonder's where I run inta your daddy one night"—he jerked a gnarled thumb at a side road —"just 'fore he went over—Over There. White drunk, and he'd run one o' them Cloud runabouts off in the ditch. Nice little filly with him, but she kept her face out o' the light, didn't get a good look at her, just the—you know, the gen'ral shape. Your daddy never got no bad liquor from *me*," he added. "Couldn't do him no good then, guess he got a log chain and got pulled out—ain't been able to do him no good since, never saw him again. All gone now, time out o' mind. Well, Nick Cloud, how're *you?*"

"I'm fine," Nick said. "Couldn't be better."

He wondered if Phyllis would be home now. And if he ought to go in and find out, anyway, after he'd put Merlin in the shed. The past was whirling around him, streaming like the leaves in the wake of the truck, beckoning like town ahead.

•　　　•　　　•

On Front Street there was obvious preparation for the coming parade. Streetlight poles with their iron candelabra and full-moon globes were wrapped with bunting. Clumps of veterans from the Spanish American War and the Great War called to one another across burning space. Rifles, immured in cosmoline most of the year, had been removed from the small armory in their packing boxes and cleaned up enough to be shouldered. The Civil War veterans had not yet been led out to go on display. Up and down this part of lower Front, down to the verdigreen water of the fountain and under the shadow of the courthouse and back, children hastened on ecstatic, high-blooded errands. Now and again the sharp report of a firecracker saved for the parade assembly alarmed the horses of the few cavalrymen who had drawn up their mounts at the head of a cross street leading to the Wolfson Block. The men slapped their horses, cursed and shouted, "Easy now, Belle!" and "Hold your fire, you damn devil!"

The locusts had reached an apogee of noise, their prelude to the strump of drum and the blast of brass shortly to rend the daylight. From water oak, catalpa, pin oak and chestnut and elm in the surrounding blocks they raised their bandsaw song.

The noise penetrated the screens of the telephone company, under sashes raised to get all the air possible above the crowns of the trees. Eugene Fisher was leaning beside a window, his blazer unwrinkled, his flannels stark, his oxfords without dust, his smile seemingly permanent. He was looking at the back of Velma Temple—sturdy, the hips sagging out in curves from either side of the seat of her caster-based chair. Her hair was deep russet, perhaps hennaed; her nape, under the thick bob, was the tender color of fresh-rising cream. Before her the operations panel was dark, but she was quietly alert. An electric fan, turned upward from the floor, oscillated ripples of air over her thighs and gently onto her breasts. The curving mouthpiece strapped to her headset was like a single horn detached from a Viking's helmet.

Eugene unbraced himself from the window jamb, one hand in his blazer pocket, made his way to her, and bending, kissed the back of her neck. His hand remained in his pocket. He had admired this attitude, one hand pocketed, as used by Rod La Rocque in *Feet of Clay*. He explored her neck with the tip of his tongue. She gave a respondent jump of appreciation and said in an undertone, "Honey, you hadn't ought to be up here. Get my mind off my work. Real sweet of you to get the sandwich—you tell Grady Flute the pork was right on the edge —but you ought to be movin' along." Her smartly plucked eyebrows, so artificially symmetrical that they didn't have much to do with the moist, plumply sensual face below them, went up. "*Any*how, since you're takin' that little *baby* to the p'rade, you'd ought to be over at her house this minute."

Eugene drew his fingertips under her left ear, traced its outline. "Lots of time. To all things there is a season; so sayeth the prophet. Half-hour yet before anything starts to move down there. M—mmmm-h . . ." He snuggled, warmly, closer. "Don't want to spend time in her living room, sugarlump, when I can be here . . . What'd Liz Cooper tell you happened last night?"

She shifted; the casters complained. "Eugene, I told you, not a blessed thing. She just left when I took over, and that's all there was to it. You know, you spout so much Bible, you ought to try gettin' it right some time."

"It's right enough. I can preach to make anybody's toes curl."

"Yeah—now *stop* that, Gene! Put both hands in your pockets. Get your hand on out." She pushed his hand aside. "Night's night, day's day. I'm on duty. You got brass nerve, anyhow, doin' this just b'fore you go to M'lissa Gardner's. Think I don't know what you got in mind for her after the dance? Drat you, stop it!"

Her breasts were agitated under the tight-stretched rosy cotton and she smelled of Trailing Arbutus face powder. As he withdrew his hand she said, nastily for her, "Quarter I give you for the sandwich's all I got with me. Case you wanted to borra. Payday's next Friday."

Eugene drew away. "Makes me really laugh when you get up steam," he said. "You do it every time. Know what? Right now you look like when I told you about Phyllis Wonderful Bellaman. Back a few years. Didn't believe it; then you did. And like when I tell you about the little sweet baby girls. You flare up, but you *like* it. Makes you feel set up, knowing you've got me and I can get anybody."

Velma's cheeks flooded with an access of blood that backed up rouge. Her headset wobbled. "Gene, get away. Now, I mean it. When they made you they busted the bastard machine." She rolled her chair swiftly backward. "Get on out of here. Stop pestering. Someday maybe I'll get a farmin' man—might not smell as good as you and know tricks. But he won't be at me all the time for pieces of inf'rmation. And he'll treat me like a lady in private."

Eugene's eyelids had lowered further. Velma's breasts shook as she rolled the chair in position again, glaring at the panel. He sighed.

Velma kept facing away from him. She heard a floorboard creak as he moved, but she didn't look around.

She addressed the panel in a low, angry, passionate declamation. "Eugene Fisher! Not a lick o' real work all his days, his mama whalin' her fingers off at the Argus, and pianna teachin', and organ playin' in the church. Maiden auntie nursin' to make all ends meet. Couldn't keep a job over a week or so, fingers too sticky. 'Bout fifteen and a half years old when he got to Miz Bellaman—lady her class, just amusin' herself, throwed him out when she couldn't stand the Bible-mouth no longer. But him, he's been tellin' it on the mountain ever since . . ."

She had wound herself up well; she hardly heard the second board protest. But she felt his hands behind her, fitting around her throat. They were holding lightly, as if he intended massage. His thumbs found the hollow of her nape. They pressed in slowly.

He said, "Poor old Velma. Period coming on, I guess. All right, fatty." His shadow loomed over the panel, quite large there. "What'd Liz Cooper tell you when you took over this morning?"

"Told me you weren't worth botherin' with!" She tried arching backward, found she couldn't. "Aw, nothin', you ignoramus. And only thing's happened while I was on is them aviation people goin' into the river, and a couple more burn cases to the hospital. That's where they took the fliers too." Her delivery was tighter. "God'll strike you dead someday, Gene. Maybe He's waitin' till you get a pulpit all your own or hit the sawdust trail. He'll bide His time and He'll smite you with a big green flame and there won't be 'nough left to sweep. Now, damn it, Gene, cut it out—" At last she said it: "Please."

Eugene was murmuring into her scalp, breath on the roots of her hair. "How long, O Lord, how long?" His misquotation of Isaiah was applied along with deeper pressure to her throat. "What'd Liz tell you, lambie? Couldn't sew her mouth shut with pearl buttons. Just spill it, you'll feel better." His breath surged out. "Give you a real good time when you're off tomorrow afternoon."

Then he said more deliberately, but without venom, "Say it, cow; I'll break your neck . . ."

Velma's eyes had shut, her eyelids and lips a little blue. She said in a flat, tired rush, "Oh, hell, Gene. Cy Bellaman shot Henry Watherall to death last night. Found Henry with her at Cy's house, their own place. They're huntin' him now— sheriff and them. Want to get him back 'thout any to-do. Now leggo."

Eugene's mouth saluted her scalp before he released her. He said with no real shine of triumph, "Meant it about the good time. Tomorrow, your place. About one, I guess. Got an Epworth League meeting in the morning." He consulted his wristwatch, a Waltham, heavily plated; on the back of the case was inscribed *George Livingston, Lt., Chillicothe, Ohio*. Lieutenant Livingston, career officer, had made the mistake of

155

washing his hands in the Arden park bathroom, leaving the watch there, and Eugene had accepted it as a fortuitous gift. " 'Bye, Velma." At the doorway he must have looked around, but she couldn't see him; she was still facing away. "You wouldn't like a farmer. You wouldn't get along with a hick." The sound of his oxfords down the stairs died away, and he slammed the door to the street.

Velma sat heavily without moving. Then she hitched her chair closer to the panel, her elbows on its counter, waiting for the blur dazzling her vision to spill over, the sick feeling that she had betrayed Doc Bowen to pass away, her fear to leave her.

Jerome Potter walked by Soames's; then past Bomasy's barbershop, its flaked wooden striped pole throwing a shadow over a poster for Lucky Tiger hair tonic; then alongside the Argus, where a scent of yesterday's buttered popcorn and disinfectant-perfume rose from the gloomy arcade and the ticket booth with its Moorish roof; then on past the Tribe of K and Melton's Funeral Parlor. He stopped when he got to the fire station, regarded three ringers stacked on a stake from the last horseshoe game, and made out Chief Gorseman sitting inside the station doorway, the heel tips of his Congress gaiters elevated on a ledge, his shirt off.

Chief Gorseman looked up at the sheriff as he stepped across the warm lawn and inside. Gorseman was fingering a brass hose fitting. Beside and behind him the scarlet Baby Doll filled the garage of the station; it was as clean and free of oil stain as the floor, from which, in a pinch, even Harky Lucas might have eaten. The firepole answered with round brass gleams.

"Do for you, J'rome?" he asked.

The sheriff said, "Think so, Ovid. You know that big head lamp?"

Gorseman frowned. "Head lamp?"

"Don't know the right name for it. About as big around as a bass drum. Used to be on the truck before you got it replaced."

Gorseman swiveled around. "Oh—searchlight!" He was a man who liked to call things by their precise names. He stood, and craned his neck until he was peering upward, past the Baby Doll's ladders and neatly folded hoses, to a rack of cross timbers holding gear not now in use.

The sheriff followed his gaze. "That's it," he said.

"Doll's got two of 'em better'n that," Gorseman said. "Fore and aft. Don't use that up there anymore. What about it?"

"Like to borrow it," the sheriff said.

Gorseman shrugged. The slack flesh under his arms swung with the movement. The sheriff noticed both their faces and foreshortened bodies, reflected in a giant arc of the Baby Doll's right front fender. "Mine not to reason why, I s'pose?" Gorseman said.

"Time being, 'fraid that's it, Ovid."

"Well, she weighs about fifty pounds. Takes wet cells to run her, too. Doll's new ones runs off her reg'lar batteries. But I got some cells back yonder in the workshop. Clammer Horston's back there; I'll have him look 'em up for you."

The sheriff said, "Appreciate it, Ovid. Don't need it yet— I'll bring my car around and load up." He was starting out again. He laid two fingers caressingly on the silk finish of the Baby Doll's fender. "God, she's beautiful," he said.

When he had taken his fingers away Gorseman, a step behind him, was polishing the fender at the spot he'd touched, with the hip-pocket handkerchief he'd brought out. "No offense, J'rome. I had her out a while ago—but them kids started swarmin' over her. Pulled her back in the cool again out o' their reach."

Potter said, "Ovid, they'll be all over her durin' the parade. Why didn't you just leave her out there, and wash her down and buff her up after?"

Gorseman shook his head stiffly. "Nosir. That lacquer she's finished with is thin stuff. Keep her from every fingermark I can." He raised his eyes. "J'rome, you eatin' right? Bowels open?"

The sheriff's eyes drew down slightly, half sheathed. "Guess so. Emma feeds me good, when I'm there."

"Just you look kind of peaky. Like you got somethin' on your plate you'd like to get rid of. Haven't seen you this way since the Ku Klux from upstate come tryin' to clean out the Colored Settlement, and my Gee, that was a month after Cal Coolidge took office."

"I'd just about forgotten that," Potter said. "They had right of assembly, only thing on their side, till it started gettin' riotous. They left in a hell of a hurry."

"Need any help? Any *more* help? I seen you and Wid and Carl and the Ridge men comin' in a while back. Noticed you had your guns with you."

"Thanks, Ovid," the sheriff said. "Guess you noticed the aviators me and Tommy took to Miss Alice's a while back, too. They didn't *help* any."

"Yuh. Asked Tommy about 'em when he come back to run the p'rade. He told me Doc Bowen says they ain't hurt bad, but need some rest and thoughtfulness. What you goin' to do with 'em?"

"When they get their rest out, put 'em up in the jail for the night. Put 'em on the road tomorrow. No, thank you kindly, Ovid . . . with the kind of luck I've been attractin' lately, if you come with me, there'd be the father of all fires, and you'd kick your butt you'd left Clammer to handle it. Do 'preciate the head lamp, though—searchlight. Be back for it before the parade starts slammin'." Potter had been looking toward the window where a point of light from the fitting shone. "Who's that?"

Chief Gorseman wheeled around. "Nobody, J'rome."

"Looked to me like Gene Fisher in the lane there and now just steppin' across the street. Yuh. There he goes."

They moved to the doorway. Gorseman shaded his eyes. "Well, can't put 'm behind bars for that."

"I ain't never had him behind bars," Potter said. "I look forward with zest to the day. When it comes, though, it'll be a mean damn duty. I like Milly and Goldy, and I liked the hell outa Jeb. Walks goosey, don't he?" He was staring after Eugene, following him until Eugene went beyond sight under leaves, toward the Wolfson Block, the Cloud Block. "Down on the heels, up on the toes. 'Varsity Drag.' " He walked out into the light. "I'll bring the car around, Ovid. Many thanks."

He returned to the Willys-Knight and cast an eye toward Melton's, sideward, raking and swift. Damn it, Henry, wait, he said to himself. I know it's all you can do now, but wait. You too, Cy. Can't ever make up for any part of what I did, but I can do what I have to. And hate it like bile on the back of my teeth. Which, also, like Eugene Fisher, just simply comes with the territory.

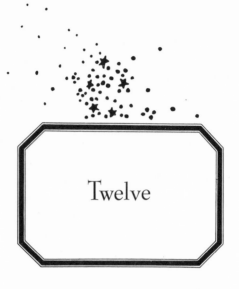

Twelve

In her hospital office, Alice Cloud clicked the receiver hook up and down, then, hearing Velma, said, "Velma, get me the Fishers." As she waited, the sound from the hallway reached her; Marty Broom, who had glumly accepted her offer of a job, was working in the halls with the mop as though bound to drive it straight through the tiles; the hissing of the mop broadcast his low and private spirits. Birdy Mathews had wound a fresh bandage around his bad leg, which had appeared to be scoriated as if he had caught it in some sort of trap; he'd not been forthcoming about his accident. When Sheriff Potter arrived, he and Tommy Beavis bringing the dripping fliers in for temporary hospitalization, Marty had elaborately avoided the sheriff as though he had leprosy. It was all a mystery, but one which didn't concern Alice much. She was aware of Marty's worth and his own keen estimate of it. But she didn't have time to placate him or tease him out of what bothered him.

Goldy Fisher came on the line, her voice muffled, obviously yawning.

Alice said, "Sorry, Goldy—I'm taking you up on your offer.

We're swamped. Birdy's doing what she can, but Mrs. Tensicott's worse—Dr. Bowen looked in, and says he doubts she'll last the night; and everything but the back room upstairs is full of people. A lot of burns, a broken neck, a couple of out-of-town barnstormers—"

"Couple of what?"

"Aviators," Alice said with impatience. "Never mind, you can find out when you get here. Dr. Bowen's had to go out again—Miller picked a grand day to go fishing."

Goldy perked up audibly. "Be right there just as soon as I get the sleep out o' my eyes, Alice. I'm all by myself . . . Milly's gone down to church to run through some stuff on the organ, Eugene's been out all morning. I—"

"Thank you," Alice said and hung up.

Aaron Kaplan had been waiting on a hall-bench with his daughter, Rebecca. When Alice was off the phone he led Rebecca across the flood of soapsuds on the tiles into the office. Alice thought that, standing there, he resembled some Venetian doge about to bless the waters. She approved of him and of Rebecca. From the office window she could see the Kaplan roadster, gorgeously decorated, its top down, Mark Kaplan's head just visible on the passenger side.

She realized that since Sheriff Potter had quietly told her the news that so far they hadn't found Cy, she had been feeling a rush of gladness—Jerome was taking it hard, but she found herself cheering Cy on. Let him get away and start anew. It was what he should have done the first time, when he was first betrayed. She realized also that if he'd packed up and left, those many years ago, she would have had great hope—been willing, if he'd come to her, to eat the humble pie of a woman welcoming the strayed penitent. But then, she had always expected him to come to her some day, some night, or stop her on the street and say, "Alice, I made a hell of a mistake."

She said, "Rebecca, if I had a hair ribbon like that, I'd go straight into a beauty contest."

Aaron sleeked his daughter's hair. Her dove's eyes inspected the slots of the rolltop, then turned brightly to Alice.

Aaron pulled out an envelope from his coat pocket. "Alice, my brothers and me got a little something here for them poor fellows from the airplane. I was saying to Jerome how it might touch their pride if we just shoved it at them. They seem peculiar people. Jerome told me maybe you'd handle it. You're so good at this kind of stuff."

Alice took the envelope, a plain one without the purple logo of the Tribe of K. "It's no talent to give away somebody else's money," she said. "And it's very thoughtful of you, Aaron. Why not come up with me? I won't say who it's from; I'll just say it's from some townspeople."

Aaron smiled. "Great. I already seen them, but I'd like to again. We were in the park when the plane went down."

"I'd really like to have seen Buck, he has natural style . . . Jerome said Nick hadn't shown up in the park when he left. Have you seen him?"

"No—him and Buck were up in the cemetery when the plane flopped and Buck dived off the wall. It was a pretty good ruckus for a while there. Carl took Buck on home to get dressed for the parade. But Nick will be fine, Alice, he knows how to take care of himself."

Alice didn't answer. She thought, In matters of physical preservation, yes. But in the other matters, the kind that ask for more than quick muscular reaction? The kind where inborn sensitivity isn't ever enough?

She glanced away from the window. "Wouldn't Mark like to come in?"

"He's kind of afraid of these flying men—the way the one with the face scars laughs." Aaron shrugged. "Poor man, I know it ain't his fault. Mark gets these bad dreams."

"So do I," said Alice, "sometimes."

As they went into the hall, skirting Marty, who stopped mopping to let them past, she took Rebecca's hand. She thought, Rebecca looks a little like Phyllis used to, when she'd be sitting in the park waiting for us, the older ones, to show up. The same carefully held trust, the great hope of acceptance, and a little of the same beauty.

But Rebecca had a sweet gaiety Phyllis never had. At the head of the stairs she put her hands on the water cooler and laughed as the inverted jug made a lurching gurgle. She laughed again as the voice of Captain Barnes came in toneless, dry upheaval behind the nearest door, from the room where Phyllis Bellaman had been earlier in the day. Sergeant Pringle's answer sounded through the door panel, "Check, sir," and then the heavy, fur-throated "Carry on, Sergeant."

"Funny men," said Rebecca.

Aaron patted his daughter's arm. "No, dear, they are sad men. Brave and sad. Not funny, Becky. You want a drink?" She nodded eagerly, and he manipulated the cooler, which talked more bubbles, handed her the paper cup and watched her drink. Alice watched Aaron, seeing on his face his adoration for Rebecca, for his family and his brothers and their families in turn, for his wife, Reba, his luck in this town, his green life.

Eugene's cocky walk was more pronounced than usual, as if there were a drum major in each knee. Encountering Mrs. Gloria Fosset, an elderly woman under a hat where a jungle of artificial flowers bobbed—she was heading toward the assembling paraders—he halted and listened to her tale of sciatica pains. When she had gone on, prodding the sidewalk with her rubber-tipped cane, he said under his breath, "And how's your mossy old twat?"

He'd been unable to hear all of the sheriff's conversation with Chief Gorseman, but there had been enough—the part about borrowing the searchlight had come through. That had been luck. Learning about the water tower from Marty had been, he considered, diplomatic genius. The discovery of *who*, and *why* from Velma had been the result of the sheer power he loved. He had wakened that morning, Melissa in mind, feeling *that* sort of anticipatory power—and the day had blossomed for him with the benison of still other kinds, until he felt, now, nearly supernaturally gifted.

His course was plain. As a pithy Argus subtitle would put it, he was Bent on Revenge.

Phyllis Bellaman's parting words, when she calmly told him she would kill him if he ever came near her again, or spoke to her, or set foot on the Wolfson place—she had said it with such ease, brushing off a fly—still burned as hotly as when she'd said them. She'd dropped him before, and had responded when he came back, but the last time was it. He detested her intelligence; it had always affronted him, even in those times when he was in her bed. She had once said, "You don't really have a mind, do you? A set of reactions, all geared for your own pleasure—but it doesn't make any difference when somebody else suffers. You're unique." And then, when he had tried to snuggle up to her again, she pushed him away and gave him some money—my God, she could afford anything—and watched him take the twenty dollars, with a kind of far-off iceberg knowledge, knowing he'd have taken less. And as for her final marching orders—well, some women, some girls, would tell you to get out, but she meant it. The really bad part was that he knew she didn't even think about him anymore, except with cold and final loathing.

And it wasn't only she who would be brought down as soon as he had told his shocking news, with a grave, concerned face, to Mr. Gardner. Mr. Gardner was a good townrouser; his indignation would be amplified by the fact that the Vigilantes had acted to keep both sin and crime from the public—he could be depended on to split the town wide open, and immediately. He would, indeed, look upon Eugene as a kind of civic hero for having come to him with this revelation. Eugene didn't know whether Cy Bellaman would be hunted down by a great many law-abiding citizens, and perhaps killed in the process, and whether Phyllis would be finally revealed as a dangerous Jezebel and scorned and reviled by all good folk. He hoped so, but at any rate, Mr. Gardner would do the job right. While doing it, he would also somehow equalize every offense against Eugene others had committed. Nick Cloud's having knocked him down; Buck Bolyard. The Clouds in general, their high and mightiness, their rejection of his face, good manners, radiance. The merchants: like Marvin Soames, for whom he'd worked eight days; Franz Otis, for whom he'd ushered an even shorter time; the Kaplans, who had reluctantly said that having a thief around might be useful to keep them on their toes, but they preferred giving to the Red Cross. Sheriff Potter, who treated him as if he couldn't be seen by a discerning eye. All of them were in Eugene's ready hands. Along with Melissa, as something extra—lagniappe.

His airy stride decreased, the sense of limitless, dark power so suddenly overwhelming that he had to stand still and relish it. From Front, a blatting of Flügelhorns and the slam of a drum announced the arrival of the band. He looked at Lieutenant Livingston's watch. Plenty of time yet to saunter along to the Gardners', to draw Mr. Gardner aside for the man-to-man talk this demanded. But the power was drumming in him, stronger than the band drums, as he moved along slowly. He saw the Kaplans' Cloud roadster parked in front of the hospital, Mark Kaplan's curly black hair shining in it. He glanced toward the hospital. Miss Alice Cloud, with whom he had seldom exchanged two words—it was always apparent that she had no wish to hear from him—had her office on this side, but she wasn't at her desk. The power became a need, knotting in him.

A man could do anything he felt like, with this crowding his chest, flowing down his arms, filling his legs, lifting his balls. Anything. Think of something.

He went to the roadster, leaning on the door.

Bored, Mark had tasted the composition of a celluloid duck's head, licked paint from its rigid feathers, taken from it all it could give. After his father and sister had vanished into the hospital, he had amused himself for a while by trying to whistle. It was an art as yet eluding him. He sat low on the leather, conscious of band music a few streets off, with other music mingled in it; he didn't know this was "Jesu, Joy of Man's Desiring" from the First M.E. organ, where Milly Fisher, finished with routine hymn practice, was now playing for herself; he knew he liked it, the sound through the heat sustaining his mood of easy safety. He felt dim happiness that his father had understood his fear of the large men—especially the one who made the loud noise—and had left him here, where he couldn't see or hear them.

Shadow falling over him, he met Eugene's smile.

He didn't know Eugene; he had seen him before, but off in a void where adults outside his family and people his own size lived. He was extremely shy, keeping long silences even in the company of the younger Kaplans.

He dropped the duck, and as Eugene said in a cheerful, promising undertone, "Don't want to sit here all day by yourself, do you? Got an *idea . . .* " he made no sense of it. He absorbed the intonation, which meant that this human being was interested in him, might be offering him something. His eyes stayed on Eugene's, as if as long as he held them there he could shield himself from this irruptive and disturbing presence.

The worst happened then, in a dream switching to nightmare. Hands came into the car, lifted him beneath his arms, swinging him over the door and down beside the curb.

With his sense of full helplessness came a need to protest, but his voice wasn't working. He was trembling, yet his feet in their white sandals held him upright; he gazed upward. He smelled hair cream and heavy body heat. A large hand was held toward him. "C'mon—I'll show you a funny place."

Fingers shut around his hand, and then he was walking beside this urgent guide, up a short hill around the hospital to the schoolyard above Shop Street. He was skirting a wall, coming out in the schoolyard. Everything was accomplished in silence, quickly; the band was far off, the organ muffled. The fingers enveloping his hand were tight, inescapable.

"There we are," said his leader.

Mark followed Eugene's eyes, staring across the yard. The oaks were tall and dusty, the ground worn by games of One-old-Cat, Duck-on-the-Rock, softball, marbles. The school's frayed dark-red bricks were dappled by shadow. But it was the fire escape he was being asked to look at.

It rose two stories, a round iron tank with rivets studding it, an iron-grilled walkway leading from the school to its upper doorway. Inside it was a chute with three spiraling curves, where in total darkness children were meant to skid downward until they came out of the lower door. It might have been devised by a master of claustrophobia. The base door, resembling the door of a baker's oven, was shut, a shimmer of heat around it, smelling, even from there, of parched iron and rust.

Mark remembered, as one recalls a voice on the edge of sleep, his cousin Alfie, ten, wiser even than Rebecca, saying as he led Mark through these grounds, "Kid died there. Smothered—they had to shovel him out." Alfie, untrustworthy, enjoyed his ability to scare, but the comment couldn't be borne.

His face was quite pale; his eyes hurt. By making his throat very tight, he managed to say "No." But it was too soft for anyone to hear. Then he was being pulled along again, his Buster Brown sandals hardly touching earth. A few drops of fire-hot wetness leaked into his BVDs, a shaming thing—at four you knew better—but not now important; his starchy suit blouse rattled faintly.

This time when Eugene lifted him, packed him under an arm, the beaten ground swam beneath. Then he heard the door groan open. He was set down again, facing Eugene; he made a lunge for the white flannels and held on with all he had. It was a few seconds before he was pried loose. The flannels still filled his nostrils with the ozonelike odor of cleaning fluid. He dug in his heels, but the hands around his wristbones tightened, and he was swung up, backward, the smell of the fire escape now solid and stagnant around him; turning his head, staring up, he caught a glimpse of the chute's lowest curve, the rest winding into blackness, glints of polished steel under the rust. Then the door slammed before him as he fell back.

For an undefined time he stopped breathing, feet pressing against the door, all of him numbed by heat, darkness.

Outside he heard Eugene. "Don't worry now, I'll let you out. Just sit tight."

The voice wasn't exultant or loud, but neither did the words convince. The tone spoke, saying *Doom, Goodbye.* Then there was no more to be heard past the door.

Facing the door, Eugene felt the silence of the schoolyard, the building and the fire escape. It was a humming, deeply alive force. A similar force, made of accomplishment and jubilation, ran through him.

The door was sealed, firmly latched. The name of a manufacturer was stamped on it in an iron scroll. Not taking his eyes from the door, he brushed at a rust smear on his blazer.

Then a strange thing happened—he found himself, as though he were out of his body, projected through the door, into blackness, into the foul, nearly airless prison. Felt his own heart stifle with unbelieving arrest, the heat press down around him, upward into him, crawling, untenable.

He became Mark. And in this duality of being, everything he had felt before increased its strength; his muscles enlarged, his shadow appeared to grow longer.

It was a moment or two before he could shake off such rapture and bring himself to look at the watch. Mr. Gardner ... the precious, blasting secret he, Eugene, knew and held like a weapon ...

He opened the door, swinging it out by an inch, then another, until it let in all possible light.

Mark crouched, a foetus shape, glittering hair taking the sun, his head in his lap, hands clutched around socks almost swallowed by sandals. On one knee a flake of rust lay like a tiny leaf on snow. His curls were wet on the back of his neck. His sandal toes were flattened, turning up sharply like Turkish slippers. What could be glimpsed of his downturned face was like white damask. Eugene touched his wrist. It was warm, and flinched a little from the touch, the fingers limpets tightening further around the ankles, fingernails bloodless. He was beyond speech.

And he was an absolute menace. Eugene realized this with a rush that passed through his whole body, sweeping away the great triumph of a few seconds before.

Freed, Mark could talk. Whether or not he would be believed—in the teeth of Eugene's own well-polished protestations of innocence—was immaterial. He could cause a loss of vital time, perhaps even cast doubt on the validity of everything Eugene was about to reveal.

For one more considering half second Eugene stared in. Then he pushed the door shut with a tight, sure clang. He had made up his mind. Surely this stupid kid—as dense as his old man—would have the sense, later, to start yelling. And surely, also later, someone would come close enough to the schoolyard to hear him and let him out. If not—well, it was really in God's lap, wasn't it? No longer at all in Eugene's. The thing now was to get away from here, to leave as swiftly as possible, without being perceived near what somebody as ungifted as, say, Sheriff Potter, might be silly enough to call the scene of the crime.

He had already started decisively out of the yard. But under the last tree he paused to straighten his lapels, then caught sight of the rust stain, which he hadn't quite removed. He had his head cocked, blazer cloth caught up between the fingers of his left hand, right hand's fingers tongued and wetted, and was scrubbing industriously when Buck Bolyard said over his shoulder, "H'lo, Gene."

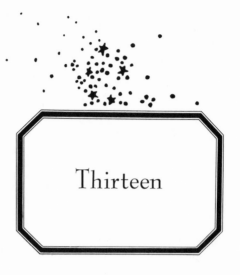

Thirteen

Wrestled into the tub by his mother, who insisted that river water stank, Buck had emerged fifteen minutes later, broad-boned and shining, had eaten half of one of the *Apfelkuchen* Maidy had prepared for the picnic, and had tried to telephone Nick. Harky, who answered, said that Nick wasn't back yet. Then he'd called Candy Pruitt and arranged to pick her up in a few jerks of a lamb's tail. In the car he finished dressing and demolished the other half of the *Apfelkuchen* in a dead heat, feeling dudish in his newly pressed blue-striped suit. The vest added dignity, and his hair was reasonably flat.

The Fourth of July band, members aged roughly eleven to sixty-eight, was warming up on Front Street, and listening, Buck felt relieved that the dancing in the park would be backed by the Colored Settlement musicians. He was moving along Shop Street—Candy lived at the end of it—when he happened to look up into the school grounds.

He braked, aimed the Dort to the curb, switched off the ignition and sat for a few breaths—puzzled and intrigued. Then he got out and quietly climbed the incline above the

Shops. Halfway to the fire escape, he stood still.

He'd been about to ask Eugene what the hell he was staring at that old door for. As a rule he wouldn't have bothered to talk to Eugene, but he thought now it was quite possible the son of a bitch had gone crazy, and if so, it was going to be interesting. Eugene should have been at Melissa's—making hay, parlor-snaking, charming the ears off everybody. Not, certainly, inspecting a fire escape like it was Vilma Banky.

Buck swallowed deeply as Eugene swung open the door. He saw from this distance what Eugene saw closer, and he said under his breath, "Holy Toledo!" In the next second he ducked around a tree, waiting while Eugene shut the fire-escape door and turned and walked off. When Eugene stopped to dab at his blazer, Buck greeted him. His voice was noncommittal, though none could have called it neighborly.

Eugene dropped the blazer fold. He was always good in emergencies. Buck remembered how he'd maintained a bronze-bound front right up to the last second he, Buck, had had to lay one on him. Eugene had been saying that fighting was for savages and he hadn't meant any harm by discussing the point that Phyllis Bellaman preferred him to anybody else in town his general age.

Eugene said in a low, mannerly voice, "Hello. Sorry, I'm sort of in a hurry . . ."

At this Buck grabbed him by the shoulder; the blazer felt as if it had considerable stuffing between its peak-edged seam and the actual flesh and bone beneath. Carefully but firmly he turned Eugene around. "You left somebody in the fire escape," he said.

Eugene looked at him, close up now, with plausible, puzzled interest. He could have been one of those shepherds in the M.E. altar window; there was the same butter-won't-melt grace. "Fire escape?"

Buck lowered his holding hand to Eugene's right arm, then he doubled that arm behind Eugene and pivoted him again, still with care to exert no more pressure than needed. He propelled Eugene back to the fire escape. Eugene didn't protest, but his eyebrows were arched and he was smiling tolerantly. His attitude was that of a man confident a case of mistaken identity will shortly be cleared up and all parties involved will exchange cards before they depart, still affable.

At the door—hot to his hand like a two-dollar pistol—Buck shifted and obtained traction on the back of Eugene's neck, pushing his head down and forward. "Open up!" he commanded.

This time there was hesitation, the smile was less certain.

Buck said quickly, reflectively, "Bakin' a little boy to death's sure different. Leopold and Loeb oughta take lessons off you. If I put *you* in there, you'd be gone in a couple hours. Flat gone. Don't know how long you was gonna leave him. Don't matter. Open it."

Eugene opened the door, its hinge-pins groaning. He said, "Lord, Buck, it's a *joke*. He's in on it. Wanted to see how long—"

"Oh, horse apples," Buck said. He kept his positive hold on Eugene, as though Eugene were genuflecting under his firm blessing, and with his other arm he managed to lift Mark. For a moment he held him close. Mark's suit was soaked through, clinging to his body, but the child seemed to weigh no more than an apple basket made of light withes. His hair was gritty, pressing up against Buck's neck, and out of his throat came a low inarticulate sound, like wind in winter-thin trees. He smelled of urine and fear.

Buck set him down, but for a while Mark refused to quite stand, leaning against Buck's legs. Buck got a hand under the delicate chin and turned the head up slightly. He spoke with extreme softness, but distinctly, warming the words like a folk singer. "Mark . . . go over there to the drinkin' fountain, corner of the yard. There's a horse block under it for kids your size. Climb up and push the lever. Works easy. Git your head soaked good. Slap a lot on the insides of your wrists and elbows . . . then go in the shade and wait for me."

His eyes on Buck like glazed dark planets, Mark took in the directions and, very slowly, seemed to recognize them as friendly, even useful. He gave a deep shudder like a colt shaking off violent swarms of flies. When at last he had started to make his way, still very slowly, toward the fountain, he stopped twice and looked back to make sure Buck was still around. Each time Buck nodded reassuringly, then Mark went on. When the boy had finally reached the horse block and was kneeing himself up as if he were an exhausted climber, Buck again switched grips on Eugene and resumed the back-of-the-spine, cross-arm hold. He said, musing, "Shadrach, Meschach, Abednego . . . man's goin' to be a true preacher ought to know about *them*."

But when Eugene looked as though he didn't, Buck only sighed. Eugene was sweating. He was moved forward again, with Buck's guidance, down a steep flight of cracked brick stairs leading to the school basement. Under the foot of the steps Buck turned a brass knob and pushed this door till it swung in. It had crusted panes, through which, for the past seconds, the interior of the basement had been dimly perceived by both, like a dungeon observed through gauze. Here Eugene made his first and last attempt to break away. Buck had obviously expected it to be as strenuous and slippery as it turned out, and quickly subdued him. Eugene was panting now and a string of saliva hung to his blazer buttons.

Pushing the door farther inward, Buck said, "Yeah, they keep this unlocked so the Woodmen of the World can git in on Wednesday nights. Lodge room's around behind the furnace. Daddy's a Woodman—dunno, mebbe I'll join up when I git his age." Buck could have been showing a group of tourists around. "They don't do much to speak of, mostly just set around and cut for high card after the minutes is read. I could borra the card pack, so you'd have somethin' to play solitaire with . . ."

He was steering Eugene to the furnace. An alarmed and underfed mouse ran off in the green drowsy light which fell from ground-level windows, illuminating ancient barrels and shovels and the debris of years of casual janitoring. There was a smell of gathered must over the whole place. From the basement door, additional light splashed over the furnace, picking out shabby asbestos sheathing around the huge pipes raised to the softly cobwebbed ceiling. Inside the open furnace door there was a large heap of ashes, with cinders and clinkers showing through.

"Hell, though," Buck said as if he had just recalled, with disappointment, a favor he'd have to withdraw. "You couldn't see to play cards, could you? Couldn't even cheat by the feel of 'em. All right, Gene—"

The heavy door slammed shut. It was still ringing as Buck dusted his hands together and then, working on the knees of his trousers, elevated one foot and then the other to the edge of a coalbin. He had finished by the time Eugene got around to speaking from inside the furnace. A cautious slither and crackle accompanied Eugene's tentative, earnest question—his assured delivery gained something meek, had improved with distance. "You coming back to get me?"

Buck raised his own voice to compete with the iron sound baffle. "Woodmen of the World don't have no meetin' *this* comin' Wednesday. Don't start regular till fall—time the heat slacks off. Tell you what, I wouldn't even try to holler. Was I you. But then, I ain't."

There was another careful rustle.

Buck's voice echoed richly. "Aw, just look at it lucky. You'll miss the mayor's speech."

Since no answer came, he walked out. He shut the basement door, shaking his head over the condition of his vest. At the top of the steps he pulled its tabs down and looked around for Mark. The child was sitting in a blue wedge of shade, knees drawn up. As Buck came near him he got up. Buck held out his hand, Mark took it, and he accommodated his pace to Mark's as they crossed the yard. Buck said, "Sure, you was scared. Everybody is once in a while. Nice thing, though, it makes the times you ain't scared a lot better. Tough findin' that out."

At the next curb he made out the Kaplan roadster in front of the hospital, and when they had reached it he lifted Mark inside. "Don't go drivin' this big thing off by yourself, now. Look, here's a duck somebody's been at. I wouldn't have a duck like that around, shows whoever owns it's got nervous teeth." He put his hand on Mark's hair and rolled it around a little. "Going to be all right now?"

Mark didn't smile, but the effort was there if anybody searched hard enough to detect it.

Buck didn't know if Mark would tell his father about Eugene and the fire escape at once, or whether it would come out in bits and pieces later on. He thought probably the bits-and-pieces approach would be most likely—when you'd been that scared, it took time putting the whole thing together. He recognized in Mark something he himself had had at that age —the ability to bide a while, to keep your most terrifying experiences from grownups, to get their meaning straight once and for all before you talked about them much. It wasn't like a cut knee or a stubbed toe. He decided that as far as he was concerned, he'd let it ride awhile—he'd tell Nick, but there wasn't any use spoiling Aaron's day, or the rest of the Kaplans'. He said to Mark, "Y' know, you're really smart as a rat and full of mustard. Ain't worried a bit about you."

He went back to the Dort, started it and meshed it into gear, wishing he had the Ingersoll but seeing on a face of the courthouse clock that there was still time to spare before the parade broke loose. He slowed the car to a crawl behind more cavalrymen, surging around a bay team which pulled a Great War cannon—more businesslike than the one in the park—with armor shield uptilted and wheels rumbling. Then, at Soames's, he parked beside a line of benches advertising Gold Dust Cleansing Powder on their slatted backs, the Gold Dust Twins grinning out like old friends. Tommy Beavis and Marvin Soames were shoving benches to the curb for a wall to keep horses and parade mules from the sidewalk. Tommy, in his regular police uniform, looked dark as a beet after a rain. The

Baby Doll had been pulled out of her home once more, straddling the line of march, Chief Gorseman scowling from her high driving seat at various children who mobbed around her. All the tradesmen whose places were open today were out in front of the awnings, except for Abe Melton.

Buck swung open the door of the pharmacy's one telephone booth and left it ajar to let some fan-air in. The booth was wide enough to hold four or five bodies if that many wanted to make a call at once, and had been one of the first in the county. Marvin Soames discouraged the young from seeing how many could fit into it in a pinch. It was painted a murky dark brown which rubbed off if one lounged while conversing. There were notations on most of its inside surface, the largest saying *Velma Temple does it with anybody,* but someone, perhaps Velma herself, had partially scratched this out. Buck drew back three inches, made a fist and pounded the phone box at the same time he lifted the receiver. It took experience; the *bong* of a nickel dropping was ideal.

Velma said, "Aw right, you're comin' through. Marvin's goin' to get that *fixed* some time, and it'll start costin'."

"Gol, Velma, only me. Bring you some stuff from the picnic when we get back tonight. Anyhow, you can see the p'rade where you're sittin'. Nick Cloud, please?"

"Oh, Buck—sorry." In a few seconds she said, "I'm ringin'. Didn't mean to bite your head off, only I'm out o' sorts. Bring me some o' Harky's cherry cake and your mom's apple if you can put your hand on 'em. Here y' go."

Buck said "Nick?" before he knew who was on.

Nick said, "Hey, Harky said you called. I'll bring your overalls and the night fireworks stuff right along to the parade."

Buck decided that Nick had a guarded sound. Which was all right; they could talk about anything Nick had to tell, later, or not talk if Nick wanted to keep something special to himself. Right now there was other, urgent news. Courteously Buck said, "Velma, you mind gettin' off just for a speck? I'll jiggle the hook when you c'n come back."

Velma said cheerfully, "All you got to do is ask." There was a hearty key click as she bowed out.

Buck said rapidly, "Eugene ain't goin' to be at M'lissa's, or even around the rest of the day. Never mind why. Gives you a clear track if you can get around ol' highpockets."

Buck heard Nick draw in his breath, then Nick said, "Damn! Thanks."

"Stay on the line," Buck said. He fingered the hook, making it dance like a gutta-percha doll with outstretched arms.

Velma said, "Aw right, I'm back, didn't listen a lick."

Buck said, "I'm ringin' off, but Nick wants the Gardners."

Velma said, not so cheerfully now, "Gene's over there."

Buck said, *"Is* he? I be dinged. Nick wants to call up anyway. B'by!" He hung up, felt in the change-return cup for a possible nickel somebody unfamiliar with the booth might have left there, found none, and, thumbs in vest pockets, went out in the greeting sun. In the Dort he headed again for Candy Pruitt's.

By turning sharp left when one got off the Kentucky-Ohio bridge and by-passing the jog leading into Arden, you could take the side trail, largely concealed by arching scrub, which led onto the Ridge. The trail led to the whole of Carmian's Hill; ran east of the Colored Settlement, then shifted westward and dropped into the white Ridge flank above the river.

Phyllis had been climbing steadily since she left the river bridge. The sound of the cicadas wasn't half as penetrating, shrill and sawing as it had been that morning around the hospital. And there were no blurts of extra sound from unexpected directions, fraying the nerves and fretting at the border of consciousness. Only a sentient humming, and birds ceasing their chatter yards ahead, flying farther off. In the distance a woodpecker, the kind people in the Colored Settlement called Lord-to-God, was drumming. A few downed oaks, riddled by borers, roots exposed to flecks of sun, lay in the long grass. Bees hung over the logfall, shifting in quick darts as if their bodies had been knocked into fresh positions, at regular intervals, on the thick, sustaining air.

One of them poised a few inches in front of her eyes. Go ahead, land and taste me, she told it silently. But it sheered off; she walked on, the scarlet purse swinging as she climbed, allowing herself to think, which she rarely did, of Rex, and of the war.

The newspapers had been lurid: "London to Be Bombed"; Belgium a cartooned peasant woman, with wide, terrified eyes, spitted through the belly by a Hun with a bloody bayonet; Marshal Foch; Joffre, Pershing. Woodrow Wilson's eyes a teacher's behind his spectacles. She thought of all of them then phasing in on Rex Cloud, all coming for him at once—German generals, ours, the whole war conspiring to take her lover. But he had been hers, no other's. He told her himself Marna had been a mistake; as they lay whispering, he told her there would be a divorce, even if it brought scandal—a divorce as soon as he came home. They spoke of Marna with what she considered extremely mature calm. "Yes, she loves me," Rex said. "As much as she can love anybody but Wilde and Bernard Shaw and Pirandello. She loves me about the way she loves Nick. He's a nice baby. There's never going to be any room for us."

He'd raised himself on an elbow then, blown smoke across her body. They lay naked in the summerhouse that was then on the slope beside the pool in the middle of the Wolfson estate; she'd had it torn down a long time back, asked her father, during the week before she married Cy, to have it razed and carted away. Tom Wolfson had said judiciously, "Well, if it's an eyesore for you, Phyl, we'll do away with it." But then it was still a summerhouse, latticed walls holding moonlight like so many white diamonds, Rex's car, a heavy fast Cloud roadster, parked back in the lane; about three in the morning. The smoke drifted in moon dust above her breasts. She gazed down at herself, reflecting that that place where he made love to her was extremely mysterious, and had no right to feel so content, so forever given to floating. They lay on an old canvas camping mattress, one of Tom Wolfson's from the days when he'd admired Teddy Roosevelt and purchased reams of patented hunting equipment, having it sent down from Abercrombie & Fitch in New York, Von Lengerke and Antoine in Chicago.

A moonlight diamond had landed fairly in Rex's eyes; he drew on the cigarette again, the glow illuminating his mouth, his upper lip and a part of his strong, daredevil jaw. He said, ". . . not her fault. She's a wonderful actress. I'm not going to fight anymore—fight her. She'll raise all the sand there is, she'll blow up—oh yes, of course she knows about us. She *didn't* know at first, but she's very perceptive, and I'm no damn good at hiding. We won't stay here—the old man won't approve, for one thing; he pours his guts in those Shops—doesn't seem to see much, but I think he's felt it, too. God, I'm glad I never went in the Shops. A good car's a fine toy, nothing to settle your life around." He leaned above her. "Phyl, where were you all that time? A kid we used to tell, 'Go home'. . .'Go roll your hoop.' All legs and eyes, and hush. You didn't talk much when you were growing up . . ."

"I'll talk the rest of our lives," she said. "I'll write every day. I'll roll bandages. I'll knit sweaters."

He said, eyes shadowed now, but only inches from hers, "It's all such balderdash, the whole thing, war. I don't intend to shirk, you know. Intend to wipe out every stinking Hun I can, be one hell of an officer. Not because the old man got so *distinguished* when he was still practically a kid. He's got a notion it's that, but it's just because I want to do my own part to get the thing over, and then sail home—I'll swim back if there aren't any fast troopships—and live ever after. Damn it, I like this town, but we can find another."

"I don't care—wherever you want to be. I don't care at all . . ." She hadn't; with him there, she didn't even have to touch him.

He said more softly, huskily, beside her throat, "Too many people around here know," and laughed. The tremor of his laughter entered her own mouth. "Blasted old Renfrew the other night—he didn't see *you*, I made sure of that. Jerome, I guess, though."

He touched her between her breasts. "Alice knows too—couldn't help finding out. Didn't give me any big-sister talk, too proud for that. Just looks at me, across the dinner table; well, thank the Lord she's got Cy. They *fit* each other, they're both stodges. No, shouldn't say that—Alice is spunky. Maybe she'll come around. What is it she's got? Compassion's not right, but that's part of it . . ."

Very softly Phyllis said, "A kind of nobility."

"Yes, that's almost it. She and Cy may side with us . . . I'd like somebody on our side. Let's not talk awhile now." His voice, its whisper-talk, had changed. "Lie here quiet—can't sleep, got to go soon . . ."

The voice drifted away from her memory like the sleep neither of them had had. She became aware of the daylight around her; she was on the Ridge. Through a screen of mock orange and wild cherry she could now see Reverend Bates's church. It rose delicately pink; there was no one near it. The world dozed here; it wasn't Independence Day. A colored child came out of a house below the church and threw water in a silver sluice from a dipper. She called back into the house, "Late for the p'rade if we don't hurry up, Mama!" Her mother answered her inside the house, and it was Independence Day again. Phyllis looked back from another angle; the church from here, river-side angels leaning high and blowing their warm-belled trumpets, was small again. She envied the true constancy of these carved figures as she envied animals, their ability only to exist. What was it Whitman had said? They do not sweat and whine about their condition, they do not lie awake in the dark and weep for their sins. Not even for Eugene Fisher—or even for Henry?

Henry, so close here on the Ridge. And now she felt herself stop again, and looked blindly into the trees. To say sorry was nonsense. No *mea culpa*, no breast-beating . . .

Cy wanted to adopt a child, he always wanted it, she thought, and I wouldn't have it. A child not mine, a child I couldn't see something of myself in, the self Rex loved? A child I couldn't see any part of Rex in? No, since I am barren, none of that. And yet it might have changed us—changed me. And you would still be here, Henry. You would be heading now for town, wearing one of those stiff, badly fitting suits you favored, hat drawn down over the fox-cub eyes, a fresh and evergreen man, with no taint of hatred or complexity in you. Alive, Henry, alive. To breathe this river-brushed air that tastes of pines and honey.

How you watched all of us at that wedding reception. You spoke to me, in a corner, while others were laughing at Marna Cloud's imitations—she frenetic, enjoying herself, actually glad Rex was dead, not quite saying it but projecting it. Alice was staring at me, bronze-brown-eyed, never saying Why? Why did you have to take Cy? You spoke, Henry, decently and well, saying, "Want you and Cy to have a real good life. Brought you a box of muscadines. They're nice and fresh, put a little ice around them and they'll last. I'm glad for friends."

It was not you, but the rest of us who were out of place at that party. And we have finally put you away.

No, no, Phyllis, she said again, heavily, the ache of it burning her tongue and throat.

I finally stopped you. Cy did it with his rifle, but that was incidental; if I hadn't wanted you, needed you as another anodyne, you'd be traipsing off-Ridge now, to the parade and later the park, enjoying everything as shy men can enjoy, with accommodating fullness.

Cy still needs me and wants me enough to kill for me, enough to have killed you—you, who turned out to be the last straw for him. He mustn't have believed, when he stepped into the living room last night, that it could be you. His eyes went from slate to black to blue, back to black again, and I still don't think he believed it was quite you as he raised the rifle.

There was a clearing below her now in which a woman stood.

And a house, its shake-shingle roof daubed with leaf shadow, the door open, a chop log on one side, vegetable and flower gardens ranged along the other, a spring welling nearby, a small barn offset behind it.

The woman had turned her head, the wool hat moving very little, as if she had merely turned to watch a leaf silently floating. The gray knitwork of a shawl was drawn tight to the bones of her shoulders. The rest of her was covered in serviceable black, the dress touching her shoe tops.

In a moment her voice came, drawn out of a quiet dry cistern. "Never would've expected you to come, but maybe it's right. The body ain't here, you know." It was a reflective voice. "Could ha' seen it down to town, to Melton's. Well." She stood just below Phyllis, the deep scored face old, a little like Henry's.

"Now you're here, come over to the bench and set a bit. Been real hard, not havin' nobody to talk to 'bout my son. Beavis—sher'f sent him up—told me they'd be obliged, them men on the Vig'lantes, if I'd keep shut awhile about it. So I ain't told a soul. Oh, I had to tell Nellis—that's Harby Nellis —when I went over there sunup, and asked him to make the coffin. But didn't tell him how. Him and his boys brought the coffin over few minutes back. It's yonder 'round the woodshed. Can see it from the bench."

She put a hand out from beneath the shawl. It had heavy veins along its back, but it was able, flint-boned, still well-muscled. She might have been about to touch Phyllis. But the hand stayed where it was.

"Yes, maybe it's right. I don't hold no blame for you, y' know. You done what you done, and you must o' give him some pleasure and sweetness. Think he felt iron in his soul 'bout it bein' Cy Bellaman's wife. Kind of half heaven, half th' other place. You know how that is?" She was looking only into Phyllis' eyes.

"I know how it is," Phyllis said.

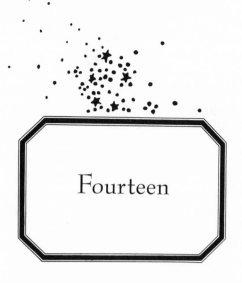

Fourteen

In the Gardner living room, from which the photograph of the thirty-first President of the United States had been removed for the time being, Roy Gardner looked unbelievingly at his daughter. He was not equipped to deal with defiance either in his own bank or at home. In the spheres of his command he expected obedience. He still felt rocky from losing sleep over Nick Cloud the night before; he considered that he'd acted then, and today about the photograph, in a Christian manner, though he was convinced Nick had smashed the glass on purpose. He thought he might need a laxative or even a new start for the holiday. He also felt somewhat as he did during school board meetings when he brought up an objection to the works of Herman Melville and Samuel Langhorne Clemens—both unfit for children—and was slapped down coolly by Alice Cloud.

His wife, Clare, sat in a corner but he didn't look at her. He said, "Call him? Call young Cloud?"

Melissa sat up straight on the mohair couch. "Yes, I want to. It's all right—he wanted to take me, Daddy. Eugene's not *here.*"

"He's been delayed for a good reason," Roy Gardner said. "He's always punctual. It's some emergency. He's considerate, above all things. Why don't you call *him*?"

Melissa said, "I don't want to argue about that. He's the one who should have called me. Daddy . . . I want to call Nick. He isn't perfect the way you think Eugene is, but he likes me more. And I don't think he'd let anybody down, or"—her lower lip did not quiver—"stand them up."

"How do you know? At your age, how can you possibly know?" Roy Gardner had gentled his delivery, with difficulty. He found himself wishing she would cry. When she cried, he knew just where he was. But she was astoundingly dry-eyed. He looked away, out into the driveway, where his Hupmobile stood simonized and decked out in full regalia. The Scout emblem was prominent on its front bumper. There were young, obedient scouts waiting for him who would line up behind the rear bumper and keep pace as he drove. He had his own official hat ready on the hatrack in the hall.

He looked back at his daughter and said, "Let's be reasonable. We'll give Eugene another few minutes. Call him myself then—if he's not already here."

"You'll do no such thing. That's up to me, Daddy—not you."

Her dress was quite short; he didn't like that, but it was established custom now. It was bright-red, trimmed with those extras which came down in cascades from the machine operated by her mother. Her hair improved the sunlight. She wore touches of Princess Pat rouge, and under it her cheeks had received the benison of Woodbury's Facial Soap. Her excellent teeth had been brushed with Kolynos, the foaming antiseptic, and since babyhood she had been guarded from rickets by Squibb's Cod Liver Oil. All she had ever eaten, drunk, gargled, laved with, been anointed by, had passed cautious family inspection first. As she sat in smooth silk stockings, knees exposed, a jaunty red hat, also of her mother's manufacture, matching the dress and crowning her brilliant hair, he thought that she could have competed with Miss Lolita Gladys Gelpi, seventeen, daughter of Mr. and Mrs. Vivian Gelpi of New Orleans, recently voted the Loveliest Sub-Deb by John Barrymore, Cornelius Vanderbilt, Jr., and Francis Scott Key Fitzgerald. She was, he thought, his golden girl, blond-inclined but with enough wild basswood-honey color in hair, eyes and flesh to be called a mid-brunette. As she stood up, she shone. She must, he was sure, be wearing some restraining device—in his mind he avoided such words as brassiere.

She said, "I'm going to call. Nick's *faithful*—and he's my friend."

She didn't add that while Eugene excited her because of his splendid manners and the rumors of conquests that trailed him like flashing weasels, Nick both excited and warmed her. She had now and again mulled the notion, not unpleasurable, that Eugene was saving her for a special treat. This was flattering, but risky; the idea of the risk might a few hours before still have given rise to a few tears. But somehow she didn't feel at all like crying now. A feeling had been growing for ten minutes that was impossible to pin down, let alone discuss with her father and mother. In the back of her head she had a vision of her father having a stroke—"Arden Banker Suffers Seizure"—or turning her out in the snow. His scout-buckle sparkling, his command final, "Go, you are no daughter of mine."

Her father, pacing, again inspected his Hupmobile. He had his watch, an Elgin on a thin chain, in his fingers. He read it again. "Give Eugene one more minute," he said. "Then we'll just take a quick turn around toward the Fishers' before we go on to Front. Sit back down, Melissa."

She didn't.

Mrs. Gardner made a noise. At once her husband and daughter regarded her as if furniture had spoken. She occupied a horsehair-stuffed, uncomfortable visitor's chair under one of the what-not cabinets. For the parade, the picnic and possibly the dance in the park—though Roy Gardner had not danced with her for a long time—she had chosen gray crêpe de chine, high at the neck, and a hat surmounted by the feathers of a sober bird. She touched a necklace of amber beads, which clicked, and said in a wavering contralto, "There are surely many other nice boys, Melissa dear, who would be glad to go with you . . ."

Whenever relatives of the Gardners came to call they were each time reintroduced to Melissa as if she were a cloisonné vase of great lustre and value so they might take home her memory and warm themselves by it. Uncles, aunts, various ungifted, unendowed cousins, were allowed to chat with her decorously, and to be filled in about her school honors and social successes. Arden possessed no country club, but Mr. Gardner belonged to the Barlton Club, across the river, having braved the rival town's scorn so he could have a place to entertain important visitors, and on Saturday afternoons he was teaching Melissa to play golf. He had planned to take Eugene along with them soon. He thought Eugene and Melissa made a striking couple and he'd voiced this to Clare Gardner. She hadn't responded, as if she recognized something about Eugene which he hadn't.

He started to say now, "Clare, that's out of the question," but Melissa was already answering quietly, fondly, "No, Mama, I don't want to go with anybody else. Just Nick."

Clare Gardner raised her chin a degree. "Melly, darling, you seem so tense. It isn't—?"

With her eyes Melissa informed her mother that no, it wasn't, and that her menstruation cycle was all right.

Mrs. Gardner settled forward again. She said, "You're not going to roll your stockings tonight are you, darling?"

Melissa said, "If the others do. It feels good."

"They look so *awful,* under the knees," Mrs. Gardner said breathily. "I wish it hadn't ever started."

"Candy always does. It looks nice on her. My knees aren't exactly horrible."

"I didn't mean that, and you know it, Melly. And I don't think in your heart of hearts you believe there's any possible comparison between my little girl and Candy Pruitt."

Melissa silently agreed. Candy did as she pleased, had five brothers and two sisters, was dark as a raven and danced like a dream. She used all the lipstick she wanted and it was right for her. Candy was frank though not prurient about what she sometimes did with Buck, and had filled Melissa in on necessary detail. The year before, Candy had won a Charleston contest over in Hamilton, taking the cup hands down. Melissa had dreamed a few nights before of Candy Pruitt, the dream vague but intense, Candy and herself in some grove with lofty trees, like the Corot picture in the Gardner front hall, the leafy trees shadowing the bodies of what they called satyrs, and nobody with a stitch on. Nick had been there, close; she should have been ashamed of the dream, but she wasn't. Yet its half-memory had firmed her will against Nick last night, as if she were afraid of herself.

She said with the direct aim of shocking, "Mama, Mrs. Bellaman doesn't wear any stockings at all, all summer, and she's the prettiest woman in the world."

Mrs. Gardner's eyelids shut. They seemed to be made of crêpe, like her dress. Neither she nor Mr. Gardner would discuss Phyllis Bellaman. They either turned the subject aside when it came along or entered a silence sealed as a mummy's tomb. Melissa knew Phyllis Bellaman well enough to smile and get a smile back when they met, which wasn't often. Once Mrs. Bellaman had had her husband's setter on a leash and Melissa had admired him and held his head. Mrs. Bellaman said, "You're Nick's girl, aren't you?" She said she was, and Mrs. Bellaman said judgingly, "You're very pretty. Please stay that way." It was more like a command than a request; it took your breath away when somebody that wonderful said it.

Then she'd walked on, and Melissa thought it was the best compliment she'd ever had. She often asked Nick about her, since Nick was the Bellamans' friend, but he didn't say a lot about them. He gave the idea there was too much to say ... As for Candy, she had strong opinions. "Maybe about half what they say about her's true. The other half's just because they wish they could be her, or if they're men, be around her. Holy Nellie, I wouldn't care if it was all true. She's got a better front and back than Clara Bow and more class than Billie Burke."

In the Gardners' house, the fourteen-carat Bellaman silence had fallen. Roy Gardner broke it: "All right, we're on our way! We'll take a swing around to the Fishers' first, and honk—" His watch case snapped. "Baskets are in the car; ready, ladies?"

Mrs. Gardner got up.

Melissa said, "No, *I'm* not," and started for the hall. Mr. Gardner was in the doorway, and as Melissa walked around him he turned all the way around to see where she went, the expression in his eyes similar to his look when he'd first found Hoover fractured. She stopped beside the Gothic wall niche, put down her handbag, and picked up the telephone. Making a call wasn't simple because the phone was draped by a creature resembling a shepherdess with many flounces. The creature had a face of silk on which tiny buttons had been sewn for eyes and nose and lips. The mouthpiece of the phone stuck out through her belly and the lower portions of the phone shaft were hidden under more silk. To get the receiver one reached under as though rifling the skirts, snaked the receiver free and pulled it and the phone wire out enough to clear the decks. Mrs. Gardner had assembled and sewn together this art object by consulting a pattern she'd clipped out of the *Woman's Home Companion*.

It wasn't till Melissa had nearly wrestled the receiver from its swaddling that Roy Gardner said loudly, "I forbid it, Melissa!"

Her mother stood behind him. "Oh, Melly—"

In ten feet of warm space between them, Melissa's eyes and her father's met and held. Suddenly they were strangers. To Melissa, the discovery wasn't stunning, but to her father it was kin to having been accused of embezzlement.

Melissa kept her eyes on his as she groped for the receiver.

She just had it untangled when the phone rang. She said, "This is Melissa," and listened.

Mr. Gardner looked around at his wife and said, "Well, now —that'll be Eugene, won't it?"

Melissa was saying, "Why, sure . . . Heavenly . . . Swell you called. Daddy's a little warm under the Arrow collar." Resenting the phrase but not saying so, Mr. Gardner patted his wife a bit. Melissa said, "Right on the corner, as fast as I can . . . No, you don't *have* to come over—I'll meet you there. Beside the benches."

Breathless, she said goodbye; her face was more radiant than the hall sun around her.

Mr. Gardner said, "He's waiting on Front?"

Melissa picked up her purse and took a few steps toward the front door. "No, Daddy, he's driving. He has to take some of those old men from the Civil War, the friends of General Cloud's—they lead off the parade." Back turned, spine straight, she could have been a dancer on point, about to soar. She was patient and polite, but in perilous balance.

Mr. Gardner said insistently, and with puzzlement, "Eugene? *Eugene*'s driving?" His voice sounded as if he knew the answer, and had known it before he asked.

Melissa was half facing him, speaking over her shoulder. "No, Daddy, Nick is. I'm going with him. There's room for me." She had a parting, helpful thought. "It'll leave more room for you and Mama, Daddy! So you could let some of the scouts ride with you. The baby ones always look so hot. Why don't you do that? I love you!"

She blew a kiss behind her, encompassing both. "I'll see you in the park . . ." Then she was gone, her voice floating back from the front-door screen. " 'Bye . . . !" Her feet were on the front steps, then swallowed by the lawn as she cut across it.

Mr. Gardner went to the hall and lifted off his Boy Scout hat, turning it over a couple of times with his fingers clock-dialing around its felt brim. Then he put it on, emblem-side-fore, though he didn't appear to care which way it went. He said softly, as if answering a spoken suggestion, "I will not, I will not chase after her." He faced Mrs. Gardner. "How would that look?" he asked. "What would the neighbors say to that?"

Mrs. Gardner murmured something, soothing and assenting.

He said, "Doesn't come from my side." He held the door open and Clare walked out. Then he shut the screen door, and after it, the outside door, rattling it to be certain it was locked against any robbery of the silver set, or the telephone's slipcase, or the Victrola, or, for that matter, of any single item among the Gardners' many possessions.

Outside General Cloud's house at the foot of the driveway, straggling along the street and around its corner, the Civil War veterans and their chaperones were waiting. The limousine, a touring model, top folded back and buckled, shone all over from Wid's polishing cloths; Lieutenant Strite sat in the middle of its broad rear seat between Captain Rance Todman and Major Belleau, and to their annoyance, roared out the chorus of "Marching through Georgia." His face was cerise, the time-refined face of Captain Todman aloof and suffering on one side of it, the close-mouthed face of Major Belleau turned away on the other. On the boot seat facing them, Harky, her lap piled high with food baskets covered with snowy cloths, looked up under the cartwheel brim of her white Leghorn hat. Sighting on Strite, she said, "Shut up! If you ain't got no more consid'ration than to sing that in the faces of them gentlemen, you make me sorry you won the war!"

Strite stopped his shouting; his shoulders shook. He leaned to tap in the vicinity of Harky's knee with a stabbing finger. "Oh, Sissy, thanks a hell of a lot! Didn't really win it all m'self, just main part of it. No 'fense, fella comrades—" He flung both arms back and brought them around the gray shoulders. "Guess Rebs c'n put up with me jist f'r today. Feelin' my oats."

Major Belleau, shifting quickly, removed the arm squeezing

him and shunted it back to its owner's side. "You'll kindly keep your body as far off as possible," he said. He coughed into a worn linen handkerchief—"Pardon me, Miz Lucas"—then tucked the handkerchief in the cuff of his gauntlet. "Times, a body of water separatin' old enemies does make a difference. Be glad to get back on my own side when this's over."

Captain Todman said to Strite, low-voiced, "Goes for me too, you blue-bellied shitheel."

Considerably mollified, Lieutenant Strite sat close-coupled, drawing in his knees. He said fretfully, "Where's the Gen'ral's grandboy? I wanta git *started*!" He rolled his head and his quid, and spat, just missing the folded fabric of the top behind him.

Wid said in Harky's ear, "If he'd hit that, I'd 'a spanked his old bottom." He was perched on the boot seat beside her.

In the front seat two very old veterans, their hair pushed like bundles of dental floss under their dark-blue campaign hats, huddled together. A daughter of the Grand Army of the Republic, blue-sashed, stopped beside them and prinked and patted their shirt collars, but they leaned away from her and continued their conversation.

Harky tapped her fingers on a basket handle in time to the band on Front Street. It had struck up "Beautiful Ohio," a waltz ill suited to its brasses, but a time filler. She said to Wid, "Song always puts me in mind o' Rex and Marna's weddin' party—orchestra Gen'ral had from Cincinnati played it four times. Wasn't even no war talk then—Tom Wolfson, bless his stuck-up old heart, said there wouldn't ever be none again, after that Spanish bumfoozle."

Wid said reminiscently, "Tom Wolfson had about the foresight of a good many rich men. Liked him a lot. Been a good thing, though, if he'd married again when the wife died, 'n not give Phyl everything she wanted. Let another woman in. Phyl got to thinkin' all she need do was stretch her hand to take what she liked." He extracted a match from his hatband and struck it on a thumbnail for the cheroot Major Belleau had taken out. In the same church-speaking aside, he went on to

Harky, "I'm like you, though, don't blame her. Can't blame Rex neither."

"Huh, you wouldn't, bein' a man!"

Wid regarded her expanse of organdy. "Always been glad I am, but can't say it's 'cause I think anybody's a weaker sex." He rubbed the arch of his nose. "Think maybe Nick's got a notion what happened back then. Couldn't hardly have grown up around here 'thout gettin' it. Think he's kept swalla'in it back, pr'tendin' it wasn't ever so, 'cause he likes the Bellamans so much. All this last night's brought it to a head. He was awful quiet when he come back from the woods today. Could tell he'd been in 'em, had mint-stains on his pants. And he smelled like dog."

"Well, you ain't his papa. Don't go readin' his mind, or puttin' things in it ought to lie back dead and buried."

"You ain't his mama neither—"

"Nearest he's got close around. Somebody's got to do that much," Harky said softly and fiercely. "Alice can't fill the whole bill."

"—and the past don't stay buried. Got a habit of rampin' right up out of its grave. Must be doin' a good deal o' that right now for Phyl. Maybe for a good many people, one way and another . . ."

"If you mean Jerome," Harky said, "don't be keepin' secrets with me. I always suspicioned there was somethin' goin' on there."

Respect touched Wid's eyes but he said with reserve, "I don't know that for a fact myself. But *not* knowin', can't say, and wouldn't anyhow. If it should be so, it's the worse for Jerome—right this minute."

Harky sat back abundantly. "Oh, fish, anyway. I'm goin' to *enjoy* the rest of this day. Try to, anyhow. Sins of the past hadn't ought to be sins no more when you got enough to eat and a mite of whippin' cream on top." In the next breath she said anxiously, "What's keepin' Nick?" She shot a glance up the hill to the house. "Where'd him and Buck go, anyhow, 'fore Buck done this week's lifesavin'?"

Wid said, "You'd ought to know you won't hear a mumble out o' either one on that score till snow flies. Had to be the cemetery, though."

She rubbed his hand. "You don't s'pose—them grand old urns—"

Wid shrugged. "Ugly as a ram's ass, all of 'em. Think Nick was goin' in to see his grandpa again a minute. Spoke of tryin' it if he could git past Angie. And if Gen'ral wasn't too tuckered from listenin' to these blatherskites."

Lieutenant Strite had gone to sleep, chin on his rumpled uniform breast. Captain Rance Todman lifted Strite's hat off and scaled it backward; one of the attendant-hero ladies went after it, but before she could pick it up, a brother officer of Strite's, who would be marching in the parade, stepped on it. She knocked its creases back into shape as she trotted back to the car, and handed it to Harky, who laid it again on Strite's lap and gave Todman an admonishing smile. The band on Front sailed into "Semper Fidelis." Todman picked up the hat again and fanned himself and Major Belleau.

Nick put Merlin in the Bellaman shed, where he gave him food and water; he hated to shut him in, since the door to the run stood open and he didn't believe Merlin had jumped the fence. The big house appeared lonely and far off, as it must have been when old Pierre built it, in those years when there was no other around for miles. He had the feeling, listening to Merlin lap up water, that the house waited for him but that there was no one in it. Foolish enough; perhaps Phyllis was there; perhaps she was asleep.

He cut across the grounds, past and around the pool. At the point where the driveway twisted down through the gates and he could have gone over to the house by a flagged, moss-fringed path or taken the drive, he hesitated. Toward the end of last winter one night after supper Cy Bellaman had taken him to the room he used as a home office. Like his office in the Shops, it was bare of much but a drawing board and some cabinets and a few pictures of geese flying in for a marsh landing. Cy showed him an old parrot cage he had unearthed from the long, cool cellars; in it a hawk perched with its talons gripping the bar as if it would break the wood. Cy said, "He's smashed a wing—maybe the high wind yesterday slammed him into a fence. I put on splints; if he doesn't rake 'em off, he may be all right." The hawk had its head drawn down between its shoulders as though it shrank away from the light Cy had snapped on, but its visible eye was cold and bright yellow. As they came closer to it, it shook its feathers and faced them more squarely. Cy said quietly, "He'd try to kill you, you know. Doesn't weigh more than two, two and a half pounds. But you don't have to be a moose to have that spirit. Marked me up pretty well when I doctored him." Nick saw, half concealed by shirt cuffs, the raking talon lines on Cy's wrists. "All he wants is to leave," Cy said. "But he knows the best way to do it—straight out, straight up. Nothing holding him . . ."

They discussed the hawk awhile, Cy saying it was a scale-shanked hawk, a male, but they did not spend much time there, and when Cy turned out the light and they started to leave, Phyllis was waiting in the hallway. It had been one of those suppers when Cy was quiet and Phyllis talked a great deal, as if she had to make up, if only to herself, for whatever had happened before Nick came. Nick liked watching her in the candlelight, hearing her, the words chiming like songs nobody else could make, a river of them running over the tight quiet of Cy.

She said as they came out of the office, "When nothing's holding you, you can go where you please, can't you?" and looked up at Cy, running a hand down his arm. There was a moment Nick did not like, while Cy's eyes widened, but the second after that it was gone and he said, "Let's play some mah-jongg." Phyllis answered, "No, dominoes," and took both their arms as they moved back into the high-ceilinged, deep-beamed living room. The fire at the end was reflected in the tiles of the hearth, and upward onto the gun rack across from the escritoire. Phyllis was inspired at dominoes that night; when she felt like it, she could win at everything. But Nick had thought of the hawk on his way home—the hawk was what Cy had wanted to be, he told himself. But there was nobody to heal him.

As he stood now, the house to his right, shrouded under generations of vines, the memory had come back in force like sunstroke. Finally, Cy wasn't held. Nick didn't think he'd ever have divorced Phyllis, or she him; they had been bound, maybe still were, by more than most people. He stood, remembering Cy's saying, "Stay away from her." No warning. Just advice. There in the cave, with his eyes level on Nick's.

After a few seconds he decided to take the driveway, thinking as he went out through the open dark iron gates, I'm not going to stay away, Cy. She needs me tonight.

On the rest of the way home he hurried, and when he came in through the kitchen Harky greeted him with her warm face, if not her words, plundering him for news. "You had sense enough not to folla Buck Bolyard inta the water, anyhow," she said. "I'm really amazed at that. He called a while back—hoo, there goes the phone again. Betcha it's him. Don't blab all day, you got to bathe and git fresh and drive all them old parties out there and—"

On the way to the phone he tried to make up his mind whether or not to tell Buck about the cave. Buck wouldn't expect him to if he didn't want to. But when he took off the receiver Buck did most of the talking; and following that, he talked to Melissa . . .

In the downstairs hall Nick knotted his tie before a wall mirror and walked along to General Cloud's bedroom. He drew a deep breath. The door was shut. He could see himself only with faint outline: the tie, the coat, the best trousers, the shoes, in its paneling. From the street below the boulevard oaks, far down, somebody was singing "Marching through Georgia," the tune bellowed but just recognizable because the voice had cracked a long time back. Then that stopped. Open the door and go in, risking Nurse Riffon's wrath? He set Buck's overalls and the fireworks against the baseboard. Straightening, he tapped lightly. There was no answer; she would be irate, asking if he didn't know any better, after the strain those old men had just put her charge through, than to come butting in here . . .

The knob turned from within, the door opened. Then the door opened farther. "Well," she said pleasantly, her voice low. "Just kind of wondered if you wasn't goin' to pay a real visit, show old—General Cloud—what his grandboy looks like when he's all spiffed up." She had noted his tie. "My! Bet you dance with all the ladies tonight!" Wistfully she added as she stood back, "I ain't been to a real bang-up dance since the robins flew back. Come on in—he's awake. Little color in his cheeks. He moved his hand kinda good a while back, too, when that—what's-his-name—that loudmouth with the real red face—"

"That's Lieutenant Strite," Nick said.

"That's the one. When he was here. As if he didn't want no more of him, but couldn't write it out or say it, so made himself articulate. Nurse word, it means moving your joints."

Nick thanked her and went to the bed. He stood at its foot, and the man in the bed saw him. She might be right, he thought; or was it the sun, lancing in more strongly now under the drawn curtains, touching a cheekbone, that brought the ghost of color. He said after a breathing space of contemplation, "Afternoon, sir. The parade's coming off in a minute. Just wanted to say hello again."

From the sheet edge a hand lifted, with infinite hesitation. The eyes of the man controlling it were deep-set, vivid, on Nick. The hand was above the sheet, then it moved side to side, a greeting, a wave of recognition from another shore. The scent of medicines and starch, the held-in atmosphere defining the room as a final trap, seemed with the hand to be banished. Then it dropped to the bed again.

"He done it again," Nurse Riffon said, marveling behind

Nick. "But he meant it nice," she added quickly. "He meant it real good this time," she assured him at the doorway as he thanked her again, retrieved his gear and went out toward the waiting, jubilating air—passing the portrait of Rex Cloud, who smiled triumphantly and ever young into the huge dark room.

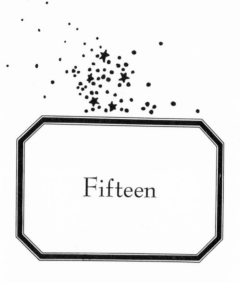

Fifteen

When the limousine had disappeared around the corner of the Cloud Block, and the sound of the parade boomed at last from Front Street, the Cloud Block was as quiet as a now deserted room where a children's party had been going on. Bits of paper bunting lay around the paving stones. A cavalryman's horse had left some evidence near a curb. An empty Mail Pouch tobacco sack was lodged in a bridal-wreath bush. The trees themselves brooded on the vacated lawns. The hitching posts topped with the heads of green iron stallions looked across the wide street with incurious blank eyes.

Then down the street came the Dodge driven by the Reverend Collis Bates. It was older than the sheriff's Willys-Knight but in better condition. It ran without tremor or fault, the bud vases attached to the headliners above the back seat holding slips of pansies in fresh water. These hardly joggled as Reverend Bates braked and parked the car at the curb. He walked up the driveway and lifted the door knocker with the *C* embraced by brass eagles. His black suit was brushed and impeccable, his white shirt flickered. He had delivered the musicians to the park, where they would wait in the pavilion for the festivities to start. When at length the front door opened to reveal Nurse Angela Riffon, he nodded pleasantly and said, "Good afternoon. I have come to see my friend the General."

Angela Riffon took a short breath. "Reverend Bates?"

"Yes, ma'am," he said. "We've met. Your brother was Joe Riffon—he worked morning shift in the Shops. You sometimes brought him his lunch when you were a little younger, before you took up nursing. He was an agreeable man; I regret his passing."

She said, holding the edge of the door, "Reverend Bates, the General's had a real strenuous day, 'cause of all them—because he had some of his old war friends in visiting. He's got to catch up on his rest."

"May I ask if he's sleeping now?"

"No, he ain't, exactly. But—"

"I'll be very quiet."

"Well," Angela Riffon said. Her face was more legible than some, and he read quite easily that she'd have been more comfortable if he had come to the back door. Since he was six or seven and his father, the second minister of the church, had said, "You will work but you will never beg," he had seldom entered a white house by a back door. The exceptions when he'd overlooked the injunction were rare, as, for instance, the time he'd been going past the mayor's house and had noticed the house was on fire.

He said now, "Even at his age we find time has passed very quickly. This might be the last time I get to see him—so I'd strongly appreciate the favor."

There was a pause of some length, some unresolved doubt, then Angela Riffon swung the door inward. "Right along here," she said rather stiffly. He saw her glance at his shoes. They weren't going to track in any obnoxious substance; they were as briskly buffed as the rest of him.

He took pleasure in the largeness and durability of the house, the fact that General Cloud had always built to last, both in the buggy days and the days of the Cloud automobiles. At the bedroom door he paused while she went in first, and when she wheeled around to motion him on, he inclined his head and followed. The deep curtains were drawn, but he found the outlines of a chair and drew it closer to the bed. The General was watching him, his eyes surveying Reverend Bates as they had often looked at him when he came into the General's office. They had worked for years on a plane of absolute appreciation for each other's abilities, as he'd worked with Cy Bellaman in the same manner; he felt at ease as he leaned from the chair with his elbows on his knees and his hands folded.

Nurse Riffon said uncertainly, "I was just about to make a cup of tea. Like one, Reverend Bates?"

He flashed her a glance of appreciation. "That'd be refreshing. Sugar, please—no cream." When she had gone he said, "Well, General. I'm sorry I haven't got around sooner. The minute I'm tiring you out, just shut your eyes—I expect that's the easiest thing you can do. Thought I might talk a bit about the old days, bring them back—they keep coming up in my own mind, especially when I'm in the Shops." Noel Cloud's eyes weren't shutting; he hadn't tried to nod, but the lids were farther apart than they had been, and he was listening. "It came to my mind this morning, the time you took your grandson with you on the test track, driving that eight the first time —and then I was recalling, too, the carburetion problem earlier, just a while after you'd taken me on . . ."

Noel Cloud's left hand was the nearest, but he didn't seem to be able to use it. His right hand came over his chest, like a deliberate old animal with a stubborn existence of its own. As Reverend Bates talked on, his quiet voice gathering the simplicities and challenges of the Shops as they had known them, the hand reached with pain but necessity from the bed and Bates took it. He held it in his closely, rebuilding the shared past as if it had never leached away, speaking of projects gone as if they were present and important; and when presently Nurse Riffon came back, she listened for a minute and then took the tray to the corner, and sat down behind a screen, drinking her own tea and waiting for a break in Reverend Bates's memories, but not able to tell him his tea would go cold if he didn't take it soon. It no longer appeared to be important to her that he hadn't come in by way of the kitchen door.

At first in the total darkness of his surroundings, panic and rage fought in him, and in spite of Buck's meditative advice to keep quiet, Eugene yelled until the ash dust clogged his throat and set him coughing. The coughing was at least as unpleasant as the results of the yelling had been, because, in its turn, it created more dust. He then settled back and down, glaring into the dark, and began, heavily, to think. He managed after a short time to reason that the furnace pipes offered the only potential exit. Standing then, with great fumbling care, ankle-deep in the leavings of burned Number Two Egg Bituminous, he reached for the lower edges of the furnace pipes, explored them with fingers which felt like borrowed tools—the skin between them was also imbedded with grit—and discovered laboriously that the pipe on his left was large enough in circumference to accommodate a good-sized body. He was by this time able to put away thoughts of Buck not coming back and his own bones being discovered by an amazed janitor, in the fall. He did have the feeling, though, that if and when he got out, the revelation to Mr. Gardner would not now take place; in this maw of a hellbox he had gained a certain perspective. It didn't actually matter; getting out was the first and only step to contemplate. Past that, of course, he would have to leave town . . . the town's dead loss, not his.

The stupid Kaplan child would chatter like a jay, and he would be hunted down and possibly strung up on a light pole in front of the Tribe of K, no matter how artful and forcible his denials. Even now Mark might be giving his fat smug daddy an earful, with Buck filling in the rest; even now there might be a posse on its way to this basement. And even if things stayed quiet awhile, the chance for revenge was blown sky-high; the need to go away from Arden was more than pressing.

He waited until the upheaval of dust around him had settled somewhat, and with no dexterity but a violent will to do it, swung himself up by the lower rim of the pipe as if he were chinning himself. Then, with the same immense effort, he managed to cram his head and shoulders into the pipe. He crawled and scrabbled farther. The pipe, its inside smelling of cold packed soot which formed a skin of grease that slipped under his hands and fingernails, took a bend upward a few feet in front of him; there was just room to kneel, and then, wriggling, stand up in this new, tighter prison. If he had been Mark Kaplan, claustrophobic by nature and gifted by an imagination like a wizard's strongbox, he would at this point have fainted. From his father he had inherited toughness of body if not spinal character and sweetness, from his mother he had learned, very young, that he was a being superior to all others, and though the rest had been formed as a paper doll is dressed with the handiest notions around, what he had was enough.

At his first assault on the inside of the pipe he felt the venerable tin give and sag outward; he then placed his hands at shoulder height, cramped but effective, and used the leverage to push with both while he rocked back and forth from one side to the other. There was a moaning of metal around him, a sagging of ancient rivets. A few minutes afterward a seam of light appeared above him. He redoubled his efforts, sweating copiously, his eyes shut against the mixture of sweat and soot and cinder flecks. When the pipe broke loose and tipped outward and down, he found himself aimed at the cellar floor, where green light swayed and the air was less polluted.

He breathed as deeply as his still-constricted chest would allow, and began working himself out. He made downward progress by inches, the chrysalis yielding with pernicious inflexibility, the shoulders of his blazer wadding about his ears. When he started sliding, he spread out his hands to take the brunt of the fall, but since it was only three or four feet, he landed without more than an extra bruise or so. For some seconds he lay heaped and free, the cool texture of the basement floor as welcome as swan's-down. He rolled over, and stood up.

He walked to a laundry tub used for washing out mops, opened a tap and splashed water in his face and eyes, sucking up some of it in passing. Then he leaned against the tub and looked at the wrecked and ripped-down pipe, reflecting that it was another point against him and would probably cost tons to repair. At the same time he was rather glad about the damage, a revenge much more modest than all he had planned earlier, yet real. He left the tap running and went up to the schoolyard, pausing as his head and shoulders came above ground level. He breathed warm air to the deepest pockets of his lungs. There was no one in sight.

He crossed to the drinking fountain, depressed the lever and drank awhile, watching himself in the water gathered in the fountain's discolored porcelain bowl. The Sta-Comb in his hair had gathered ashes like a Voodoo hat, and his eyelashes were plastered with a paste of powder. No matter—he was fit and able to move, and movement was important. The exterior Eugene could be repaired.

For a couple of clearer breaths he thought about going home now, quietly, bathing, changing—his blue serge was fit for travel, he had other shoes—but gradually his thoughts switched direction; to leave, get the hell out, was the vital target, which couldn't be accomplished without money. He did not intend to ride any rods or travel in discomfort. He heard the organ from the First M.E., and hoped his mother, wound up in the music, would stay there for hours. At any rate, there might be time before she quit to do what had to be done, then go home by back lanes and clean himself up. If Aunt Goldy was at home, she would be snoring her head off after the night work at the hospital. She might have something in her pocketbook, but that was small fry, like the few dollars and quarters and nickels and dimes in his mother's piano bench. He was after higher financing.

There were the mite boxes, stacked in the First M.E. closet with the choir robes and collection plate. But their potential yield was also slim. There were also private houses; but who knew when somebody might show up, and though perhaps not recognizing him in his pillar-of-ashes disguise, cause an embarrassing furor? But in the vicinity of the parade, in the lane running along behind the back entrances of Soames's, Flute's, the Argus, even Abe Melton's . . . while everybody was gathered on Front Street . . . ah, there you had opportunity.

Filled with new purpose, he left the schoolyard by a rear corner. And Eugene, like the Red Shadow sweeping with the Riff across plains of sand, went fast.

Out of the courthouse tower flew the pigeons. They scudded over the fountain and sent shadows skimming in blind caress over the fallen fliers, Captain Barnes and Sergeant Pringle. The two men sat morosely on the rim of the fountain and watched the parade start. They had been released from the hospital and brought to the jail by Tommy Beavis, and given the option of strolling in and out of the open cell. They had been fed after a fashion with blue-plate specials from Flute's, and they had the money anonymously donated by the Kaplans. They looked upon the beginning of the parade with eyes dour and proud, the scar-sprinkled face of the captain haughty, the pugnacious jaw of the sergeant sardonic.

Captain Barnes said, "Sergeant, there's the old offer—the mail job." His laugh was incipient, but did not quite explode.

"Oh, cat's sake, Captain. The mail. Have to keep regular hours, sir. Fly when they say, where they say." Pringle's tone had the rubbed quality of old argument. "No stunts. Straight as a meaching string. Chicken in our pot; car in our garage. Like streetcar conductors, cat's sake, sir."

"It's how the cards fall. Boche got us this time. Got old Jenny at last. Loved her as much as you. Not much left of her, soupy engine, had to compensate her like loving an old trull. They'll never make another one like her, she tried to the last

... thought at first these solid citizens did it, shot her up. Blast off the bluff, poom-poom in the park. But she did it herself, died on her own. Salute Jenny, Sergeant—her heart, her leaking valves. Her watery grave. Salute her, and damn the Boche —prepare yourself for Omaha in the morning, Sergeant, and good little mail planes. And salute!"

He passed the jar of Renfrew's best, which Tommy had treated them to. As Sergeant Pringle drank the parade advanced another ten feet, the lead vehicle aiming toward the courthouse fountain, the bulk of the parade noisy and imminent.

Pringle lifted the jar high. "All right then, sir. On this Fourth of July, country a hundred and fifty three, old enough to cut its teeth—to the country, to the old outfit, even to Omaha and mail routes, and to Jenny forever!" His eyes blazed.

Captain Barnes lifted his chin, his aquiline nose glittering with scar tissue. "To us all," he intoned, and this time he let the terrible laugh snort out. "Carry on, Sergeant!"

"Check, sir, and right!" said Pringle.

Nick drove the limousine in the lead. Beside him sat Buck and Melissa, and Candy occupied the right-hand side of the front seat. In the tonneau Lieutenant John Strite had defiantly, in counterpoint to the band, begun again: "Sherman's dashing Yankee boys are marching to the sea—" Major Belleau sat erect in gray and fading gold; Captain Rance Todman shouted, "I've chewed blue meat you had to hold on a bayonet to cook —but it smelled better'n this Yank!" Harky kept the peace as best she could, passing around a thermos of iced tea.

Nick thought, Whatever happens on this day and tonight, I'll remember it all my life. Everything seemed brighter than usual, outlined with meaning, everyone more his inmost self than ever before. Buck had finished telling him about Eugene; he found himself feeling a touch of sorrow for Eugene, almost the quick stab of regret he felt for what had happened to Mark. He nearly told Buck about Cy in the cave, swallowing it back with difficulty. Instead, he remembered his implied pledge to Cy, as important as the promise to Phyllis, and gazed in the rear-view mirror. Out behind the limousine those Civil War veterans who insisted on marching slogged along, their veins starting to purple, their faces slick. Their herders, the watchful ladies, trotted close to them, handkerchiefs soaked with sal volatile and spirits of ammonia handy for emergency.

Following the old veterans came the Kaplan roadster, with Mark, now in a blue sailor suit, sitting on Aaron's lap, his eyes enormous, his face unsmiling. Julian drove, and Leon and some of the other children threw confetti. Cheers accompanied the old veterans, but they were too intent on holding heads up, eyes on the line of march, to respond.

As the limousine drifted under the telephone-company windows Velma Temple leaned out and called, "M'lissa! Where's Gene?"

Melissa looked up and spread her hands in an I-don't-know answer, her face brilliant as she turned again to Candy Pruitt. She said, "That's right, it's a one-piece suit, yellow. Daddy doesn't even know I bought it. I had a terrible time talking Mama into it."

Their heads were close. Candy wore her sister's cloche hat of dull gold cloth, appropriated for the parade and picnic and dance. Her dress was also gold, with a fringe of beads that swished and tinkled about her knees. She had intense black eyes, her full lips were raked with lipstick, and because she projected a constant sense of celebration, holiday or no holiday, she seemed now at her best. She said with relish, "Buck's going to take us swimming—right after we eat but not so quick we get cramps and die. He knows a cove downriver . . . we'll shoot off their night fireworks before we go back to the park for the Kaplans'. Lissa, didn't your daddy just roll over and pant when you walked out?"

Lightly Melissa said, "If he did, he got over it. Look—he isn't even letting the little scouts ride." She frowned, then, bringing her eyes from the rear to the front again, and leaned closer to Candy, whose lips bee-buzzed at her ear. Under the band, which had now segued to "The Stars and Stripes Forever," Candy whispered, "Maybe we'll go skinny, won't need any suits at all. I've done it before and it's nice that way. The water just silks around you and you feel free as a bird. And, listen, about that other, don't worry about getting a baby . . . I mean if it happens. Nick thinks you hung the moon seven times over, and he—"

Reversing positions, Melissa said into Candy's small flushed ear through her polished jet hair, "I wouldn't care if there was a baby, right now I just don't care. I'll take my chances."

They drew back, looked at each other and suddenly laughed together in delight.

Hearing them, Wid thought, By God, they'll never sound that young again, and they don't even know it. He stared back past the Kaplans' overloaded car to the Great War veterans. Only two Vigilantes were now represented there—Muff Raintree and Slim Thomas. Tommy Beavis was hurrying from one parade end to the other, trying to discourage children from patting the fenders of the Baby Doll, cautioning cavalrymen to curb in their mounts. Muff, in his old line-sergeant's voice, which had no relation to his Ridge-man's drawl, rasped, "Dress it up, dress it *hup!*" Slim, a color-guardsman, balanced the flag butt in its holder on his belt, colors streaming above him like a sail flapping. Cannons rumbled darkly, the clatter and fire of draft-horse hoofs making sparks like little firecrackers under the horses' moist, veined bellies. The heels of the Great War marchers struck in rhythm, their uniforms weighing like heated lead, hats bobbing in unison. Wid thought of trench muck, rats, Red Cross ambulances, the smell of mud and death. In his mind a star shell burst over fields of ragged darkness. He sighted on the flag and came to a salute, detesting himself for it, but nobody was watching as his fingers touched his forehead, and as he felt both shame and pride at the salt passion stinging behind his eyes.

In the mirror, Nick made out the Spanish American veterans

in position behind the Great War soldiers, their rifles few, their marching casual, some of them singing hoarsely, "Oh, we'll put 'em in a bag—civilize 'em with a Krag . . ." Several of the rifles were actually Krags.

The Baby Doll rolled, majestic, Chief Gorseman at her wheel, fire hoses coiled tight, the chief vigilant, but Clammer Horston, his assistant, riding carelessly beside him, tilting a bottle of birch beer into his plowboy face. The five-foot thermometer, clamped to the post-office bricks on Front, registered one hundred and two in the tinted alcohol of its capillary bore. But it took the full sun, so that could be discounted. It was probably only ninety-eight or so in the shade.

Nick called back to Harky, "Want me to put up the top?"

She leaned forward. "No thanks! We're all bearin' up! Melissa, you and Candy are eatin' with us and the Bolyards, ain't you? Got enough loaves and fishes here for a multitude!"

Melissa nodded yes eagerly. Harky settled back and waved to the Bolyards in their car behind the Baby Doll, Carl beaming, Maidy's cheeks like cherry juice. Maidy answered the wave and patted Carl's right hand, which cupped her knee. "Going to dance with me tonight?" she asked.

Carl said, "Bunny Hug, Camel Walk, you name it. Fred and Adele Astaire, that's us."

"You said it," Maidy agreed. "Real Fanchon and Marco production." She nodded to Abe Melton, and his equally grave-faced helper Cuff Ainslee, both coatless, both soberly gazing out under the funeral parlor's awning. Then she looked back briefly at the Gardner Hupmobile, turned immediately to the front again and said, "Sometimes I'm downright glad you're a man."

Garnished by scouts trailing from its rear bumper, their neckerchiefs soaked, the Gardner car progressed, Roy Gardner's nostrils seemingly afflicted by smells of horse and mule. Clare Gardner said tentatively, "Melly has such poise, she will be perfectly all right." She glanced at her husband. "Are we planning to stay for the dancing?"

"Dancing?" Roy Gardner exclaimed as if she had said "orgy."

She looked away from him, rearward, where more cavalry clattered, and where farm wagons with agricultural exhibits bumped along, sheaves of very dry wheat bobbing, girls in patriotic muslin clinging to them; Elks, Rotarians, Woodmen of the World, Sons and Daughters of Church Groups; a popular local quartet whose "Won't You Come Home, Bill Bailey?" quarreled faintly with the band; then a line of the cars put out by the Shops, fenders quivering ominously. She inspected the parade's tail, and faced forward once more, folding her hands.

A glint of light from a tuba bell spangled Buck's ears, then lit up his fingers as he put his hands over his ears. He grunted to Nick, " 'Member the year Linicome fell down the manhole?"

Nick smiled. It had been wonderful; Linicome was a fearless clarinetist, near-sighted, of middle years. Stepping onto a manhole cover left askew, he had plummeted out of sight; they said if he hadn't hung by his elbows from sewer pipes, he'd have been swept clear to the river. He had continued to play, not missing a note.

Buck said, "That's what I like, every year it's different." He took his hands from his ears and sat up higher. In the tonneau the bickering of Strite, Belleau and Todman continued, on a steady but more exhausted note. Buck indicated them, and their marching brothers behind them. "Feel real bad about the old geezers, though. Feel that way *every* year."

Nick agreed, thinking of the old men, wondering how many would be back next year, thinking of them waiting for this through the winter. Buck was still sitting high, his eyes narrow, a plan spreading the corners of his mouth. "Well, hey, now. Let's just give 'em a little extra thrill this time." He pointed ahead to the fountain, the breakup point, where a clump of linns shadow-freckled the aviators. "Give them a little good cheer too." Then he took off his shoes and handed them along to Candy, saying, "Don't throw 'em overboard, they just *look* like lifesavers." As he stood up he said to Nick, "Try not to hit no sizable bumps."

With a light lift, as if he floated, Buck stepped over the windshield. He walked the long polished hood to the radiator, his shadow on it rippling. At the radiator cap he stood on one leg, extending the other backward, leaning far forward, raising his arms to form a hoop, his fingertips touching, his head lifted. He stared up at the sun.

Lieutenant Strite shouted for joy, then choked, Harky pounding his spine; Belleau and Todman and others called encouragement. Beside the fountain at last, Nick braked as if his foot were a feather. Standing on the fountain rim, Captain Barnes called, "Good show! Strafe 'em where they live . . . same man pulled me out, Sergeant! Croix de Guerre with palms!" Candy and Melissa wound their arms around each other, dissolving slightly. Buck jumped down, dusted his hands, bowed briefly and returned for his shoes, Candy kissing him as he took them.

The wave of good feeling cut through the usual regretful farewells to the old veterans; when Wid helped them down they were still laughing, and even as their chaperones took charge of them, they looked back with appreciation. Todman called, "Next war, you boys fight on the right side! Keep your peckers up—wish Noel the same!"

The band had stopped. A few pigeons were circling back to the courthouse eaves. The day was ripe, unending with promise. Nick caught Melissa's eye and they looked at each other for a moment as though they had never met, discovery leaping between them; then they looked away as if this were too much to take in, in a single second. Settling back, Buck said, "There goes the Kaplans, first headin' for the park."

Wid said, "Yeah, let's us move out, Nick." His eyes gauged the sun. "P'rade an hour late, this year. Two hours, last. Life's goin' faster all the time. Come on—I been piecin', but I got an appetite to shock a snappin' turtle."

As Nick backed and turned, Wid said to him softly, "Little worried about Jerome. Him, off on his own out there." His eyes lifted to Carmian's Hill and the Ridge. "Wish I could be with him. He's Lucky Lindy now. Him and Cy, off in the blue."

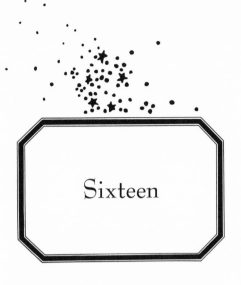

Sixteen

The sheriff crouched under a stand of loblolly pine and cedar, a dozen yards from the quarry rim. His hat brim down, shoulders slumped, he relaxed. The searchlight might weigh fifty pounds in the firehouse; as he packed it up-trail, it had gained a pound for every step. His arms still answered the pull and sparks swam before his eyes. The six wet-cell batteries hadn't been any easy haul, either.

Now the searchlight stood above the quarry, batteries ranged behind it like square black rocks. Remembering the lash-up Clammer Horston had advocated—wires strung in series, positive and negative poles linked—he rubbed his fingertips together gingerly, where copper wire ends had torn them. Neither electrician nor handyman, he felt the accomplishment of the amateur when something works which he knows little about.

He had tested the light. From the quarry edge, the beam it cast onto the railroad tracks and trestle was, in this glare, tenuous and faltering. But when darkness came it would be good enough.

He pushed his hat back. A house was nested on the opposite rim of the quarry, just under its lip, a building once used to store dynamite and blasting caps, cedar-shingled roof green with age, door hanging open, a haven for barn owls. Nobody had used it since the middle of the war. Quarrying limestone hadn't been rated essential in wartime, there weren't enough able bodies left for a big-scale operation, and after the war, things never got back to full time. A few people from the Colored Settlement chipped out baskets of stone with hand mallets, but on the whole, the quarry stayed lonesome as a loon's call all summer. In winter it had many human visitors; when the smooth, tabletlike floor had frozen over, it made a natural rink. Skaters would light fires around the base of the high-sloped walls and swing out freely, confident their playground wasn't going to turn into the often treacherous cat-ice of the river. You could play crack-the-whip, jump-the-barrels, to your heart's content. Sheriff Potter tried to remember when he'd last been there just to enjoy himself; it took quite a bit of casting back.

He'd been nineteen, and it was a night when fires leaped up with brilliant tongues, pine boughs snapping red and blue around the quarry flanks. The Clouds were having a skating party, Marna and Rex as hosts, Cy and Alice Cloud their attendants. A nine-year-old Phyllis Wolfson, wrapped in furs, standing with one of the Wolfson servants, Ike Hazer, beside the fire he'd built for her, watched them with longing and a certain anger in her huge quiet eyes. It had been well before the war, then; she was an aloof, watchful child who hadn't even gone into the local school yet, but accepted all the cosseting her parents gave her. He recalled her skating out on her own suddenly, and doing a tee-to-tum series of spins, starting upright, gaining speed, gradually stooping as her skates flashed and her skirts fanned out, then standing again and easing to stillness with perfect control. The Clouds and Marna Davenanter and Cy were watching, and in a moment Rex applauded, lazily, as one applauds a child who has done or said something beyond its years. He said, "Good kid! Looked like Pavlova for a minute!" Phyllis, cheeks flushed, stared at him without smiling, then turned slowly and skated back to Ike and her own lonesome fire.

Potter stood, digging hard fingers into his shoulder muscles. He doubted that Cy would make a move before dusk. There was no reason he should risk it. Wherever he might have holed up, he would wait, and move like a good woods ghost in the dark of the trees, to the water tower. Staying right there, watching for the least motion between the trees south of the trestle and the tower, would be Potter's job then; and then he would be positioned behind the searchlight, and ready. But it was too hot out there at the searchlight to breathe right now. In cedar-leaf shadow, he dug into a pocket for the crushed ham sandwich, wrapped in wrinkled waxpaper, he'd brought from Flute's Café. He peeled off the paper, inspected the bread as though it had spoken to him insultingly, then ate the sandwich conscientiously and drank from the bottle of body-warm coffee he'd also brought from Flute's; both sandwich and coffee were awful. He laid the bottle beside a pine root, balled up the paper and put it in the bottle mouth. Then he sat again, his back against a cedar trunk, and considered tactics.

Cy was by far the best shot. To wait for him under the water tower would have been to risk a shootout when they confronted each other.

On the other hand, pinning Cy with the searchlight, calling out that he was covered, wouldn't be enough; Cy might well get off a snap shot at the light. In which case Cy would have to be hit before he'd had a chance to raise that fine old rifle. But hitting a man where you wanted to, at this distance, demanded more than artful work; it called for out-and-out luck —you took the chance of killing him or missing. And there were myriad other possibilities . . . among them the one that if Cy did get off the first shot, even with the light in his eyes, he might hit you. Well, you stepped up to the booth at this fun fair, you paid your dime and took your choice. And you didn't walk off with a kewpie doll . . . you just walked off with Cy or you didn't. If everything went perfectly—which nothing made a habit of doing—Cy would keep his rifle down, realize he was well covered by a man with a searchlight advantage and start coming this way, around the north rim of the quarry, while the searchlight tracked him. The trouble with that was, Cy didn't happen to be a possum, easily dazed by a bull's-eye lantern, ready to curl up and wait for the tree to shake enough to toss him down to the dogs. The good part of it was, he wouldn't know how many people were after him and might well decide that several of his escape routes were covered.

Sheriff Potter felt satisfied on one count alone; this was he alone against Cy, no other contestants.

Yes, Cy and me, and whatever other wild cards the night deals, he told himself. He'd left the Willys-Knight steaming—because you had to put oatmeal in its radiator to plug the leaks, and he'd forgotten to do it today—at the foot of the trail where it couldn't be seen from the road. He had locked it because it had the rest of the Vigilantes' guns in it. There was no earthly use trying to cover the searchlight and batteries with grass or leaves; camouflage was impossible in this light, but when the moon rose from this side of the quarry, they would turn into mere extra shadows.

He tried not to think about Phyllis.

Yet, trying, he failed. She ran her own kingdom, its only ruler. For a while he'd been part of that kingdom, and maybe, for the same time, an important part. But thought of her now overwhelmed him for a few breaths, rushed in upon him, with affection he had never lost, and old longing that came back no matter what. And a pain as if he'd been struck a low blow in the groin.

He willed himself to think about the searchlight, about flicking its lever with his left hand, his right holding the Winchester. That much at least would be all right. Unless fate or Marty Broom intervened.

He watched the heat-quaking space between the distant

water tower and the end of the trestle. Phyllis . . . he was absolutely sure he wasn't going to get any sleep.

With care, silence and celerity, Eugene entered the back door of Soames's Pharmacy. This was the section where prescriptions were compounded, its drawers full of bottles labeled with the cabalistic writing only Marvin Soames could read. On a side counter the sunlight from the lane outlined a mortar and pestle; under the counter Marvin's cat slept. She was semi-Persian, with dark silver fur. As Eugene's soiled flannel cuffs appeared near her, she woke, and extended a paw to touch his shoes; then, fastidious, she pulled away, licking her fur, lifting a back leg as if she were bowing a cello. She didn't bother to look up as the drawer of the cash register slid out or as it shut. The trouser cuffs passed her again and the door closed, inaudible over the roar of the parade out on Front Street.

In the lane again, Eugene slid past the barbershop, but hesitated behind Flute's. He pressed his nose to the screen door. Grady Flute hunched at the end of the counter, in a shaft of sun; ignoring the parade, he had last Sunday's Cincinnati paper spread out and was following the adventures of the Katzenjammer Kids on one side, Rose O'Neill's Kewpies on the other. Eugene drifted along.

At the rear of the Argus, he pulled a dime-store comb from his hip pocket and inserted it between lock flange and plate, then opened the door and went in. He was in darkness as warm and close as a black velvet hat, air heavy with popcorn, cracker-jack, strong-scented chewing gum, disinfectant. He made his way around the piano pit, below the screen, where, the next night, his mother would play the overture to *William Tell* for chase scenes, variants of "Hearts and Flowers" for emotional close-ups; along the center aisle he traveled past splintered seat backs to Franz Otis' office, just off the lobby. He found the light switch. A wall poster of Theda Bara, kohl-eyed, moody, watched as he opened a desk drawer and attacked the cashbox. He slammed it against the floor in unison with the beat of the bass drum sounding from the street. It sprang open.

Once more in the lane, he approached Abe Melton's. Where was the cash in a funeral home? Not, he decided, in the viewing room, where coffins were displayed, and when occupied, banked with flowers. But the rear precincts would be worth trying. The lane door gave, and he found himself in a dim hall, another door ahead on his left; he tried this and it, too, opened. Inside, the darkness was as complete as that of the Argus, but much cooler—clammy. Somewhere, water plashed. He groped for a switch. An overhead fixture came on, bright as sustained lightning.

On a granite slab under it lay Henry Watherall, his body light-flooded, as if each crevice were entered by unsparing, colorless illumination; the intricate stitchery of army hospitals, on his right thigh and kneecap, an indelible-pencil blue; his hair, normally soft and rough, soaked and slicked back tightly from the forehead; his brown skin faded; and the lips, angleworm pale, drawn up in a broad artificial smile. The eyes were shut, and a pale-pink substance, now drying, had been worked into the right eye corner where bone had been shattered; his arms hung like clock pendula, and his feet turned outward. Rubber tubes leading from various points in his punctured flesh ended in a floor gutter beside the wall, and the plashing came from a garden hose which was washing away the blood.

Eugene examined the short muscular body, surveyed the sex and said aloud, "What did she ever see in you?" Then he made for the coatrack and Abe Melton's alpaca jacket, hanging there like the husk of its owner. Beside the rack a ledge held wide-mouthed jars of embalming fluid, one of them open and giving off a raw smell like varnish mixed with formaldehyde.

In Abe's pockets was a tin of Copenhagen snuff and a bill-fold. Eugene stripped it, replaced it and the snuff, and left. It was interesting to know how these things were done; a piece of information that might be useful. If you could put together enough pieces you got rich and respected. The power he had felt when he first put Mark in the fire escape was coming back; he felt himself martyred, but capable again.

He weighed his chances of visiting the Tribe of K, but remembered that its back door lock was sturdy. No need to crowd this luck. At that moment he glanced into the alleyway leading between Abe's and the Argus to Front Street, and in the same moment the Kaplan roadster appeared at the heels of the Civil War veterans, and Eugene saw all the Kaplans, Mark included. Everybody in the car except Mark was smiling, waving, and Eugene had the instant conviction that nobody else knew about the fire escape. Anyhow, not yet.

He dropped into the lane ditch, and a few minutes later came out on one of the somnolent streets he'd used to reach the lane; here, the noise of the parade was fainter, but he could no longer make out his mother's music from the First M.E. Stooping low, like a raiding Indian from *The Birth of a Nation*, he kept to obscuring hydrangea and sheltering oak until he reached the row of neat fences on which the Fisher bungalow backed. With growing hope he went in at the rear gate, then paused in the shade of the catalpas which Jeb Fisher had planted some years before going overseas. He looked at the baking stucco, the back porch. A change of clothing . . . perhaps a small rest before he put the town behind him. He climbed the porch steps and went into the kitchen.

The icebox, dripping steadily into its pan tray, was tempting; he had a hand on the door latch when his mother's voice, plaintive, vaguely frightened, came from her bedroom. "Eugene? Is that *you*, buddy boy?"

He moved from the kitchen to the head of the hall, where he could see her shut bedroom door. She shared the room with his Aunt Goldy; his own, larger, cooler—and warmer in winter —was across the hall. In the hall hung what amounted to an exhibit of Eugene photographs, even more than those of Melissa in the Gardners' living room; he could be seen on a photographer's bearskin rug, through Sunday school, into Epworth League, and in many scout activities. Among all the

Eugeniana was a small yellowing snapshot of his father. He remembered that there had once been a framed picture of Jeb with a lot of men from the old Cloud Shops, their arms around each other, Jeb standing beside the Reverend Collis Bates, but that his mother had long since removed that picture, saying that his father had had rough tastes, and that she knew Eugene's would always be refined, and that one didn't associate with Negroes.

He drew in his breath, gazed past the hall into the front room at the Chickering upright, the fumed-oak piano bench, the ferns, the Czerny exercise book open above the keys, and called very gently, "Mama, I had to come home from the parade."

In the same tone he went on, "There was this little boy, he fell right under one of the horses, and there wasn't anything for me to do but run and get him. It just kind of ruined my clothes, so . . ." He waited, and heard a bedspring creak. With great solicitude he asked, "Now, have you got one of your old, bad sick headaches?"

Milly Fisher's tremulous voice admitted it, but it was more concerned for him: "Yes, yes—but, buddy boy, you're missing all the fun. The Gardners, Melissa, your friends, the dancing . . ." Then she waited, as if she expected a denial.

"Oh, Mama," Eugene said. He laughed soothingly. "You know that all that's never been important to me. You know I have more worthwhile things to do . . ." His voice took on a lower, fonder quality. "It's real funny, Mama, I was thinking about you all morning. Kind of worrying. I could hear you in the church—it was beautiful—and I kept thinking, I hope those silly fireworks don't bring on one of her headaches, I hope she can just go on playing away, and shut out the noise. And then later I had this conviction, it was like a sign, it was right after I'd saved that poor little child . . . I thought, *Mama needs me.*" He paused, and this time his voice was lifted, resonant. "So do the righteous sustain one another in time of stress and travail." More or less to the door, he whispered "Amen."

Faintly, sighing, Milly called, "I'm always so *proud* of you . . ." When she spoke again it was flatter, as if she regretted having to come down from this plane to mention her sister-in-law. "Your Aunt Goldy left a note—she had to go back to the hospital, I don't expect she'll be home till late." Then she returned to the other tone. "Now you're here, I'll be able to sleep awhile. Oh, I'm glad you're home, I'm glad you're not going! And I don't mean it selfishly, it's just that all that crude music, all that noise at the park—they're beneath you." Then she sounded farther away, drowsy. "Buddy boy, do have something to eat, there's some of that nice tutti-frutti you like . . . take a nice bath . . . don't worry about me . . ."

In the kitchen Eugene extracted from his blazer the proceeds of his trip to the Front Street lane, counted it and left the money on the table while he stood at the icebox. For five minutes he ate steadily, then took off his trousers, shoes, socks, blazer and shirt, and in his grayed BVDs went into the front room. He lifted the lid of the piano bench and from under sheet music by Beethoven, and Ethelbert Nevin, took out the lesson money; then he visited the bookcase, removed a couple of the works of Ella Wheeler Wilcox, a copy of *Bunny Brown and His Sister Sue and Their Shetland Pony* and *The Little Shepherd of the Hills* and *Sermons of the Reverend Mavius Ackman,* drew out *Fanny Hill,* replaced the other books and went back to the kitchen. He put the lesson money with the other, dropped his underwear and went along to the bathroom. He shut the bathroom door, turned the tub taps, and while the tub filled, read *Fanny.* But she was nothing to the real thing; her exploits had, for years, been tame, so he cast her aside and admired himself in the mirror, noting that even the coating of dust had a virtue; it made him resemble Richard Dix, as seen in *The Vanishing American.*

Presently, lying in the tub, he found himself recalling with satisfaction how Mark had looked, crouched and still; he flexed his soapy fingers, reaching high and exultantly into the air. Suppose Mark had died? Nobody would have known, and if

Buck hadn't come along, it wouldn't have mattered anyway. And he would always be above all Buck Bolyards, all stupidity, and people of discernment would always appreciate him . . . he had a glimpse of them growing nicer and nicer, richer and richer; of himself, on a dais, swaying those people, moving them to do as the power suggested. Attendant maidens, white-robed, approached with offerings, and he ran his hands over them, solaced them, taught them how to solace him.

Out of the tub, he used four towels; then, in his own room —where Boy Scout knot boards, and butterflies mounted on cotton and bound in glass, spoke of past adventures, the little peaks of childhood—he dressed in sober serge, good for travel, and his second-best oxfords. His tie was a muted clergy-gray.

Back in the kitchen he pocketed his fund, and in the front room once more, took from a closet a handsome Gladstone bag, lined with kid, which Aunt Goldy sometimes used when visiting outpatients. There was nothing he wanted to put in it as yet; it would hold what he bought, and gleaned, wherever he was going. Out of a taboret drawer, from beneath a pile of mimeographed recital programs, he lifted the Smith & Wesson .38, which had been his father's. An ancient box of ammunition lay beside it. After experimenting awhile, since he didn't quite know how it worked, he broke the action, spun the empty chamber, filled the chamber and locked the action again. Joining the money, it made a heady weight in his pocket. Besides the snapshot, it was the single memento of his father left in this bungalow. He felt no sentiment over it. He had been told from an early age that his father had been a lout, and when he wasn't told, his mother implied it.

In the antimacassared armchair beside the window, where he could see the streetlight through leaves, he sat, the Gladstone at his feet, touching the owl heads on the grip of the gun. When the streetlight came on, he would leave. The sky around it was still bright, but subtly westering. The parade was as silenced as his mother. The locusts had the air to themselves.

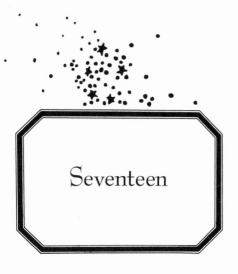

Seventeen

."My favorite time of day," said Candy. With Melissa, she sprawled face down on the rear thwart of the scow, a board so ample they could lie on it side by side, their toes pointing to the Kentucky shore. Now and then when they looked up they could see the park as if it were a miniature painted on the bank, the landing nearest, then lofty trees filtering golden light, the picnic tables oblongs of color, then the lacy pavilion, and the park gates far, far away. Melissa's one-piece swimsuit, the color of a fresh buttercup, fitted her closely—infinitely more daring than the old two-piece kind with their aprons dangling over short trouserlike legs; she felt the sun sinking through the wool, which was, so far, dry. She murmured, "Daddy's watching me; I can feel it. See if you can see him . . ."

Candy raised her head. "Honest, Lissa, I can't tell. He's still at that table with your mama. But I can't make out if he's looking or just sitting. Too far off . . ." She yawned, more with excitement than ennui, and rolled over. Her bathing cap was cornflower-blue, like her suit; the rubber earlaps clung to her cheeks; she trailed fingers in the soup-warm water. "Maybe he thinks you got poisoned 'cause you didn't eat with him . . . I ate too much myself, but I bet I could swim right now . . ."

Buck, on the middle thwart, had just finished spitting into the oarlocks to lubricate the tholepins of the oars. He said, "Just kindly hold your horses, lady. Nobody's swimmin' till we get to the cove. I'm gonna float us off downriver, 'n ride current till we're out o' sight. Nobody'll even know we're gone."

Melissa spoke down into her warm crossed arms. "He'll notice. He always notices."

Buck's bathing suit consisted of a striped top and sagging black trunks. Now he had started easing up the anchor, pulling the rope slowly over the gunwale with a gentle rasp; he bent to watch the anchor rise, and the watery halo of sand and marl that came up with it. When it was over the gunwale, he lowered the concrete-and-iron weight, wound the wet rope around it where it wouldn't touch the fireworks bag, and said to Nick, in the head of the scow, "Okay, Captain, get that ol' dingus out o' the river. None of us is ever goin' to see hide or hair o' that airplane again in our tender young lives. You'll ruin your eyes lookin'."

Nick could barely hear him; his head was encased in the viewing box which someone, years before, had donated to the park for the study of underwater phenomena. Made of rough boards, and glass-viewing panes sealed in by tar, it was frustrating to stare into, because time had greened the glass and algae flourished within it; one became interested in the life of the box instead of the life of the river. A water spider was trapped in it now; Nick watched it climb, fall back and climb again, and wished he could rescue it, but since he didn't know how it had got in there, felt powerless. Down below the bottom pane, river weeds floated in dark-green tendrils; sometimes there came a teasing glimpse of what might have been an aircraft, but was, more likely, a school of minnows.

Voice muffled in the box, he said, "But we're right smack over where she sank . . ." He pulled his head out, blinking, and sighted back to Melissa, whose right eye gazed at him over the curve of her arm, thoughtful, assessing, amber.

Buck had the tholepins settled, the oars trailing from them, his hands around the grips. He shook pickerelweed from an oar blade and said, "Where she went in don't make no never mind, I told you. Current's runnin' so strong down there, that Jenny's halfway to the Gulf. Bet it went into the Mississip' hours back, and'll hit New Orleans this evenin'."

Melissa gave a slight shudder. "Scary . . . thinking about things—all drowned . . ."

Buck said, "Well, don't think about 'em." As Nick hauled up the viewing box, Buck went on softly, "Don't anybody look towards the park now. Just pr'tend we don't even know we're driftin'." He had the oar blades feathered lightly backward along the scow's gunwale.

Nick could feel the pull of the river under the boards. Like the rest—even Buck, disobeying his own admonition—Nick risked a glance into the park. His aunt had joined them halfway through the picnic supper. He could see a flash of her red-gold hair from there and catch the outline of Harky's hat; he could also see the tiny *v* of the Kaplans' rocket trough, in front of the cannon, aimed toward the river, and the Kaplans at their table, but he couldn't see much of Mr. and Mrs. Gardner, whose table was set apart from most others. He looked away then, toward the Kentucky shore, and then to the water riffling around the square-cut prow. It was like being in large hands which took you wherever they wanted, served you up to the river.

He slapped at a mosquito. Buck said, "Citronella bottle, inside my towel." Nick, bathing-suit pants drooping as much as Buck's, his jersey top a washed-out puce, reached for the towel. Candy said, "Rub some on Lissa and me, Nicky . . . I love the smell . . ."

As Nick started back over the middle thwart Buck murmured beside him, "Oh-oh. Highpockets is onto us."

Melissa and Candy heard Buck, too; everyone was staring back into the park and at the raft, where young children had been flat-diving, and where, now, Roy Gardner had appeared. Small in distance, face a pale oval under the Scout hat, he had cupped his hands to megaphone his voice, which reached the scow clearly: "Melissa—that's enough now—your mother and I don't want you traipsing off there—it's dangerous . . ."

Melissa had raised herself to her elbows. "Oh, Lordy, oh, Lord. Please stop it, Daddy. Please, please stop it . . ."

Buck said gently, "Brick wall couldn't stop him, M'liss. We can go back if you want . . ."

Nick stared under his tangled hair at Roy Gardner. "It's me he can't stand. If I was somebody else, he wouldn't mind so much. Maybe we better—"

"No," Melissa said firmly. She was looking at water-lily pads slipping by, not at her father. Her voice was lower than the sound of lapping water. "We're not going back, so don't say anything like that. Let's just forget him for a while . . ."

Candy said, "You're a real brick, Lissa."

The voice lifted again, forlorn, indignant, weak but commanding. Like a heron's, thought Nick, when it's missed a fish. "Melissa! Your mother and I—are laying down the law! If you're not back in ten minutes—don't come home tonight! The door will be—locked!"

There was quiet after the last, just audible words. Then, even lower, muffled, Melissa said, "Mama hasn't got a single living thing to do with this. She never, in her whole life, said anything like that." Her face was flushed. "He hasn't got any right, any right to yell all those things where everybody can hear. Oh, Lordy, oh, Lordy woe . . ." She buried her head in her arms.

Candy rubbed her shoulder. After a moment Candy said, "All right, it's over, honey, you can sit up and look around." She smiled, fully. "Nobody here but us chickens."

Melissa's head came up. The west shore had intervened in a green curtain. The park was invisible; ahead, the river glittered, mocha and blood-red, the Kentucky bridge far to the south, a splatter of ironwork and boards arching east and west.

Inching backward, Nick opened the citronella bottle. Candy

sat up, thrusting out her legs; Nick cupped oil and worked it around her calves, her knees and her arms. Her fingertips turned up, and she began to glisten. Nick thought it was no wonder she was never chosen to play the part of a mother in any school drama—you just didn't think of Candy that way. Like Melissa, she would get older, but something in her would always shout, say "Hooray!" He felt himself respond to her muscles, the bright flesh. But there was cameraderie between them; it wasn't like touching Melissa. With Melissa, beneath the friendship pulsed the need, the blind wishing.

Finished with Candy, he knelt over Melissa, sprinkling oil on the backs of her long thighs, her tapering calves; massaging it in, he felt his need grow, also blindly, and was glad his suit sagged at the crotch, accommodating this. The pungent oil filled the air. Melissa sat up, looking downriver, and he rubbed her spine, liking each small bump there, the beauty of the nape as it rose like a flower's calyx out of the shoulders, the heated skin over the sturdy yet delicate shoulder bones. Women were all miracles, this one a special wonder . . .

Buck hauled on the heavy starboard oar, keeping them straight in the current. Over his shoulder he said, "Tell you what, Lucky Louis, you can do the rowin' when we head back. Won't be till dark since we want to shoot off our own stuff. Might miss the Kaplans' rocket. You git over to their table, take a look at it? Goin' to tear up Barlton. Candy, slap some o' that stuff on me. These damn midges think I'm their ice cream."

Candy crowded forward, working over Buck's back and arms; Nick, sitting beside Melissa, their thighs together, said, "Sure I saw the rocket. Wonderful!" And to what was visible of Melissa's ear under her bathing cap, he said, "He didn't mean that about locking the door."

"I don't know if he did," said Melissa. "I don't care now." Her eyes were wild; it was the mood of the Victrola session again, but with something else, more reckless, more sure of itself. Nick put his arm around her, and she turned to him as if she were famished and he was food; they kissed as the cry of a bird tumbled through brilliant air above the bank reeds. When they drew apart her lips were open, moist, the lipstick she had borrowed from Candy smeared on her upper lip.

Candy glanced back from Buck's rippling shoulder blades. "Lissa, you can stay at our place if you want. Mom won't mind —in the morning I'll show you the new kittens, there's a batch, that old cat turns them out like lemon drops . . ." She tossed the citronella to Melissa, who raised it above Nick's shoulders and, palms flat, spread it on.

Melissa said, "I'll be all right, honest." Nick wished she had sounded more sure about it. Out of the corner of his eye he saw Melissa and Candy exchange a long and knowing look, summing up their own secrets, which were interesting, and yeasted in his own consciousness. Melissa dabbed oil behind his ears; he caught one of her fingers and put it to his lips; the citronella tasted like revolting medicine, but it didn't matter.

Then Buck was shouting in a rooster crow, "Ladies, passengers, we're here!" His voice lowered. "Couldn't even tell it was a cove, could you, now?" His tone complimented the hush of the shoreline where they drifted. He rested on the oars and nodded to the west. "Right in there . . . prettiest thing since buttered popcorn. Get set, hang on, we'll smush some sand goin' in through the grass. Then there's a creek, a stream—you'll see."

He was angling sharply toward Kentucky; as the scow swung, nothing they saw ahead resembled a landing. Tall grasses shrouding lily pads grew in a half-circle from the shoreline, small frogs leaping from the pads as the scow drove into them. A turtle dropped into the water, surfacing at once, periscope head alert. The smell of shore mud walled out the sharp citronella. Then the scow was blundering through grasses, Buck taking long, deep sweeps of the oars. Nick leaned to grasp a willow trunk, and pulled; his neck muscles stood out like cables. Then the scow had wallowed on, Buck was shipping the oars, their blades tip-ended with muck, and as he shipped them he said, "Everybody out, and haul like hell!"

They jumped out in cool sand and mud while fingerlings with transparent bodies darted under them and crawdads scuttled away. Hands on the gunwales, they pulled the scow through the last of the marsh grass until, suddenly, it was floating again—this time in clear water. When they had it a few yards upstream they pulled it onto the bank and turned to look at the hurrying, dancing stream. It rolled down over a series of dark rocks with pink and blue veins shining through the waterfall; a long flat rock hung above it, over a pool round, deep and gin-clear to the sandy bed.

Buck gave an enormous stretch. "Ain't the *worst* cove in the world," he said happily. " 'N the water's good as gold . . ." He stooped, cupped and drank; then all of them were drinking alongside him. He was first to rise and slap his belly. *"Now* we can swim," he said. "Dive right from the ol' dornick up there." He was putting an arm around Candy, drawing her with him up the slope. Her hips were joyous, Nick thought; they seemed to strive as if she were a willing pony in a race. He took Melissa's hand; they climbed behind Buck and Candy. The rocks were slippery, water flowing around their feet. Buck and Candy reached the diving rock, Buck suddenly outlined against the sky, Candy appearing beside him, and both of them taking off their bathing suits as though they couldn't stand the feel of them for another second, Buck yodeling as he tossed his trunks away and they sailed like a black misshapen bird almost to the scow. Candy's suit followed, landing downstream, to snag on the bank. Nick pulled Melissa the last yard.

Beside him, Candy was wearing a suit made entirely of her own skin, the cream and gold of her body defined by her darker arms and legs; her buttocks were tensed, her body arched as she raised her arms, the line of the fleece between her legs like a sleek nest, her breasts lifting and taken by the full sunlight. Her face was alive with freedom. Buck, head back, heels planted like trees on the rock, legs muscled and copper-shining, scrotum tightening in the updraft from the pool, reached to pluck off her bathing cap, sent it skimming away. Her hair puffed out in black brilliance; she shook her head like a young colt. And this time when Buck called out it wasn't with words, the need to sing and praise ululating from him, and still sounding as he and Candy were gone into the pool.

Then it cut off with their resounding double splash. Nick, Melissa's hand in his, watched the shiver of sand at the edge of the pool as the splash wave touched it, then Candy and Buck gleaming as they came up. Candy's hair was in soaked love-locks and mare's tails, arms and legs churning as she swam ashore, her buttocks rolling sweetly with her strokes. Buck emerged beside her, passed her like a brown flashing distance runner surging for the tape, and she raced after him as he vanished inland, both of them dappled with gold for an instant before they were out of sight.

Nick looked away from them, straight at Melissa. Her eyes were deer-wide and wild; under the yellow wool her nipples were outlined clearly. She moved her hand in his, then pulled it away and said "Yes!" And in the next breath her hands were on her shoulder straps. Nick felt a flood of warmth rushing through him, and under it a passing curiousness. How do I look to her? he thought, pulling at his own suit, tossing away the top, stepping out of the trunks, feeling the stream-updraft wash around balls and penis head, touch the skin of his belly, breathing it up through flared nostrils.

For a moment he didn't move, staring at Melissa. She had dropped her bright suit on the rock. The bathing cap lay with it. Her hands were on her hips, clasping the hipbones like buckles. But when he took a half-step and swung against her, drawing her to him, her arms shot around him, her breath a warm slipstream in his ear, nipples sheltering against his chest —he thought of young woods strawberries. When they stepped a few inches apart he felt his growing, rising, not-to-be-stopped hardness, his testicles climbing again in the fire-and-chill of the air. She looked at him, down at him, her eyes skimming to his nearly standing penis, back to his face. She smiled, half willow, half woman; her arms went up, and she dived. He was off the rock a second behind her.

In the water's shock he opened his eyes, saw her body, turning to surface like his, breasts buoyed and sustained by the pool. They swam, together, to a log. Her hair had turned to a golden animal's, water beads diamonding her forehead, cheekbones. He clambered onto the log, reaching for her. She steadied, with the arch of a foot against the log, which dipped, then he had pulled her up, and she wound an arm tight around him as he laced his around her, his fingers firm on the cleft of her spine at her haunches.

Dry grasses hissed around their legs. They had gone far enough into shadow, and they drew each other downward, into the soft, billowing grass tent. Her eyes were so close that he could not see the rest of her. Seeing didn't matter. They moved into one another, and she cried out, then said, "It's all right, I'm fine, Nick," and kissed him, her tongue working, her head far back, her eyes so drowned they were both white and amber. A last thought came: if you deflowered somebody, it was good to do it near running water. Then, no thought—the syrupy sound they made, and a certain lightning, in the sky over them.

As Alice Cloud walked past the mayor's house—far too large for him and Corabelle, but inherited and so prized forever— she noticed that some superbly enterprising child had blown two tines from the antlers of the iron deer in the mayor's front yard. No doubt he and Corabelle would grieve over this awhile.

But most of Alice's mind, free for a while from the hospital, was taken up by Phyllis Bellaman. She told herself that she should have abstained from anger; talked to her, reached through the tough shell of loneliness. Too late now. It was always too late when it came to Phyllis, and Cy . . . it was like him to leave town now, this way. He would detest a trial as much as Phyllis would. The judge would ponder at unconscionable, dutiful length; the lawyers would rattle papers and drone on in the high, fly-specked courtroom chamber; and all of it would have not a scintilla to do with Cy or with Phyllis, or even with Henry . . .

Or with me, she had thought, walking quickly in the breathless air. What Cy and I were was overtaken many years ago; my own innocence hasn't recovered; I just became someone else. Now she thought about Henry Watherall, the victim of those years that had fused for Cy in an instant of rage.

By the time she came in through the park gates, the plain action of walking had cleared her mind. She found herself enjoying Harky and Wid as she always had when she and Rex were children; closer to them than she had been to Rex, or to her father and her mother. She listened to Wid and Carl Bolyard as they remarked with wonder at Melissa Gardner's riding in the parade with Nick, and that she had gone with Buck and Nick and Candy in the scow. Alice said, "Don't upset the applecart. Roy Gardner's back is turned on me, as usual. He's as full of himself as two eggs."

Alice had missed the sheriff at the park, and when Wid whispered to her that he had insisted on going after Cy on his own, she still wasn't going to wish the sheriff luck. Through lowered lashes she watched the sun spangling the river, the scow balanced against the current, far out, and thought that this hour was, after all, placid; eating, drinking, celebration went on wherever you were, linked to life and death, their quality measured by how much the eaters and drinkers believed in living . . .

Tommy Beavis, uniform coat unbuttoned and spread to let in air, sat at the bench end in a technical argument with Aaron Kaplan at the next table, over how far ten rockets, lashed into a unit, could travel. Aaron said he believed five miles; Tommy said no, only a mile or so, because their combined force was offset by the extra weight and they would drop faster. Rebecca Kaplan sidled along, then perched near Alice, allowing herself to be admired; Mark Kaplan stayed next to his father, eying the impressive, consolidated rocket which was now balanced in its trough, destined to be the forerunner of the Kaplan night entertainment. At the pavilion the Colored Settlement band blew preparatory notes on cornet, trombone and saxophone, and the bass fiddle growled. Alice looked over at the rocket and thought, amused, that it was perfectly phallic, which seemed right—ready to make rude love to the sky.

Then she turned her head, listening to Roy Gardner speak to Tommy. She hadn't heard him approach across the grass, threading his way around men who were hunkering on their heels, blowing on grass blades, talking crops, murmuring about sales figures for the cars now produced in the Shops. Maidy Bolyard leaned toward Alice and murmured, "Oh me, the scow's gone. Here we go."

Alice shaded her eyes against glare; yes, the scow was out of sight. She looked back at Roy Gardner as he said to Tommy, "All right, you're the law. Potter didn't even bother to show up here this afternoon, did he? Go on, get a boat—I want my daughter back." Tommy's face remained blank as Gardner went on, "She's been kidnapped."

Harky sat up with the appearance of a considerable seahorse sighting down its nose. She leaned on the table, one hand beside the remains of a latticework cherry pie, the other beside a platter of chicken bones. She said, with some majesty, "Yessir, Roy. I seen it all. Just like in *The Black Pirate*. Nick and Buck, they slid down the sail on that scow, cuttin' it with a knife, yelled like banshees and sailed it off right into the sunset, with a young lady under each o' their arms." She shook her head. "Aw, Roy, heaven's sakes, go on back and set with Clare —since you don't want to mix with no other hoi polloi around here."

Roy Gardner glanced at Harky. "I didn't come over to talk to the Cloud servants, or the Clouds. I'm asking Tommy what he's going to do about this."

Wid unkinked himself from the bench and walked to Roy. He said, "We've worked for Gen'ral Cloud longer'n anybody else around the house ever did, but we ain't servants. He don't think we are, and we don't either. We do a job and that's the

232

whole ticket." He was inspecting Gardner steadily, calmly. "I got some advice, Roy. Take a walk and cool your britches."

Turning away from Wid, Gardner said to Tommy, "Well?"

Tommy said, "Look, them kids didn't do a thing but start downriver. If you'd like to do some rowin' yourself, I'll help you tote one of them boats over 'side the pavilion into the river. Except most of 'em are dried out, so you'll have to bail awhile."

Gardner said, "Is that all you're going to do?"

Tommy said, "What else?"

For a moment Roy Gardner appeared to regret his loss of control; even his loud calling after his daughter. But he had gone too far to back down now; Alice noticed a tic in his left eyelid. He said in a tight, slightly overloud voice, "I warned her. My house is shut to her. Clare and I are going home now . . ."

Carl Bolyard rumbled, "Roy, I don't give a damn if you never buy no more meat from me, I'm here to tell you that's an assy thing to say. She ain't a bad girl, she's a good girl, like Candy, and she's in hands that'll take care of her. Won't let her drown . . . and Tommy ain't goin' to take out after her. They ain't robbed a single bank, includin' yours."

Gardner pointed a forefinger. Alice thought it was sharp, like a wasp's stinger. His voice was even tighter, a half-tone higher. "Your son's nobody to brag about, Bolyard, nor that girl Candy. And young Cloud hasn't had any rearing at all that I know about. Raised to do as he pleases, mother showing herself off onstage—"

Carl stood with such force that the bench rocked. Wid had taken a step closer to Gardner, which put him in body touch.

Alice exhaled and said thoughtfully, "Roy, just hold it down. You're confusing law with morality. You do that a great deal, you know. As for Nick's raising, I know something about that —it's been casual but it's been solid. If he didn't like Melissa, he wouldn't be with her now. If he wanted someone for mutually satisfactory rape, there are plenty of those around. I know you're upset—possibly Melissa's talked back to you. But that's

233

your own problem, not my business, or anyone else's at this table."

She saw his lips moving until he found his voice. "It's your fault, Alice Cloud—you and people like you! Putting up with the mayor's incompetence, letting Potter and that crowd run roughshod—"

She bowed her head briefly, wanting to laugh but holding it in; her tall body cast a trim shadow on the table, her green suit gathered light from across the river. Raising her head, she said, "There are elections coming—you have a vote, and influence, Roy. I've never wanted to run this community myself or pull its strings—there are due processes, you know. Father never wanted to run it, either. He wanted to make a car as good as, or better, than any other made, and for a while he did. And about Marna—she's not here to answer you. She'd do it more succinctly and wittily than I. Jerome Potter, too—I may not always agree with him, but when he's out of office you'll never get another man as good. I guess that's about all, Roy, and a happy Fourth to you and Clare, anyhow." With her eyes, she signaled to Wid and Carl to stay where they were. "I'm defending all this, reluctantly, Roy, because it doesn't really need any defense."

Gardner turned and walked away and Harky said to Wid, "You done just right, not hittin' him, Widdicomb Lucas. Ain't supposed to hit anything punier'n you. Showed good judgment."

Carl said, "The fart wouldn't fight, anyhow. Beg pardon, Alice."

They watched Gardner and Mrs. Gardner gathering up their baskets and belongings. Then they watched them leave the park by the far side, Clare a few paces behind, hat feathers subdued, dress hem floating softly in her wake.

The incident had unsettled Alice. She found that her hands wanted to shake again, that within, she was raging, at the years and at time, even at Cy now; why couldn't he have resisted Phyllis? Why, back then, couldn't he have stood with Alice

234

Cloud and shored *her* up? Why did being alive require so much accommodation, so much compassionate flexibility, which was harder to come by than any diamond? She thought of going home to her quarters behind the hospital tonight, of reading Molière or anything crisp and sane. And of being by herself; sufficiently. Alone, some said.

Aaron Kaplan bent from the adjacent table. He said, "Here," offering her a linen handkerchief. "Got one of those little gnats in your eye, I guess. They swarm all over, this time of evening . . . Reba was just saying to me, you are always so collected. Like a field of wheat, you know . . . calm like that." She returned the handkerchief and he added, "We'll wait for the first star to show, then send the rocket to Barlton. I think it'll please you."

Alice said, "Of course, it will be magnificent, Aaron."

Her eyes met Mark, who was standing now, looking at her. She thought, Why, he looks as though he's grown today, as though something has come that wasn't there before; a sagacity, a knowledge not leaving him disillusioned, but making him see farther than he has until now. They inspected each other gravely, then both gave the merest trace of a recognizing smile, and looked away once more.

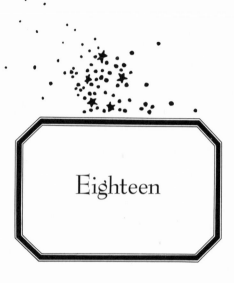

Eighteen

All day sun had beaten on the truck garden and the flower patch beside the path through the Watherall's clearing. The ground under the rows of carrots and radishes, onions, beets and squash, friable but hard on its surface, turned to clods that broke between the fingers and exploded in dust; but beneath, it was wet with dark river-earth, and the roots of the weeds slipped up through it as Phyllis reached and pulled, reached and eased them out; there was a rhythm to it which pleased her. It sent the mind to sleep, used only the body like a well-lubricated machine; with her thighs stretched, the tendons of her heels tight under the steady strain, she moved from plant to plant, placing the weeds in the old split-cane basket. She was now working on the onion sets; her hair swung like a dark cape under which she could barely see Tilda Watherall, weeding two rows over; she breathed deeply, thinking that these onions lacked the sharp scent of new spring onions; these were fat with summer, pungent with a heavier odor.

As she inched along, knocking each weed on the earth after it was extracted, returning earth to earth, then thrusting it in the basket without looking behind her, she considered the sources from which she sprang: Pierre Wolfson, who, in the steel engravings, looked fierce and arrogant—taker rather than giver—a man who gathered in his fists every inch of land he could claim for his own. With the softening, veiling influence of local historians, he was called a benefactor; she'd never thought so. He, Carmian and Roberts had cut up the spoils, buccaneers around the treasure chest. She put her head back. Tilda Watherall was speaking, for the first time in minutes: "You're a handy worker, Miz Bellaman, but you're overdoin' yourself. Get sunstroke, mebbe." The tone was patient, dry as this surface soil. Against it played the chill sound of spring water welling from stones at the end of the clearing. "You c'n go in, take one o' Henry's old hats—on pegs, back o' the door."

Phyllis let her fingers rest on warm soil. She said, "I never wear a hat outside at home." She shook her hair back to see Tilda better. And found herself asking what she had wanted to ask for an hour, "Why don't you hate me?" There was no answer; she listened to the spring water for a moment and went on, "I took your last boy. My husband did . . . but I was the reason. Why didn't you order me off the place?"

"Ain't much use blamin'." The voice was slow, tired, but strong, weighing the question fully. "No more use than in cryin'. Blame's not yours, or even Cy's. Not with Henry, neither. And cryin's just for ourselves, it ain't for the dead . . . Why, I like your company. You don't chatter and carry on. Needed company today—didn't know it, till you come, but it's been an easing. Mebbe we even need each other."

Phyllis said, "Maybe we do . . . I wish you'd been my mother."

Tilda's voice was now only loud enough to touch the moist, still air. "Wouldn't have been easy for you. You'd ha' married on the Ridge; lived harder, lived different. But it don't signify, anyhow. You're a Wolfson—born that, stayin' that. Last of 'em." Almost delicately she said then, "Never wanted no children?"

"Oh, yes," Phyllis said. "I wanted a child."

"Couldn't have your own, why'n't you take one to raise?"

"I didn't want one that wasn't mine," Phyllis said.

"Blood kin . . . well, I had blood kin. And I'm the last, too." She was working again, talking as she stooped along her row. "Soon's we get cleaned up down to the fence there, we'll have a bite. Got greens and side meat on . . . then, I'd like a hand up, loadin' the coffin on the wagon. It ain't so heavy, empty like it is—good pine, just light and stout—but I ain't got the grit I had once. Can ride with me down into town a ways, if you want to. And help me pick out which shirt I'd ought to take with the good suit—the stripéd, or the plain white." She paused, then said, "Harby Nellis and his boys'll help with the buryin' at sunup, tomorrow. If you been thinkin' you'd ought to help out with money, you can put the thought away. Henry's war insurance'll do me all right. The papers is made out to me."

"Yes," Phyllis said. How fatuous I was, she told herself, thinking I could intrude here, send money. This is a wholeness I have never had.

She took hold of another weed; this one deep, calling for a side twist to bring the root webs out. When she had tossed it back and was reaching for another, she saw the intruder. It was uncoiled, a flake of sun touching the triangular, turned-away head. The serrate, arid scales looked as though, if touched, they would whisper like autumn leaves. The body of the copperhead was a thick single muscle, relaxing. She sat back, hand hanging in air, then withdrew it gradually, from shade to sun. She called quietly, "Tilda, would you bring me the trowel? I think it's alongside your basket."

Tilda squatted, sun from the river casting red light over her eyes, her dusty dress, the snub ends of her shoes. "If it's a cottonmouth, or copperhead, you set quiet—I'll get a rifle. They come up from the water—got their nests in the bank. Start plaguin' in spring, don't leave off till first frost." As she stood, her shadow fell long on the rows.

Phyllis said, "Just the trowel. I can handle it. I'll hold my hand back—just put the trowel in it."

Unmoving, watching the copperhead, she heard Tilda's footfalls softly approaching. Then the caked trowel handle settled into the palm of her hand. She adjusted her grip, turning the handle as if it were a knife haft. She could hear Tilda's breath and her own, and feel the waiting copperhead, and smell it.

Her right arm swept down, pinning the body just behind the head, where the triangle narrowed. Under the blade of the trowel the head flattened, then canted up, the jaws opening, the fangs, ivory-white, arching from the lining of the lips; the body was suddenly an electric cable. Leaves trembled as it fought. The tip of the tail swung in a blur, the body frantic against the stabbing pressure, trying to come free and coil.

Phyllis brought her left hand to bear with her right, digging in with full force, wanting to laugh for exultance. She shook her head to clear her eyes and then felt the flesh sever. And while the body still writhed, she took off the pressure and straightened, handing the trowel to Tilda, who bent and cleaned its wet, blackened point in the earth until it shone again like polished coin silver.

Phyllis said, "At home sometimes there are garters, blue racers—but they're good for keeping down insects and mice."

Tilda answered, inspecting the snake, "Big 'un. It'll thrash awhile. I'll get a spade and put it on the woodpile." Her gaze came up to Phyllis. " 'Bout ruined that pretty dress. What I said—you're a Wolfson. They never went under easy, what I've heard. You done enough today. So've I." She looked down to the river through willows, birch, an arcade of water oaks. "Them greens and the meat's about ready. We'll go in and wash up and take our bite. Time then to harness Tobe—dark drops quick this side the Ridge, it's a good ways comin' back." This time when she reached, her hand did touch Phyllis' arm. "Strong and hale," she said. "You come on in the cool of the house now."

When she'd gone for the spade, Phyllis stood brushing

crumbs of splattered earth from her arms and from around her face. She went to the spring, cupped water and drank thirstily. She remembered her father, Tom Wolfson, telling a family legend about old Pierre. The winter Pierre's father had died, only he and his mother were left in the cabin where Pierre later staked out the Wolfson house. Pierre and his mother had buried the father behind the cabin, on a dark frozen night, heaping stones on the grave to keep the Indians from knowing the man of the house was gone. Phyllis didn't remember what tribes her father had said they were: Algonquins, Pottowatto-mies, a strayed Sac or two. This country had still been theirs then in fee simple, the cheating treaties not even begun. Tom Wolfson had told her about the dwindling cornmeal in the cabin, the remorseless snow; their stomachs hollow and stretch-ing with starvation.

And then one day there was a knock at the door. Pierre, two or three years old, was grasped by the arm by his mother and pushed behind her. Then the knock again, and the woman went to the door and pulled the latch string through, a rifle in her hand. The door was flung open and an Indian was standing there, half in furs and half naked, his face not even interroga-tory but fixed in silence, his shoulders bearing the body of a fresh deer, rear hoofs lashed. He had taken two strides into the cabin, flung the deer on the table and left, not even glancing at the rifle in the woman's hand, leaving the door open behind him on a league of snow and bare trees. The Indians had fed her great-great-grandfather Pierre and his mother the rest of that winter; they must have found the cairn of stones over the grave almost as swiftly as the father had been buried there. Pierre had passed the tale along, as perhaps a luck piece for his kinsmen, and Phyllis had always relished it.

Yes, she thought, I have that strength. Losing is not final; death takes away, but what was stolen can be replaced. I'll not have to use a wall to keep me from knowing myself anymore. It has been shattered too. She saw, again, Nick standing before her in the hospital room.

Balancing her weed basket and Tilda's, she walked up the path between the rows of flowers and vegetable plants, hungry, already savoring the food on the roots of her tongue.

Because it was still too hot for the hunting coat, Cy folded it over his arm, and with the rifle in his other hand, left the cave. Harbingers of dusk hung through the heat; he tested the air, feeling the change, enjoying it. He had had, since his boyhood, the hunter's ability to be swallowed by any terrain, like a leaf, a log. It wasn't just a matter of soft-walking, but of fraternizing with whatever was around, of settling in. Henry had had that quality down to the marrow. Sit quiet, go quiet, feel quiet.

At the mint-bed creek he drank again, then worked the second chocolate bar from his pocket and ate it, crushing the wrapper into a pellet he slipped back into the coat pocket. He angled up through fiddle fern and wet, bright-green moss to the peak of an incline where Robert's Gulch started, its water twilight-green in its four-foot depth. The uprights of the trestle were black as a grid against the sky. He skirted this creek, moved nimbly in the shadow of the next trestle, then, past it, climbed the embankment to the railroad tracks, and followed them until the sound of Foe Killer grew. He paused at the north end of the trestle and lay full length between the ties. Through them he could see water, rocks, spinning white foam. He folded the coat and propped his arms on it, chin on his hands, rifle alongside, and waited. From the south end of the trestle he would have been, in this light, a mere trick of shadow. An early-out barn owl cruised across the trestle a few feet above him, wings silent, face a malevolent ghost's; it drifted downward as he watched, into the trees near the river.

When the sun went under he waited still, feeling the mist rising, and on his arms, under the small hairs, the difference in the violet air. Gazing between the ties, he saw the shadows already around the water stones, the wild cress now gone from liquid, vivid green to dark blue, the racing water plumage, foam and sliding bubble, standing out above the polished hastening onyx. Before a star had showed and while it was as blue around him as though lighted by a single gas flame, he got up and went on. Stepping off the trestle, he stood quiet. From here he could see the leaves like the walls of a tunnel ahead, then the open space, still rosily burning, past that; at the end of the lighted area was the water tower. There was too much light as yet. He folded himself off the tracks, between sugarbushes, sitting cross-legged in the dark hollow, hearing the creek bustling, and an animal—badger, he thought—coming out of its earth.

Ahead of him the light decreased steadily; far down across the tracks at the other flank of the stone quarry there was complete darkness. When he couldn't make out the shapes of grasses growing outside the rails, he got up and let himself down the embankment, through wild cherry and leggy daisies, until he stood at the west rim of the quarry. He made his way to the stairs leading to the quarry-house walkway and the door. The boards had spread in the heat and he took them one at a time, putting his weight down carefully, then settling forward; aside from one creak, which might have been a bat, he accomplished the door without other noise. When he was inside the house he laid his coat on the floor and sat down on it, nostrils wrinkling at the musty deserted tang of the place; there was no window, but he could see out through the doorway.

A quarter-moon was rising; it had not yet reached the other quarry rim, but sent light spreading around the pines, outlining their needles in rough dull pewter. The quarry house had trapped and held the heat, but aside from that, it was ideal. He would hear the whistle of the Nickel Plate long before it arrived. He didn't know whether all the Vigilantes would be clustered near the water tower, hiding around it and waiting; it was hard estimating where Jerome might have deployed them. But from the house back up to the tower would be a kiss-your-hand jaunt in full dark, and from the trackside to the train a few steps. He did not intend to wait under the tower unless he had to; if Nick came to see him off, he would be in the grasses near it at that time, and attract his attention; he regretted his own sentimentality at asking Nick in the first place, but it was done now.

In the cove the contents of the night fireworks sack had decreased until all that remained were the two fire balloons. Buck had built a modest fire of driftwood ends beside the stream. Now he parted the thin, whispering balloon paper, unfolding the package with caution, the pale-blue, egg-white and primrose panels unfolding slowly from their creases, the first balloon already promising magical expansion. Nick thought, It will be about five feet high when it's full and floating, and how do the people in China pack it all in that little space?

Candy, lolling back, one leg extended, her ukulele resting in a transverse position on her re-suited stomach, strummed and sang, "Throw a silver dollar—on the ground—and it'll ro-oh-oll —because it's row-ow-ownd—"

Nick turned his attention from Candy to Melissa, who joined in, her voice smaller than Candy's, as if she couldn't at the moment put much heart in it. He felt another dagger of remorse, one of a thousand which had visited him in the past few hours. Along with it went sympathy, in protective waves; he wanted to step through the firelight and comfort her, say some enchanted word which could smooth away her trouble. She would never, now, be the Melissa of the porch swing again, and that might be splendid, but there was bitterness in it, along with the charge of joy, and the wanting her again that had come back afterward. The bitterness was against himself, for doing what could be called "taking advantage"—the joy was an unsaid, ready-to-burst feeling of vast tenderness, for which he had no name. Love—to tell yourself you loved her—was too small for the feeling. It was a feeling of constancy, of having been pledged. He dug his fingers into the sand, sifted it and felt the grains fall, his chin on his knees. And he tried to catch Melissa's eye, but Candy's rich alto had stopped, and she and Melissa were leaning together, whispering.

Buck said affably, "They got all these secrets. Come on and help me get this thing off the ground."

Nick brushed sand from his trunks, firelight filling his eyes as he rose. He helped Buck stretch the fragile paper; then, as Buck said, "That'll do 'er—now touch off the candle," caught the matchbox Buck tossed him, knelt and held a match to the candle in the paper cup which swung in a string cradle below the balloon. As the flame blossomed and the balloon began filling with warm air, crackling gently, Candy and Melissa stopped whispering and leaned back to watch. Candy struck a low chord on her ukulele. "I just love those things—they're kind of like a good dream . . . who ever knows how far up they go?" Nick looked around at Melissa, but she sat, knees drawn up, pinpoints of candle flame reflected in her eyes, watching the balloon, not him. Buck, his hands now holding the balloon as its swelling upper curve pressed against them, said with fondness, "Yeah, like girls, pretty and soft and floatin' around . . ."

Then he said, "Here she goes," and took his hands off. For another instant the balloon stayed where it was, then began ascending. Its frailty was its strength; only something so light could have become so much part of the air. Ten feet above their lifted heads it was touched by a thermal rising from the stream, in which it shivered daintily. Then it moved toward the mouth of the stream as if drawn by the river, illuminated inside by the pulsing candleshine, still rising, bearing a secret message to an unknown place. Suddenly Melissa clasped her hands and said passionately, "Oh, it's lovely," and then her eyes were on Nick's. "It's so rare, isn't it? I'll always, always remember . . ."

Her voice was small, rough, nearly breaking, but she wasn't going to cry again; her eyes were as dry as they had been after the love-making. Her eyes stayed on Nick's while Buck clapped his hands. Buck's voice broke the spell of the balloon, but not this other spell: "Okay, crew! Man the boats! Don't leave nothin' behind—scoop up that towel, Candy, don't forget your fancy bathin' bonnet—we're sayin' goodbye to this here cove for now . . ." He jostled Nick, holding out the remaining balloon, still in its tidy and remarkably small package. "Here, this 'un's yours, that other was mine. Send it up some winter night 'n tickle the natives."

Nick took the package. Splashing water on the fire, which steamed and went out, Buck stepped away, hoisting Candy, ukulele, towels and gear and all, to his shoulder and stalking with her to the scow, while she beat a light tattoo on his shoulder blades and shouted for joy. In the fading dusk Melissa's eyes were still full of the vanished balloon, and of something else; Nick held out his hand, she took it, and they walked after the others to the scow. Then Melissa said, "Can I have it?" For a moment Nick didn't know what she meant; if it was the moon, he thought, he would try to get it for her. Words struggled in him, half formed, as if memories of some enormous eloquence out of a past life were nearly, for a few seconds, audible; his arm in hers, he stopped walking, and she stopped with him.

"The other balloon," she said, whispering under the steady stream sound.

He put the package in her hand. She held it between her breasts and gave him a brushing kiss. "You taste like smoke and water . . ." Her voice shook. She looked down at the package. "I won't keep it for long. I'll send it up, so you'll see it, after I get home . . . so you'll know I'm there, and everything's all right."

Nick found his own voice, no eloquence in it at all, only his urgency—to protect, to affirm. And he said what, after all, he had never brought himself to say on the swing, or in the back row of the Argus, or even in his head, hearing it come out without amazement, knowing all it meant had been battered and worn by overuse and misuse, yet feeling its life and strength: "I love you." Perhaps when you said it so, nobody had really ever said it before. Different for everyone. Light as a valentine, just as strong as death.

Her head lifted. This time, not to kiss. And not even now to speak, with everything accepted, acknowledged, answered.

Buck was roaring from the scow. "Get crackin', troops, we'll miss the rocket! You're rowin', Cloud, this thing ain't got no Gar Wood engine—highball it, will you?"

Running for the scow then, where it had been pushed by Buck back into the stream water, Nick gripped Melissa's hand as she ran with him, and said, "I can take you right home, if you want to go—your father . . ."

Her water-stiff hair flew, and she said, "No, I want to dance with you—tonight. We can leave the dance early . . . don't even walk me to the door later. Just put me down outside— I'll do the rest . . ."

In the scow he leaped for the middle thwart, Melissa crouching below out of oar-sweep range. Buck, toes spraddled on the bow thwart, facing back toward the cove, said, "Pull like Billy-be-damned till we hit the river, the way I did comin' in." He kissed his fingers to the diving rock, the rambling, importunate stream, the daylight gone and the pleasure. Nick took the oar grips; the locks creaked, the blades caught, raised, caught again; Buck splayed the heels of his hands against a willow, pushing, leaning like a bridge between boat and water; then, as the scow came loose, he threw himself backward, Candy catching him and both of them tumbling on the floorboards. Then the stream was buoying the flat keel, reeds and grass were releasing them, and they were swinging into the river. It was a dark glittering wide lane leading north, and south, across the world. Candy struck her ukulele strings: "In the evening—by the moonlight—you could hear those banjos—ringing . . ."

Nick, pulling against the current, felt Melissa's voice against his knees at the same time he heard it. "I hurt, a little. But it'll go away . . . I guess nobody can ever tell you about it, not even Candy . . ."

Buck's minstrel-show baritone blended with Candy's lucid singing.

Nick said, "Maybe nobody can, even if they want to. You

were a flower. You're a flower. You always will be."

But I can't call her a Paul Scarlet rose, he thought, because Phyllis is that; and that's no robbery, is it, saving that for somebody else? Maybe Melissa would understand that, sometime, but it didn't have to be explained right now. The feeling of having betrayed Melissa was almost a ghost, as if he had, when he declared himself, entered a free new dimension; jubilation worked in his muscles, sent the oar blades dipping in deep-sprung rhythm. In a little while Buck, turning his head to peer northward, broke off his particular rendition of "Mary Ann McCarthy She Went Out to Gather Clams" with "Let up a little now, Noah, the ark's comin' in safe to port."

But Nick had already seen the growing red shine of water in their wake. He lifted the oar blades, let them drip and over his shoulder saw the park. It was a green cave, lit with crimson; railroad flares were signaling from the diving raft. On the raft stood Wid, hands on hips. He bent to help warp the scow alongside, nodding to them all. "Could hear you threshin' water half a mile off, figured you'd wanta git back for the big blast. Just made it in time." He was helping Candy to the raft, then Melissa. "M'liss, your papa's right upset—guess you already knew that. Anyhow, him and your mama seem to've left the party. Dunno how serious he is about what he said, but me and Harky got an extra cot over the carriage house if you want it."

Melissa held her purse, towels, her bathing cap, loosely in one arm, the little balloon package tightly in her other hand. Candy moved over to her, laying her arm across her shoulders. Melissa said, "Thanks a lot, Mr. Lucas, but I'm going home no matter what." There was no quaver in her now; she didn't have to glance at Nick for him to know she felt him there, sustaining.

He and Buck upended the scow and turned it over, river slugs and snails shining along its keel. Nick wedged the viewing box safely under it and stepped with Buck onto the raft, and for another moment all of them looked back into the park. Wid said at Nick's side, "You c'n take M'liss home in the big car, Cap. Whenever you want to leave. Guess most of us'll stick around here tonight till the last dog's hung . . ."

Buck said, "Hey, we ain't none of us even goin' to have time to get decent duds on to see the rocket go up." He gestured to the rocket trough, surrounded by a knot of people.

Wid cast a glance over his shoulder, at the sky. Above the river hung the first star, like a seed pearl. "That's so. Aaron said the first star'd be the go-ahead." He swung his head back. "Well, everybody hold tight, and don't breathe much. And if it shoots straight at us, everybody just go straight overboard—ladies first," he added, bowing slightly to Candy, who laughed delightedly.

Nick felt a communal silence; it reached throughout the park, from the river to the cannon, the pavilion to the rest rooms, to the gates. Faces of children and adults, in the waiting instant, shared the same wonder. He saw his aunt, her fingers on the shoulders of Mark Kaplan. He took Melissa's arm just as the rocket was touched off.

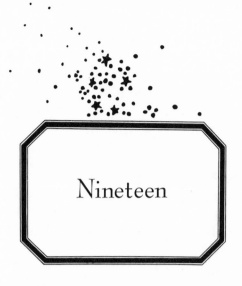

Nineteen

The Kaplan rocket launch marked a division, a special moment of demarcation everyone in Arden—and in the Colored Settlement, and on the white side of the Ridge—afterward held to be important. In the autumn the stock market would fail, Black Friday come; the United States would go into a cataclysmic depression, and Arden change forever with it—and many would look back to the Kaplan rocket as the peak of the old days. Traveling across the velvet sky, it was like a moving finger, a summing up of things past and an augury of things to come. Even those who, for one reason or another, weren't in the park, or didn't happen to see the rocket; those who were tuned in to WLW, Cincinnati, or listening to Carlton Coon and Joe Sanders' Nighthawks from Kansas City, or asleep, or ill—even those were touched.

Alice Cloud, with her fingertips on Mark Kaplan's bird-boned shoulder blades, felt her heart expand like a filling wine-skin as the rocket shuddered in its trough and left. It left smoothly, a trail of roaring, varicolored brilliance behind it, and a pall of smoke rising above the trees. It left with dignity, speed and precision. By the time it reached the river, Leon Kaplan had not had a chance to drop the match with which he'd lit its central fuse. And Julian was still open-mouthed beside the trough, and Aaron was steadying its boards with his foot. The ground shook as if a minor quake had happened. No one shouted now; there had been no time to shout. Spewing flame from ten cylinders, the rocket burned in a great trajectory over the river, which was suddenly flaming with turquoise, lapis lazuli, garnet, gentian, emerald and sardonyx, keeping these colors for bright seconds after the rocket had reached Kentucky. Then, at last, breath was released, there was a victorious outcry; the Kaplan brothers congratulated one another; they were congratulated. But no one looked away from the rocket.

Alice felt it as if she herself rode upward and out, as if it transported her to an earlier, simpler and assured time when each incident held doubled meaning because Cy had been there with her. She sucked in her breath and said to Mark, "Look, look at all the little fire folk sitting on the air!" The poet's line was meant to apply to stars, but this man-made star had perfect qualification. She knew its furious surge as though she arched with it into the distance; she was allied to the child in her and the child she touched; they shared the flight.

Nick and Melissa watched, holding each other with fierceness that transcended their individual emotions. Wid and Harky murmured, "Ah, damn now!". . ."Ah me!" As the rocket took off, Tommy Beavis had forgotten his job of keeping children and adults from coming too close to the firing point; Muff Raintree and Phil Thomas, Great War helmets long set aside, sucked in their cheeks and slid their eyes to each other. They smiled and forgot their concern about Jerome Potter's whereabouts. The rocket swept aside the tragedies of the day and consideration of the night to come. Behind it the air was different; it held more ozone. Harky said, for the rest of the night, at intervals, that she didn't mind now having missed Halley's Comet, because she'd seen its superior.

No one was ever certain, but it may have been the Colored

Settlement band, waiting in the pavilion to begin the music, which first noticed that the rocket was coming back. By then, it had been out of eyeshot for about half a minute; nearly everybody had blinked, cleared his vision and turned again to the picnic tables to start cleaning up odds and ends, anticipating the pinwheels, Roman candles, generous fire fountains and sky bombs to come. But the band had a better view of the whole sky than those closer to the riverside. It was Henny Dervis, cornet in hand, who leaped to the railing of the pavilion and sang out, "Here she comes again!" Buck, Candy, Nick and Melissa had started toward the men's and ladies' facilities around behind the pavilion, to change to dry clothing; they were the butts of a little cross-talk by their peers, answering catcalls, and questions about where they'd been, when Henny's call rang out. They turned around, as did, gradually, everybody else, to see what Henny's lifted cornet was now indicating. Buck said, "Well, God sweet damn!" Melissa's eyes widened; she stiffened as if her father had appeared, breathing retribution. Alice Cloud, seated on the bench again, took Mark's head in her hands; she let him nuzzle into her bosom as though he were hiding from Nemesis.

Everybody, later, agreed that the return was at least as awesome as the outgoing flight. It came quickly, staggering back above the river; losing nothing of its fire, but erratic as a loco horse, dipping and rising, yawing from side to side, searing air above the treetops so oak leaves were scorched, and passing above the pavilion. Then it flattened out and veered southwest, disappearing.

This time it left behind more than congratulations. The Kaplans were murmuring, "Maybe it'll show up *again!*". . . "Anyhow, it did fine on the way out." Rebecca Kaplan was so pleased, and uncontainable, that she threw up. Tommy Beavis asked, "How much powder'd you put in that catamount, anyhow?" and Julian confessed that in the heat of invention, he might have added force to the original rockets, but didn't remember how much. Carl Bolyard bellowed soothingly, "All it'll do is land in some corncrib way past town!" Most people concurred with this. After all, it was only a home-built device with an adventurous extra load to it, wasn't it? Couldn't last forever, or keep circling and showing off. It had had its chance to show Barlton that Arden existed and was kicking. It had made its legend. The Kaplans nailed pinwheels to the oaks with tenpenny spikes and set them going. Presently everything was almost back to Fourth-normal again, with Harky rubbing butter on the foot sole of a child—Morgan Hargis—who had stepped on a radiant sparkler wire.

Meantime the rocket had been seen, well marked, both going and coming, by more people than those now gathered in Arden Park.

On its outward, confident climb to the dusky west, it spread magnificent color backward over the limestone quarry. Here it brought the sterility of neglected stone alive, making the northern quarry depths stand out as though winter skating fires had been lit in the basin—bringing Sheriff Potter to his feet as if he had been gigged by the throat. With dusk, he had left the pines and stretched himself behind and above the searchlight, his Winchester handy on the harsh, rocky soil, his hand ready to flip the searchlight's activating lever at a second's warning. He hadn't slept at all; there was too much to think about. Not the least of it, his worry that in the treeless space between Foe Killer's trestle end and the water tower, he would somehow let Cy get by in that moth-wing moment between the end of twilight and darkness—a time when you saw what wasn't there, didn't see what was; when if you were ever going to hallucinate, you would. But when the moon came up, its light would fill the questionable area. Then a squirrel would be noticed if it scampered over the ballast and ties toward the tower.

West of the embankment, past the trestle, there was a drop-off straight down through thick trees to bottomland; Cy wouldn't try to go down that way and get around.

Potter moved very little. He cursed in silence when an image of Phyllis Bellaman came to touch his secret parts, handling them with scorn and dexterity. If he could have brought himself to hate the thought of her, he would have. As sweat dried on his forehead, his arms, the backs of his legs, he wished they had never met—that he, Cy and Phyllis had never lived in the same town, not even the same county, state or country. A red ant climbed his arm; he blew it off without looking away from the railroad tracks and the trestle end.

He had fallen into a frozen mood which had nothing to do with comfort or discomfort, when the rocket appeared to the north. Even as reaction and alarm brought him up standing, he remembered Aaron talking about this, and hated himself for not remembering a few seconds sooner. But he doubted that anyone watching now would have seen him; Cy, if he were around, would have been distracted, too. The rocket's trail spread majestically, incandescent peacock feathers brushing the roof of the quarry house before they slid on over the river; then it was gone, its brilliance still in his eyes in aftermath, as if he'd been staring at an electric light and now had to blink away the filament burn. He lowered himself again behind the searchlight.

There was no movement at all between the trestle and the tower.

When the rocket came back, he refused at first to believe it; it was completely odd, as aberrations must be; it appeared northward, park-aiming, then changed direction once more and swooped erratically straight overhead, a spirit trailing hairs of fire, and landed somewhere on the other side of the quarry in the trees. And as it went over, it brought him, the searchlight and the batteries into full, staring relief.

He hadn't risen this time. He was staring out where the rocket had fallen when the shot came. He heard the glass in the face of the searchlight shatter, the bullet hit home on the inner curve of the reflector and then sing away in a long ricochet through the quarry.

Glass was still falling from the searchlight as he got to his knees. The humming whine of the ricochet died.

Rage filled him as though he had been shot, not the searchlight. He bent over and around its face; the heavy lens was gone, and glass shards clung to the circle of metal like uneven teeth. He stayed on his knees and picked up the Winchester. Out before him the quarry was tomb-silent, yet something seemed to be quietly laughing. He stood up all the way, stepped over the searchlight and moved quickly to the extreme rim of the quarry, down so far that warning shale bits dribbled and clicked under his feet, spun off into the depths. He lifted the Winchester, took a breath and aimed at the railroad tracks where the trestle ended. He squeezed off, heard his shot break and then the back echo taken up by the quarry, bouncing from stone to stone.

He had reloaded before he realized with sickening conviction where the shot had come from.

He aimed at the quarry house. There was no one on the walkway or the stairs leading down to it. Cy would have left the house the second he'd put the searchlight out of commission. A good place, Potter thought; a damn good place—and one he'd never once considered. He realized now that Cy hadn't meant to get to the tower till the last second. And now he was out of the house; and the whole thing would be hide-and-go-seek around the tower.

He kept the Winchester up. Right back where we started last night, he thought. Most of the luck and skill still on the other side. His anger was going down; he felt a spasm of admiration. Cy's skill at chess; his hunting patience—they added up, and the searchlight had been so perfectly eliminated . . .

Bet he even recognized it, he thought. And figured it better be put out of the way, even if it would tell me he was in the vicinity. And got a kick out of thinking about me borrowing it from Ovid.

Sighting at the trestle, the sheriff whispered. "Oh, come on. Just step out of those trees around the near side of the trestle, where I know you are now, and we'll call it a day." But Cy wasn't going to, and anyhow, it was a donkey ride from here to there.

Let's see now, he thought. I could find a trail down, and cross the quarry, and go up the other wall, and come out below the trestle. But I'd be a walking target down there because the moon's starting to come up higher now. He's watching the moonlight just the way I am, and he knows that when it gets past that open space between the trestle and the tower, it'll be dark enough so he can cross there. Easy, with Ovid's searchlight gutted.

Well, there's only one way for me now. And there's time for it. I can skirt around the whole north rim of the quarry, weasel up through brush on the embankment, and try to get a bead on him when the train stops.

He lowered the Winchester.

He kicked the searchlight—which rolled over with a crash —and started back for the pines and cedars, and the circuitous route around the quarry rim. He felt somehow closer to Cy than he had for a long, long time. He breathed and walked carelessly now, not caring whether the other heard him on this first part of the journey, and even snorting, once, as he thought about the great rocket. Thank you, Aaron, Julian, Leon, he said in his mind. I hope you enjoyed it, and I hope everybody else did too. In both directions.

Leaning against a pine at the trestle end, watching from resin-smelling shadow the moonlight on the rails in front of him, Cy got back the breath it had taken to come from the quarry house and climb there, and felt admiration for Jerome Potter. He himself would never have thought of that old searchlight, and if he had, he would have thought twice about the difficulty of hauling it into place. It indicated a doggedness, even a certain caring, which he liked. He was fairly sure Jerome was the only one out for him now—he had listened carefully for other voices, after shooting out the light—a simple target, no danger of hitting anything or anyone else—and as soon as he was sure there weren't any, he had climbed the stairs and taken the embankment like a rabbit running. Then as he settled into this place, there'd come the shot from the other side—whipping well above him, whistling on toward the river. But no more shots, and no noise except the flat crash of the searchlight, which, in his mind, he saw Jerome kick as surely as if he'd been standing beside him. He'd once had Jerome kick over the chessboard just after he'd quietly pointed out a checkmate. The rest of the Vigilantes would by now have made a lot more noise than that—they wouldn't have meant to, but it would have been there.

Filling his lungs, he felt remotely amused at the flight of the rocket, and simultaneously, a surge of sexual memory: Phyllis, only night before last—before last night and Henry. She'd been very loving, very quiet; he'd been almost sure, for hours, as he stayed awake and watched her sleeping, that the years of driving unfaithfulness were over. Not because she'd simply grown older—at thirty-one she could have been in her twenties, years had only put a bloom on her—but because she'd arrived at some truce with herself. He'd known, for most of his life with her, it was a truce he couldn't bring about. But maybe, he'd thought, it had finally happened . . .

Then, yesterday morning, when he'd left for a day in the woods, she hadn't even said goodbye—she was on her knees beside a bed of zinnias near the lane when he walked by with Merlin at his heels; she'd barely waved, as if she couldn't stand him and was ashamed of the brimming passion she'd brought, like an old gift, the night before.

He stopped thinking, shut thought off like a water tap, and listened.

The usual night noises from the river, frogs, birds; no humans sounding out, no matter how quiet they might think they were. Yes, this was just Jerome, who'd now be trailing him around the quarry, by this time coming slower, raising his head from time to time to see that Cy didn't make a dash over the still moon-bright rail bed to the tower. He straightened, and took a soft step closer to the treeless stretch in front of him. In a few seconds the moonlight would be at the right angle to let shadow cover those tracks out there. He was irritated to find that he was, in spite of himself, thinking of Phyllis once again. Would he keep on doing that, wherever he was, years from now? Why hadn't he ever been unfaithful to her? Well—possibly because she'd have known; without one hint, she'd still have known, and though he couldn't close her wound, he wouldn't make it wider.

He was breathing calmly again, ready for this hundred-yard dash. The pines were tonic. There was a huge one, down fifteen yards below the trestle, a venerable giant that must have a hundred years under its bark, rising above the rest like a castle above humble houses. Where in God's earth would he ever find land loved as much, known as well? There was other hunting country but it was spoiled if you hadn't walked it young, seen it change. With the sale of the Shops he'd never wanted another job, and if it hadn't been for the land, the woods, he would have shriveled. They had kept him, and so had the hope of Phyllis changing, and so had Henry—Henry, the holder, the anchor.

The rails were dark. He hung his coat around his shoulders, buttoned one button, and, shoulders low, ran. The smell of train-burned short grasses lifted around him, his boots made soft spurts in the ballast, sounded on the ties. He looked down and to the east only once, seeing nothing but acres of green, no Jerome, and keeping his rifle low and on the riverside so no flash of it could be made out from this darkness. Then he was under the tower, where, earlier, he'd never intended to be at all; but it would do very well for the time being, and it was a marvelous listening post by itself. He decided to leave his coat on till he had cooled out completely from the climb and the run. The night was going to be fresher than he had anticipated while he was in the cave. Good, benevolent holiday weather.

•　　•　　•

The road angling down to Arden from the Watheralls' clearing was moderately rutted, worn first by the heels of pioneers through long grass, widened by oxcart and timber sledge in later days, further expanded by automobile tires in times following. The vegetable wagon, riding its crown, made a continual rumbling. Phyllis sat on the wagon box beside Tilda, her head lifted, drawing in the night as though she could drink it and be made strong. Now and then she looked backward, to see if the coffin, on this slant, had shifted on the bed; but it was solid, its new-cut-pine smell raw and sweet, a good job of craftsmanship done in a fairly short time, even its lid beveled, and staying firmly in position.

At the point where the road came out to join a curving dusty farm road, white with new moonlight, Tilda pulled the bay to a stop—"Hoo up now, Tobe"—and with a grunt, leaned to shift the brake post from the inside forewheel. She looked tired, straightening, her face as gray as a weathered wasp's nest. Phyllis said urgently, "Let me drive awhile now."

Tilda nodded. She hung the reins on the post and moved over as Phyllis got down and walked around the wagon. Phyllis got up, took the reins and was about to cluck to Tobe, when Tilda touched her arm. Tilda's head was back, her seam-cornered eyes wider. "Now, there goes somethin' right sizable."

They watched as the rocket sailed out from the park, changing moonlight to dayshine, spilling light and fire over the nearby roof of a barn as though it had leaped from blackness, and bringing, for a few seconds, the tattered poster on the side of the barn into sharp relief. Announcing the imminent arrival of the Hagenbeck-Wallace circus, the poster depicted a lurid tiger in the act of bounding through a burning hoop. For a few beats, the tiger reared and glared, twice life-size. And Phyllis thought, I was ten, then, a Fourth of July night like this one; the whole night's still with me, just the way that tiger came out of nothing, waiting there all the while . . . She had been allowed to go to the park, to watch the Clouds as they sent their Roman candles from the landing over the water; her mother hadn't allowed her to indulge in anything but tame lady crackers. She'd edged her way onto the raft, and Rex, noticing her, had said, "Here, you can hold this awhile." She'd taken the Roman candle, a little fearful at first, then entranced by feeling the small hop and skip in the muscles of her arm as the gold, green and blue spherules shot from its mouth, watching them double in the water as they fell, then drown in marvelous hissing. She hadn't been able to say "Thank you," only to nod as she left the raft; that night she'd dreamed she was holding a Roman candle again while Rex, beside her, said, "You can have all you want."

It was a dream of making love, yet more; at that age, enchantment, perhaps innocence. She'd played Roman Candle–Rex Cloud to herself all summer, holding her arm so, and so, and feeling the trembling flame balls pass from her into a wild and gracious river of her own.

She held her gaze on the sky, the column of her throat lifted, undistracted from the memory even as the rocket returned, following with her eyes its erratic path until it was blacked out in the darkness of Carmian's Woods on the other side of the quarry, but still caught in the flood of her own remembrance.

Tilda said huskily, "That play-pretty's gone like a strayed shoat . . . kind of like to've gone down and seen the doin's this year—went last. Henry took me, it was right fun . . ."

Phyllis looked back at the coffin. Then she slapped the reins, clucked to Tobe, and the wheels churned briskly in this road's soft flatness. A farm dog charged the wagon from beneath a clump of alianthus trees, barking routinely, and she took the whip from its socket and snapped it down at the dog to silence it, Tobe surging into a fox trot, his best gait, his fly netting swinging smartly. The lights of town shone ahead, still far in the distance, screened by peppery dust.

Tilda sat hunched, hands supported by her skirt which sagged between her braced legs. Phyllis could feel her getting ready to speak before it came. "I'll miss you. Don't expect we'll get together again. You bein' you—and me, me. Nothin' happens twice."

But she turned her head, curious, at Phyllis' voice. "Anything can happen twice, Tilda." The voice was low but fierce as an order for execution, with an undertone that made Tilda think of the old river in spate, over its banks. "Anything."

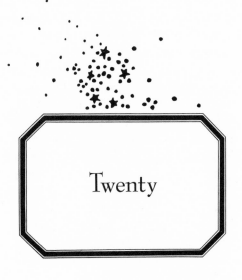

Twenty

Angela Riffon had looped back the curtains, letting in the night's breath. A night light brought out points of color in the medicine bottles and water carafe on the sideboard. Here on the Cloud Block the distant rocket flash was only a flicker in the sky, might have been a touch of summer lightning. Noel Cloud felt the change through his closed eyelids; he could still hear and sense Reverend Bates close by the bed. If he could have talked, he would have asked Nurse Riffon to bring his guest a bite of supper. But as it was, he was still grateful for Bates's solid company. He kept his eyes shut, still in the grip of the recaptured experience of a night long ago—a time not dreamed, relived. Again he was taking his regiment, battered, forlorn, beaten, down Pennsylvania Avenue in Washington on the rain-sodden night following First Bull Run.

Another July then; the downpour incessant, as it had been since the troops were driven from Virginia. The road back in the darkness, the road called Cat Bend a mass of mud, where the overloaded carriages, landaus, barouches and gigs of congressmen who'd come joyfully to Manassas to see the South whipped had bogged and stalled. He and his aide, Custis, had been glad about those floundering congressmen. They'd brought their wives, doxies, children, whiskey and picnic baskets, to watch men die. They deserved to be stripped of office, hanged. On the bloody retreat, Noel had fully understood that now he'd never rise past his brevet command. Because about two o'clock the day before—an hour before the battle's turning point; an hour before Jackson held, men swore with tears in their eyes, like a stone wall—he'd found himself on his lathered roan near a carriage full of congressional dandies. And he'd lunged in the stirrups, throat aching with rage, and bawled down into their faces, "Home, go home, sirs, God damn you! I'd rather Jefferson Davis had the White House than your filthy kind!" They'd heard him well; they'd remember; they'd keep him from advancement. But it didn't matter. A minute later the roan was shot out from under him; he took time to put a pistol ball through its wild-eyed face—a sweet mare, tough, gaited like a dancer. And the Union was rolled back like stones under an avalanche. Nine of his regiment, then attached by General McDowell to the Second Ohio, killed; most wounded. Generals Beauregard and Joe Johnston unbeatable, working together like flame and a battering ram, the North between them. Those who'd come to crow over the South eating crow, chewing it themselves to the last cud of hard meat.

As his men reeled, puppets with their strings gone, down the avenue in the eternal rain, Noel felt the unbearable fact of having betrayed them utterly. The Bedouin caps of the Second Ohio rags, the littered wounded moaning like cattle in slaughter pens, the rain unremitting as if God scorned all war and its enterprise; those men still able to pretend they could march, looking back over their shoulders as if they already saw the South cantering into Washington.

Black the night then; not simple defeat, but defeat rubbed in the soul. Colonel Custis, drilled through the wrist, his arm in the sling like the wing of an exhausted bird, said, *"Silent leges inter arma,* Noel." Noel, weak in Latin, thought it meant something about laws being of no use in wartime. Custis coughed rackingly. "Has it struck you the Rebs believe their cause just as much as we do ours? That all this ruck and bobtail"—he spread his good hand, sweeping it around the crippled, the crawling, the remnant of what had waited, dry-mouthed but whole, for the opening guns on the morning before—"is futile, deadly futile? Even if they don't chase after us now, and take the war, even if it goes on, we're all fools? With the country so riven it can't heal?" He coughed again. He was six months younger than Noel, his voice already old. "Treason, Noel, I speak treason. Yet now we're committed, what the devil does that signify? What any man *thinks* means less than this arm rag."

Agreeing, Noel had kept his silence. Later Custis grew a wartime shell he never lost, not even when dysentery rotted him away in Andersonville, with no fine or conclusive words on his dried-out tongue. He died before Noel and a handful of others had escaped through the tunnel under the deadline fence; died without his insigne, as anonymous and unremarked as the fifteen thousand others who died there.

But he had been right. All one did in any battle, in that war or the one in which Rex had gone, was endure the result of other people's commitment; it was what the high-flown memoirs and the eager, contentious historians forgot. And as Custis had also said, dying was extremely easy. It was living, learning the true core of one's self, that took talent.

Well: he had built an excellent buggy, some were still in use; he had built a superb automobile, which men and women would enjoy for its integrity until the last one ended up in some museum. But he'd never been able to tell his son, or his grandson, how he truly felt about such matters as life and death. And it was too late to speak now; he could no longer even write his name.

He opened his eyes. A soft free night, leafy, a touch of airiness at the windows; a night of national celebration.

Nurse Riffon, approaching the bed, saw his eyes come open.

So did Reverend Bates. She said immediately, "Now it's time for our broth, isn't it?" She glanced at Bates. The ridge of bone around his eyes was as hard as the bezel of a watch; his graying eyebrows tufted above it; he sat comfortingly, a serene, tightly packed companion. "If the Minister wants to stay a while longer, why, I guess it's all right . . ." In spite of having let him in, she was still doubtful, edgy; she cocked her capped head; the decision hovered.

Reverend Bates stretched his legs; the chair under him creaked. He said, "I'll stay. Not in the mood for anything to eat myself, thank you. I had a bite before I took the boys to the park. Yes, I'll linger awhile yet."

She let her lips move, but didn't answer. Noel would have laughed if he'd been capable of it.

At the first ring of the telephone in the bungalow's front room, Eugene answered; his voice, shaded with caution, could have been a visitor's: "Fisher residence, Mrs. Fisher's sleeping."

His Aunt Goldy said, "You, Geney? My God, boy, didn't you go with the Gardners?"

He relaxed, breathing out. "No, Mama was real bad off, so I just stuck here."

"Geney, you're a bunch of sweetness and a beauty-man, all rolled up. Well, it's gettin' quiet here for a change, but I'm hangin' around till Miss Alice gets back. Tell Milly if she wakes up, but don't wake her to do it. I'll fix my own supper when I get there, and if you're still up, we'll have a real good gabfest about some o' the things happened here since I been back." Her tone lowered confidentially. "You and me, we enjoy talkin' about folks, more'n your mama does."

"Oh, you just bet, Aunt Goldy." He waited for a few seconds, then asked casually, "Did anybody bring in a little boy today? I heard some little boy got hurt . . ."

"Nope, no real little kids . . . Aaron Kaplan was in for a minute, Birdy told me he come in 'fore I got back, he give some money to the aviators fell in the river, 'n Birdy said he had

Becky with him, but Mark stayed in the car . . . You heard about them aviators, didn't you? 'S'pect everybody has . . . but lemme tell you, I never did see such down-in-the-mouth souls . . ."

"Save it and tell me later," Eugene said genially. Assurance had been swelling steadily since he came home from Front Street; this was its capstone. He looked out the window at the streetlight, which had come on a few minutes before. Caution would still be necessary, he didn't want anyone to see him leaving town, but at least holiday spirit had staved off retribution; either Mark hadn't talked yet and Buck had stayed quiet or the Kaplans were too taken up by their fireworks to act until later. Impossible now to even think about approaching Mr. Gardner, while still surrounded by possible discovery, but in his mind the town was already practically left behind. He practiced a smile into the receiver. Someday his aunt would pick up a newspaper and read about him and how rich he was. She'd have to recognize him from the photograph, though; for the past minutes he'd been sure Fisher was too dull—Delancy, Du Pont, Morgan, Vanderbilt, would fit better. He said gently, with a vocal caress, "You're my favorite person, you know that? Bless you."

"Oh, you fool, Geney, sometimes I think you're just too wonderful even to be a preacher . . ."

He saluted her with a telephonic kiss, the last she'd be getting. She'd been a good source of information, giddy as a guinea fowl, but actually, he thought, she was *good riddance* —he drew the revolver from his pocket and touched its muzzle to the mouthpiece before he hung up.

He repocketed the Smith & Wesson, picked up the Gladstone bag, and softly opened and shut the front screen door.

When he reached a spreading oak, its lower leaves bowering a horse block, no streetlights near at hand, he sat and gazed across to the railroad station—the depot, as the unenlightened called it. He had already decided to walk behind it, following the tracks, until he attained the Front Street lane again, which would take him out to the bridge-highway, from which he could get a lift going north. He studied the street for signs of human life, found none, and was on his feet once more and had taken a few steps toward the station when he heard the wagon.

It rolled with a clatter, coming from the country end of town, aiming for either Front Street or the lane abutting. There was no other traffic there, but why take a chance on being spotted when you didn't yet know who the spotter might be? He returned to the protective shadow, setting the bag down at his feet, but this time not sitting, alert and swathed in leaf-pungent darkness. The horse's head appeared from a wall of dark leaves, flecked with moonlight; next he saw under her hat the face of Henry Watherall's mother, whom he knew as no more than a useless parcel of sticks at the rim of consciousness, as he had known Henry. But she wasn't driving—face thrust forward, expressionless, her hands hanging like weights in her lap. The driver sat back, still shadowed for a moment, and in the same moment he thought, Sure, some Ridge runner, helping her collect Henry from Melton's. His eyes had almost moved to the wagon bed, to see if there was a coffin on it, and his face was sardonic, ready to break into a pitying smile if there was a coffin and it was as cheap and Ridge-made as it would have to be, when the driver's hands slid into the light . . . then the driver, on the box side nearest him. He didn't know he had taken a step out of the oak leaves until he realized he'd done it inadvertently, and that she was looking straight down at his face.

Fear fitted over him, became intrinsic to him, as it hadn't even been with the clanging home of the school-furnace door. He could not step back or forward. Remotely he understood that he was smiling—the smile of lofty pity had been so near that it had grown, become a rictus. She had checked the horse a little, and as she came up level with him and reached for the whip, he did try to move, but was held as if the tree-darkness, covering all but his face, were an iron maiden. The whip flicked once. He felt the warm cut on his earlobe. The wagon rolled past, the resinous smell of the coffin wafting over him, wagon hubs so close that they eddied air at his shirt. She had not looked back.

After a moment he retrieved the bag and crossed to the station, almost running and almost blindly, this time not caring who saw him, though there was no one else to see. In the station rest room he groped for the string pull, and as the sickly bulb came on, swinging, he gazed with horror at his reflection in the tarnished mirror. Dark, light, dark, it showed him blood running from his ear, staining his shirt collar. He stanched it with a wet handkerchief, dabbing frenziedly to discover the range of damage, but it was only a small cut, even now beginning to close. For another quarter-hour he stood repairing himself, touching up the collar as well as he could, now and then bringing his ear close to the mirror, a finger behind it, as if he were a mother inspecting a wounded child. Picking up the bag, issuing forth into the half-lit waiting room, he stood with moist palms, swinging the bag nervously, his shadow, elongated by the platform window over the foot-beaten boards, repeating each motion in large. The station was an odoriferous trap, the gum-machine mirror, the zinc ticket counter with its wicket shut, glinting at him slyly. Outside he made his way under the dark windows to the platform, and as he set the Gladstone on a baggage truck below a rear window, the gun in his coat pocket struck against the truck with a cloth-muted thud. He pulled it out, the butt momentarily resisting his pocket lining, and looked at it intently. *Should have shot her,* he thought. His features were moving toward calm again, with a hint of angelic quiet in them, as he aimed at the rails. His usual regnant expression, that of an adored child, had returned; he leaned back against the window sill, slipping the gun again in his pocket. It would make too much noise out here; he might try it out, briefly, inside the station, before he went on. Now he had been, somehow, delivered from the hands of somebody who no longer even detested him, who didn't care if he lived or died, who had gone beyond caring at all. His own sort of

267

gods still favored him. He rested more comfortably, nape braced by the sill, shoulders and hips supported by the truck, legs dangling symmetrically off the truck. Lowering his eyelids, he produced a righteous sigh.

The last pinwheel had whirled, sputtered, rested empty; action centered on the pavilion, where Japanese lanterns swayed in rice-paper kimonos. The older set had had its first turn on the floor, to "Dardanella," "Japansy," "Diane," "Roses of Picardy," "The Naughty Waltz," "Whispering," and a judicious spurt of "Black Bottom." To these and other melodies Wid had manipulated Harky in increasingly dangerous circles; Carl and Maidy demanded even more room while they Turkey-Trotted, Bunny-Hugged and Camel-Walked. Alice had danced with Aaron, Leon and Julian—and with Principal Randolph Sutton, with whom she found light conversation—or intelligent—impossible. Now the young had the floor. And the band had come back to its natural style, close to that of Reverend Bates's church, from the same well.

They'd already blown the blues—"Beale Street," "Memphis," "St. Louis," "Empty Bed," "Basin Street." Then "Jack the Bear," then "San," and the water-wheel whirligig of "High Society," and "Creole Belles," and "Down by the Riverside." They played from the chest and the roots of the knuckles and the heels and the insteps. Raw, and right, Henny Dervis' cornet riding out the first chorus, the trombone slamming in for another, the saxophone for his, Gladstone Phillips on slap bass —the bow was for church—then all in concert on the last.

Nobody could tell for sure if it was the rocket or something else charging the air like sodawater. All anybody could say was that when it came time for the Charleston, a spirit was on the band, and on Candy. She and Buck were the matrix of the crowd, and after the kneesies—clasping your knees, crossing hands over them in lightning strokes—they had risen to better heights. Buck, vest flapping, tie askew, was now merely watching, having joined Nick and Melissa and the others, surrounding Candy in a circle, while her legs flew as if she had twenty of them, and came in again to a point that brought her heels together like caliper ends, and her gold dress took all the light and her hat stayed on by centrifugal force, and her skirt fringes spun like out-of-control mouse tails.

Only Nick and Melissa watched each other, looking away from Candy. As he maintained the unison beat, clapping for Candy—*Charle*ston, *Charle*ston, over stabbing cornet and deep-mouthed trombone—a warm part of Nick's mind wanted to be closer to Melissa than he had been in the cove. And yet the urge toward Phyllis was there, too. It was mystifying that a man could simultaneously hold this much urgency and need for two people . . . Melissa's eyes stayed on his, trusting, yet still, he thought, assessing; as if she, like him, considered what had been done in the cove secondary, but what was ahead, vital.

Around the pavilion, darkness gathered from all corners. Here, cored by light and agreeable noise, the tensions of the daylight knotted instead of loosening. The need for Phyllis burned in Nick's blood. And why from time to time did he find himself responding to Melissa's look as if he read there that she was cast adrift, that no one would ever speak to her again, once she'd gone home to the Gardners'? All at once, between one sound blast and another, it was too much; her elbow firm under his palm, he steered her away from the others, then down the steps, past Wid, Harky and his Aunt Alice, who, hands clasped around her knees, sat inspecting dark treetops, as if still relishing the flight of the rocket.

The nearest picnic table, ten yards off, retained a smell of lemonade and home-churned peach ice cream. Nick said, "You wanted to leave early. We can go now."

Melissa's red hat, moving, made a negative stronger than her actual head shake. "Isn't fair to you. Just because *I'm* in trouble . . ."

Nick's voice turned rough, reaching past the band. "Who got you in it? Wouldn't be in hot water if we hadn't gone to the cove . . ."

Melissa, head down, had turned away; her slipper toe investigated a clump of grass. "I loved the cove. Didn't you?"

I've said I love her, Nick thought; she knows that—it isn't anything you ever have to keep on saying, and she knows that, too. He heard himself say in half a groan, "Oh, my Lord. All I meant was, I should've had more sense . . ."

Her eyes were hidden, her voice even farther off than they were. "Well, I didn't have any more sense than you did . . . and all I know now is, I'm not going to cry anymore." Listening closely, he could just hear her. "Today with President Hoover . . . I should've backed you up. Daddy's not—king of the whole universe." Her purse was open a little; he saw her fingers touching the balloon package. Swiftly, making him think of the hurrying cove water, she said, "Watch for the balloon, around midnight. It'll tell you everything's all right. And, sure, maybe I better go home now."

Nick said thoughtfully, "Look, if the door's locked, I could help jimmy it open . . ." He had a vivid picture of himself in the act of burgling, Mr. Gardner opening the door in his face. In which case, he thought, he might say he'd just dropped over to borrow a cup of sugar.

From the pavilion, the Charleston reached a fresh and crashing plateau; as Nick gazed there, feeling abstract envy for Buck's wholeheartedness, Candy's emancipation, he put his arm around Melissa, caressing the small of her back. Her skin below the short sleeves was cool, pleasant. She said, "No, I told you I'll go to the door myself. If I don't do it tonight, I never will." Somebody who'd owlishly observed them from the pavilion shouted, "Spooners!" Nick increased his arm's pressure. Melissa was murmuring, nearly speaking to herself, "Oh, I'm the whole house there. Everything I do's so cute. I'm so cute it just makes me sick . . . I feel kind of sick, anyhow." He could see her lips, now, under the hat; he wished he could spend millennia with her, even without touching, in some airy craft suspended a few feet under the moon.

But Melissa was continuing her own self-assessment, excluding him for the moment. "I want to feel different; I want to feel like Candy; I want to stay here with you till they play 'Good Night, Ladies,' and then I want to sleep and sleep and think it's the best Fourth of July I ever had. Just the best, all around, in the cove and everything. But I can't do it because I don't feel like Candy. It's not even worrying about having any baby."

Nick found himself saying as if he had, quite naturally, jumped from a springboard, "I'll marry you."

And her eyes were suddenly upturned, as direct as the startlingly honest face. "But I'm not even talking about that . . . that's not important for a while."

Would Phyllis Bellaman have been as impatient? He didn't think so; didn't think she was going to be.

He thought of the wide fieldstone fireplace in the Wolfson-Bellaman house. It wouldn't have changed, nothing in that house could change, Phyllis herself never alter, only become more herself. And if she was turning to him . . . all right—he let himself think it, bring it out for the first time to himself. It felt raw, as if he had swallowed something too huge for his throat.

All right, my father knew her, and I'm going to.

But Melissa was here, needing him. He pulled his arm away, shook himself and said quickly, "I'll just tell Aunt Alice we've got to go now."

His aunt was still on the lower step of the pavilion, Mark Kaplan beside her. Their commonality of quiet made him think for an instant of himself at Mark's age, the world unfolding in directions mysterious, frightening, but always hopeful; he said, "Good night. Melissa and I have to leave now."

Over the band she said, "Au 'voir, Nick. It's been a good day, in spite of many things. Good. I want to remember it this way."

He bent closer, kissing her forehead. She whispered, "Cy will be all right. And Phyllis. Don't worry about them."

How had she known? But it wasn't about him and Phyllis;

it was just a certain confidence she sometimes had. As he raised his head Carl Bolyard waved from a higher step, Maidy flickered her fingers to him, Harky called, "Now try to git in by some decent time," and Wid touched his fedora. Past them, on the pavilion floor, Buck, Candy and the applauders were still violently engaged as he went back to Melissa.

They walked in silence to the gates. Most of the limousine was shadowed, only a front wheel showing moonlit wires around its hub like silver stalks. As they drove away, the music followed like rising bubbles, but it had nothing to do with them, thinking their own thoughts, as disparate as though there had been no parade, picnic, scow or cove. This distance obtained for a minute.

Then, as he held it to her, she took his hand and moved closer to him. Street lamps showed blue and dim on the horizon.

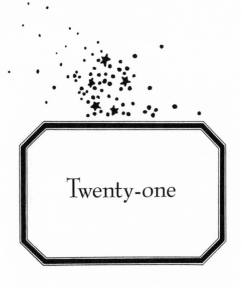

Twenty-one

The driveway gateposts of the Wolfson estate had been sunk there when the house was built, rooted five feet underground, with their finials snarling stone griffins, whose beaks slanted outward and down to the Wolfson Block. The iron fence had been added in the late 1800s, its spikes twined through with ivy and clematis. The drive took long upward curves before it flattened out at the house, running beside scythe-mown routes which led to the poolside, to groups of statuary and to vine-gripped sundials, some of which said they counted only the sunny hours.

Phyllis went a little way up the drive, then followed sunken flagstones around the south flank of the house, its windows staring at her like black glare ice. Under the ledge of a back porch she stooped to pick up a fallen gutter tile and laid it against the gutter pipe. Brushing hair back from her forehead, she looked up at the chimney, which was swathed in ivy leaves like loose chain mail. Before long she would ask Marty to put up the ladders and help him clear out a few vines; not cutting back heavily, but removing just those root suckers which might spread the rosy, hand-baked bricks. She didn't think she could have lived without the half wilderness of vine, leaf, long grass —without growing things, which didn't blame, didn't talk.

She took a path to the dog run, saw its gate open and stood still. Then she whistled, but there was no answer from the doghouse; the whistle itself seemed an intrusion on natural night sounds. Then she saw the shed and the peg in the door hasp, and as she approached the door she heard Merlin moving inside. Opening the door, she knelt and ruffled his fur. "Well, he didn't have to put you in the shed. Little boys don't know you don't like the shed, do they?" She buried her face in a silky shoulder. "Anyhow, your ribs are all full." She thumped him; his plume waved and he trailed at her heels into the high-ceilinged kitchen, then stood watching as she took an apple from a bowl and bit into it.

She went on talking to him softly as they moved into the hall with its Adam, Sheraton and Shaker pieces, and the benches Pierre Wolfson had had carpentered from heart pine; in the doorway to the front room she stood a moment, breathing its polish and wax, watching moonlight spill from high windows to the peg-laid floor and over the fireplace stones. At the other end of the room, shadows climbed the stair. She turned on a lamp, then said directly to the dog, and gravely, "Listen, Cy's not coming back. I'm sorry. But it's the way things are . . . We'll walk a lot, we'll run. I promise."

Again she knelt, stroking his head, then looked down at her dress in the lamplight. "This is a disgrace," she said. "Look at me. Even cockleburrs. Down now. Wait for me right here."

Merlin lay down on the cool hearth, dropping his haunches first, forepads tipped with the light as he slid them out and extended them, his head lifted; he looked up at her steadily. She moved to turn on another lamp, and its light, brightening ruby tiles, also brought out a few dark spots, near the tapestried sofa. Phyllis went to her knees, brought out a crumpled handkerchief from her dress pocket and attacked the spots, scrubbing industriously. After half a minute she stood once more.

"Wood ash and lye," she said. "We'll get all that out tomorrow."

She retrieved her purse from where she'd dropped it on the sofa and went on to the stairs. She could see the escritoire midway between the staircase and the entrance hall, and the gun rack across from it, the glow of its low polish, and glints of the derringer, the dueling pistol, rifle and shotgun, target pistol and Luger. There were bookcases beyond, and above them, a painting of ducks in a tide marsh, and silver-framed photographs of Tom and Betty Wolfson. From the forty feet between Phyllis, and Merlin on the hearth, her voice reached him, quietly. "You tell me when he's here," she said. She took her hand from the newel post. A few steps up, she stood on one leg, then the other, removing the walking shoes; after that her feet were almost silent on the broad treads. When she had gone Merlin looked out into the room, his gaze constant on the entrance hall.

Nick pulled the limousine to the curb in front of the Gardners', before the neat and moonlit lawn, past which the house was dark and waiting. He got out, but by the time he'd gone around the hood, Melissa had opened her door; she stood with her purse, fattened by bathing suit, towels and paper balloon package, clutched in both hands at breast height. Elm leaves, shrouding a streetlight, touched her face with faint green as she lifted it. Holding her head between his palms, he kissed her. Then he said urgently, "Let me go with you, anyhow, to the door."

She shook her head, saying very softly into his chest, "Go ahead now. Don't stay and watch. I'm just fine. Watch out for the balloon, later." As his hands slid from her hair she added with a return of impatience, "I'm dandy."

She waited until he had driven off, which he did slowly, the headlights, massive owl eyes, finally fanning past the hospital, the taillights a slumberous red. Then, the limousine out of sight, she stayed where she was for another minute.

She could still feel him around her. The time of wondering how it would be to have a man was behind her; it had been, she now understood, wholly idealized. Borrowed from romance —*Graustark, Chickie,* the adult-proscribed *The Green Hat* of Mr. Michael Arlen, and from what happened, on screen, at the Argus. Nick was in the immediate now. But he was, essentially, reassuring; she felt she could count on him. He'd tried to suffer with her . . . When he'd said what he said, she was sure he had meant it.

She turned quickly and cut across the barbered lawn, dew around her ankles. The front steps to the porch were narrow, tidy, upright. Facing them, she stopped.

The small, secret object people whispered about, made jokes about, called the cherry or, more genteelly, the maidenhead, couldn't, by itself, be important. But she was a swan regretting cygnet days.

The brass door knocker was a miniature hand, wrist and grasping knuckles on a pivot over the plate. For a few seconds she held it, poised, then eased it down and silently shut the screen door, which she had been holding aside with her shoulder.

She felt ghostly, weightless, here on the porch. She glanced at the chains of the swing, their links in shadow. She retreated to the foot of the steps, her own shadow long on the grass, and stood, her head lowered, wholly indecisive. Lordy, Lordy woe, she thought. Courage, held all the way here from the park, had gone.

Beneath the noises of the night lay a listening quiet. She tried to remember Candy's encouragement, the good music at the pavilion, but these were at once defeated by the silence.

Her parents didn't share a bedroom; in her memory they hadn't, though clearly they must have, if only for a short time, in the past. So she could try going around under her mother's window, rapping, taking her chances in that direction. But after the cold-creamed face looked out, what then? Would even her mother let her in? Did she wear the earmarks, plain to the knowing, of having been handled, ruined? And even if her mother let her in anyhow, wouldn't this be hard on her mother, in her father's accusations to follow?

The beautiful cove was light-years away—magic stream, amiable rocks, freedom. Nick exciting as wildfire, naked; she'd never looked on her father even seminude, unless you counted him as such in pajamas and bathrobe, and certainly never in such condition. The feeling of sun and air on her own flesh, all of it. Nick, Nick . . .

Maybe he'd been clumsy—there wasn't anyone to compare him to, and if there had been, she couldn't have thought about it, because he was Nick. But careful. Maybe it was all a talent you had to learn by degrees, like really wonderful ice-skating, or a gift like double-jointedness or the ability to whistle back, in kind, to a mockingbird. Maybe it was the special talent Mrs. Bellaman had that made her mysterious, along with her looks. Maybe Candy had been born with it but it had been left out when Melissa Gardner was born.

She crossed the side lawn into the backyard, skirting the walk and the closed sprinklers aligned beside it. She looked levelly at the steps where, a child, she'd shelled peas with her mother before Nick came along this morning. She went on to the glider, which was bound to be more quiet than the porch swing, opened her purse, took out a damp towel and wiped a little dew from a slatted seat.

She sat, her legs stretched out, heels on the opposing glider seat. With her hands behind her neck, weighing her hair under the bob, she thought about Iris March, whose often puzzling adventures she had followed closely in the novel, because Candy had recommended it. "Hot stuff," Candy had said. But if you just had to kill yourself, it was a mannerly method, in a Hispano-Suiza automobile, hitting an oak at full speed, leaving a trail of bleeding male hearts behind. If she herself wanted to do it, Nick might be willing to furnish the car; the Cloud limousine must be as big as a Hispano.

She thought of her own room, full of ruffles, old toys, a

luxuriant bed, a room into which her father never came. Now he had turned into a resident ogre, barring her from it; no longer the man she'd blithely walked around to the telephone; not Daddy, with thin hair.

This time she took the path to a side street, then walked swiftly under the trees until she was on the residential side of Front, facing the railroad station. Her footfalls stopped chasing her along the sidewalks as she gazed at the Front Street business block, carved out of the night as if framed and set off there. There, taking moonlight, was the courthouse far down in the square, and the dark fountain, and those buildings with a suggestion of light in them, like grounded stars.

Her rhythm, across Front to the station, was bold, she swung the purse as though conscious of fixed attention—there goes Melissa Gardner, toast of three continents—and it lasted as she climbed the station steps. When she had turned the greasy knob, the wave of cinder effluvia balked her for another breath, but she went in. Train schedules, thumb-tacked to distempered walls, fluttered gently as she shut the door.

She decided on a rear bench, under a window, as best for purposes of stretching full length. Its iron armrests had loosened and spread; at least it offered abundant room. The ash pan under the stove shook a trifle as she passed it, in elderly, fireless comment. At the bench she put down her purse—an adequate pillow—and stood looking out over the platform to the tracks. A baggage-truck handle blocked several panes, the rest of the truck obscured. With a bed of bright weeds between them, the rails shone like her mother's tea service. She lay back on the bench, inspected the dust motes still agitated by the mild breeze she had raised, thinking they made casual fireworks of their own, in random streaks of moonlight, and to her own gentle surprise, fell asleep at once.

She didn't know what had wakened her. It could have been the creak of a board or the opening and shutting of the door to the station steps. But on later reflection she was sure this would have been done in near-silence, and that after she had been observed, and recognized, from the platform window, every motion of her visitor would have been as hushed as possible. She did know that her eyes came open as if she had been dreaming strongly and had been shaken awake by the dream's force, and then, at once, she also knew where she was, and who was with her.

Looking down at her, Eugene said on a warm breath, "It's just old me, Melissa."

Nick left the limousine in the lane, entering the Wolfson grounds from there. Halfway up the path under brushing leaves, he made out the open shed door—Merlin was released, Phyllis was at home. He walked for the first few steps around the house, then found himself breaking into a light half-run. And through his rising excitement, Cy was everywhere. He was beside the dog run, whose creosoted cedar posts he had tamped in and shown Nick with pride; he was on the terrace, stretched in a chair beside the game table. He wasn't talking much, because he never had, but he was companionable—and watchful. He didn't go away as Nick moved across the drive to the walk and to the front door, but leaned somewhere near the door, and watched Nick raise the eagle knocker and let it fall.

He stayed there, hearing the house with Nick.

From the hall came the ticking of Merlin's pads on the floor; Nick drew in one lungful of air, then opened the door.

The room he had always liked, as much as he liked its generous counterpart in the Cloud house, was lamplit, cool, cavernous. The lamps were islands, soft darkness between them. He shut the door and felt Cy come in with him just before the latch caught, so that now there seemed to be three of them in the hall—Nick, Cy, Merlin. He went on into the room, Merlin close beside him. He supposed Merlin had heard him even as he stepped onto the grounds. And had given one soft bark, the signal that the grounds had been entered. Crossing to the hearth, Merlin with him, he touched the dog's head.

He stood before the cold hearth and noted that there was

no feeling of fresh terror there. The familiar sofa, and at its end, a stack of magazines, and past it, the ivory and walnut chessboard, the pieces set out for a game. He knew he should have been thinking about Phyllis; in the morning, her hands warm, all of her lifting toward him in the sun-blazed hospital room. But it was Cy, a little rumpled from a day in the woods, who stood in the nearest pocket of shadow, without comment, eyes steady.

And it was still Cy, there with everything else, as Phyllis came from the stairway. Her feet were bare, quick, the belt of the robe carelessly knotted; her shining hair swung free; Merlin had turned his head to watch, too. She stopped before him, perfect, all need and ready to answer it, speaking without a least word.

It was the time to touch her, to bring her to him.

Cy seemed to have stirred slightly. A lift of the head, where he stood.

Nick heard himself breaking the quiet ridiculously, saying like an oaf, "I can't stay. Grandfather's worse." The words had come to him as simply as though he had thought them over, all the distance from Melissa's.

She stood where she was, something—a light?—dying out in her face. Then it came back slowly as she smiled. "Nick, I won't eat you, you know." She was tipping her head to one side, studying him carefully. It was as though she had never seen him before, even this morning; as though now that he was there, she was delighted with all she saw. Walking over to the sofa, she said, "You've always been remarkably self-possessed —for your age. I don't mean bland or smug. You're too craggy for that. Well . . ." She sighed and relaxed against the armrest. Looking past her, he made out a few dark blotches on the tapestry. Anything could have made them; yet he had a hard time pulling his eyes back to her. She said, nodding a little, "It's nice to be visited, anyway. By somebody who wants to visit me. Nice to have you here."

Merlin had gone to her silently; he stood alongside her. She gazed away, down the length of the room. "When I was a little girl I used to pretend I was the last person on earth. That everybody else had died or gone away to another planet and left me alone. It was a luxurious feeling—thrilling. When my mother and father were out, I'd pretend there wasn't any cook in the kitchen or a maid upstairs, and prowl through this place." She was looking at him again. "Did you ever feel like that?"

Nick felt sympathy stir in him, with a kind of joy. After a moment, not breaking his gaze, he said, "Yes, lots of times. It's not like Robinson Crusoe—you don't even want a Man Friday. You're by yourself, really by yourself, and around the next corner—down a hall, or wherever—you're going to find out something tremendously important. It's always been there, and you know it's there, but nobody knows it but you."

"That's it, Nick." She was leaning forward now. It doesn't make any difference that her robe is a little open, he thought; it wouldn't make any difference if she wasn't wearing a robe. In his mind she had been there so long, in this light, in this way, that it was natural. And a thousand miles removed from any drawing on a bedroom's wallpaper. "And don't you know how sad that is? Nick, that's the saddest thing on earth . . ." She was speaking a shade faster now, but the words weren't running together, only mingling with her wish to get them out. "Two people who have that, that loneliness and that seeking, never coming together? Never knowing each other, only cast back into the darkness of themselves, never journeying together?"

Her breath went in, then out quickly. She said, "Don't disappear in the dark. I don't think I could stand it if you did." She had straightened. She stood—proudly, he thought, because she couldn't stand any other way—and said, "There's nobody else left now. Nobody I'd ever want." Then her voice changed, folded back, melted inward, and she said quickly, "Ah, my dear, ah, Rex . . ."

Less than an instant afterward she stood with the name

frozen in her throat, her eyes widening, and then she said, not clearly at all, even though he heard it, "My God, I didn't mean . . ." And then, this time more plainly, "Is that what I meant, is that what I meant for you? For me?"

She had turned; he couldn't see her eyes. He stood quite still, the joy gone, but not the sympathy—but it was more than sympathy, at last. He understood the need to love many people, in many special and different ways, and the need each had for his own love. Yet, in that instant, it was as if he had been struck by lightning that would always burn. He took a step toward her, the dog looking around and up at him. But she hadn't looked back, was turned away. She shook her head, the collar of the robe slipping to show a small square of bandage on her shoulder near the throat, alien against the fine skin.

Her voice was controlled, even, all of her dissolving behind it. "Good night, Nick. I love you, and I'm sorry. This is—my fault. Go away now, and I'll call you sometime . . . You're my friend."

For still another second he was rooted. To touch her now would be treacherous; even to say good night, too much. She had been horrified by herself, every line of her body said that. As he made himself walk away, starting down the room, he felt that he was leaving himself there, and, not strangely, his father as well. He had reached the hall doorway before he glanced back. It wouldn't have surprised him to see his father then, no painting, only the man he hadn't known. Yes, he thought, but I do know him. Now I do, and I like him.

But all he saw at the hearthside was Phyllis, her head still turned from him. And when he had let himself out, an image of Phyllis, Merlin unmoving beside her, printed on his eyes, Cy was also somehow there once more, reassuringly. He thought, I'll go see Cy, I'll say goodbye. It wasn't much to ask of anybody.

In the lane he backed and turned, ran the heavy lever through gears, and saw from the dashboard clock, which worked well like everything else in this Cloud car, that it was still too early for the Nickel Plate to be coming. All right; he would wait for Cy at the water tower.

When he was clear of the town, he pronounced Phyllis' name, once, and it whipped back in the slipstream of air while he drove toward Carmian's Hill. Then, more quietly, he spoke Melissa's.

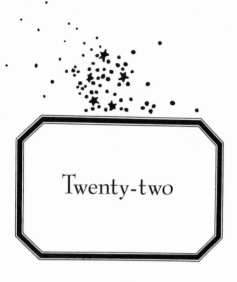

Twenty-two

Propped on an elbow under the water tower, in grass shut off from the sun so long it was faintly white even in the minor groundlight, Cy watched the tall, even monumental pine fifteen yards or so to the south and below him. Passing minutes had made him very familiar with the tree; given a pad of paper, a pencil, he could have done a more than creditable sketch of it even in this half dark, doing justice to its great height, the spread of its lower boughs, its prideful sweep of limb and its outstanding green thrust above its neighbors. He had known the tree for years, often used it as a landmark when hunting on this side of the Ridge. What made it special now was his conviction that Jerome Potter lay beneath it. He reflected that outwitting Jerome was like outwitting a really splendid buck, a wary, scarred animal that knew all the tricks of evasion and, after the first hour, made the contest worthwhile; it was the kind of game Henry had enjoyed.

There was no slightest stir of wind, a fact which had helped him trace Potter's progress to the pine. He had heard nothing, but a patch of dog fennel had moved—then a high stand of fuchsia-headed clover trembled—then, considerably later, the bearded, sappy grass stalks nearest the pine's coal-black, almost purple shadow swayed. In his mind's eye he could visualize, as obviously as if it were blueprinted, Jerome's Winchester aimed up and under the tower, and Jerome's face, bleak, patient and waiting, sweating under the pine's enveloping darkness. He rolled over, without sound, lifting his own rifle as he stood. There was a clearance of three inches between the crown of his head and the water-tank's dark belly. From the pine it would have been impossible for Jerome to make out a hint of motion beneath the tower. For Cy to leave the tower and fade through its own rigid, starkly outlined shadow a dozen yards to the north would be a simple matter. When the train came, which Cy estimated would be about an hour yet, under cover of its grinding tumult of brakes and steam and the rattle of the waterspout, it would be equally simple to slip across the tracks and board from the other side, with the bulk of the engine and the cars blocking him from Jerome. He moved his feet noiselessly, boot soles settling into the pale grasses like rain mist, and was about to step into the tower's projected shadow, free of the close, iron-smelling heat trapped beneath it, when he heard the noise from the other end of the Foe Killer trestle.

Looking over his shoulder, he let only his head move, and that slowly. In this position he could see the stretch of track he had raced across, pitch-dark under leaves, and beyond, the whole of the trestle, the tracks and ties emerging from their leafy tunnel, the bridge spanning the creek in crystal-bright outline. The intrusive noise was as clear as his vision. Someone was walking the ties. The sound, and its immediate echo, blended above the creek. While he waited, Nick came in sight. He was walking quickly, not running, sure of himself, head up, eyes on the tower. For a few seconds Cy had another imaginative vision of Jerome, arrested in his vigil, staring up at the trestle, astonished.

Then, as his eye followed his thought, and he turned halfway around to take sight again on the deep pine shadow, he was, in his own turn, as astounded as he had estimated Jerome might be.

Jerome had broken cover. Out of bough-darkness he had stood, indeed shot up, and he was beating wildly, blindly, at his arms and shoulders, as though in the middle of a swarm of bees. And making enough noise about it to raise the county. Branches went crashing, the lower, knuckly limbs of the great pine heaved and spread, and suddenly, even in this windless air, there was a malodorous smell of burning from the pine— burning cloth, and behind it, a stench of gunpowder. The Winchester had been flung aside; in the same instant, Cy saw its stock leaning from the brush. And saw, as well, the fiery, widening holes in Jerome's shirt, across his chest, and then across his back as he twisted and fought. But the instant of recognition, realization, was over, and Cy was already running.

As he slid and flung himself down the slope, through grasping brush, throwing his own rifle down at the last moment and then, within diving range of the sheriff, launching himself at Jerome's legs in a long tackle, he saw the still-smoldering, sputtering shape of the rocket, plainly caught for a while in the thin topmost twigs of the pine, then by insistent gravity, having worked its way down the immense trunk, and now fulminating in heavy boughs, a few feet over head height. From its nose dripped tags of fire, catching resinous bark slivers which flared, died like doused torches, and flared again. Then the sight was blotted out as he hit Jerome, his right shoulder catching him behind the knees, Jerome grunting once, then rolling, Cy rolling with him and catching him again, kneeling beside him, rolling him once more, finally both of them sitting, breathing in gasps which died out as they regarded each other.

Cy was the first to speak. "Get that damn shirt off!"

Potter nodded. He was working on the buttons, lifting the shirt away from his body, easing his shoulders out of it, balling it up with disgust and throwing it aside, looking first at Cy, then at the rocket in the pine, then around and up, toward the trestle, and back to Cy. After his second full reconnaissance Cy got up, brushing off his coat, brushing the palms of his hands on his trousers, and walking a few feet toward the pine, where he stood for a second, hands on hips, then stooped and picked up the sheriff's hat and brought it back to him. "It'll burn itself out now," he said. "Too much rock fern and green brush under it to spread. Let me look at you. Sit still."

He walked around the sheriff in a circle, bending close, eyes narrowed. Then he stopped in front of him. "Not a thing butter won't cure. How'd you get that blue mark on your spine?"

Potter had put his hat on and drawn up his galluses over his lean shoulders. "Shrapnel. Soissons."

"Just wondered," Cy said. Then, a beat later, and as if casually: "Henry's leg—looked the same."

Their eyes met and held. They were still holding as the sheriff got up. His face, sooted, seemed composed mainly of bone. "My rifle's yonder in the brush. Yours is right close to hand. You can get to both of 'em quicker'n I can." He blinked, wiping a bothersome smut from the bridge of his nose. "I'd have burned right up. Remembered not to run—but I didn't remember to roll." He dropped his hand. "That's Nick Cloud I saw, ain't it?" He listened. "Off the trestle now. Comin' down . . . he may complicate things a little for you. But you'll get around it some way. Me, I'm bowin' out." He was staring off to where a crackle of brush, a slither of grass, announced Nick. "I surrender—take your train."

Cy had made a quarter turn to watch Nick, who came off the embankment, saw Cy and the sheriff and paused, lifting his hand. Cy motioned him on, then said, "No. I'm not taking it. But you go back with Nick. It'll be easier riding; you could use it right now. He'll have the limousine tonight. Probably left it at the hill trail. Your car's downtrail from the quarry, isn't it?" The sheriff nodded, but not as if he had yet understood. Cy said matter-of-factly, "Give me your keys. I'll drive it back." He hesitated fractionally. "Back to the jail," he said.

Potter's eyes creased as he shut them, shaking his head, still unbelieving; but he dug into his hip pocket, and Cy caught the keys. Cy said, "I'd ride with you, but I want to be by myself just a while longer. Don't grudge me that. And don't get to thinking I'll spill my guts, tonight or ever." Watching Nick, who was coming closer, he said, "That was smart—the searchlight."

The sheriff seemed afraid to stare foursquare at Cy, as if he might disappear. Finding his voice again, he brought out tentatively, "So was shootin' it out."

Their eyes met, scanned for much less than a moment, and turned away to Nick again, who was walking slower as he neared.

At last the sheriff said, still not able to look at Cy, "Lock the car up when you get to the station house. It's full o' guns."

After the shock of being wakened from first sleep, Melissa felt more irritated than apprehensive. True, being alone with Eugene was always cause for tremors, but surely the reputation was overblown, the human a mere gifted and dashing fellowman? All the same, she would have preferred his absence; he seemed—sitting beside her, placing a serge arm around her as she, too, sat up—larger than life, making her shabby sleeping place shabbier. She worked her toes back into her slippers, which she'd half kicked off while comatose, and looked helplessly out at the stove. Eugene's hand moved like a river finding a new bed, across her throat and downward. She admired his fingernails, any girl would have.

His voice thrummed through her ribs. "Melissa, I've got to apologize right now . . ." Whatever it was he was saying then, something about rescuing a small boy—or was it an old man? —from some dire fate, and ruining his clothes in the process, and being too late to even call, slipped past her actual consciousness; it was no doubt thrilling, but not at this hour, and not here. The hand descended, its fingers finding the lace edging of her brassiere, while he spoke of his worthy mother, and his worry about her health. If you just sat back and listened to the voice, it would have been reassuring; in conjunction with the hand, it was irksome. She made a sudden semi-leap, temporarily freeing her bosom. Eugene was saying at that point, "And what on earth is Melissa Gardner doing in this dirty old room?"

Melissa felt a wild need to extemporize; a summer Nature Study project, brought over from the school year, the study of cockroaches in their native habitat? She suppressed it, along with the truth, by murmuring, "Couldn't sleep, I took a walk and ended up here . . ."

She had immediately realized that the truth would be fatal, inducing a Eugene-lecture about being tolerant of one's father. While the hand returned she considered biting it, but instead shifted to her right—it was a long bench, its space would last awhile—and said, "Were you taking a walk too?"

He said he had been because the condition of Mama had been preying on his mind. He said he had been talking with the Lord. He came closer, the arm lowered, and she moved again, this time more slowly. He followed, homing in with precision, and his earlobe came into a spot of light. Melissa sat up straighter, welcoming a fresh topic. "You've hurt yourself!"

He frowned, eyes, also sharing the small light, instantly flatter and, she thought, somehow scared. But he said, "It's just a speck," and went on to explain that it was one of the results of his recent rescuing adventure, as he rubbed the lobe. Then he was in business again, in full cry, dimples moving like creases in velvet as he spoke of his good fortune at having been touched by the Lord, and this time clamped his arm firmly around her, giving the hand free play. She reflected that his every mention of the Deity had the ring of her father when he spoke of Andrew Mellon, but that there was no awe in his fingers. The lace tore slightly as she jerked away. His breathing sounded like a through train's, chuffing like a hotbox. It was past time to stand up, which she did abruptly. She cast a glance at her purse, now lonesome at the other end of the bench, and said brightly, "Well, it's been nice talking, Eugene, but I've got to go along now. Mama and Daddy don't even know I'm out . . ."

That had been a mistake, a serious error, she understood, as she attempted a wide detour past his knees and found herself stopped as he rose, his arms locking behind her. He said, "Don't they?" With the question the game was over, and she felt panic touch her. He was still only Eugene, yet now a much more substantial and genuine Eugene, one with the skin stripped and the understructure showing. After swimming, she had once looked down to find a leech on her thigh; at this moment she remembered it with exactness. There in the good water, the sweet air—the glossy slug, drinking. It wasn't like Nick, it wasn't like most men; it was very much like these hands, both holding her now, in a secure grip, and fumbling, smoothing as they held. Pressing inward, pulling her.

His nose was buried in her neck, and she was too close to attain leverage. Fighting against the rising panic, as well as the need to beg—she had the overwhelming feeling that he wanted her to plead with him—she managed a short step to the rear. And brought up her right knee as hard as she could, feeling it go between his knees and something crush under it. It had been only instinct. She had touched Nick there, marveling at the softness of the skin, a new baby's. She had a second of complete revulsion, horror at herself—had she killed him? and if she hadn't, would he kill her?—which drained away into near-compassion as he let go of her, doubling over, clutching himself. Then he was on his side, floored, legs drawn up, the ubiquitous hands centered.

Melissa stood back. Then she saw the revolver slide halfway out of his coat pocket, recognizing it as one exactly like her father's, owl heads on the grip, bought a dozen or so years before when the model was popular. Mr. Gardner used it solemnly from time to time to shoot tin cans from the back fence, explaining to Melissa and her mother that this was in case the Chinese invaded Arden, or the Negroes came down from the Ridge in ravening hordes.

She drew in a breath. He was moaning now, saying words she couldn't quite unravel. Shakily, and with complete sincerity, she said above him, "Eugene, I don't think you better come over to our house for a while." He seemed to notice neither her counsel nor her presence. And with his hands so surely occupied, she didn't think he would remember the gun or be able to use it. Nevertheless, she hastened to pick up her purse, and out in the night, floated down the steps and walked briskly away, breathing the air as if it were the first she had ever enjoyed.

Her mood was presently buoyant, firm, invincible. Visible above leaf webs, the courthouse clock registered a few minutes past eleven. Soon the dance would be breaking up, those who had stayed for its end coming back to Soames's for sodas, Black Cows, Cherry Frappés in vessels with frosted ears. Next year, she thought, I'll be among them. At the Gardners' front walk she didn't pause to consider the hushed grass route, but made a solid noise going over the cement, up the steps, across the porch to the door. For a demiquaver of time she looked back at the moonlit walk. Even the legend marked in the cement when fresh—*Laid by Jno. Evans, 1910*, three years before she'd been born—was friendly, welcoming. She pushed aside the screen frame, lifted the doorknocker's prim wrist and let it bang down, roundly—then again, and then once more. The third time it struck, her father opened the door, so she decided it must not have been locked, and he must have been waiting all the while.

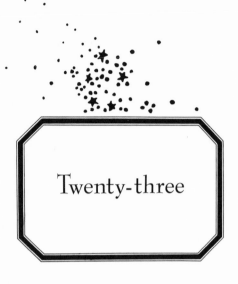

Twenty-three

There were times, Nick considered, when it was wrong to ask too many questions—the sort of questions a child might have asked, the kind that nudged in him and wanted to leap out. There was a quality of settlement, a truce, between the sheriff and Cy; it was uneasy and delicate, something you didn't want to break or spoil by the intrusion of your own ideas. He could feel, tacitly, the sheriff's absolute trust that Cy would drive to the jail and not head out into the blue night with a back seat full of weapons and ammunition. He could feel, as well, Cy's assurance that he would keep his word. Little enough had been said about this—Potter and Cy had greeted him with a minimum of conversation, the sheriff listening without comment while he, in turn, explained about meeting Merlin, finding Cy in the cave and trying to keep the rendezvous at the tower. Dryly, Cy corroborated this—his mind seemed a long way off, his whole self aimed at summing up the past and realizing his place in the present.

The sheriff said as they walked around the quarry rim, "I might've done the same thing at your age—come to see a friend off. It wouldn't have made much difference to my nabbin' Cy or not nabbin' him. Except, showin' up early like you did, you took a pretty fair chance of gettin' caught in a crossfire."

They had almost reached the trail down from the quarry on the town side. Cy walked behind, carrying his own rifle and the sheriff's, a little out of earshot. And the sheriff was speaking quietly. "I've never felt bad about standin' beside a friend," he went on. "It's when you don't that it eats into you." He cast a sidewise look at Nick, his set face still smudged and blackened, his bare chest singed as though he had been exposed to a blast of birdshot from a distance or developed smallpox.

Nick could sense his self-disgust at having chosen the pine for a lookout point; his carefully muffled anger at the fact that the rocket had been, in a manner of speaking, lying in wait for him there. His anger wasn't directed toward the Kaplans or even, for that matter, at the vagaries of circumstance, but it was turned inward upon himself. And beneath it there was some vast, hardly repressed regret as if, even though he might have won and got his man, there was no trace of victory in it.

Nick stood and waited while Potter squatted beside a stillwater pool cupped in rocks. Rubbing water on his face, applying it gently over his chest and back, he said, still softly, "I got to lock him up now. I guess that's what bein' a public servant means." Then he added, speaking not to Nick but to himself, "And I got to go tell Phyl."

Nick had an instant's urge to tell the sheriff he had seen Phyllis a little while before and that he didn't think this was a good time to visit her; but it would have meant too many other explanations, and in any event, it was too late now. Cy had come up, was standing with them, a few steps away.

The sheriff straightened, water streaming over his cheekbones. He spoke to Cy. "There's a couple of old grads from the Army Air Corps in one o' the cells. Don't think they'll bother you much, since I asked Tommy to get 'em some of Renfrew's bug juice to quiet 'em down for the night. But in case they get to singin' and carryin' on, ask Tommy to put you in the end cell—it's a little airier than the others, anyhow, and got better blankets." He spoke more loudly. "I'm goin' to ask Nick to take me on to see Phyl a minute, then I'll be back. If you want some grub or anything, Tommy'll get you somethin' from Soames's while it's still open." Then his voice dropped to a whisper and he asked what he must have been carrying with him since they had come from the pine. "Cy, just this, then I won't bother you no more tonight 'n less you want me to—how come you're knucklin' under?"

Cy shifted the rifles in his arms. The crease in his forehead reminded Nick of his grandfather when Noel Cloud had attempted, after the last stroke, to speak. Then his face cleared and he said, "Who the hell can hide out from himself, Jerome? Came to me when you were sitting on the ground—after we'd wallowed around under that tree." His face was still clear, and bitter, and lined more deeply than Nick had noticed in the cave. The trail head was to the east, just behind him. He turned and started down, his voice reaching back as his legs vanished on the down slope and his shoulders and bright hair were still in sight. "I decided what I had planned was a losing proposition and I ought to cut my losses. And anyhow, God damn your eyes, I couldn't stand you killing yourself any more over what's past and gone . . ."

There was a susuration of trail brush below, but no more words. When Nick turned to the sheriff he saw what he considered remarkable. The sheriff smiled rarely, and when he was perturbed or at ease, he merely hummed or purred, so that you actually couldn't tell what he felt. But now he was smiling, and his shoulders had relaxed, and he was looking at the place where Cy had gone as if everything he had done today had been worth it. It didn't last. His face drew down again, and he motioned to Nick to come on, but he was walking more quickly, like a much younger man; Nick had a hard time keeping up. When they had reached the hill trail and were picking their way down, the sheriff called over his shoulder, "How was the dance?"

"Good," Nick said. Then: "I took Melissa. Took her to the parade too."

"Fine girl," the sheriff said. "Trouble with the old man?"

Nick didn't answer for a moment, and the sheriff, going on, said, "Don't have to ask, do I? You wouldn't think it, but I was a fair dancer in my puppy time. Known far and wide for wickedness and steam . . . sorry I missed it." He kept silence then, as did Nick, until they had reached the limousine, nosed in from the road; then, leaning on a fender, he said, "Drive easy, I ain't in haste now, and I want to get straight in my mind how to break this to Phyl Bellaman. Leave the top down, air'll feel good on my fool hide." His mouth corner turned wryly. "Won't ask you how the rocket went, I know how it went." He peered into the tonneau. "I'll borra one o' them lap robes when we get there. Can't walk in half naked." A flickering of what Nick took for memory—some girl or woman he'd once known, hadn't worried about being naked with?—passed over his face this time, and his eyes changed as well, then everything was what it had been before, and he got in carefully, sitting forward, inspecting the dashboard as if it were a crystal ball.

How to explain how much Phyllis was upset, how to put over to this silent man the moment of self-revelation in her astonished, widening eyes when she'd called him *Rex*? Nick wrestled with the need to tell, and the impossibility of doing so, while the road to town passed under the wheels. But as the outpost houses of town came closer, he gave it up, knowing he could never tell even Buck about that; instead, listening to the murmur of the engine, he found himself thinking, not of Phyllis at all, but of the time Noel Cloud had let him go along on a car-test run . . .

Noel didn't test all the Cloud automobiles himself in those days; this one, he'd wanted to, because it was a one-off job, no other like it ever to be built. Styled like this limousine, but a two-seater, supercharging pipes bulging from the fairing of the hood. It had been a cold morning, so that, stepping onto the track, Nick's nostrils widened, full of autumn; Noel, a Borsalino hat low on his forehead, greeted Cy, who'd designed the car, nodded to Reverend Bates, who held the stopwatch, a watch finger-worn to the brass. No one spoke much, except that Cy mentioned a last-second point about the brakes; then Noel had his hands at ten and two o'clock on the steering wheel, the engine drummed, and they were off.

The quarter-mile track was in four sections, four road surfaces. On the first, silvery concrete, Noel brought the speed to fifty. The next section, rough brick, curved into the far side of the oval, like the Indianapolis Raceway. Noel brought the needle to sixty, the tire sound altered, the windstream changed its tune. The third part was logs, a punishing, bone-shaking strip. But the tremor in the chassis was rhythmic, the sensation magnificent. Then came the sand. Noel hit it at sixty-five, braked midway, held the wheel firmly, and the car itself did the recovery. Sand plumed, the tires plowed—then, on the concrete straight again, the needle touched seventy-five, held there for the next three surfaces, and on the last circuit came up and stayed fixed at eighty-five. Ending the three laps, Noel braked down quickly, hands now light on the wheel, and he, Cy, and Bates listened—there was a low mutter under the hood. The supercharger pipes gave off a shimmer of heat. And the three men were looking at one another, and Noel was saying, "She is fit, gentlemen . . ." It was a very good thing to be able to make with your vision and will power, something like that. It was what he would think about next, in his own life.

Nick glanced at the sheriff. They were crossing Front to the Wolfson Block; a line of cars, Bolyard's Dort with them, faced inward toward Soames's; the glass jardinieres of aquamarine and ruby water lit the pharmacy window. Flute's was dark, its awning cranked up for the night.

His voice made the sheriff sit higher, look around. "I'll go in with you to see her if you want me to . . ."

The offer had to be made; he didn't think he showed any relief when the sheriff shook his head. "No thanks, Nick. You know the Bellamans pretty well, but this is just business. It wouldn't take the edge off, and even if it did, you might be in the way." He had swerved his head, straight on. He said bluntly, "Think a good deal of Phyllis yourself, don't you? For Christ's sake, don't give me any blather . . . I know it, shouldn't have asked it." Reaching behind him, he pulled the lap robe from its holding strap, thumb and forefinger feeling a fold of it. "Soft as a sheep—I can wear it, all right." Draping it around his shoulders, he resembled a sachem whose tribe had died out or deserted him.

Nick was making the Wolfson Block turn. He let up on the accelerator, swung out before the stone and snarling griffins on the gateposts, and geared down for the incline of the drive. The paths to the statues, the sundials, the pool drifted past—a corner of the house appeared ahead. As he braked and cut the engine Potter said, "This is a place I like. I hope if it ever gets sold or cut up, I'll be dead myself then so I won't have to see it go. I know things have to change, but some shouldn't." Out of the car, he said, "You notice my car's back in the jailyard, steamin' like a kettle? Seen it when we come over Front . . . no, you were dreamin' about somethin'."

Nick didn't know precisely why he felt so close to Jerome Potter, but it was as if the silence of the grounds pulled them together, as if there was something he ought to say, something equally important the sheriff ought to say to him, about Phyllis, about Cy, about this day and this darkness. And as if perception hung like a fragile vase between them, which could be lifted and looked into, containing gifts too large for workaday examining.

He said, "I was thinking about my grandfather, about one time when he was trying out a car."

"Yeah," the sheriff said. He looked up into the trees over the walk. And slapped the limousine. "When he goes, this'll be here awhile. And even when it's gone, it'll have been here." His gaze came down to the windows of the house. "Don't see a light—hate to rouse her if she's sleepin'. . ." And under the laprobe his shoulders went straight, as he walked away. "God, I hate to wake anybody up."

Nick watched him go up the steps and approach the door. He looked more alone than he had beside the pine or at any time on the ride here. He had braced his legs, wide apart, and was lifting a hand to the door, when it moved inward. Nick caught a glimpse of soft light, the single hall lamp burning, and saw the sheriff's shadow elongate, then Merlin's head, illuminated from behind, and then a glimpse of Phyllis' face. She was waiting, he thought, there in the big room all the time. Not waiting for me, she meant it when she said she loves me, and she meant it when she told me to go away, but waiting all the same. Her strength and loneliness compounded in him as the sheriff's did. He held the steering wheel as if it were a bulwark, keeping himself from getting out, following the sheriff inside. But the door had been shut again, and after a few more breaths a light appeared in the room. He could see it painting a window.

For a few seconds Sheriff Potter stood still in the hallway, watching Phyllis move ahead of him, pause and turn on another lamp. As she faced him again, her eyes, that unbeaten, steady blue, studying him as if he were a somewhat interesting stranger, he saw none of last night's remoteness. She might not be concerned about him now, or anticipating the news he brought, but something had stripped her to the bone. He had wondered, waiting outside, if it might not be right, when and if she answered, to hold her for a little in his arms, to attempt to speak without words. But when the door came open the thought vanished; she was no more his to handle, to touch now, than she was any man's, and the fire-tipped needles in his blood, so sharpened for nearly twenty-four hours, were absorbed by dull cold. Beautiful—ah, God, yes; more so than she'd been last night while he and Tommy and the rest milled around there. But the beauty was not even conscious now; she had forgotten she had it.

He drew the lap robe more closely around him and went to a chair. He sat on the edge, pulling in his knees, knowing what he must look like—half a wild man, fresh from the woods, face thrusting into the light like a blunt, soiled ax blade.

Her own robe covered her tightly, drawn up close to the throat, a deep knot in its snugged belt. She was barefoot, but she could have been wearing a ballgown.

Speeches, some too lofty to be considered for more than a second, had charged through his mind all the distance from Carmian's Hill. He had always had trouble bearing bad news, always felt there was death in it even before he started to speak. A child drowned, a man shot, plagued him weeks after the event, as he wondered if he could have said it better. Not many people made it easier for you, and why should they? They waited, as she was waiting, and the waiting only increased the pain.

He had opened his mouth, to say it simply, when she said, "Did you just do it? Just take him to jail?" She hadn't spoken loudly, but it filled even the length of this room.

He found himself capable of answering, without merely nodding, and even of clarifying, "Didn't take him, Phyl. He went by himself. Because of me, sure." Some imperious quality, something so old it couldn't abide its owner's new humility, had lashed out with her question. Last night she had seemed if not careless about what happened to Cy, at least a fatalist about it. And last night, in all the moiling and muddle, he had wanted her so badly it hurt. Now he felt the cold grow inside his veins.

Something's wrong here, he thought. More than any of this we're talking about. Something she's seen, found out.

He shook his head, folding his hand around the chair's armrest, as if for ballast. "Phyl, I'm not glossin' it over. It'll be a bad trial, and it'll go on a long time, and you'll have to show up every day. But"—he took a needed breath, thinking, I haven't got the wind I had, for this or anything like it—"but it's a hell of a lot better than it would have been with half the county chasin' him. And he's got the chance, tomorrow, to tell his story to us on the committee, just how it happened. That'll have weight in court. I'm willin' to say he gave himself up. And even if it took him a day, that ain't far from the truth."

But the something wrong was so wrong he could feel what he had said fall away, die in a corner; he might better have been speaking to the dog—she wasn't hearing it. Absently he snapped his fingers to the dog, who lifted his head higher but stayed beside Phyllis.

Then Merlin stirred, and paced after her as she left the lamp and came to stand before him. There wasn't so much light there, with her against it, but he could make out the beating of a vein in her throat. He remembered a time beside the pool, one of those go-to-Satan afternoons, when he'd opened his eyes first after the long, hard, sated loving, and examined every inch of her while she slept. Mapping a country of pleasure, the tiny forks of blue veins in her breasts, the Venus mount at rest, the thighs relaxed as she lay on her flank in birch-dappled sun, the intelligent repose of her face; and then her voice as she came out of sleep, for a moment wrapped in anonymous drowsiness, as if their identities had for a moment flowed together and become the same: "Hello . . ." A fingersnap later she'd become brazen, sitting up, lifting his prick, rolling its head between her fingers, urging him on as if he existed only for her and had no meaning aside from that. But there had been, in that split second of full acceptance, at least a shadow of tenderness.

Now she stood straight as one of those pool birches before him, but far away, yet with her eyes speaking almost more than the words meant as she said, "Listen to me now. Listen, Jerome." Her arms were folded in on the robe's belt, fingers cupping her elbows as if the pleasantly cool room were a glacier.

His battered hat lay on his trouser leg. She looked down at its crown, not seeing it, then back to him directly. "You've taken the wrong one to jail. Do you understand? It's not your fault—but Cy didn't shoot Henry." It's what she's studied saying, he thought; he had listened, in wearisome trials, to enough witnesses to recognize the patness, the patness she was trying to bring fully alive. But, he thought, even Marna Cloud couldn't make me believe this, and Phyl's no actress. He checked himself from saying, "Then who did?," looking up into her eyes and waiting. Perhaps the question was transmitted without words, because she nodded. "I shot him."

With an effort he kept himself from sitting back, even perhaps smiling. The hell you did, he thought. There wasn't any reason, and even if there was an outside chance there'd been one, I don't even think you know how to load a gun. And it was plain as daylight where you were, on the sofa, and where Cy was when he stepped into this room, and where Henry was, jaybird-raw and dazed by Cy and without a chance when that quick, head-smashing shot came. There are so many things to say now, but of course you can't say them. Not with her standing over you, saying the moon is green cheese and down is up and inside out is outside in, and making herself mean it.

He did, this time, reach to touch her arm, but she drew back, and went on with everything nicely spaced, as if some goddamn lawyer had drilled her in the desperate part: "I was angry, it was something Henry said . . ." Very breakable ice, right there, he thought; Henry never said anything to anybody that could rile a rabbit. He kept his mouth still, his eyes unmoving, his head raised, listening. Listening with courtesy like a mask that pinched him a little. "Cy had just come in, he'd found us, he was yelling, and Henry said what he said, and I grabbed Cy's rifle . . ."

Yes, he told himself, sure, yes, certainly, and after you killed Henry you upended that rifle of Cy's and managed to give yourself a nice little flesh wound. We didn't find the second bullet, we only found the one that'd blasted Henry's skull and then gone on to flick your skin, but that's incidental. Maybe that other bullet just walked away. Like I ought to do, but won't, because you're Phyllis and you want me to hear all this.

She was going on, not loudly, trying to make the story plausible to herself at the same time that she tried to drive it home to him, as if he were some clodhopper who only mattered because he also happened to be the law; he wasn't, actually, listening any longer, because it didn't matter—all that mattered was why she was saying it—but he caught part of the spiel from time to time, ". . . then Cy said he'd hide out and take the blame and protect me . . ."

He waited, holding his head stiffly, meeting her eyes. When she'd finished she stepped back, the dog pacing her exactly, flanking her. Waiting for him now. He cleared his throat, pinched his hat by the crown, lifted it an inch, noting that the sweatband had for a long time needed replacing, settled it again on his leg and said thoughtfully, "Phyl, it changes things a lot." High time to go, get out, sift this over in his own mind, tell Cy about it. His eyebrows arched, but not sardonically. "If you want to make a confession, sign it—"

She said so rapidly that this time he hardly caught it, not at all the way she'd said the rest of the deliberate, pre-rehearsed speech, "Oh, I'll do that. When, Jerome? Do you want it now?"

He shook his head. "Morning'll be time . . . you'd ought to get some real sleep tonight." He was standing, gazing past her at the gunrack, realizing there were bruises on the backs of his legs where Cy had tackled him, saved him; the chair had augmented the ache. But there was another ache in the room, huge, as big as the house and the grounds, the town and the river, and it was centered in her. For a breath he nearly put his finger on it.

But it went like gauze, a veil whose outlines he'd nearly made out, and seen through . . . By God, he thought, the way she stands now, arms still crossed and close as if ice surrounded her, she's holding whatever this is she means, or has found out, inside her in a burning brighter than any rocket. And when she started with him now to the door as he murmured "Good night, Phyl," the air of talking to a clodhopper was gone like a dirty garment; she was taking his arm, and there was nothing planned, nothing but herself speaking in nakedness when she said, "Jerome, I'm so sorry for what I've done to you—made you do to Cy . . ."

He could feel the warmth of her hand through the lap robe, which kept, somehow, holding the warmth after she'd taken it away, in the hall. When she kissed his cheekbone it was a dry quick feeling, sudden as a hummingbird wing there, and for an uncounted space, a time he'd remember, he wanted to rush into her, absolve her, lift her high out of the house and night, cleanse both of them of everything they'd done, become what they could have been. He said, "Careful, I just come from the woods and I stink."

He heard the door close as he went down the steps. He got in the limousine heavily, shut the door without much noise, and said to Nick, who was sitting quite straight, and patently not looking at him, not waiting to hear, as if he didn't love her in some lasting way himself, "Okay, if you'll kindly drop me back at the station house now."

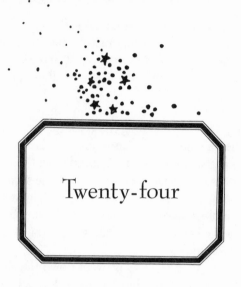

Twenty-four

Reverend Bates left the Cloud house later than he'd meant to, but sure the boys could stand waiting for him a few extra minutes. Time well spent; he was pierced by the communion he'd felt with General Cloud. Peace, satisfaction . . . he pointed the nose of his car across Front Street, slowing for the crossing. Soames's was lighted, a cluster of cars near it; down farther from courthouse shadows a cool, catatonic lamp burned on a pole above the jailyard.

He was unsurprised when the boy in the dark neat suit, holding a Gladstone bag, stepped out from linden-shadow and leaned into the car window. He said, "Eugene? Eugene Fisher?" He didn't know him well, but that wasn't odd; there was hardly what you'd call steady fraternization between white children and the Settlement.

He was slightly more surprised, but didn't show it to speak of, when the muzzle of the revolver appeared and the boy said, "Don't ask any questions, Uncle. Start driving north." The words, the tone, sounded to Reverend Bates borrowed from something else; some manner of speaking the boy thought appropriate to the action. Not springing from himself. He sat quiet, letting the boy get in and put the bag on the seat between them. The child was breathing like a one-man tornado, all sulled up, and didn't handle the gun with much assurance. "Go right down Front to the jog, turn north at the bridge."

Reverend Bates accomplished the Front Street curve; it would take him a bit out of his way, but he was intrigued now. As they passed Soames's, the telephone company, other buildings, the fountain, courthouse and jail, his passenger sat low, only the top of his hair-cream-polished head visible from the street; the gun pointed at Reverend Bates's torso, wavering with the car's motion. At street's end, Reverend Bates negotiated the slanting jog to the bridge. There was room, here at the peak, to back and turn; he slowed, noting that his passenger was sitting upright again. Automobiles, traveling south on the bridge, shot headlight brilliance into river mist, and those heading north skimmed onto the highway, their taillights flushing the dark cement. Gearing to neutral, Reverend Bates braked, examining the gun pointing at him. He raised his eyes to study the face. "How far were you planning for us to go?"

Breath spilled, hissing, through the sparkling teeth. "Just north, I said. We'll hit a city some time tonight . . . if we run out of gas, we'll get some more, but I'll have you covered." All nerved up. The gun jerked. "Come on, I'm in a hurry—I'll let you go when I'm ready."

Reverend Bates switched off the ignition casually. Before the other had a chance to talk or stir again, he said, "That piece has got a safety. The safety's on. It's that little slide, right next to your thumb. You push it forward to take it off." He slid his own thumb along his forefinger illustratively. "Belonged to your daddy, didn't it, Eugene?"

The other walled his eyes, then looked down, alarmed, at the weapon; there was finally a click as the safety went off. Reverend Bates leaned back. "Jeb and I worked side by side, in the Shops, about—oh, say ten years before he went off to the war.

305

Once, when the shad were good, we went shadding on a week-end." He was remembering it fondly; his fingers lay motionless on the steering-wheel rim. "You must've been about knicker-bocker size when he left for the service." His tone was, like the river's, ruminant. "I recall the day, just as if it was last week, when he brought that Smith and Wesson in. Wanted to ma-chine off the firing pin—file it down so it wouldn't reach a cartridge center. I helped him do it." He gazed through the immaculate windshield to the north, where, under an end-of-the-bridge lamp, automobiles slowed before assuming highway speed. "He didn't want to take the least little chance that his boy, just a smart little baby then, would go looking around for fun, the way babies do, find the gun, maybe hurt himself with it . . . him being overseas, fighting. Turned out, Jeb didn't come back. But I guess the gun's doing a little hurting anyhow, and that kind of hurts me, you know . . ." He faced around, stretching out his hand. "Give it here, will you? It won't do you any good, and I don't think your mama needs it or your aunt wants it much. I'll keep it, for remembrance."

Without lowering his eyes to the gun itself, he heard the spring stretch as the trigger was pulled, the empty snap of the blunted pin, the cylinder turn. A trace of anger went red in his eyes and his hand went out farther, over the smooth wrist, around it; he held his pressure until the hand opened like flaccid jaws, Eugene made a low noise and the gun dropped. Bates reached over the bag, scooped up the gun, brought it to his pocket and dropped it in. "Oh, me," he said. "If you hadn't done that . . . I was going to see if I could help. Sort of, for Jeb. But it wouldn't work. I can't be of use. You've gone past that, and when they get past that, colored or white, words are just sand . . . Well, you slide on out, now, scamper on up to that bridge light. You'll get a ride right off, with your looks and bearing. I won't bother a soul, telling about you. Wouldn't want to hurt your mama, or your auntie—or what I feel about your dad. Skedaddle . . ."

Quickly, fumbling for the latch a second, Eugene opened

the door, bumping the bag out, stooping to get it; he didn't look over his shoulder as Reverend Bates reshut the door, or turn as the car started. But Reverend Bates stayed where he was a little longer, watching Eugene climb to the haloing light, and bag in hand, stand under it, outlined in brightness. He was in traveler's luck because in the next few seconds a car slowed and stopped—a Pierce-Arrow, Reverend Bates saw, maybe without Cloud stamina, but a respectable thing. The license plate was from Illinois, a woman was driving; she let Eugene in and the car was gone.

Reverend Bates said, like a bass drum commenting perhaps not quite to itself, but softly, "There is a place prepared for you . . ." He reversed, made a turn, then drove off the bridge, faster now on his way to the town, the park and the Ridge, wanting to collect the boys, get back up where the wooden weather-beaten guardians blew their horns.

With a sure intonation, telling Melissa what he said had been ready for a while, Roy Gardner said, "We'll discuss this in the morning at breakfast, before I go to the bank. It's much too serious to hash out at this hour."

While he made a rite of locking the door, always a weighty matter, this time prolonged, Melissa went along the hall, through the living room, into the parlor, where she pulled a lamp chain; here, everything was wicker, creaking even if you sneezed heartily. But it had the air of a sanctum as well, fit for dedicated argument. She selected the settee, which complained like a brittle forest, laid her purse down, crossed her ankles and waited for her father to find her. When he did, he stayed in the doorway, fingers nervous under his bathrobe cuffs. He repeated, "In the morning, Melissa. Go to bed."

"I'm not sleepy at all now. I had such a wonderful day—I'm still thinking about it. Haven't you ever had a day like that?" Receiving no answer, and telling herself that very probably he hadn't, she laced her fingers around her knee, which, she realized at the same moment, was still bare, the stocking having been rolled like Candy's, and went on, "I was dead tired a while ago. But I went down to the depot and took a nap."

His sucked-in breath made his pajamas tremble. "The *station?* Do you realize—" All pre-prepared words had failed him in this emergency, as she had trusted they would, though she knew he was capable of going on at length with a Boy Scout manual or the Banker's Guide for reference. He said, "At night, a public place, sleeping—"

"I didn't sleep long. But you're right, it's not a very nice place to stay. I just stayed till I felt better." She was briefly tempted to tell him Eugene had been present, and with what in mind, choosing her words with nicety for their euphemistic value, but an immediate understanding of what this would bring on, along with the common cruelty of undermining his faith in his power of judgment, decided her on silence. Whatever happened to Eugene from now on, she didn't want to hear about or be part of.

She drew a shallow breath and said quite easily what, after all, she had drawn him there to announce, "And Daddy, I don't want to have any talk in the morning, or ever again about today. I just want to say right now, I like Nick, and he'll be coming here, I guess, once in a while. And when he does, if it bothers you having us around together, we'll take long walks or something." It was all reeling out spontaneously, as she had known, walking home, it would. "I love you and Mama very much, but I'm not any better than anybody else, and not as good as some, and your having the bank doesn't make me different, and I won't let it. And when Cousin Margitta and Cousin Trilby and Aunt Millicent and Uncle Joe come for a visit, I don't want to sit around and be a doll and listen to how good I am. I'd rather take them down to the park and play softball and eat peanuts. If I ever do anything good, not just getting good grades, I'll know it, and that'll be enough, and I want to work this summer, before school starts again, maybe at Marvin Soames's; he'd like somebody to help serve sometimes. So I can buy my own dresses, pick them out myself, and not have Mama sew them, or put them on a bill . . ."

She opened her purse, disturbing the balloon packet; then
setting it aside with approving fingers, pulling out the wadded
towel, then the daring bathing suit. "You saw me wear this
today—I think it made you as mad as anything, even if you
were already mad about Nick and Mr. Hoover. Maybe Mama
told you she'd approved it, and you talked to her mean about
it. But if she did, she was just telling you that to protect me
because she'd never seen it before I got it at Neilsen's Empo-
rium without telling anybody but Candy." She patted the
damp cloth. "It's my favorite suit, maybe I'll wear it every
summer till I'm eighty."

She had run out of a modicum of breath, but felt more
coming. With Candy's family, she had once been allowed to
travel forty miles off to a baseball game featuring Rube Wad-
dell, on a day when the great pitcher could do no wrong, his
arm like both of Samson's, his speed uncanny, his eye falcon-
true, and she knew now how he felt in that searing light, on
that god-blessed afternoon.

She looked brightly, openly, at her father. "Well, Daddy, I
guess that's all. I'm glad you waited up. I wish I'd had the
gu—I wish I'd been brave enough to come in the first time.
Maybe you heard me at the door then." She swept off her hat,
her hair shining. "Hit me if you want to."

With what sounded a great deal like an injured neigh, but
with pride, Roy Gardner said, "I have never struck you in my
life."

It seemed to be his parting word. He was already moving
backward, preparing to leave, though still watching her. A
sector of him, though invisible, had somehow crumbled, and
sadness touched her, not a crying sadness—tears were for real
grief, not summer showers or killed worms. She got up, crossed
to him, touched her lips to his forehead, which was cool and
tasted a trifle of Bay Rum. In the wingbeat of the instant she
wanted to pat his head, rumple his hair, but what there was of
it was so perfectly arranged that it seemed a desecration; and

anyway, it proved he hadn't been to bed yet at all, and would need his sleep for the strenuous banking day tomorrow. He took her hand, pressed it, turned, the set of his shoulders baffled but holding up under onslaught, and his slippers, shined each Saturday along with his outdoor shoes, went off over the carpet.

When his bedroom door had shut, she kicked off her own shoes, scuffed from the dance, and made her way leisurely to the kitchen, pulling open the high door of the General Electric, which she thought of as a Hindu prince because all around its head it wore a turban of intricate, enameled white mesh. From this rajah's interior she chose leftover picnic food and ate ravenously, chasing it with milk. The milk came from one of the few town-edge farms where her father would buy, since he held the mortgage on it and personally tested its germlessness. She took from her mother's Nappanee cabinet a sizable box of Diamond matches and talked back to the Harz Mountain roller when it made a dry, investigative chirp under its cage hood.

In the parlor once more, she knelt on the settee and pushed a window higher, then lifted its screen. A moth miller flew in, bumbled around the lamp and settled. She shook out the balloon, preparing to admire it for a while, to dream over it before it went on its journey. It spread out over her dress, making an overdress of lightest paper, most delicate tints and rustling shadows. The parlor clock, she saw, was ticking along gradually, moving toward twelve. She felt herself in the heart of the night, and alive, alive—alive like the canary, but unhooded.

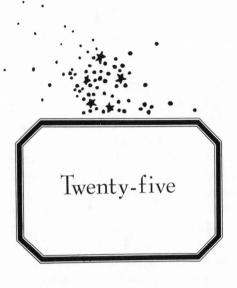

Twenty-five

Alice Cloud knew the pressure of mortality which could be at
its worst on a perfect night in summer. Winter braced the
mind and spirit and skin for its blows; ideal weather stretched
old longings to the breaking point and could make even a leaf
a reminder of the past, broken promises, far-off and unredeem-
able minutes. At times like these she walked very purposefully,
as if she must be somewhere specific inside a settled time—
keeping a date with herself. She was sorry Marty Broom had
joined her as she left Soames's, but here he was, causing her
to keep her pace down to his slower one, brimful of his own
self-pity bred from indignation. Hailing her as she headed from
Soames's—she'd told the Bolyards and the Kaplans and the
circle of people around them good night, saying she wanted to
walk—he had begun sputtering like a leftover firecracker, and
now, as they started along the Wolfson Block, he clung beside
her, evidently sure of a sympathetic ear. She wanted to make
the circuit of this block and cross over to the hospital as soon
as possible. But without showing pain, she listened.

The tale he had told her of offering his services to the

Vigilante Committee and being, in some manner she wasn't quite sure of, spurned, had a fuzzy ring to it, as if he were keeping back part of the details. It must have something to do with how he'd reinjured his game leg earlier today. As he expounded on what he called his constitutional rights, she made brief noises to prove she was attentive. But with the major part of herself she was looking up at the griffin-adorned gateposts as she came closer to them, thinking how many years it was since she had gone up that drive, and telling herself as well that the griffins exactly summed up Phyllis Bellaman's hands-off and stay-away attitude. A thorny branch, extruding from the ivy clinging around the fence posts, brushed at her stockings irritatingly, and as she paused, turning up her suit skirt to remove the branch, Marty's voice wrangled on: ". . . didn't even give 'em the satisfaction of goin' to the park this year. Guess this whole place could get along fine without me. Might even march over to Barlton, some mornin', git me a room—I got my good hands to work with, and the pay might be better, for all I know . . ."

She straightened, flicking the branch aside, looking at the run in the silk on her leg. Then she gazed at Marty, who had ceased in mid-note. His head was back, and he had raised a stubby hand in a gesture meant to keep them both quiet, though he'd been the one doing all the talking. He said, "My Gee, Miss Alice, never heard him do that before . . ."

Alice took a step onward, unaware of what he could mean. But he stood where he was, head tipped on one side, and this time she heard it too—a long, low whine, ascending half a scale and then dipping again, moving down and across the grounds, distant and muffled . . . it must be coming from the house, she thought—yet heavy with portent, and repeated again as they waited. Marty muttered, "That big setter. Cy's. But he ain't a noisy dog. God damn—pardon me, Miss Alice—sounds like a wolf, don't he?"

Nodding, Alice said under her breath, "He sounds haunted." Marty didn't hear her, but he had taken a step between the gateposts and stood staring up the drive. The low, searching cry came again. Alice thought, I am not psychic, I have no talents in that direction at all; reading tea leaves and crossing the palms of gypsies with silver has always seemed to me a dead end of inanity, but that dog is either dying or announcing something I'll have to find out about.

She found herself beside Marty, then moving ahead of him up the driveway, without time to reflect that this was alien country, a place where she had not walked for so long it was a wonder that she remembered the grounds so well. Those years ago, Tom Wolfson still alive, the grounds had been cut back farther, pruned more neatly; yet she liked this half-rough appearance, and told herself approvingly that it suited Phyllis —a perfectly kept sweep of lawns, trees, hedges would have been more welcoming, but this fitted remoteness, an alien soul.

She could see a little of the house now, still far ahead, and the overgrown path nearby where she thought a summerhouse had once stood. Marty, beginning to puff behind her, said, "I cut all them side-swaths towards the pool and them fancy statues. Need scythin' again b'fore long. She won't let me even scrub the green off the statues." There was pride for her in his tone. "Says leave 'em like they are, the green's natural—"

The low, intense wailing was filling the darkness. As it reached its long-drawn high note now, then died out and started again on the dark starting note, Marty said, five yards behind Alice, "Hey now, somebody's foolin' around the pool. I told her a thousand times kids'll come in if they leave them gates open. Kids ain't what they used to be, riffraff around—"

She heard his sharp intake of breath and whirled as it came. Then, because he was silent, she walked back beside him, not minding his hand which gripped her arm and went on tightening. Again the shivering wail rose, fell and started its rise. She stared where Marty was staring, through a half screen of hickories, proud trees whose roots were nourished by the water in the grotto, and birches with bark like the flesh of white, still ladies.

But the leaf-shaded body of the woman in the pool was no tree, and as she watched, it floated nearer, on a slight pulse of the water, the face, upturned, coming in gentle sight, a few inches under the surface, yet so perfectly lit by the shafts of light between trees that it might have been spotlighted. The long, wet, rich black hair was spread around it. Alice thought, No, no, in a moment she'll turn over there, and swim toward us and climb out, unconscious of her nakedness, treating me with scorn, her great eyes opening wide at my temerity at trying to break through to her . . .

Marty was mumbling something incomprehensible, and she pried his fingers from her arm, and walked ahead of him, through the rough, clinging strong grasses, to the pool. The rocks on this side were granitic, taupe-gray and shadowed by high grasses. On the largest rock was a robe, spread out neatly. A stone had been placed on the sheet of paper centering the robe's soft lining. As she bent to read the bold, right-slanting calligraphy of the note, forcing herself not to look past it at the face, its eyes shut, below her in the water, a glimmer of glass caught her attention; she stooped further, and held the little bottle that had contained the sleeping pills. It was empty. Dr. Bowen had said, "One or two at a time"; she was back in the sun-spangled room, handing the pills to Phyllis . . . she could not actually hear the dog crying now, though it was going on. She read the note. It was admirably short, a few words shining in dark ink; *I killed Henry—among other things.* And the signature was forceful, done with a dash, underlined once, the name appended with boldness, style, as on the old land-deed documents and letters preserved for posterity Pierre Wolfson had signed his name.

She gazed outward and down once again at the body that could swim so capably, that was, she was certain, matchless at love-making, that Rex had loved, Cy had been held by—that she had tried not to detest because it could not help what it was. The beautiful hands, water winnowing between the fingers, were a little higher than the face, and one was moving softly, but only with the buoyancy of the water.

When she turned, Marty was behind her again, and she took him by the shoulders and pressed him down until he sat on a lower rock beside the robe and the note. He sat there looking straight ahead, like a frog. She said, "Stay there, I'll call Jerome." And others, she thought; Dr. Len Bowen, a formality; Abe Melton, a necessity. Marty put his face in his hands; she patted him on the back, and went back along the fragrant grass path to the drive. The dog had continued its lament, so she hurried a little more at the drive, wanting to reassure it with her hands, talk to it, stop its voice. Though she would go on hearing it—and not only tonight, she was sure.

Beneath the sheriff's much scarred desk, in the room graced by the name of office, a paraplegic squirrel lived in an apple box; a wire-stove grid, with a couple of bricks holding it down, lay over the box. The squirrel, which had no name, had been brought in the year before by Tommy Beavis, who had casually rescued it after its spine had been nipped by a dog. Its hind legs had shriveled, but its forequarters were like those of a miniature Japanese wrestler, and it had a habit of clinging to the wires of the grid, swinging its way along, and playing a small tune on the grid wires by plucking them with its front teeth. The sound was rather like that of an out-of-tune harp, signaling that the squirrel was either hungry or wanted its head scratched. For some time now, the tune had grown increasingly insistent; as Sheriff Potter hung up the telephone and stared down at the smudged blotter, then up at a coal calendar with a picture of an undraped Comanche maiden saluting the rising sun, the sound twanged steadily. He opened a sack of boiled peanuts on the desk, shelled a handful, and reaching down, scattered them through the grid, then rubbed the squirrel's head with his forefinger until, with a chirp, the animal released the grid, dropped into the straw and began eating. Then Potter got up and walked slowly into the next room, where Tommy Beavis sat trying to win a game of solitaire. When Tommy looked up, he stopped with a card held in midair, then laid it down and sat back, waiting. The sheriff talked to him for a few minutes, his voice subdued and sometimes sinking to near-tonelessness, so that Tommy had to lean forward to hear. The only other sound, outside his voice, was the snoring of the fliers in the darkened cell across the hall. When he had finished, Tommy got up and shrugged into his uniform coat and went out into the hall, the sheriff following him, and in the front doorway, holding him for a moment longer with a few more parting directions: "Tell Abe to take the lane and go the long way 'round. No use makin' people wonder this time of night. Alice's already callin' Doc Bowen and Abe. She'll ride back with you." He had washed up, and rubbed goose grease on his chest, arms, back and face, and put on a clean shirt. His face glistened, high-lighted sharply in the cold light from the yard. "Put a little water in the radiator before you go, or that engine'll freeze up for good."

Tommy nodded and went down the steps, and the sheriff moved out onto the top step, from where he could see a portion of Front Street past the courthouse, the only cars now visible there the Cloud limousine, parked under the telephone company windows, and the Bolyard Dort in front of Soames's, whose windows were dark, its awnings rolled up. He saw Nick and Buck in the limousine, and reflected that tomorrow would be soon enough for them to know. As Tommy went off, the sheriff breathed the night for a moment, then turned and made his way back along the hall to the cell at the end. He made an extra fuss opening the door, shutting it behind him louder than he might have done, and Cy, stretched on the cot, rolled over and looked up at him.

The sheriff leaned back against the bars, and presently Cy sat up. The sheriff moved on into the cell, swung the single chair around and sat on it facing the chair back. Then, as Cy waited, he said very gently, "Didn't want to wake you up earlier, when I got back from tellin' Phyl you were here. She's dead, Cy. Just got the word."

There was little intonation in his voice, but the muscles in his jaw were stretched, and his hands, on the chair back, gripped heavily. The man on the cot did not move, after the first upward jerk of the head at Potter's last words, and he went on waiting while the sheriff said, "She left this little note—Alice found her, in the pool. Alice and Marty, passin', heard your dog, went to see what was wrong, found her. She'd swallowed a bunch of pills first." Cy's hair, touched by a streak of hall light, was a small flash of yellow; the sheriff couldn't see his eyes, but he knew he had shut them. Then he knew when they were open again. "In the note she said she killed Henry. Same thing she'd already told me when I went out to tell her you were here." He made his hands go slack, stop tightening on the chair and went on, "I don't believe a word of it. Judge will. Alice read it to me on the phone. It's a straight confession. Likely there won't even be a jury, just the inquest."

He didn't say that the note Alice had read was incised on his mind and would be for more time than he could guess at. It could be, he thought, that Cy had already known that. There wasn't too much left to strip away between him and Cy. It's funny, he thought, how men can read each other when all the foolishness drops away. He'd known it in the war, and Cy knew it in his own war, which was just as tough as the real one. Christ, he thought, that's what makes the real wars easier to bear—when the flags are waving and there's plenty of whoop-to-do, your own wars get by-passed.

He pushed away the chair and stood up. Hardest of all to say what he ought to say now. "You can stick to sayin' you shot Henry, which I know damn well you did, be a mule and go through a lot of legal fracas. Other hand, you can take this the way I think Phyl meant it—kind of tryin' to pay you back, and even, maybe, pay Henry back a little, pay everybody back for what she must have figured, at the last, was her fault."

Cy's face came out of shadow, his hands pushing down on the cot. "And pay you back too, Jerome. Don't leave yourself out."

317

The sheriff said, "I ain't. But then, I never figured she owed me much. Other way around."

Cy had got up, and they were both in the hall light now. Cy came closer, boot soles quiet, and said, "I'll take her gift. I'm glad for it. And this is the only time I'll say this, because you rate it. I wasn't aiming at Henry. I was aiming at her. It was a snap shot, there wasn't much light, and in the last second Henry threw himself in front of her. Trying to protect her." He drew in a breath, and let it out, a long one. "I don't think she even knew that." Then he said, "I'm glad she never will."

You couldn't shake hands with Cy—he wasn't offering his hand—and in any event, handshaking was overrated as a custom; what you could do was stand for a second longer, then turn around and fiddle with the door, and shut it finally and go back to your office, where the squirrel, impatient, was again holding forth. Then you could sit down, wondering if you ought to call Emma and tell her you might be home a good bit later, and deciding not to, since she'd be long asleep now. After that you could sit hoping Tommy would remember to tell Abe to take the back lane, and remember to tell Marty, who'd have to be a witness at the inquest, to keep his mouth on the hinge at least till tomorrow—Lord, God, he'd talk himself blue in the face at the inquest, carrying on like William Jennings Bryan defending the rights of all commoners; and you could think of Phyllis, mainly. As you'd do, anyway, always.

He was looking out along the hall when Tommy showed up again, ushering Alice Cloud ahead of him. Tommy inclined his head to say everything had gone all right, but Alice had paused at the cell on the end, so Potter got up and walked out there. He'd guessed Cy was still standing beside the cell door, which turned out to be the case. It had crossed his mind that, food from Soames's being passable but tiresome after a spell, he'd have to make plans for bringing Cy something home-cooked once in a while until the inquest. But then, over Tommy's head, he saw the look on Alice's face, and a second after that, the look on Cy's, and he didn't think Cy was, by any definition, going to go hungry.

Buck had deposited his parents, and Harky and Wid, and then more lingeringly, Candy at their respective homes, then visited the school basement. Not favoring post-mortems, he was, all the same, in a summing-up mood. He'd encountered Nick, just after delivering a package of rich cake to Velma, and as he stepped into the street from the phone company. His hands cradled the back of his head, his knees were elevated and supported by the limousine dashboard, and he looked up into the leaves of Front Street, here and there illuminated by ghostly globes. Nick had said nothing of his visit to Phyllis, or the sheriff's. That was other business . . . but Cy in custody, Eugene out of the basement, the ultimate and unique landing of the rocket—all these had been discussed.

Buck was concerned now about Velma. "Says she ain't ever goin' to listen in no more," he murmured. "Now, a big sociable girl like that's goin' to miss the gossip. Says she swore to God above she wouldn't. Think I'll have to make up things to tell her—like that the mayor, say, eloped with a Gossard Corset saleslady—just to keep her chin up. Well . . ." He yawned, opened like a jackknife from his position, hit Nick on the shoulder and leaped over the car door. "I'll git off swampin' out the best meat market in Ohio 'bout five-thirty t'morra. Come around and we'll pick up Candy 'n M'liss 'n have some Christian fellowship." He was in the middle of the street when he turned around and called, "How's your old Independence Day?"

Nick considered, and then said, "Over the average!"

Nodding, Buck jumped for the Dort, put it in action, made a bravura turn and drove away. When he had gone, Nick restarted the limousine, contemplated going past Melissa's to watch for signs of life, read from the courthouse clock that the day had nearly spun itself out, and recalling her promise to send up a message, drove to the Cloud Block. It was quiet, yet not, he thought, completely sleeping, vibrant with some nameless promise. The very hitching posts seemed to know something they didn't tell, and might soon reveal. Making the turn up the drive, he touched the brakes as the headlights swept Harky's flower beds, bringing out clumps of roses, Paul Scarlets among them. He saw them turned away from him, bud cores tightening in secrecy, as Phyllis had turned her back to him. Yet their brightness was the more valued for that, as if, by denying him something, they were giving him more . . .

When he came out of the carriage house, limousine put away, Wid was standing in the moonlight. He held the depleted contents of a Mason jar to Nick. "No heel taps," he said solemnly. "That's what them Britishers used t' say, 'fore they went to Blighty or got 'emselves shot up, when they was drinkin' serious. Means, finish it up. And keep quiet. Harky's gone t' bed, asked me t' wait up for you." Nick drank, handed the jar back to Wid, who turned it over, shook it and set it down on the back steps as they approached them. "Tommy Beavis called a while back," he said. "Rang up the rest o' the Vigilantes too. I know Jerome's got Cy. Tommy rang just after Cy drove in." He flicked Nick's tie, which jumped under his finger. "I know you was in it some way too. Somethin' Tommy said, that Cy'd mentioned in passin'." He stood back, thumbs hooking in his belt at his kidneys. "Think you'll live to vote?"

"Maybe," Nick said. "If Hoover's not running then."

Wid's adam's apple moved, but he didn't smile. "Sometimes I think you will, at that. 'Night, Cap."

He was still standing there, assessing the moon, as Nick said "Good night" and went in. The kitchen was shadowy, the sink's pump handle passing coolness to his hand as he drank again here, without a glass. In the hall there was an undershine of light; this, he thought, was a time when you expected the whole house could speak, attics to cellars, talking about Noel, Grandma Marie, Rex, Alice; with his mother's voice, the one she used when she wasn't on stage, commenting as well: "Nick, you ought to think about tomorrow. It's a fine old town, but it's not your world." You could answer that when you knew what your world was, couldn't you?

He hadn't meant to stop and listen at his grandfather's door, but he did, anyhow, and Nurse Riffon must have sensed him because the door opened silently; looking up at him, she whispered, "He's in a good sleep. Talk to you a minute?"

They walked together toward the living room, away from the quiet room. She said, "About that dust-up this mornin'. I regret it. I'm saying I'm sorry." There was warm pride in her, but she'd muffled it, and said, to prove this mastery, "Got kind of above myself. He hasn't got long. You'll be the man of the house."

"Thanks," Nick said. Her hand was callused, brisk in his, briefly there. "I was snotty," he said.

Without denying that, for which he liked her better even than for the apology, she went hush-rustling back to the bedroom, and its door shut. And then, in the front room, he tried to see his father's portrait, but it was too far away, and too dark to make it out.

Almost on the third-story landing, he stopped. Moonlight fell around him from a window. The courthouse clock had begun. He stood, counting, hearing the day go away with the chimes. Then the Nickel Plate's whistle, on time at the water tower. Then, shortly, the train closer, sweeping through, sad and jubilant together, roughening hair on his spine as it always did. A burst of cracking thunder overrode the fading echoes of the whistle—a last salute, saved for now, a pure revolutionary roar. Then the cricket could be heard once more.

He had started for the stair head when the fire balloon appeared. It had already soared high above the Gardners', on windless air, making its way in its own free course toward the river. He watched it until he couldn't see the lovely light at all, until the town it was over could have been any town, and it was a star among others.

ABOUT THE AUTHOR

PAUL BOLES is the author of many books, including *The Mississippi Run, The Limner, Parton's Island, A Million Guitars* and *The Streak.* Several of his books have been made into films and have been book-club selections. He regularly contributes short stories to major magazines in the country. He won the Friends of American Writers Award in 1959 for *Parton's Island;* the Freedom Foundation Citation in 1957 for *Deadline;* the Distinguished Fiction Award of Indiana University in 1969 for *A Million Guitars;* the award for a body of work in 1970 by the Georgia Writers' Association; and the best-novel award by the Dixie Council of Authors and Journalists in 1975 for *The Limner.* He is interested in old cars, music, horses, archery and painting, and lives with his wife Dorothy in Atlanta. They have three sons, Shawn Michael, Patric Laurence and Terence Ross.